"You want me to help y

Aiz shook his head. "The Farians call them gods. They are not gods. They are powerful beings, devious and deceptive. It will not be easy. But they can be killed." There was no humor in his voice or his eyes. Mia's back was straight and her gray eyes were locked on me.

"Why do you think I am even remotely capable of succeeding where you have failed?"

Aiz smiled and lifted a shoulder. "You are the Star of Indrana and my sister has seen you standing in triumph over our defeated enemies." His smile vanished. "It's why we can't send you home. If we don't fight, if you're not there, we won't win. And the light that comes after burns everything to the ground."

Praise for K. B. Wagers

THE FARIAN WAR

THERE BEFORE THE CHAOS

"Twisty and clever and magnificent, full of political maneuvers, space action, and genuine feeling. The end broke my heart in the best sort of way. I cannot wait for the next book."   —Beth Cato

"A perfect blend of political intrigue and realistically conveyed action.... Kick-butt women, space battles, complex relationships, and fiendish plots abound."   —B&N Sci-Fi & Fantasy Blog

"Wagers achieves a rare balance of action...tension, and quiet moments, keeping pages turning while deepening the portraits of Hail and the friends and foes around her. Fans of the original trilogy will welcome Hail's return, and any space opera reader can easily jump in here."   —Publishers Weekly

"An exciting dose of space opera and political intrigue peppered with hard choices. Highly recommended for fans of science fiction with assertive female characters."   —Booklist

THE INDRANAN WAR

BEHIND THE THRONE

"This debut ranks among the best political SF novels in years, largely because of the indomitable, prickly Hail.... [A] fast-paced, twisty space opera."   —Library Journal (starred review)

"Taut suspense, strong characterization, and dark, rapid-fire humor are the highlights of this excellent SF adventure debut."

—*Publishers Weekly* (starred review)

"Full of fast-paced action and brutal palace intrigue, starring the fiercest princess this side of Westeros."

—*B&N Sci-Fi & Fantasy Blog*

AFTER THE CROWN

"*Crown* is fast paced, and its focus on a female action heroine defined by her decisions rather than romance is refreshing and fun."

—*Washington Post*

"Craving a galactic adventure? K. B. Wagers' second Indranan War novel is just the ticket."

—*Bookish*

"Two books in, this series has exemplified political plotting as compelling as the badass heroine at its center."

—*B&N Sci-Fi & Fantasy Blog*

BEYOND THE EMPIRE

"Nerve-wracking action on the ground and in space, dark humor, and the characters' til-the-end loyalty to one another....A satisfyingly thunderous end to Hail's quest for vengeance that makes an excellent addition to any SF collection."

—*Publishers Weekly* (starred review)

DOWN AMONG THE DEAD

By K. B. Wagers

THE INDRANAN WAR

Behind the Throne

After the Crown

Beyond the Empire

THE FARIAN WAR

There Before the Chaos

Down Among the Dead

DOWN AMONG THE DEAD

THE FARIAN WAR: BOOK 2

K. B. WAGERS

www.orbitbooks.net

Copyright © 2019 by Katy B. Wagers
Excerpt from *Out Past the Stars* copyright © 2019 by Katy B. Wagers

Author photograph by Donald Branum
Cover design by Lauren Panepinto
Cover illustration by Stephan Martiniere
Cover copyright © 2019 by Hachette Book Group, Inc.

Orbit
Hachette Book Group
1290 Avenue of the Americas
New York, NY 10104
orbitbooks.net

First Edition: December 2019
Simultaneously published in Great Britain by Orbit

Orbit is an imprint of Hachette Book Group.
The Orbit name and logo are trademarks of Little, Brown Book Group Limited.

The publisher is not responsible for websites (or their content) that are not owned by the publisher.

The Hachette Speakers Bureau provides a wide range of authors for speaking events. To find out more, go to www.hachettespeakersbureau.com or call (866) 376-6591.

Library of Congress Cataloging-in-Publication Data

Names: Wagers, K. B., author.
Title: Down among the dead / K.B. Wagers.
Description: First edition. | New York, NY : Orbit, 2019. | Series: The Farian War; book 2 | Summary: "Gunrunner empress Hail Bristol must navigate alien politics and deadly plots to prevent an interspecies war in this second novel in the Farian War space opera trilogy. In a surprise attack that killed many of her dearest subjects, Hail Bristol, empress of Indrana, has been captured by the Shen—the most ruthless and fearsome aliens humanity has ever encountered. As she plots her escape, the centuries-long war between her captors and the Farians, their mortal enemies and Indrana's oldest allies, finally comes to a head. When her captors reveal a shocking vision of the future, Hail must make the unexpectedly difficult decision she's been avoiding: whether to back the Shen or the Farians. Staying neutral is no longer an option. Will Hail fight? Or will she fall?" —Provided by publisher.
Identifiers: LCCN 2019032463 (print) | LCCN 2019032464 (ebook) | ISBN 9780316411257 (paperback) | ISBN 9780316411264 (ebook) | ISBN 9780316411240
Subjects: GSAFD: Science Fiction.
Classification: LCC PS3623.A35245 D69 2019 (print) | LCC PS3623.A35245 (ebook) | DDC 813/.6—dc23
LC record available at https://lccn.loc.gov/2019032463
LC ebook record available at https://lccn.loc.gov/2019032464

ISBNs: 978-0-316-41125-7 (paperback), 978-0-316-41126-4 (ebook)

Printed in the United States of America

LSC-C

10 9 8 7 6 5 4 3 2 1

This one is for those who have lost everything and somehow found the strength to rise again.

AUTHOR'S NOTE

Dear readers, there are some difficult moments in this book pertaining to grief, suicidal ideation, and self-harm. Please proceed according to your comfort level.

I am royalty by blood, but there is little else one would consider noble about me. I drink too much, swear even more, and can't seem to keep my hands from closing into fists when I'm angry. As a princess I got into far too many fights for my parents' liking, and once I'd slipped the bonds of Pashati to disappear into the black, there was nothing left but to embrace who I truly was.

A liar. A thief and smuggler. A killer through and through.

I'd thought that was all I was, but I was dragged home by those who'd convinced themselves I was an empress worthy of the throne, and somewhere along the way I started to believe it myself.

I am a killer. I am also an empress.

I am the Star of Indrana and there is no one who can stand in my way.

1

*W*e're coming up on the embassy. It looks like the mercs pulled back when the Solies flew in," Emmory said over the com link. "Majesty—"

I jerked awake, the concussion wave of the explosion in my dream carrying into the real world in the form of my heart slamming against my rib cage. The room was dim, the early-morning light crawling in through the windows. The breathing of the other three women was rhythmic as they slept on, unaware of my nightmare.

Gita Desai had protested when I'd turned my bios off, but I was glad I'd insisted. There was no reason to wake my *Ekam* up night after night just because I couldn't sleep.

My *Ekam*. Strange how a single word could cause so much pain.

I curled into a ball, holding in the grief that always followed on the heels of the dream. Because it wasn't a figment of my imagination, it was my reality: My brothers were dead. Most of my Body-Guards were dead. All I had left were Gita, Johar, and Alba.

And we were in the questionable safety of Shen custody.

I'd been betrayed, taken prisoner, and dragged away from Earth. Shortly after our arrival Aiz Cevalla had tried to make it seem as though we were guests on this planet across the galaxy from home, but with no way to leave and very little freedom over the last month it was hard to believe the lie.

Prisoners or guests, either way it made little difference in the end.

We were simply four people very far away from everything we'd ever known. My fury had snuffed out like an explosion exposed to the black, leaving me floundering the moment we'd touched boots down to the soil of this planet.

While the others had set to the task of finding a way to get us out of here and back to Pashati, I'd drowned in my grief over the loss of everything I knew.

I ate when my *Ekam* told me to, answered questions that were asked of me as the trio of women continued to plan for an escape or some way to contact home, but otherwise I stayed silent, staring out the window at the jungle beyond.

Our captors, or hosts, left us alone. They had a war to run, after all, and I got the impression that the events on Earth had caught them off guard just as badly as they had us. Or they were responsible for it all and playing the shock up for my edification. I poked at the tangled ball of details sometimes but could never seem to find the energy to grab a thread and pull.

I did not want to be alive, yet here I was. The universe was once again cold and uncaring about what I wanted—as it had been with the deaths of my parents and my sisters. This dream echoed night after night in my head, and the ghosts whispered endlessly in my ear during the day. They were my new companions, and I welcomed them into my shattered life.

A voice somewhere in the back of my head screamed at me. It scolded me for giving up. It shamed me for letting the empire down, for turning my back on everything I'd ever believed in. For betraying Hao and all the others by curling into myself instead of seeking revenge. It wanted me to get up and keep fighting, but I ignored it even more than I ignored my companions and my captors.

The ghosts who haunted me were easier to talk to. They understood that it was better for me to stay down, that fighting would only kill more people I cared about. They knew what would happen if I raged.

Baby, you should go back to sleep.

"There's nothing to do but sleep," I murmured back, imagining the feel of Portis's hand in my hair as his ghost whispered in my ear.

He didn't answer. Sometimes the ghosts spoke and vanished; other times I could have whole conversations and would look up to find Gita watching me with concern heavy in her brown eyes.

I'd mentioned it once, curious if the others were seeing the same, if I was hallucinating or being drugged. But no one else could see the figments of my slowly cracking mind, and all Gita's scans came up clean. The Shen weren't poisoning me. So I stopped asking and tried to pretend they weren't there.

At least not when anyone else could see me.

I slipped from my bunk, moving slow to keep from disturbing the others, and padded my way on bare feet to the window.

The twin moons of Sparkos were setting, bathing everything in their silvery light. The jungle was filled with shadows, having one last dance in the breeze before they gave way to the pink light of sunrise. I could smell the thick salt of the sea and the heaviness of decaying vegetation seeping in around the edges of the window.

It made me miss home.

I pressed my hand to the thick pane and felt the slight give of the plastic. Johar had been diligently working on loosening the foundation of the sturdy window, and it wouldn't be long before it would come free entirely. Then we could escape. To where I didn't know. It felt very much like jumping from the frying pan into the fire.

"Majesty, where are you?"

I turned my head from the window at the sound of Fasé's voice. My Farian ghost was more insistent than the others, constantly questioning my whereabouts as though she couldn't see right where I was for herself if she'd just show her face.

My anger at her was worse than the grief. I knew it was useless to blame the dead for their failures, knew even better that it

5

wasn't Fasé's fault she hadn't seen this coming and saved us all. It was mine.

Your crew, your responsibility, little sister. Never forget that.

"Hail?"

I squeezed my eyes shut. Johar's whisper seemed loud in comparison to Hao's voice in my head, and the touch of her hand on my back was almost unbearable.

The former gunrunner and smuggler from Santa Pirata had chosen to stay by my side. Her plans to retire and live in my empire were a decision that had ultimately led her here with me. I would have apologized if I could have forced the words out of my throat.

"I couldn't sleep." It wasn't really a lie.

"I know. It's close enough to morning, though," she murmured, slipping into the space next to me at the window; the warmth of her body chased away some of the graveyard chill that had settled into my bones. She smoothed her hand over my back, resting it gently on my hip and tugging me against her. "We notice it, even if we don't say anything. Don't need access to your bios to know you're not sleeping."

I didn't want the comfort. It hammered away at the wall of grief I'd built around my rage. But my body was a traitor and leaned into Jo's embrace before I could stop it. I wanted to curl against her, bury my face in her shoulder and weep, but if I started crying I didn't think I'd ever stop.

"Shiva, why do the gods take the good ones and leave me here?" My hands were shaking as I curled them into fists, hating the plaintive question that slipped free.

"You *are* one of the good ones," Johar said, fingers tightening on my hip. "Don't argue with me, Hail, you know you are. I love you for it and so do your people. We'll get out of here and go home. Then we can figure out what to do from there. Figure out who was responsible for Earth."

Earth—the attack on the peace negotiations between the Farians

6

and the Shen and our desperate run through the streets filled my head once more along with a burning fury.

Though no matter who'd fired the shots and blew up the embassy—Farian, Shen, mercenary—I'd been the one who brought them there. My foolish belief that I could somehow stop this brewing war between two alien races had been hubris. In the end I was responsible for the deaths of my people.

Shame burned in my throat.

"You know they're dead, don't you?"

Johar took a deep breath and then exhaled. "You and I have a hard time trusting to hope, Hail. We've seen too much. We know the miraculous survival of the crew doesn't happen but in the stories. I don't begrudge Alba and Gita for wanting to hold on to that flicker in the darkness, though. It's a small comfort."

It was no comfort for me. Jo was right, the real world didn't give second chances and happy endings. It gave out death and grief, and bits of justice on the rarest of occasions.

I'd already had my justice; I couldn't hope for more.

"I have led you all to disaster. Loving me is a curse none of you deserve to bear."

Johar reached across and cupped my face with her other hand, forcing me to meet her eyes. "I have good news and bad news for you, Hail. The bad news is love doesn't win, entropy does. We all die, the stars will explode, the Milky Way will collapse, and the universe will tear itself apart."

She leaned in, pressing her forehead to mine. "The good news is we get to choose to love every day, which makes it even better, because it's a choice."

"It's the wro—"

"Listen to me. We need you back. I understand the darkness you've been in for these past weeks, and none of us begrudge you it. However, it's time you come back to us."

"I don't know how much of me is left." *I don't know if you want*

7

to see this rage fly free, Jo, it might burn the whole galaxy down. Those words remained unsaid even though I shook with the effort of keeping them inside.

"There's enough of you." Johar smiled as she pulled away. "You're still alive, aren't you?"

It should have been an easy answer. My heart was beating. There was air in my lungs.

But the soul of me was gone. Gone like Hao. Like Emmory and Zin. It was nothing but ash.

"I have lost the best parts of me."

The smile slipped off Jo's face like water sheeting down a window in Krishan's rainy season. "Hail," she said again. "Don't go out like this. You know they wouldn't—"

"Don't." I stopped her with a hand on her mouth as I pulled away. "Please, don't say it."

I was expecting cruelty, harsh words of disappointment over how I'd let down Emmory and Zin and all the others who'd died. Instead Johar pulled me into a hug.

"I would take your pain away, if I could," she whispered, releasing me and slipping back to her bunk as silently as she'd arrived.

I turned my face, now wet with tears, back to the window and the setting moons.

She's right, you know. Jet rested his head on my shoulder, and I let my imagination convince me there was weight to it.

"About what?" I asked my dead BodyGuard. It felt like so long ago that Jet had died. But it had only been a little over a year since he'd sacrificed himself to save me from a bomb on a cold Pratimas day. "That love doesn't matter? I suppose so. It only ever brings pain."

That's not what she said, and you know it, he countered. *She's right about them needing you. The whole galaxy needs you. You didn't quit when Wilson had you on the ropes, don't do it now.*

"This is different."

No, it's not. He chuckled, lifting his head to look at me with dark gray eyes. *You know it's not, stop lying to yourself, ma'am. You got knocked down. It happens to the best of us. Get up, spit blood at them, and keep going.*

Jet vanished and I rubbed the tears from my face as his words echoed in my ears.

2

The tears soaked into the long sleeves of the shirt I wore, leaving little wet patches on the smooth gray fabric. It was reminiscent of Fasé's outfit in the days after she'd tried to kill herself.

The resurrection of my previous *Ekam* had been so taboo, so against everything Fasé had believed in as to drive her to suicide. But I'd refused to let her do it and grabbed for her hand, insisting if she was going to die she'd have to take me with her.

I won't abandon you, not when you need me the most.

At the time I hadn't realized she would come back. Her soul reborn on Faria. I don't even know if she'd realized that in the moment. All I knew was that I couldn't stand by and watch her go without doing something to stop it. I closed my eyes as my memory threw my own words back at me. "Bugger me."

The time for fooling myself was over. I wasn't going to roll over and die; no matter how many of my people I lost, I'd keep fighting to the end. I was too damn stubborn to do anything but that.

Besides, we weren't anywhere close to the end, and this was my mess to fix. Jo was right about that. The dead wouldn't let me walk away without at least making the attempt.

Gita stirred in her bunk, waking slowly. I knew from experience Alba would sleep for another hour, as she often stayed up later than the rest of us, doing research and calculations on her *smati*. We would need to wake her.

I checked my own *smati*. The brain-computer interfaces we all had were still online. We could communicate with each other on our internal coms, but we were locked out of the bulk of the compound's systems. Alba, of course, had found a way in past the security at the basic levels but hadn't made it any further than that. The rest of us made do with only our internal network to avoid raising the Shen's suspicions. It limited our communication distance, but I was planning on us all staying together so it wouldn't be an issue.

The sun was rising. This little jungle base we were on was always moving, but the majority of the Shen would be starting their daily routines in a little over an hour. Right now they would be either groggily ending a shift or headed to one.

I'd seen as much even while I'd been lost to my grief, part of my brain cataloging the information and filing it away for a time when it would be useful.

I pushed away from the window and pulled the sheet off my bunk. Tapping on Alba's bunk on my way by, I issued the quiet order. "Get up."

Johar was lying on her bunk flipping a makeshift knife between her fingers. It didn't surprise me that she had it; Johar wasn't the type to stay unarmed for long. My movement caught her attention and she rolled to her side to watch me but didn't say anything.

I sat on the edge of her bunk and held my hand out for her knife, cutting and then tearing the sheet into strips.

The noise roused Gita the rest of the way and she climbed from the bunk above us, rubbing the sleep from her eyes.

"Good morning, Majesty."

"Good morning, Gita," I replied, watching as my greeting caused my *Ekam* to stutter-step on her way to the bathroom.

"Majesty?"

"Don't make a fuss—" My protest was muffled as Gita dropped to her knees and wrapped me into a hug.

As I hugged her back I realized that my *Ekam* had been grieving as much as I had. The loss of her fellow BodyGuards, of Hao, and even of her mother had to have weighed on her heart.

The latter had been killed by Wilson's treachery not that long ago, and I knew she had to still be grieving for Clara. I did, too.

"I'm sorry."

I waved off her apology when she released me. "I should be the one apologizing. I have not been the empress you deserve these last few weeks."

Gita's smile was watery. "You had every reason, Majesty. I am just glad you are back."

There was so much hope in her words I couldn't bring myself to argue and instead offered a smile before I returned to the destruction of my sheet.

"Majesty, what are you doing?"

"You have an escape plan, I'm assuming?" I replied, wrapping the first strip around my wrist and then my hand, covering up any piece of exposed skin.

"Nothing concrete yet, we've been waiting." Gita's exhale spoke louder than her words.

Waiting for me to wake up.

"Don't make it too tight," Johar said, sitting up and reaching for my arm. "You'll limit your movement."

My *Ekam* didn't protest; instead she moved to my other side with a frown. "You'll want your throat covered also, Majesty." She reached for the remaining sheet and took Jo's knife from the bed, cutting a triangular-shaped wedge and wrapping it twice around my neck. "You can pull this piece up to get some coverage on your face."

"It's better than nothing." I looked at her as Johar finished tying off my other hand. "I'm surprised there's no protest."

"Emmory always said I indulged you too much." Gita's smile flickered to life, edged with pain. "But I understand this need to hit something and I'm trusting you have a reason for this beyond recklessness."

"A shuttle came in last night. We're right at shift change, plus the early-morning hour will help us. We need to move now."

It took us less than ten minutes to shred the remaining sheets and protect the others. Alba had snapped awake once she realized what was happening and scrambled for the packs of food they'd stashed around the room.

"Back," I whispered, and headed for the door. Gita, surprising me again, didn't argue. I pulled open the door and the two Shen Aiz so charitably called escorts rather than guards came to attention. Hamah and Sere, if my memory served me right.

"Your Majesty?"

Hamah stiffened when I stepped from the room, finger creeping to the trigger on the Koros 201, the cousin weapon to the Koros 101 Aiz had shown me when we'd first been taken. It fired miniature projectiles at high speed. I hadn't seen a demonstration of their destructive power and didn't really want to be present for one.

"Are you feeling better? Mia asked that she be notified if you wished to see her." Sere, the shorter of the pair, smiled at me as he spoke. "If you'll wait here."

Neither of them had clued in to my attire and I punched Hamah in the throat as a response, jerking up the scarf to cover the lower half of my face as I kicked Sere in the knee and dropped him to the floor. Another kick to Sere's head knocked him out as he fell, and I brought my covered arm up to block the first guard's swing.

It was wild; Hamah's palm spread as he instinctively tried to find a bare patch of skin to touch instead of just leading with the force of a punch that would have stunned me had it connected. I dodged out of the way, planting my booted foot in his solar plexus, and kicked. His head hit the wall and he slid to the floor unconscious.

"Let's move," I said, picking up the guns and tossing one to Gita. "Alba, which way?"

She pointed to her right. "Down to the end of the hallway and right again, but there will be guards at the outside door and possibly some inside as well."

"Is the door locked?"

"I don't know," she replied with a shake of her head as we took off down the hallway. I glanced behind us at Gita.

"It seems unlikely," she replied. "We couldn't—or rather—Alba couldn't find any programs in the base system for door locks. So they're either unlocked or manual."

"Either way," Johar said. "Let me give it a good kick, we'll be fine."

The door when we reached it was not only not locked but not guarded, and I shared a worried look with my *Ekam* as we slipped into the predawn light.

"Too quiet," she whispered as we moved around the exterior of the low-slung compound.

"Yeah."

The Shen couldn't have anticipated this escape. They had no way of knowing I'd come out of my stupor and—

"You will, Majesty. I've seen it." Mia's words on the bridge of her ship came back to me faster than the speed of light.

"Fuck." I skidded to a halt as we came around the corner. Mia Cevalla stood by the shuttle, her hands folded in front of her.

"Good morning, Majesty." She smiled a slow, knowing smile but otherwise didn't react, even when I brought the Koros 201 up and pointed it at her.

I tugged the scarf down, moving toward her with Gita at my back. "Get out of my way. I really don't want to shoot you, but I will if you don't let us go."

Mia took a deep breath, looked down at her hands and then back at me. Her second smile made my gut twist with want and I muttered a curse under my breath. I did not need this ill-timed distraction, so I kicked it back out of view where it belonged.

"Aiz will come through that door in just a moment. You should hear the ruckus he's making on the coms. There are three ways this can play out, Your Majesty," she said. "Kill me, get on the ship, and everyone dies. Kill me, and Gita and Alba will die in the firefight that will happen when Aiz arrives. You and Johar will survive, for a while at least. Or drop your weapons and everyone lives."

I put my hand out, stopping Gita from bringing her own weapon up as the door to our right flew open.

"Only two options now," Mia murmured. "I am fine, Aiz." She put her hand up.

Aiz Cevalla was dressed only in a pair of black pants, leaving his lean torso bare, and his brown hair was disheveled as though he'd just rolled out of bed. It gave him a charming, slightly carefree appearance, but the glare he directed at me could have leveled a city block, and I was reasonably sure he could kill all of us with the pistol that was in his hand. "She broke her promise. Twice."

"Perhaps," Mia admitted. "It should have been expected, but you all got lazy thinking she would drift in her grief forever. Don't be reactionary. She will apologize. I've already forgiven her for it."

"Majesty." Gita shifted just enough to put herself in between me and Aiz. "I want you to go."

She had to have known what her words would do to me, coming on the heels of Mia's warning. There was no way I'd let anyone else die if I had the slightest control over it.

"No." I put my left hand up, my eyes locked on Mia as I lowered the gun to the ground. "Gita, put it down."

For the barest of moments I didn't think she would obey me, but finally, with her jaw muscles flexing, she slowly lowered her weapon to the ground as a host of Shen spilled out of the building.

"Crisis averted," Mia said, and blew out a breath. "Now, Your Majesty, I was about to sit down to breakfast. Would you like to join me?"

Judging from the look Aiz shot her, he wasn't on board with that plan, which made me more than happy to agree.

"Sure."

"Aiz, why don't you see Hail's people back to their rooms. Be nice." She gave him a look that was then transferred to me. "You didn't kill Sere and Hamah, did you?"

"They should be fine except for the headaches," I replied.

"Consequences for underestimating you, then, though a broken promise from you is surprising. You can apologize to me as we walk." She turned for the door; I shared a look with Gita and then followed Mia.

I held Aiz's gaze as I passed him. "Not a hair out of place on them," I said.

His expression didn't flicker. "I give you my word."

Point to the Shen, I thought, but I had to trust he'd follow his sister's orders and leave my people unharmed. *Two losses before breakfast; at this rate you're going to lose this game, Hail.*

3

If we're your prisoners my oath not to escape is pretty much useless. I'm honor-bound to get my people out of here safely, by any means necessary," I said as Mia and I headed down the hallway.

"You're not our prisoner."

"Then I'm sorry for the broken oath and for the injuries. Can we go home now?" It was a strange formal dance we were doing, but it blessed me with another of her smiles.

She ignored the question. "It is good to see you feeling better, Hail. Can I call you Hail? I'd like for us to be friends."

"Is Aiz going to retaliate against my people?"

"No." Mia seemed so certain. "Mostly he's mad because he was wrong and I was right. He really hates it when that happens."

"You can see the future, like Fasé."

"Yes." Mia stopped at an opened doorway and gestured inside. The room was so plain as to be familiar. I'd seen concrete bunkers like this on dozens of planets in our arm of the galaxy. The only difference was most of the rooms here were circular, with curving walls and domed ceilings. "Have a seat."

I sat at the table in the center of the room and looked over the simple spread, feeling my appetite wake up for the first time since Earth.

"This was inventive," Mia said, tapping my wrapped arm as she sat next to me.

I somehow managed not to jerk away from her. "Your people are too focused on their advantage against a human opponent," I replied, reaching for a dish of unfamiliar orange fruit. "It's a weakness if you're fighting someone intent on winning."

Mia's laughter was as bright as the fruit. "They are all under orders not to hurt you. That's also something of a disadvantage."

"Why?"

"Why what?"

"Why are they not supposed to hurt me?"

"Hail," Mia replied, and my name was an exhale, though her smile was as patient as her tone. "You are the Star of Indrana. We have not lied to you. We want your help. We want you on our side. We brought you here because leaving you on Earth was far too dangerous, especially after what happened to your embassy."

"Who blew up my embassy?"

Mia reached for a steaming dish, spooning the purple grains into a smaller bowl. "Try this, I think you will like it."

I took the bowl, pouring in a vanilla-scented milk from the pitcher Mia pushed my way. It was clear she wasn't going to answer my question, so I asked a different one. "Who's in charge?" I gestured at her with the pitcher. "On Earth it seemed as though Aiz was, but—"

"It was easier to let him be on Earth. Adora was distracted, is constantly distracted, by him. She discounts me because of who I am." Mia lifted a shoulder and picked up the pitcher to pour milk over her own bowl. "Speaking of Aiz, he'll go see to Hamah and Sere but then he'll be back and won't leave again. All I've really done is bought us some time alone." Her laugh lingered in the air, tangling itself into my brain.

So much for ignoring distractions.

"If you have any questions you'd rather he not hear, now would be the time to ask them."

"You seem awfully certain I won't hurt you."

"You have no reason to." Again with the patient smile, though this time I caught the surety behind it. "And you won't make the mistake of thinking I am defenseless."

"Fair enough." I took another bite, chewing as I studied her. "Are you going to answer my question? Who's in charge?"

"We are the co-leaders of the Shen, Hail. I trust my brother and he trusts me. We make decisions together whenever we can, but there are times when it is easier to just believe the other will handle it the best way possible."

"Who made the call to kill my people? You or him?"

Mia didn't blink at the venom in my words. "Neither of us, Hail. I believe a man named Jamison was responsible for the destruction of your embassy."

We'd known Jamison was there even before the embassy blew. His men had attacked the party, hounded us through the streets, blown up a shuttle and the building we'd been hiding in before finally destroying the embassy.

It appeared my long-running feud with the mercenary smuggler was reaching critical mass.

"That's what happens when you hire shit mercenaries," I said finally. "They do things like blow up embassies and shoot heads of state." I struggled to put the memory of the flight from the party to the embassy out of my head, but it insisted on playing just behind my eyes. "Is President Hudson alive?"

"I believe he survived."

"My people didn't." I put my spoon down, my appetite gone. "Your mercs killed them."

Mia raised an eyebrow at my snarl and shook her head. "They were not our mercenaries, Hail. I would not have hired Jamison. I certainly wouldn't have been so thoughtless as to have him attack the party like that. And there is nothing in this universe that would have convinced me to attack your embassy."

"Then your brother did it. Why else was Jamison there?" The

words had barely left my mouth before the voice in my head whispered that Aiz had been as surprised as I was by the attack. I'd seen it. Not to mention I'd seen the merc bring his weapon to bear on Mia.

Jamison could have been after Hao. Though his reckless, head-on attack had cost him the bounty Po-Sin had levied against his nephew for leaving the Cheng gang and swearing his loyalty to me.

"Hiring the mercenaries was my decision," Mia said. "We used Aiz to offer the contracts because we assumed they would react better to his face than mine." She rolled her eyes toward the ceiling. "Men are strange. I prefer your empire's way of doing things." She set her spoon down and laid her hand palm up across the edge of the table at me. "I picked the mercenaries we offered contracts to, and you have my word that Jamison was not among them."

"Why not?" I ignored the way my hand itched to reach out to hers. My attraction to Mia hadn't dimmed the least little bit in my grief, it seemed, but at the moment it was an unwelcome feeling. I fisted my hands and shoved them into my lap.

"You don't like him and for good reason," Mia replied, pulling her hand away with a tiny smile. "I know you, Hail. If I wanted your help—and I do—why would I bring someone you hate on board? I picked the mercenaries we hired with careful consideration—they are all groups you worked with or for in the past. Groups you respect. Jamison does not have your respect. Moreover, he's reckless and cruel. Sloppy and without the kind of control I know you value."

"You know an awful lot about me."

Mia dipped her head and I wondered if I was imagining the blush that seemed to stain her cheeks. "It's the same reason Aiz approached Hao for help on Pashati. Though I understand that caused far more disruption than any of us intended." She lifted her head and smiled. "I misjudged how much Hao cares for you. I did not think it would cause such a ripple effect. Po-Sin is still quite upset over his defection."

I blinked at her, unable to hide my shock. The Shen's tone was matter-of-fact, and as much as I cursed myself for a fool—I didn't think she was lying to me.

"Po-Sin will go after Jamison for killing Hao." I shoved a hand into my hair. "I need you to let me go so I can get to him first."

"It is not an option I can consider."

"If I am not a prisoner I'm free to leave."

"You are, but at what cost?" Her expression was clean of any amusement. "I have no ships I'm willing to lend you right now, so you have no way off this planet and no way to get back to the human sector of this galaxy."

"This doesn't engender any goodwill on my side, you know."

Mia leaned back in her seat. "You believed me when I said if you left on that shuttle everyone would die. Why don't you believe it now?"

"I—"

I was saved my fumbling by Aiz's arrival. He came into the room through the open door, reaching back and closing it behind him. Now he was fully dressed, not barefoot and shirtless, and with the pistol hanging from a holster under his left arm.

"Mia, *no den asfalés.*"

"*Ahora,*" she replied, her lips twitching into a smile. Aiz nodded and sat by her side, fixing his eyes on me. She rolled her eyes with an amused look at me that clearly said, *See?*

There was a long moment of silence as I met Aiz's gaze. Mia seemed content to let us have this staring contest, and it went on for several minutes before Aiz conceded with a tiny smile.

I went back to my food, hiding my surprise over the victory.

"Hail, I knew trust would be difficult, given your people's associations with the Farians, but—"

"A Shen tried to kill me at that party, my *Ekam*—" My voice cracked as I interrupted Mia, but I ignored it.

It didn't matter now that I'd killed a Shen while his hands had been on Emmory and my *Ekam* hadn't died. Emmory was dead now. They all were.

"What am I supposed to make of that?"

"What would be the point of killing you there?" Mia countered. "When we could have killed you so many times before? I hope you believe me when I say that flashy statements and worthless pomp are not our way. If I'd wanted you dead, I would have walked into your hotel room back on Pashati and killed you myself. I could kill you right now, Hail." Her tiny smile should have chilled me to the bone, but that vicious voice in my head whispered that maybe baring my throat to her and getting it over with would be better for everyone.

"Do it, then. What's stopping you?"

Aiz stopped shoveling food into his mouth and chewed as he stared thoughtfully at me.

Mia's calm gray eyes met mine and a sudden sorrow flooded them as she shook her head. "Oh, Hail. I wish I could take that pain away from you."

I pushed out of my chair and spun away from them, pressing my fingers to my eyes. "I don't want your fucking pity."

"You don't have it. You have my sympathy. You have my respect. Hail, we need your help—"

I froze at the touch on my arm; even through the fabric I could feel the heat of her skin. I dropped my hands and looked at her. "I am not in any position to help you. Especially here."

"That's where you're wrong. You are the Star of Indrana. The one who can see through the light. The one who calls out the rot from its beautiful façade. The one who loses everything and saves everything in return. Without you, it all burns to ashes.

"We don't want you dead, Hail. It's the worst thing that could happen."

I am already dead. My body just hasn't figured it out yet.

Her words were like frozen needles under my fingernails, but somehow I found my footing and sidestepped my grief, taking refuge in the anger. "Here we go again," I said. "I am not your savior. I am not your prophecy. I am not your weapon! Give me something real to hold on to or let me go so I can hunt Jamison down and cut him into pieces for what he's taken from me."

Mia inhaled and flexed her hand on my arm before she released me and stepped back. "We have gotten off track. Hail, sit down, please. Finish your breakfast."

I told myself I was choosing to go back to the table, not following an order that—no matter how delicately it was phrased—was still an order. I picked up my spoon again and poked at the food in my bowl.

Aiz had been silent the whole time, eating as though nothing unusual were happening. Now he put down his fork and folded his hands together on the tabletop. "The man who attacked you in the embassy wasn't a Shen. He was a Farian, but I have seen the surveillance footage so I understand your confusion. He was not after you, he was after your people. The Farians have a use for those who look like us. They are too obvious to blend in well," he said.

"What would be the point of the Farians trying to kill my people?"

Aiz pinned me with a look. "After the last month, do you really have to ask?"

This time I was the one who looked away.

"You care about your people, Hail. It's not a weakness, it's an admirable thing," he continued. "But it is something the Farians would exploit. Six months ago I would have sworn the Farians would have protected you to the end, but the inclusion of Fasé and her rising power may have tipped the balance. Fear makes people dangerous."

"You think the assassin was there unconnected to Jamison?"

Mia and Aiz shared a look before she answered. "It's possible. However much I would like to blame the Farians for what happened on Earth, I have to say it's more likely Jamison was the one responsible for it all." A smile flickered to life. "As you said, he is a shit mercenary."

I shoved at the sympathy in her voice that dragged at the pain in the depths of my chest. "Let's back up a minute. There are Shen who work for the Farians?"

Mia sighed. "Yes and no. They are not Shen, but they have been separated from their gods and so they look more like us than Farians. They are still Farian to the core, more so if the truth be told because they are willing to sacrifice themselves for the cause."

I remembered what Fasé had told us about how the Shen came to look more like humans than Farians. "Why does the separation change you?"

"The Farians are linked to their gods. Rooted to the soil of Faria. It is that connection which makes them look the way they do. I do not know the specifics, but Aiz could tell you." She gestured at her face. "Aiz and our father, the others who were with them. They are the first Shen. They shattered that link with the gods and with the breaking lost their connection to our home. It was an easy sacrifice. But there were other sacrifices they did not realize at the time. Things that took a far greater toll on them."

"Like what?"

"The loss of our immortality."

4

blinked at her. "You aren't immortal? But the Shen came from Farians, Aiz said—"

"We make no distinction between those who chose to break from the Farians and become Shen and those who are born from human-Shen pairings." Aiz shook his head. "The universe, however, is not so kind."

"My people," Mia said. "Those of us who are blessed with human kin are different from my brother's people, though we are all Shen."

"When I die, my soul is reborn," Aiz said. "But my sister and the others—"

"We just die," Mia said, picking up when her brother lapsed into silence, and I watched Aiz's shoulders jerk.

He reached out, closing his fingers around Mia's. "My sister will die. I will not." Aiz shook his head. "I also will not accept that."

"I am sorry," I said. "However, I still don't understand how you expect me to help you."

"If we go home," Mia said, her voice soft, "we can be reborn."

"Home?"

"To Faria. We will go home and finish what we started." Aiz's smile was slight, dying before it made the climb from his mouth to his eyes. "I wasn't lying to you. That part of the negotiations wasn't up for discussion."

"You were lying about just wanting a settlement on the planet."

"If, as Mia said, it were to happen, it would be a miracle. I don't have enough faith left that Adora and the Pedalion will see reason in this. So we will take the whole planet as our due. The Farians who choose to rise up against the Pedalion and their worthless gods are welcome to stay. Fasé's rebellion has proven, however unintentionally, to be most beneficial to our cause. I was hoping she would join us, but her death at your embassy will be a significant setback for her plans."

I realized then that Fasé and Sybil and her siblings wouldn't stay dead, and I wondered how long my brain would insist on hearing her ghost whispering in my ear. Swallowing down the pain, I shook my head at the pair of Shen and grabbed for the bravado that had always saved me. "You've got a lot of fancy ships here, but I doubt it's enough to match the Farians."

Mia's laughter spilled out into the air, a sound as brittle as old-fashioned castings raining down on a metal floor. "These are not our only ships. We have dozens of outposts, Hail. All with just as many ships as this one. This war has been going a long time, but now we are finally winning."

"How do you finance all this?"

"Our people live all over the galaxy, Majesty. It's easy for us to blend in with humanity, to make sure we are among our own kind in case of emergency. The Farians can't spot us, and you humans are rather involved in your own worries most of the time. Our people have businesses in every sector imaginable—manufacturing, pharmaceuticals, finance, construction, shipping." Her mouth quirked upward in a smile. "We also do business in your former line of work. It is all done in service to the cause. We have built a nation in the shadows of humanity, safe from Farian attack, all to fuel this endless war. When I call, they will come and fight."

"How many?"

Mia shrugged. "Enough."

Her words confirmed my suspicions that the Shen had integrated themselves into human society, and I wondered just how many thousands, if not millions, were hidden in plain sight.

"Assume for the moment I believe your claim that it was Jamison who attacked us and blew up the embassy," I said as I set my spoon down next to my bowl.

"You don't believe us."

I studied her and then shook my head. "I don't have a reason to, and you don't have any proof. I've known people like you—granted, they were human—but it's no different. You've both forgotten I sold guns to the leaders of hundreds of petty wars for decades. Everyone thinks their side is the righteous one, the justified one. What do you want with me? Because I'm not about to believe you rescued me and my people from Earth out of the goodness of your hearts."

Mia laid a hand on Aiz's forearm, stopping his rebuttal. "Assuming for the moment that you believe us, we want your help, Hail. Freely given. To finish what my brother started and help us be whole again."

"What are you offering me in return?"

"In exchange, we will help you visit justice on whoever it was that attacked you and your people. We will keep Indrana safe from the Farians and whatever else is coming. The Shen will be your allies."

"I cannot make an alliance with you. Not while Indrana and Faria are allied." I shook my head. "And there is no way we can break that alliance without bloodshed."

"The alliance is already fracturing, Hail, and you will soon no longer be empress." Mia shrugged. "We are not interested in your empire, though we would welcome such a friendship should it happen. I agree with you that it would be unlikely as long as the Pedalion holds power. Your people's lives are too entangled with the Farians. Ripping you apart would be most dangerous."

"So what then?" I set my spoon down. "I'll admit I am not the most politically savvy person, but even I know that an alliance with a single person isn't worth a lot."

"Hail, a single person can move the stars themselves." Mia reached her hand out again, a hopeful smile on her dark lips. "Did Fasé ever show you what the future holds for you?"

I stared at her hand, heart aching in response to the memories flooding my brain. "Yes. No. I mean, she showed me futures that didn't happen. Ones where the choice had already been made. We talked about the others, including the one from the Council of Eyes. All of it, I'll be honest, is asking me for a lot of faith I don't have."

Mia rolled her eyes. "Farians. I had hoped Fasé was better than the superstitions of her upbringing. What is the point of sending a soldier into battle without all the information, all the weapons to defend themselves?"

"She said it wasn't wise to know too much."

Mia muttered something in Shen that I was reasonably sure was a curse, and looked at the ceiling before responding. "Is it wise to fight not knowing why? Not knowing what you're trying to save? Let me show you what is coming."

I reached out, intent on pressing the exposed tips of my fingers to her palm, when Hao's ghost whispered in my ear.

Cas knew what was coming. It cost him his life.

I jerked back, scrambling out of my chair and away from Mia before I consciously realized I was moving. Aiz moved in front of his sister, his hands raised, and I put my own up as I backed away.

"No." My voice was raw in my throat.

"You can't dodge this, Star of Indrana. There's no escape from what is coming," Aiz said. "The light will swallow us all up. Bodies and souls."

"Aiz, it's fine." Mia rose from her own seat and moved around him. "Hail, if you will just let me—"

"No."

Taking a step toward me, Mia thought better of it when I snarled and she dipped her head. "Okay. You're not ready. It's okay."

It wasn't okay. I fisted my hands, battling the desperate desire to throw a punch at something, anything. "I should go back to our rooms," I managed.

"We'll take you."

There were new guards outside our door. They stiffened when we approached.

"We're not going anywhere," I said. "And we're not your prisoners. Is this really necessary?"

"Probably not," Mia admitted. "If I give you leave to come and go from your rooms as you please, do you agree to a guard?"

"Sure."

"Aiz can send you what footage we have from the attack at the party and what information we've gathered. I have a meeting to attend tomorrow morning," Mia said with a smile. "But I will send someone to get you for dinner and we will talk again." She looped her arm through Aiz's and headed back down the corridor. I slipped through the door after watching them go.

"Majesty, are you hurt?"

I shook my head, flinching when Gita closed a hand on my arm. She released me with a murmured apology.

"What happened?"

Johar and Alba joined us as I sank down at the table in the corner. My left hand was still locked in a fist and I spread it open against my thigh.

"Jamison is the one who attacked us." I rubbed at my forehead. "The Farians may have also been involved, or they may have only been trying to kill all of you. I don't know for sure. They want me to help Aiz finish the fight he and his father started. They want an alliance." I frowned. "With me, not Indrana."

"You can't be serious—" Gita stared at me, wide-eyed, and blew out a breath before she dropped her hands from her hair. "I'm sorry, Majesty. That's—"

"I know. I know I shouldn't believe them, that there's no reason to believe them. But what else am I supposed to do?" I lifted my hands helplessly.

"We all know it was Jamison's men at the party, right? I hate to say the Shen might be telling the truth, but Adora left just before the shooting started," Alba said.

I sucked in a breath. The memory of Adora leaving the party had slammed into my head before my chamberlain even finished speaking. A red haze of fury dropped itself over my world.

I was a weapon seeking a target, and a part of me knew there was a very real chance Mia was using that to her advantage; but it was drowned out by the louder voice in my brain screaming for vengeance. "Fuck," I muttered, because it seemed a better idea than screaming.

"And Aiz took out a waiter who was about to shoot his sister." Alba smiled when we all stared at her. "I've been over my recordings from that night. There's no outward sign of nervousness from Adora, but her timing is impeccable. And Aiz wasn't pretending to be surprised. Believe me, I'm not defending them, but he really was caught off guard and Mia was in real danger there."

Relief flooded through me, stronger than a shot of whiskey at the confirmation that I hadn't been imagining Aiz's surprise. That I hadn't been grasping at something, anything, to justify my belief in Mia's words.

"What are we going to do?" Johar asked.

"I don't know." I shook my head, hunting for the right words. "I need to talk to her more, figure out what they actually mean. If they want me to fight with them, or what." I sighed and lifted my hands. "I know you three don't need to be here. I was going to ask them— we got sidetracked. Mia wanted to show me the future."

"Did you let her?"

"No, I—" The words stuck in my throat again and I pushed to my feet, suddenly desperately in need of motion to keep the scream from crawling out of me. "They could kill all of us, but here we are still alive," I said when I could speak again. "They took us off Earth because it was safer than leaving us there. And I'll be honest, I'm not sure I can blame Aiz for that decision."

"Why don't they just take us home, then?" Gita's question cut like razor wire.

"They need my help. Even if we don't believe it, Mia believes that me going home will kill everyone." I knew the answer didn't satisfy her. It didn't satisfy any of them, judging from the looks I was getting.

"You could help better from Indrana."

The thought of going home, of facing everyone's pity, of having to go through my days with a whole crowd of new BodyGuards around me, made an explosion of pain go off in my chest. I wanted to curl up around it and never get up. "I don't think they will let me go," I said. "We can move around the compound as long as a guard accompanies us. She didn't say anything expressly about not going off the base, but I suspect that's more because she assumes the jungle will stop us than anything."

Johar made a dismissive noise. "I've been in worse jungles. Find me a long-distance ship we can get to and I'll get us out of here."

"You think we should try to escape again?" I looked around as all three women nodded, but I spotted Jagana's ghost shaking her head at me in the corner of the room.

"Majesty, what are you planning?" Gita asked.

"I am considering our options." It was a cowshit answer and we both knew it.

"See that." Gita pointed at me. "That makes me nervous."

"Wrapping me up to go toe-to-toe with guards who could kill me with a touch didn't?"

Gita laughed. "The only part of this I believe is that they don't want you dead. I don't know why, and I don't trust that it's for our good or the good of Indrana. But you are right that they could have killed us all at any point here and they haven't. The question is why?"

"Mia said she—they—needed me." I shrugged. "And Aiz seemed to agree. They need me to get them back home so their half-human offspring can be as immortal as the others. They need me to scare some sense into the Pedalion. I don't know." I pinched the bridge of my nose as I sat back down in my original spot. "When did my life become a vid-drama?"

The chuckling that echoed unknotted some of the grief in my heart, and Gita sat next to me, her shoulder pressing into mine. "If it is, Majesty, that gives me some hope."

"Why?"

She smiled. "Because the good people always win in the end in those vids."

I laughed bitterly, then turned into Gita's embrace and wept.

5

The Shen who knocked on the door to our room the next evening favored me with a smile when I opened it. "Star of Indrana, I am Talos. It is a great pleasure to meet you," he said in heavily accented Indranan. He was taller than me, by a few centimeters only, but it was a rare enough thing among Indranans and even more unheard-of among the Shen and Farians. His brown eyes were warm as he extended a bare hand to me, palm facing out.

I studied him for a moment. "A test?"

"A greeting," he replied, his smile never wavering.

I pressed my palm to his, and his smile spread as he gestured toward the doorway. Despite my wariness, my gut liked him and I smiled back.

"I will bring you and your *Dve* to the *Thínos* for dinner. There is food coming for the rest of your companions soon."

"Gita is my *Ekam*, Talos."

"Of course, Star of Indrana, my Indranan is not very good. I'm sorry."

I followed him into the empty corridor, Gita at my side. True to her word, Mia had left us to roam as long as we had a guard, but I decided to wait a day or two before we explored just to see how serious she was about agreeing to my request.

Talos escorted us away from our room and through another series of twisting corridors before we ended up in a softly lit room.

Aiz and Mia were in quiet conversation on the far side and they turned as we came in. They were wearing the same gray clothing as both Gita and I were.

"Thank you."

"Star of Indrana. *Dve*— My apologies. *Ekam* Desai. *Thinos*." Talos bowed and left us alone in the room.

"Majesty, Gita, have a seat," Aiz gestured at the table. "We'll talk about killing gods." He grinned. "That's good dinner conversation."

Mia rolled her eyes. "This is why no one invites you to dinner, brother."

"Killing gods," I repeated, an eyebrow arched upward as I took the seat Gita pulled out. She sat on my right, between me and Aiz, and though I admired her determination to protect me, I wasn't sure Mia was any safer.

"When you say that, it's a metaphor for something, right? You didn't really fight and kill gods when you and your family came back to Faria?" I asked.

Aiz continued to grin at me.

I stared back for a long moment until Hao's ghost whispered in my ear. *Find out what they want, Hail. You can't operate on zero information.*

Mia rose from her seat and poured wine into a glass, studying Gita when she waved it off and passing it along to me with a smile. "My brother is a trifle too blunt at times and incredibly obnoxious at others. However, I would appreciate it if you wouldn't kill him with that."

I smiled. "You heard that story, huh?"

"Everyone has heard that story," Aiz replied. "The great Hail Bristol, getting her revenge on the man who destroyed her family and tried to steal her throne. Killing him with the broken stem of a wineglass. It's a thrilling tale." He looked like Hao used to at the promise of an easy job with a high payoff. So very pleased with himself. "But my sister and I rejoiced because we knew it meant it was finally time."

"Time for what?"

"Time for the Pedalion to fall. Time for the Farians' so-called gods to meet their long overdue justice."

"The Farians are not the only ones with plans for the future," Mia said. Her smile was gentle. "I meant what I said. I would like for us to be friends."

I passed the wine to Gita so she could scan it; as much as I was sure the Cevallas wouldn't kill me, not scanning it seemed like an insult to Emmory's memory.

"It's clean, ma'am." She handed it back to me.

"To friendship and victories."

"I don't expect either of those things to happen, but cheers," I replied, and took a sip, and the earthy scent of it morphed into cherries on my tongue.

"Start talking." I picked up my fork and dug into the plate in front of me. "Tell me why all this cowshit showmanship with the negotiations, which did nothing but put my people in harm's way, when you could have just told me from the outset what you wanted. Tell me what the fuck is going on here and hope to whatever gods it is you follow that I believe you. Because if I don't, I promise you that fighting gods will be the least of your worries."

The challenge was snarled, my anger and grief almost slipping free from the box I'd shoved them into, and I felt Gita tense at my side. Part of me was tempted to let it out, let it free to wreak the kind of havoc I knew it would. I'd kill Aiz, kill Jamison, and kill anyone else in my way. I'd burn this whole damn galaxy to the ground and then set the ashes on fire out of spite.

Some undefinable emotion crossed Aiz's face. "We follow no gods, Hail. We are bound by nothing outside of our own hearts and the vows we choose to make to each other. That is Shen law. Not some dogma dictated from a council lording over the masses. People pledging themselves to the cause of a greater good."

I watched him over the rim of my glass. In another world, we could have been friends—his words echoed so deeply in my soul—but we weren't in that world.

We were in my own personal Naraka.

Aiz continued. "I realize how little my word means to you right now, but we didn't kill your people. Don't you realize that would be counter to our desire to enlist your cooperation?"

"Prove it. Tell me what you want from me." Setting my glass down, I leaned back and crossed my arms.

The siblings shared a look, timeworn and battle-tested. It said a hundred things in the span of a heartbeat and reached an agreement without use of *smati* or silent coms. I'd shared that look with Hao in what felt like another life entirely. I'd seen that look passing between Emmory and Zin, and it made my heart ache to see it now.

"The Shen have been the rebels from the beginning," Aiz said, looking from his sister to me. "You've heard of our return home. How my family and others brought justice to some of those who'd enslaved us."

I had heard it; moreover, I'd heard it from enough varied sources that I had to admit to myself the story as I knew it was probably true.

The Shen had been Farians who were sacrificed into the black, Farians who'd then returned and slain their gods. All but three of them. If I were to believe Adora, Aiz and his parents were the ones responsible. They would have been her parents, too, I realized.

"I've heard it," I replied.

"We want your expertise in the fight against the Farians. You know the mercenaries we have hired. They respect you. They will follow you."

"You are assuming an awful lot." I blew out a breath and laughed. "But go on."

"And I want you to help me kill those who escaped me before."

My amusement fled, and Gita stiffened at my side. "You want me to help you kill gods."

Aiz shook his head. "The Farians call them gods. They are not gods. They are powerful beings, devious and deceptive. It will not be easy. But they can be killed." There was no humor in his voice or his eyes. Mia's back was straight and her gray eyes were locked on me.

"Why do you think I am even remotely capable of succeeding where you have failed?"

Aiz smiled and lifted a shoulder. "You are the Star of Indrana and my sister has seen you standing in triumph over our defeated enemies." His smile vanished. "It's why we can't send you home. If we don't fight, if you're not there, we won't win. And the light that comes after burns everything to the ground."

"Fight a god. They were serious about that?" Alba blinked at me as I recounted the conversation later that evening.

"Three to be precise, or the universe goes up in flames. Though according to Aiz they're not gods." I tapped my palms on my knees and then pushed to my feet to pace the room. Alba sat cross-legged on a nearby bunk doing something on her *smati*. Gita was at the table, meticulously drying out her hair.

"They want you to fight several beings that the Farians believe are gods." Gita threw her hands in the air, her laugh sharp enough to draw Alba's attention for a moment. "It's madness. Never mind the cryptic: Something worse is coming if we fail."

"Something worse is always coming," I replied, unperturbed by my *Ekam*'s outburst.

"Mortals don't fight gods, Majesty."

I chuckled. "You and I both know that's not true. Not if we're to believe the stories of our own gods."

"The more I hear of this, the more I think the Farians and the Shen are off the rails." Johar was in the corner, braced against Alba's bunk. "But then, I don't believe in gods," she muttered, not looking up from her work of painstakingly chipping away at the concrete wall holding the thick plastic window in place.

37

"Honestly, I'm not going to get hung up on the god bit," I replied with a shrug of my own. "Aiz may have been telling the truth there—that these are just powerful beings. *Hai Ram*, they're probably unknown aliens who played themselves off as gods to the Farians. Whatever they are though, Aiz wants me to fight them and the idea holds more than a little appeal." I sighed, raking a hand through my hair, knowing Gita was going to protest my next words. "I did what Fasé asked and tried to stay out of this fight.

"I followed that future and all it got us was chaos and lot of dead bodies. I need to pick a side here, and even though the Farians may not have been responsible directly for what happened on Earth, they knew what was coming." Images of Adora leaving the party filled my brain, and my hands shook with the need to hit something. "What choice do I have but to join the Shen in this fight?"

"Majesty, no."

"I know it's not ideal. Alice wasn't ever supposed to be on the throne unless something happened to me, but now she'll be on it whether she likes it or not. She can rule until Ravalina is of age." Alice's newborn daughter had become the true heir to the throne at the moment of her birth.

"What happened to trying to escape again?" Johar asked.

"If they won't let you go, I say yes, keep working on it." I shook my head. "But I won't go with you. I'll stay here and make sure the galaxy is safe. Or at least I'll make sure Indrana is safe, because if we can't trust the Farians, then I should be fighting with the Shen to stop them."

"You can't trust them," Gita protested.

"I can trust my own eyes." I very pointedly did not look to where Jet's ghost was sitting on the bunk above Alba watching our discussion. "This war between the Shen and the Farians needs to stop because it will spread and it will continue to kill people. I will do what I can to stop it." My tone was ominous enough to have everyone frowning.

"Majesty, I can't leave you." Gita closed her eyes and shook her head. "Emmory will—"

"Emmory is dead, Gita." I hated that it got easier every time I said the words out loud.

"You want to sell yourself in exchange for our lives."

"I am empress, Gita, for the moment anyway. That's kind of the job description."

Jet smiled at my words. They were an echo of the ones he'd said to me once upon a time.

"I won't ask anyone else to die. Not when I can stop it." If it meant my death I was okay with that also, but I didn't think it would help my argument to say that out loud to Gita.

"This is a horrible idea," Gita replied.

"The one I had that ended with Hao jumping off a building on Pluto was worse," I replied with a bitter laugh. "I can't deal in maybes or hope, Gita," I replied. "I have to look at what's in front of me, and my priorities are very clear here. Your safety. The safety of the empire."

"With respect, Majesty, *you're* my priority."

"If the councils do their damn duties, they'll declare Alice as empress once we hit the two-month mark of my absence." I spread my hands wide. "Problem solved. I will no longer be your problem."

"You'll always be my empress." She met my look with a calm expression that kicked at the wall I'd built around my broken heart. "No matter what. You can order me to quit, I won't. You can try to fire me. It won't make any difference. It's not something you or anyone else can take from me, ma'am."

Tears threatened to break free and I rubbed my hands over my face to hide them as I wrestled with the emotions digging their claws into the raw place in my chest. "I need you all safe," I whispered. "After what happened, I can't—"

Gita got up and wrapped her arms around me, holding on even when I stiffened at the contact. "I know you do, but you can't shut us out. You can't sell yourself for our safety. It doesn't work like that."

"How's it supposed to work? You want me to stand here and watch you all die?" My words were muffled against her shoulder.

"I'm not planning on dying, but yes. If it comes to that. I—we expect you to be the last person standing. We expect you to survive and to lead Indrana." Her voice caught. "I won't dishonor the memory of my fellow BodyGuards by leaving you alone here." Gita pulled back, cupping my face in her hands and pressing her forehead to mine. "Do what you need to do, Majesty. I promise I won't fight you on it as long as you let us stay. Don't make us leave you here."

"It sounds like I can't make you do anything, *Ekam*," I whispered.

"Maybe not." Gita smiled. "I'm reasonably sure that goes both ways."

"Gita, I'm in." Alba's announcement broke us apart, and I frowned first at my chamberlain and then at my *Ekam*.

"In what?"

Alba smiled, holding out a hand, which I took. Her palm was warm and solid against mine, a reminder that I had a duty to keep them all safe that went above and beyond Gita's comfort level.

"When we first arrived I could see several signals on the base, Majesty," Alba said. "They were all on lockdown, though, and two were military-grade encryption that I can't hack." Her fingers tightened around mine. "But I poked around at one of the smaller ones for the last month to see if I could find a way to piggyback off it. I've got access to their network. I may be able to find out where we are, maybe even get a signal out to Em—" She broke off, and worried at her lower lip.

"Emmory's gone, Alba."

"I don't want to believe you, ma'am."

"I know. I don't want to either, but it doesn't change the truth of it." I sighed, knowing I should tell Alba to leave it be and let me handle our hosts.

"Majesty," Gita said, leaning against the bunk. "Let us do this while you see what you can learn from the Cevallas."

"All right." I nodded, glancing in Johar's direction.

She didn't look up from her work on the window. "You could cut my hands off and I'd still keep working on a way to get this window open."

"You know we can walk out the front door, right?" I replied.

"Yeah, with a guard."

"Jo." I shouldn't be smiling, but I couldn't help myself. "It'll be easier to walk out the front even if we're escaping."

Johar muttered a curse and turned to glare at me. "Why do you ruin all my fun?"

6

Tell Aiz to look at these." Mia smiled up at Talos as she handed back the tablet. "I want all those troops ready to move out of there in the next ten standard days to the rendezvous point."

"Yes, ma'am." Talos nodded once and headed for the door.

"Why can't you fight the gods with Aiz?" I asked. "I understand the risks of you dying, but he can still bring you back from the dead if you're killed, right?"

"He can." Mia watched Talos leave the room, a smile on her face. They'd interacted so much like me and my BodyGuards it was almost painful to watch. All the Shen who spoke with Mia came away with smiles on their faces, yet I could already tell there were a handful at this base she was closer to—Talos and Hamah among them. The latter stood in the doorway, ignoring Gita, who was on the opposite side.

True to their word, most of the Shen didn't seem to consider us prisoners even with our constant guards; however, I could pick up on the little pieces of concern that some of the others couldn't quite hide. Gita wasn't armed, a fact that was still a point of contention with our hosts, but I had faith that she could get Hamah's weapon from him if the need was dire.

Especially if he kept gripping it that tight. There was no way he could get a shot off before she'd be on him.

And I'd be right behind.

"But you can't help him?" I dragged my attention away from my *Ekam* and back to Mia.

"It's not a matter of me not being able to help him, Hail. It's that I won't."

"You won't?"

Mia's smile at the shock in my voice was fleeting. She lifted a shoulder and then carefully set her fork to the side. "I have agreed to lead the fleet. What Aiz wants—what he needs as far as the fight with the gods goes? That is not something I can give to him."

"I'm not sure I understand."

"There is killing and then there is *killing*, yes? You know the difference. Between firing the weapons of a ship, and firing a gun, and killing someone with your bare hands. Cutting their throat and watching them bleed out on the polished wood floor of your family's summer home."

Air clogged in my throat.

Mia got up from her seat, her movements echoing a restlessness I felt in my own chest. "I went down that road once. It was necessary to get us where we are now. If I do it again I will not return. If I try to do it again, it will lead us all to a place where everything is lost. I am not the one to do this. The futures I have seen where I fight at my brother's side only bring us to disaster. Aiz understands and forgives me for my failure, but it means we need your help."

"You want me to kill gods," I said, the memory of Aiz's words floating into my head as I pushed away from the table and crossed the room to her. "I don't believe in gods. And even if I did, I am human, Mia. I have no special powers. I am not—"

"You are the Star of Indrana and they are not gods."

"So everyone keeps saying." I shoved my hands into the pockets of my gray pants. "Not sure just what that's supposed to mean, though. They are powerful, yes? And me?" I lifted a shoulder. "Star of Indrana is just a title, Mia."

"No." Mia poked me in the chest and Gita stiffened.

I pulled my hands free and held one up, stopping my *Ekam* before she could cross to us, and caught Mia's hand in one smooth motion with the other. "You know enough about me to know what happens when people poke me, right?" I asked with a smile.

Mia's reaction was minute, a slight widening of her eyes that told me she had, in fact, heard the story about my hapless cousin and her broken finger.

Hamah, by contrast, snapped something in Shen and brought his gun up. I was all too aware of the dangerous line I was walking. I trusted Gita not to move, but Hamah was an unknown quantity who seemed to lean more on the side of react first, think later.

"His reaction time needs to be better if he's supposed to be keeping you safe," I murmured.

"You're touching my bare skin, Hail." Mia's eyes darkened into the color of rain-drenched stone. "I'm reasonably sure that I have the upper hand here."

The memory of Aiz stopping everything inside me back on Earth flashed through my head, but Mia wasn't as old as her brother, nor was she fully Shen, and I wondered what kind of odds that gave me.

"Being half human and younger than my brother doesn't lessen my abilities," Mia said as if she'd read my thoughts, her smile never wavering. "I will apologize for my rudeness, though."

"Apology accepted." I couldn't stop myself from rubbing my thumb over the back of her hand before I let her go. "Star of Indrana," I said, spreading my arms wide and giving a sarcastic bow. "Enlighten me, since I am not up to date on just what this means and you all appear to be working off a different future than the one Fasé and Sybil told me about."

Mia shook her head. "I think we can both acknowledge that this is a bit like explaining to a tiger just what she is. You are yourself, Hail. As for the future, yes. We are aware of the one Sybil has seen, I have seen parts of it myself. There are more, though, parts that

44

impact the Shen, so either Sybil left them out or the Pedalion struck them from the record."

"So you lied to me on Pashati?"

"We were dealing with the matter at hand, which was keeping you from helping the Farians." Mia met my gaze without the slightest hint of remorse. "A lie by omission, maybe, but we were a little pressed for time. Plus, the Farians have us at a disadvantage where Indrana is concerned."

I hummed. Caspel's initial notes on the Cevallas were being re-sorted in my head with every conversation. Mia was far more politically savvy than I'd been led to believe, and I wondered if her competence extended to her battle strategies. The Shen didn't seem the least concerned about how this war might play out, and I wondered if it was—once again—because I was at the center of whatever they were planning.

That was fine. I was game for a fight.

"You've seen me fight these beings."

"I have."

"And we win?"

Mia considered her answer for several heartbeats. "I have seen you win. I have seen you lose. I've seen you fight the gods to a standstill. I have seen the fight interrupted by treachery." She shook her head. "It is too far out to see the outcome as a certainty. There are many choices between here and there."

"But it's where you and Aiz want me." I took a deep breath. "You want me to fight because you won't."

"Yes." Mia dipped her head. "Because despite the chaos in the futures I see, it is always you in the winning ones. You are the one who will stand at my brother's side and defeat the gods."

"I appreciate the honesty at least," I murmured, and glanced in Gita's direction, knowing my *Ekam* would likely protest my next words. "Will you send my people back to Indrana?"

"No."

"What if I refuse to help unless you do?" I asked.

"Hail." My name was a sigh on her lips. "I want you to choose to help us, not be forced into it. We are running out of time. The galaxy is running out of time. Your people need to stay with you."

"As leverage."

"As reminders," Mia countered, looking down at her hands before she looked up at me. "You said everyone you loved had died, but that's not really true, is it? You need to be reminded there are things in this galaxy worth fighting for. Believe me, you will need the reminder."

I hate it when the bad guys have good points, Hao whispered in my ear, and I jerked away from my brother's ghost.

"I want you to make this choice on your own, Hail. The circumstances are not ideal, but we will make the best of them. We had planned to try to speak with you again at the party and try to convince you—to show you what would happen. Obviously, that didn't go so well. I am sorry for the loss of your people; I know how much it hurts."

It was hard to focus on Mia's words as Hao's ghost strolled around us and leaned in close to study the Shen. He looked back at me and winked.

How you always gravitated toward the prettiest and the most dangerous ones I'll never know, he said, and I hissed.

Mia arched a delicate eyebrow. "Are you all right?"

"Fine." I gritted the word out and rubbed both hands over my eyes. When I removed them, Hao's ghost was gone, and Mia was frowning at me. "Thank you for breakfast," I said, and headed for the door.

Gita followed me out without a sound and we made it halfway back to our rooms before she said anything. Her voice was pitched low to prevent Hamah from hearing where he trailed behind us.

"Majesty." The beleaguered sigh was a painful reminder of Emmory, and grief poured through me again. "You said you wouldn't—"

"I know where this is headed, *Ekam*."

"Shiva, I wish you would stop calling me that."

"You're my *Ekam*."

"Emmory is your *Ekam*, ma'am."

"Emmory is dead!" I knew we had Hamah's attention now. Seething, I continued down the corridor and into our rooms. Johar and Alba jerked in surprise as I came through the doorway with enough force to make the door slam against the wall. "Fires of Naraka, Gita, I'm just trying to keep the rest of you safe."

"You're trying to sideline us. You said you wouldn't send us away, but first chance you get you're trying to bargain with them by selling yourself for our lives!"

Johar raised an eyebrow at me, and I dragged a hand through my hair with a muttered curse. "It was worth asking the question."

"Majesty?"

I only just kept myself from shouting at Fasé's sudden interruption. Ignoring the look that passed between Jo and Gita, I strode back out the door into the silence of the hallway.

Hamah didn't follow; instead a smaller Shen whose name I couldn't remember took his place. I was both relieved and disappointed by the change in guard. Hamah I could have provoked into a fight. This woman behind me had far too much awe in her eyes.

My stomach was a sharp-edged mass of grief and anger all tangled together. It cut so deep I was surprised I hadn't bled out.

You'll keep going, ma'am, it's what you're good at. The rest of us die but you just push forward untouched by the chaos.

Willimet's ghost strolled beside me down the corridor. My Body-Guard looked the same as she had before she died, crushed by a wall on Red Cliff when the king of the Saxons had attempted to kill me. The tiny, dark-skinned woman winked at me as we turned a corner and went the opposite direction, vanishing a moment later.

I didn't know if her words were meant to be comforting or a challenge. Either way I couldn't argue. I kept going, somehow, through some cruel twist of fate. That was what Gita and the others didn't understand. Being near me was deadly. The only thing I had left was to try to keep them safe.

"Majesty, I need you to focus, this is difficult."

"You think it's difficult? You're dead." I shook my head and kept going, thankful when Fasé fell silent once more and my guard didn't say a word.

The calls and sounds of fists connecting with flesh filtered down the hallway. I followed them until I came to a dead end and a wide, arched entrance.

The room had all the trappings of a bare-bones military gym: weight benches and punching bags but little else. A rack of weights in the far corner. The mats under my feet had stains on them that were decidedly old-blood in color.

Aiz and Talos fought, both Shen stripped to the waist and streaked with blood. A handful of men and women watched from the side, none of them noticing me as I slipped through the doorway.

Talos had a longer reach than Aiz, and he used it, driving his opponent back several steps. But he took one swing too many and I winced, seeing the hit before Aiz threw it.

The sound of breaking ribs shot through the air.

"D'asto," Aiz said with a shake of his head, grinning at Talos's muttered reply. "It was your own fault," he continued in Indranan. "Even she saw it coming." He jerked a thumb in my direction and six pairs of eyes swung my way.

"So much for not being noticed," I muttered.

"Thino Aiz notices everything, Star of Indrana," my guard murmured.

Aiz didn't break off the fight as I expected, but gestured to Talos and barked an order in Shen. The pair collided again, fists flying with a speed I could barely follow. My breath stuck in my lungs, clotted by an unexpected desire to be in the middle of that fight.

If I was fighting I could stop thinking for a little while. If I was fighting I could stop feeling.

It would wash away these unpleasant feelings, but at what cost, Majesty? Emmory whispered in my ear, the words like a blade carving out my heart.

Aiz caught Talos, snapping his neck with such cool precision that the gasp which tried to escape from my throat got lodged there and I stared as he lowered the Shen's lifeless body to the mat.

7

Aiz went to a knee, touching a hand to Talos's chest, and I watched in fascinated horror as the man came back to life.

There was no ceremony, no words. Aiz didn't look the least bit exhausted, whereas Fasé had been wiped out both times she'd brought someone back from the dead. Aiz merely leaned in and touched his forehead to Talos's, a smile peeking through his dark beard.

I couldn't hear what Aiz said to him and it was probably in Shen anyway, but Talos laughed and Aiz hauled him to his feet, giving the Shen a gentle shove toward the others before crossing the room to me.

"You killed him." I hadn't meant to let the words out, but they found their way into the air regardless.

Aiz smirked, grabbed a towel, and scrubbed at his face. The white surface came away red and I couldn't tear my eyes away from it.

"We're in a fight to the death, Hail. We practice like we fight." The smile continued to play across his face as he rubbed the towel across his torso.

"You're not the least bit winded." I frowned at him. "You're not injured. You brought him back from the dead and healed yourself as if it were nothing."

Aiz's smile grew. "Mia will answer your questions about that." He gestured at the mats. "I was going to do this tomorrow, but the universe appears to have different ideas."

"Do what?" I asked, still frowning.

"Mia said I should convince you to help us. She said I should be charming and explain things to you, show the ropes and see what you think. I am too old for charming and you have no patience for it anyway."

"You're not wrong about that."

"I thought of something that would be more suited to us. Something that would allow us to get to know each other better. Showing you is easier than explaining it all."

"So, what was your plan?" I asked. "Challenge me to a fight? Best two out of three has to join the campaign or you let us go?"

"I didn't think about best two out of three," Aiz replied with a smile, and spread his hands wide. "But the fighting part is right. It's what I know. It's what you need to learn. I am the best one to teach you."

"I don't want to fight you."

"Liar." He shook his head, tossed the towel to the side. "It's written all over your face, you're practically vibrating with the need. You've needed to kill someone since Earth. Here is your chance. Consequence-free."

I felt the tone of the room shift, the other Shen suddenly watching us with interest.

He was lying. There was always a price.

"I thought you didn't want to fight me?" It was a desperate bid to distract him, but the easy challenge had reminded me too much of Emmory and it hurt.

"I didn't, and still don't, want Indrana to help the Farians. I don't want you anywhere but here." He lifted a shoulder. "I have been waiting a very long time for this. It's a great honor to get to fight the Star. Even greater to fight at your side against the so-called gods."

"You want this from me without giving me anything in return," I replied. "Send my people home safely."

"I'm giving you something back, you just don't want to admit it."

Aiz shook his head. "Mia already told me you asked, Hail. You need them here. My sister is right about that. What we are attempting to do, it is not easy." He moved in on me and I backed away toward the center of the mat. "I will push you beyond what you can stand because it must be done. You need people you trust around you to balance that out."

"You're acting like I've already agreed to help you."

"You have," he replied. "Your heart did it already because you are the person who will put herself between the chaos and all she loves. You will stand against the tide. Sacrifice everything to see the galaxy safe. You have always made that choice and you always will."

Somewhere in the back of my head, I knew what he was doing, that his taunting words were designed for dragging a singular response from me. I just couldn't bring myself to care when my fury was snarling to be let out of its box. "I am not supposed to fight for you."

"Maybe once," Aiz admitted, and then spoke the words as if he had pulled them from my head. "You stayed out of the fight and what did it bring you? Nothing good. You and I both know a few moments of peace before the storm isn't worth much when you can see the destruction coming."

I scrambled for purchase on uncertain footing. "You're very good at speeches. It's a pity I can't trust a single thing coming out of your mouth."

"If you fought me you'd know I was telling the truth." He shrugged, grinning at the flat look I shot him. "You know as well as I do the best way to understand someone is to fight them. Shen fight, it's who we are. It's all we've ever known."

"I promised your sister I wouldn't hurt you," I said, this time holding my ground when Aiz moved in.

"I release you from that promise."

My blood surged with the desire to drive my fist through his throat. Johar's warning about not letting him get to me beat it back down into a quiet whimper. "Tempting. Still not interested."

"Come on, Empress, it's just a friendly sparring match to start. You'll need to learn how to fight our way to defeat the gods." He reached out, laughing when I slapped his hand away.

"Nothing about us is friendly."

"True, but I respect you. And I would value the chance to earn your respect in return." Aiz tipped his head, smiled. It was a cold look. One that said he knew exactly how to twist the knife. "You want to fight. I can feel it rolling around inside you like a caged monster." He shook his head. "Why are you resisting?"

Less violence, not more, is always an option. Dailun's ghost whispered the words in my ear, but they were drowned out by the rush of blood in my head. Aiz was right. I wanted the fight. There wasn't anything I wanted more in this moment.

I threw the punch without thinking. My fist connected with his mouth and Aiz staggered backward, laughter and blood flying into the air. With my rage off the leash, I rushed him, tackling him to the mat and knocking the air out of both of us.

Aiz punched me in the head with such force I don't know how it didn't break most of the bones in his hand and crack my skull. He didn't react, or at least I didn't see him react as I rolled away, my ears ringing.

I pulled myself to my feet with the help of a bench, aware that the other Shen were watching now, fully engaged but apparently without any intent to join the fight. I caught a flash of Talos's smile as I straightened just in time to block a flurry of punches from Aiz.

Think, Hail, watch him. Where are his weaknesses? Portis whispered the order in my ear.

He doesn't have any, I protested under the pressure of the assault. *He's so quick, I can't keep this up—wait—right there.*

Aiz moved fast, but he had too much weight on his front leg, and his right arm lifted a little too high when he swung, leaving his ribs open.

I feigned at his head with my left hand, following up with a punch from the right that slipped under his elbow and slammed into his ribs.

"Good one," Aiz wheezed, clearly in pain, and I felt a surge of triumph. But then he straightened and gestured. "You can do better, come on."

"You healed yourself." I dropped my hands, stepped back. "I'm not fighting you. You've got an endless advantage. What's the point?"

"Don't worry. I'll heal you when you need it until you learn to do it yourself. The point right now is the fight." Stepping in, he threw a punch. I didn't block it and the blow snapped my head to the left. He drove a knee into my gut, holding me up when I would have dropped to the mat, all the air gone from my lungs.

"You fight, you die," Aiz whispered in my ear. "You come back and do it all over tomorrow. It's the only thing that matters. You know this. It's in your blood. You're not an empress made for sitting on a throne. You're a fighter. You always have been. Let your grief go, Hail, and let the rage take its place."

I dragged in a breath, beating back the nausea through sheer force of will alone, and caught his hand before he could grab my face.

I didn't recognize the sound coming out of my throat, the snarling rage of a wounded animal, but Aiz did. His smile was patient, his right hand dug into my shoulder; then he twisted sharply, and I felt the socket give.

"Get up."

I stumbled to my feet, pain screaming through every nerve ending. According to my *smati* we'd been fighting for an hour, far longer than should have been possible. Aiz had healed me twice, bursts of energy that kept me going past the point of collapse. His energy was fire and pain almost worse than the injuries they healed, not the heat of Mia's energy that seemed to make the whole world come alive.

I reveled in it. It was the punishment I deserved for letting everyone around me die and being unable to follow.

I was bleeding from a cut above my left eye. Three of my ribs were broken and every breath was a hot lancing stab of pain. There was something wrong with my right knee and my right wrist, but I threw a punch at him anyway and he slapped it away with a sigh.

The other Shen had trickled out, my guard included, though Talos and a woman I didn't know still remained propped up on a bench on the far wall, their heads bent together as they critiqued my performance.

Aiz wasn't uninjured, but I was the worse off of the two of us, almost staggering drunk with the pain and the residual energy of his healing. That sang through me like an entire bottle of Hestian whiskey.

"You need to move faster."

"You need to hold still," I replied.

He blocked my second punch, catching my fist and stepping into me, kicking my leg out and slamming me to the mat again.

"When you go up against these beings, Hail, there is only pain. You have to learn to get past it and fight on the other side." Aiz's voice sounded like he was teaching a roomful of children, not standing above my battered and bruised body.

Rolling to my side, coughing blood up into my mouth, and spitting it at his boot was the only defense I had against the kick I knew was coming. My remaining ribs shattered under the impact, pain blotting out my vision, and my scream was only a low moan of air escaping.

"There are two lessons, Hail. The first one is this. Fighting is pain and death. Nothing more, nothing less. It is not your brain. It is your heart. When you know this, when you realize there is no difference between breath and no breath. You can use it to win instead of letting the fear of dying drag you down among the dead." Aiz bent over and touched three fingers to my cheek. More pain lanced through me, the healing worse than the injuries he fixed, and this time my scream bounced off the walls.

"Take her back to her rooms," he said.

Talos went to a knee at my side and put a hand on my chest as I tried to sit up. "Give it a second, take a few breaths. That first time gets you a little out of sorts."

"What he means is he threw up twice the first time."

I blinked up at the woman smiling down at me over Talos's shoulder. Her head was half shaved, the remaining hair so pale blond it seemed almost silver, and her eyes were the same warm brown as Talos's.

"I am Vais," she said, stepping around to my other side. "Take a deep breath, kiddo, and we'll get you on your feet."

Two Shen grabbed me by the arms, pulling me to my feet and holding me upright as my legs refused to support my weight. With their help I stumbled down the corridor. They opened the door without knocking and I flinched away from the sudden exclamations of my people.

"What did you do to her?"

"Easy." Talos lowered me to the ground and backed away. "She's fine. Might be a little wobbly but otherwise unharmed."

"She's covered in blood," Johar snarled.

Talos's reply was garbled and then cut off by the sound of a slamming door.

"Dark Mother." Gita fell to her knees next to me, Alba right behind her. "Hail, what did they do to you?"

"I'm all right," I managed, my voice slurred as I rolled onto my back.

"You're bleeding."

"Was. Not anymore." Smearing the blood from my face with the back of my hand, I lay there and waited for the universe to stop spinning around me. The laughter was inappropriate, but I couldn't stop myself. "That was wild."

The answering silence was oppressive, and I cracked open an eye to watch as Johar and Gita alternated between staring at each other and at me. "I'm fine. It was a lesson," I said, though my legs still failed me when I tried to get to my feet and I landed heavily on my hands and knees.

Johar muttered a curse, reached down, and lifted me with one arm around my waist, practically carrying me into the bathroom. "Alba, get the water on."

"I can do this myself." My protest was nothing but bravado.

"Shut up." Johar stripped my clothes off, muttering under her breath the whole time. She walked me into the tiny shower, holding me against the wall with one hand while she scrubbed me down with the other.

I clung to consciousness, protests and curses of my own bouncing around the bathroom as Gita and Johar wrestled me out of the shower and into clean clothes.

"There's no sign of a drug in her system," Gita said as they laid me out on the bunk.

"Judging from the amount of blood, he beat the shit out of her and then healed her," Jo replied.

"Couple of times." I managed, this time, to swallow my laughter. "It's fine."

"Pendejo." The simmering anger in Johar's voice should have worried me, but the edges of my vision were closing in around me. "I'm no expert on the Shen but that's probably what's got her high as a kite."

"Why would he do that to her?"

"I don't know," Johar replied, her fingers gentle in my hair. "Whatever the reason, it's not good."

"M'okay." I reached up, missed her hand, then caught it on the second try. "This is good. I deserve this." I gave up and let the blackness drag me under.

8

I slept through the night without a nightmare, only the strange echo of Fasé's ghost calling my name. My people were subdued the next morning, their sidelong glances driving me from the rooms and toward Mia's an hour earlier than our normal breakfast time. She still welcomed me in, though she stared into my soul with those gray eyes of hers and sighed sadly. "Oh, Hail. I am sorry for this."

"Aiz said you were special, why?" I sat with my back pressed against the wall and my knees pulled up to my chest. Something about her sorrow ate away at the furious desire to fight that Aiz had woken, and I didn't know what to make of the new conflict in my soul. I didn't want to go back to the grief, I wanted to stay in the heat of rage and the taste of blood in my mouth.

Mia moved to the counter nearby, and the smell of something that was almost—but not quite—like chai filled the air.

"When my father and brother broke from the Farians, some Farians went with them. Including a member of the Council of Eyes." She looked up at the ceiling for a moment and then returned to her task. "I sometimes wonder if so much of the Farians' hostility is tied into the idea that we stole him. But Jibun just wanted out from under the Pedalion's rule."

"So he came with them when they left Faria?"

"Yes, and he's been with us ever since." Mia grabbed a pair of glasses and the delicate teapot and set them on the floor next to me.

She sat on the opposite side, wrapping her own arms around her knees. "He died shortly after my father, but I was there and stopped the assassin from stealing his soul."

I recognized that smile, having seen similar ones on my own face, and knew that the assassin hadn't survived the encounter.

"Jibun is safe and guarding the place of return."

"Place of return?"

Mia nodded. "The place where Shen go when they die. Thanks to Jibun, we were able to prevent our souls from returning to Faria when we died. Aiz, the others who can, are reborn there and grow up safe from the grasping claws of the Pedalion.

"Occasionally some take the risk of being reborn for the cause. They come back on Faria and try to evade detection by the Pedalion, try to whisper our truths to others. It is dangerous and valiant work. They are heroes far more than my brother or I."

"This is all fascinating, but it doesn't answer my question," I said.

"Oh, yes." Mia's laughter danced through the air. She poured the tea; the purple liquid filled the cups, steam curling into the air.

That looks like the moment just after sunset on Yaga, Hao's ghost said.

"I liked it there," I murmured before I could catch myself, and took the cup Mia offered with a smile. "Sorry, I was remembering something."

There was sadness and understanding in her gray eyes. "The weight of your grief will crush you if you don't learn to let it go. The rage doesn't make it go away, Hail; it only hides it from your heart."

"My question?" I prompted, lifting the cup to my lips and taking a sip. Whatever this was it definitely wasn't chai, but it wasn't bad. There was smoke and flame in the inhale, a softer floral that faded under the onslaught.

Mia waited a beat, sipping her own tea, before she spoke. "I am like Fasé, like Sybil and Jibun. I am even more improbable because of my mother's humanity, but the universe wanted me to see—and so I do. According to some, that makes me special.

"According to the Pedalion, it makes me an abomination. They cannot have an uncontrolled seer. Let alone one who is half human. It's why they were so quick to have Fasé come home once word reached them of what she'd done."

"And I helped them."

"Don't blame yourself, Hail. They would have taken her by force if you'd resisted, and at that point it only would have led to disaster."

"It must be a comfort to be so certain you know how our lives are going to play out." I put my cup down. "I'm sorry, that was unnecessary."

"No, it's fine. And yes, sometimes it is a comfort. Other times it is an unbearable weight. I am not sorry for the choices I've made. They've all been done with a full awareness of the outcomes. Make no mistake, Hail. I am committed to this path I'm walking. You will need to make a decision which way to go and soon."

"I already made a commitment to protect my people." The words burned in my throat. I hadn't. I hadn't protected anyone. Not my sisters, not my mother. Not Emmory and the others.

"And you still can, but this is more," Mia said, holding out her hand. "Going to Faria with us and fighting these beings is just the first step. Let me show you what is coming and then you can choose."

I stared at her hand for a long moment, desire and fear going to war in my chest. But there were no ghosts to save me this time. "Dailun used to say to me—less violence, not more, is always an option. But everywhere I turn, there it is."

Mia tipped her head curiously at my words. "I promise not to stop you if you still want to go home after what you see," she whispered. "I will take you home myself. You can withdraw to your empire. It will keep you safe for a time. There is some blessing to the amount of empty space between you and the rest of humanity. But death will come to wipe away everything. If you're lucky you'll die before you see Indrana in ruins, but it's unlikely."

I looked up at her and whistled. "That's blunt."

"I have no time for anything else. You need to see, Hail. You need to let go of your grief and channel your anger into this fight. It is the only way to keep everyone you love safe."

Mia's hand was steady, unwavering as she held it out to me. I looked at my own and dragged in a breath. I reached out, slapping my palm down and closing my fingers around hers with a muttered "Bugger me."

Heat lanced through me and my vision whited out. Her hand was smaller than I'd expected, her fingers slender, but her grip was firm. It anchored me to the ground even as the images slammed into me.

Death and destruction. Beings of light so bright it hurt to look directly at them. Emmory dying, his hand sliding out of mine. Pashati under fire from ships that looked like upgraded versions of the Shen and Farian ships, sleek and deadly. I was alone on a battlefield soaked in blood, one arm bound to my chest, the other clutching a gun.

It was endless. So much I could barely take it all in. Battles in the black. Graveyards of thousands of destroyed ships. The skies filled with fire. More bodies than the survivors could bury and so the funeral pyres lit up the night. My empire and all of humanity in utter ruin.

I jerked away, knocking over my cup as I scrambled a meter away from Mia, my eyes wide and my heart hammering in my chest.

"Take a breath, Hail. It's overwhelming."

"It was a jumbled mess."

"I can't force you to see, Hail. That's not how it works. If it was a mess it's because you're not ready to trust me."

"Apparently my instincts are on point even if my brain isn't." I only just managed to keep from saying *body* instead of *brain* and bit down on my tongue so hard I tasted blood for real. "What the fuck was that?" I rubbed both hands over my face.

Emmory. I'd seen him dying. But how was that even possible when he was already dead?

"That's what's coming, Hail." Mia put her hand on my arm and I stiffened, my thoughts flying away like a flock of startled birds. "We don't know what they are, but if you and my brother don't kill the gods, then these things will come from outside the galaxy, somewhere out past the stars, and kill us all. They are the fire that will burn everything down—humans, Shen, Farians. No one is safe."

"She said she deserved it, Gita, like it was some kind of punishment."

I paused just outside the door to our rooms as Alba's declaration reached my ears, and leaned against the wall. Mia had held Talos back with a smile and an "I trust you to go back to your quarters, Hail."

Eavesdropping? How un-imperial of you, Hao said.

"I know," Gita replied. "She's convinced herself they're all dead and that she's responsible. Aiz is only going to encourage that because it feeds into what he wants from her."

"Which is to go on some suicide mission with him," Johar said.

"Precisely." Gita sighed. "And she's going to say yes. You know her; even if she weren't bound up in grief, if you dangle the choice of walking away or saving the world, which one do you think Hail's going to choose?"

Jo's laugh was humorless. "Saving the world, every fucking time."

"What are we going to do?" Alba asked.

"I don't know yet," Gita replied. "You keep digging, though. We need to get word out somehow. Even if everyone died in that explosion, someone is looking for us. The least we can do is wave a fucking flag around and scream that we're here."

They're going to get themselves killed.

I waved an annoyed hand through Hao's face and he vanished, but not before rolling his eyes at me.

The trio had fallen silent. I backed up a few steps as silently as I could manage and then shoved my hands into my pockets and strolled for the door.

The future Mia had shown me was still bouncing around the inside of my brain like a hot coal in a pot—all fire and loud fury. Only now it had to contend with the conversation I'd just overheard. How could I tell the three women pretending not to watch me what was coming? How could I tell them that I was going to have to do the one thing we'd tried so hard to avoid?

Fighting was my only option—Indrana's only option.

I sat down on my bunk with a sigh, trying to get the words in order in my head so I didn't sound like a babbling fool.

"Hail."

I looked up at Gita, raising an eyebrow at the absence of my title. "Gita. Sit." I patted the bunk next to me. "You two come here."

Johar and Alba crossed the room, sitting on the other bunk facing us.

"I have made a decision, but I wanted you three to hear it before I tell the Cevallas. Yesterday's fight was a lesson, not a punishment, not some sadistic fetish of Aiz's. What I've seen today is—" I blew out a breath. "I am, as you can see, fine. I don't expect you to understand this, but I do expect you to not challenge my decisions."

"With respect, Majesty, you're not fine," Gita replied. "I know I said do what you needed to and I wouldn't protest, but this? This is not what I meant. You can't let him do this to you."

I looked at her. "I can and I will. He's not going to do anything to me I don't agree to. Let's be honest, Gita, fighting is my greatest talent. And when the whole galaxy is at stake, it seems a small price to pay. If I fight these beings with Aiz, there's a chance of stopping what's coming."

"What's coming?" She frowned. "What do you mean?"

"Mia showed me." I held my hand out, but Gita didn't take it.

"We're not meant to see the future, Hail. Cas—"

"Is dead," I said flatly. "So is Emmory and Zin and Hao and anyone else who can get us out of this mess. We're it. The last ones standing. I've been wallowing for weeks, but it's time to get over it and move on."

She pressed a hand to her mouth and closed her eyes, and when she opened them again the brown depths were filled with desperation. "Please don't ask me to stand by while these two kill you."

"That is exactly what I'm asking of you," I replied, reaching out and linking my fingers through hers. "Not as my *Ekam*, but as my friend. I won't lie to you and say this isn't terrifying and painful, or even that I don't enjoy it." Those words hurt to admit but I made myself say them. "It's not without a purpose. If it's the only way I have a chance of defeating a being so powerful the Farians think it a god, then I'll do it. If it keeps Indrana safe and keeps the galaxy safe, I'll do it."

"You can't trust—"

"I saw it." It was hard to get the words out. "Indrana in flames. The rest of the galaxy burning. So much death and destruction. Not from a war between the Farians and Shen." I shook my head. "All the things we feared, they're so inconsequential compared to what's coming."

"Majesty—"

"I know. I want you to see this but I won't force it on you." I squeezed her hand and then released it. "Believe me. I know. Maybe Emmory would yell at me, maybe he would let me do this. Either way, he's not here, Gita. We are."

"What if they're not dead, Majesty? Can't you have a little hope?"

I remembered the vision of Emmory but pushed it away as a trick of my brain trying so hard to deny what was real. I'd lost my faith a long time ago, watched it bleed out with my father as he died from an assassin's old-fashioned bullet. For a brief moment back on

Pashati I'd thought maybe I could believe in our gods again, but it was gone. It had been swept away like the colored grains of sand of a mandala in a vicious wind.

"I admire your faith," I whispered. "I don't have any left."

"Hail." My name was a breath of air from my *Ekam*'s mouth as she dragged me into a hug. "Please don't give up." I clung to her, unsure how to explain that I wasn't. That this was me fighting as hard as I could to save us all. But the words to explain it in a way that made sense wouldn't leave my mouth. I just knew with the same kind of bone-deep certainty that Cas must have known when he walked into the palace that I had to do this. No matter the cost.

Or everyone left was going to die.

9

When I sought Aiz out after telling Mia of my decision, the last thing I expected to see was Emmory standing in the middle of the otherwise empty room.

"Empress." He turned with a greeting and frowned at me when I nodded back.

"What?" I asked. "You're going to lecture me about this plan, too? It didn't go that well for Gita and she's alive."

"You don't seem surprised to see me."

I shrugged. "You've been less visible than the other ghosts, but I figured you'd show up eventually." I passed him by, reaching a hand out for his arm even though I knew it would pass right through.

Only this time it didn't. My hand met the solid flesh of his arm. The world tilted sideways and dumped me on my head.

I blinked; my *smati* was registering him. Standing right in front of me—alive.

"I—" I pressed my fingers to my eyes, removed them to find Emmory still there watching me. "How are you here?" But then his greeting to me cut through everything else. "Emmory never called me 'Empress.'" I backed away. "Not even when he was mad at me. You're not Emmory."

Not-Emmory's smile was awful, a slow baring of teeth like a predator who'd just cornered his prey. Then the image of Emmory wavered and vanished.

Aiz grinned in his place. "You asked me down in the tunnels how I got past your BodyGuards, but there wasn't time for me to answer." He spread his arms wide. "This is how."

"My *smati* was showing you as Emmory." I stared at him in wonder, my relief a strange heat in my chest. "No glitch, no sign it was anything but him. Is that what you used back on Pashati? We'd assumed you had some sort of masking program from Hao."

"We don't need a program. What you see is just light," Aiz said with a shrug. "And light is energy. We can channel it, shape it, create and destroy it." He passed a hand in front of his face, and it morphed back to Emmory.

"Don't." I turned my head, squeezing my eyes shut. "They're really dead, aren't they?"

"At this point would you believe any answer I gave you besides *yes*?"

I laughed; it was brittle and fell to the floor in pieces. "No. I wouldn't. I know they're gone." I looked at Aiz and took a deep breath. "Aiz Cevalla, I will help you fight these beings, whoever or whatever they are, to stop this future your sister sees. I will help you reclaim your homeworld, or a piece of it at the very least so that your people can have their lives back.

"Understand this, I would prefer a peaceful resolution, but if the Pedalion will not listen to reason, I will help your forces defeat them."

"Very good," he said, and stuck out his hand, grabbing my forearm when I reached for it. He tugged me forward until we were nose to nose. "Thank you, Hail. I mean that."

"Thank me when this is still over and we're still alive."

His grin flashed and he released me. "You want to tell me what you meant by 'less visible than the other ghosts'?"

"Nope," I said, and walked out the door.

"Aiz brought Talos back from the dead without batting an eye and then went on to fight me, heal me, bring me back." I shook my head in amazement several days later. Mia and Aiz had left the compound the same day I'd agreed to help, though the reasons hadn't been explained to me. My repeated questions to Talos had been met with "The *Thínos* have a rebellion to run, remember?"

"He did it all without breaking a sweat. He made himself look like Hao, like Emmory. They were near-perfect copies and the only thing that gave him away was how he walked as Hao and that he assumed a formality between me and Emmory that never existed. How?"

Mia laughed but didn't look up from the tablet as she paged through her now familiar morning sign-offs. Vais stood next to her chair, hands folded as she waited. She winked at me, her easy grin smoothing over some of my anxious tension.

"The Farians have taught you this is something amazing," Mia said finally as she handed the tablet back to Vais with a smile. "Thank you, Vais."

"Of course, *Thína.*" Vais gave a short bow, threw me another wink, and headed for the door. She paused, exchanging words with Hamah.

"This, Hail, this is just energy." Mia held up her hands, tiny blue sparks arcing between her fingers dragging my attention away from the Shen at the doorway. "That Farian talent you humans revere so deeply? It's just energy. Anyone can learn to manipulate it—Shen, Farian, human."

This time I was unable to stop myself from reaching out to meet the hand she held out to me, and those same sparks jumped from her hand to mine, skittering over my palm and settling under the surface of my skin. I stared at my hand in fascination until the sharp sting on my other arm jerked me out of my awe.

"Bugger me!"

Mia slipped the tiny silver blade back into the sheath at her wrist. "Fix it."

"You cut me."

"Of course I did." She looked pointedly at the blood running down my left arm. "Fix it. It's easier and safer to learn it on yourself.

All you're really doing is transferring the energy I gave you from one arm to the other."

I frowned but put my hand over the cut. It was shallow, less than ten centimeters, and already the bleeding had slowed. My right palm was warm, the heat soaking into my forearm, and I closed my eyes.

Nothing happened.

"It's all right." Mia smiled and put her hand on mine. The strangest sensation of what I could only assume was her forcing the energy through my hand and into my skin rolled through me. "I would have been stunned if you'd figured it out right away. I will teach you this. Aiz will teach you how to fight."

"I know how to fight." Even as I said it, the memory of the fight with Aiz flooded my head. I tried to ignore the feelings that swarmed to life along with it, but it was like trying to stomp out a wildfire.

Mia shook her head. "Not like Shen. You are fighting beings of immense power, Hail, not brawling in some lonely space port bar. You will have to learn how to fight like a Shen in order to have a chance. As well as this." She extended the knife to me. "Try again. This time envision your skin as if the wound had never existed."

The surge of energy. The sharpness of the pain. These things were familiar.

The warmth of healing was not, and my frustration grew as it eluded me. We practiced it over and over again as the hours passed. Shen came and went in the room, Mia conducted her business in between watching me, and the whole time the healing hovered just out of my reach.

There was endless motion on this base, always someone needing something from Mia. She seemed glad to give it, so settled and sure in her place among her people.

I wondered what that felt like.

If you had stayed home you would have known. Instead my unfit, ungrateful daughter chose the black over her own family and left us all to die.

My mother's voice made my hand slip, and I cut deeper into my arm than I'd intended.

"Hail." Mia turned away from Hamah as her knife clattered on the floor. "Too deep."

Not deep enough, a voice insisted.

I couldn't stop Mia from wrapping both hands around my forearm, nor could I stop the shudder that rolled through me as she healed the wound.

I was unfit and ungrateful. Too fascinated with this woman instead of finding a way out of here and back to my empire.

"You don't look well. You've pushed yourself too hard; come sit down."

"No!" I jerked out of her hands and Hamah snarled a warning at me in Shen from the door. Unlike so many other Shen, Hamah had not warmed up to me at all, and the sound of his weapon powering up was more comprehensible than his words.

I put my hands in the air. "I'm going to go back to my rooms," I said.

Mia watched me with curious gray eyes before she nodded and waved a hand at Hamah, who followed me. He waited until I was out the door and out of her line of sight before giving me a shove.

Instinct kicked in and I spun, jamming two fingers into the base of his throat. He dropped, gagging and gasping for air, and I stepped on his hand before he could bring the gun up. "You should be more fucking careful about who you shove," I whispered.

The clapping startled us both.

I glanced over my shoulder. Aiz was leaning against the wall at the juncture, clapping his hands in exaggerated approval. He pushed away from the wall with a smile and tipped his head to the side as he approached.

The signal for me to let the Shen up was clear, and I removed my foot from Hamah's hand, taking a step back as he got to his feet.

"Hamah, you really do need to be careful," Aiz said. "You've been bested twice now. The empress will kill you if given half a chance. In fact, I'm rather surprised she didn't."

"Dead men don't learn lessons," I replied.

"They do when they're Shen," Aiz said, and my stomach clenched when he glanced pointedly at Hamah's throat. "Next time kill him. He deserves it for not paying better attention."

"Lo syngo, Thíno." Hamah bowed his head.

Aiz smiled and ruffled the Shen's dark curls. "Don't let it happen again," he replied in Indranan. "I will walk her back to her rooms; you go get some breakfast."

"Lo syngo?" I asked as we headed down the hallway.

Aiz glanced my way and chuckled. "It means 'I'm sorry.'"

"I thought as much. And *Thíno* is?"

"An awkward title that comes with the job." Aiz made a face. "It is much like 'Your Majesty,' I suppose. Mia got used to it faster than I did."

"She is not the killer you are."

Aiz chuckled. "How little you know. Mia has killed her share, Your Majesty. Don't let her sweet face and kind smile fool you. We were not granted leadership of the Shen simply because of our father. We fought for it. Proved our worth in a contest of skill, and strength, and intelligence. It was a ritual not used since the days when we first split from the Farians."

It would be too easy to fall into a rhythm with Aiz. Part of me hated him for what had happened on Earth no matter how much he protested they hadn't blown up the embassy, because it was his feud with the Farians that had put us there. I knew how dangerous he was, how determined to see this through no matter the cost.

Another part of me was far too interested in both of them. It was shameful to admit I admired their dedication to their cause. That the more I learned about the Farians, the more I questioned just who was wrong and who was right in this conflict. I felt a curious little tug at my soul when either of them spoke.

"So you and Hamah and the others are extra protective of her even though she can handle herself in a fight? Is that because she can die, or because she won't defend herself?"

Aiz stopped at a crossroad as a group of soldiers passed. They murmured greetings to him and eyed me with curiosity. "My sister is special, Hail. Her birth was celebrated by my people. The Farians denounced her immediately. They tried to have her killed as a child." His dark eyes waited for my reaction, and it took all my self-control not to give him one.

But the fury was there, no matter how well I hid it from him. The thought of the Farians trying to kill a child was bad enough, but I had to admit to myself it was the thought of Mia almost dying that brought the anger to life in my chest.

"We already knew about the soul problem for the human-born Shen, but my father was in love," he continued, turning down the now-empty corridor and leaving me to catch up. "Even with the heavy guard on my sister, the Farians nearly succeeded in stealing her from us." He glanced my way. "I was almost too late to save her, almost killed myself to do it. You should ask her to show you the scar sometime. She was six years old and yet she asked me to leave it, so she would remember."

I glanced down at Aiz's hand. He clenched and unclenched his fist as the memory consumed him, and I swallowed. I knew that pain. Only I hadn't been around to save my sisters. They'd died.

Everyone you love dies, sister. Pace wrapped her fingers around mine, the cold seeping into my bones, and walked with us down the hallway. She was wearing the same lavender dress she'd been in the last time I'd seen her, her golden curls piled on her head and a smile on her dark face. I'd seen images of her from after I'd left home, but this picture of her was burned into my brain.

"Mia is special," Aiz repeated, unaware of our companion. "She was the first piece of the puzzle of our redemption. You are the last."

10

The days blurred into one another: a haze of pain and violence, broken bones, and crushed windpipes, always followed by the jarring electricity of Aiz's healing. He killed me more times than I could count, or else I killed myself by refusing to submit long after I'd lost the fight. Weeks stretched into months. Fasé's ghost pestered me about our location until I wanted to scream, and I started to ignore her persistent questions.

My grief took a grateful back seat to the sense of purpose the fights brought me as I threw myself into fighting with Aiz. I preferred the fights; there was a strange peace woven into the violence. There were often spectators for our fights, but Mia did not watch us, and when I pressed her about her absence she only gave me a sad shake of her head as a reply.

What she did do was insist on endless attempts at teaching me how to use the energy the same way the Shen did.

Johar joined us on occasion, far more interested in this talent of the Shen's than either of the Indranan women, and she took to it startlingly quickly. Whereas I failed at it, over and over again. Pain was easier than healing. Healing meant comfort, and there wasn't any to be had in the wasteland of my heart.

In between all of it, I watched as Mia and Aiz ran a rebellion against an enemy who still outnumbered them and had a tenacity in fights that was impressive despite their somewhat straightlaced tactics. Bit by bit I did what I could to influence their strategy into something that I knew would confound the Farians even further.

I slowly learned Shen as the months passed, from listening to endless meetings and lessons with Talos in our rooms when Aiz and Mia were too occupied to bother with me. Gita, Alba, and Johar often joined us for those, and I was grateful that it seemed my people had given up on their plans to escape.

The Shen had, with my urging, pulled their ships from the human sectors and were running missions closer and closer to Faria. The tactic worked as I'd hoped, forcing the Farian ships out of the human sector and closer to their homeworld to deal with the threat.

They'd left the mercenaries on their payroll on standby, and despite my queries Mia didn't seem interested in having me coordinate anything with them. I didn't blame her. There was a decent chance Po-Sin would blame me for Hao's death, and it was friction this operation didn't need.

The guards vanished from our quarters and as the days passed I was left to wander more freely, though I noticed there always seemed to be someone trailing behind the others when they left our rooms.

I felt more and more at home here in Mia's office instead of with my own people. The ghosts reminded me of my betrayal, but most of the time I simply ignored them.

Blood welled up from the blade as I drew it across my skin. The bright flare of pain faded too quickly, a casualty of the hours I'd spent with Aiz fighting. It was intentional, this dulling of feeling. The increased tolerance for pain meant I could fight longer and through more injuries than even Johar's enhanced abilities allowed, certainly longer than any normal human.

But it also meant the feelings crept back in as the pain faded.

I longed to jam the dull black point straight through my arm, but I knew it would attract Mia's attention from where she spoke quietly with Aiz by the door.

Especially since I still hadn't figured out how to heal myself.

Hail. Emmory's ghost made a soft noise of distress as the blood dripped down my arm. *Why are you doing this to yourself?*

"What do you care?" I murmured, tracing a finger through the drops on my skin before I slid it up to the cut and pressed down. The pain woke up again for just a moment and then vanished. More blood welled.

You need to fix this.

"You're just as maddening as a ghost as you were alive, you know that?"

Emmory smiled and put his hand over mine. *Fix it.*

I blinked away the tears and laid the flat of my palm onto the cut.

Fix it. With an exhale I pictured the muscle knitting itself back together, the skin drawing closed until all that was left behind was a patch of blood-smeared dark brown skin.

I pulled my hand away, the rushing sound in my ears drowning out Mia's delighted exclamation. The wound was gone, the only evidence that it had been there at all in a slender scar and the last of the blood still dripping from my arm. I could still feel some of Mia's energy rolling around in my gut, though after a moment it settled down to something more familiar.

"You left a scar." She smiled. "You don't have to."

"Leave it," I said before she could put her hand on me. "It's a momentous occasion, isn't it? I should have something to remember it by."

Mia pulled her hand back, a curious, assessing look on her face. "That's new."

"What is?"

"The sarcasm."

I laughed and flipped the knife between my fingers. "No, it's not new at all. Hao could have—" I bit my tongue and turned away, but not before I saw the strange flash of sympathy on Mia's face. "I have always been a sarcastic bitch," I said. "Putting my ass on a throne didn't change that."

"I'm reasonably sure everyone who backed you doesn't care in the slightest."

"I was the last woman standing. That's why they backed me." The words felt like they left my throat cut and bleeding, but there wasn't any way to heal that wound, not with a thousand Shen.

"No, Hail," Mia said softly. "It was so much more than that. I— your people love you and you'll see them again, I promise."

I knew I would. I'd either die fighting or die old and weary in my bed, and I'd be a ghost like all the people I cared about. I was okay with that outcome. "I know," I said, moving back to the table and sitting down again. I cut another bright line of pain into my skin, then set the knife on the table and put my hand over the wound.

An inhale followed by a slow exhale and I felt the energy that had been coiled in my stomach wake up and flow up through my hand like warm honey in the sunshine.

I pulled my hand away and held up my healed arm for Mia to see. The little voice in the back of my head that was getting weaker with every passing hour whispered that she looked concerned rather than happy, but I brushed it away.

I had a purpose to keep me going. If there was nothing else, that would have to do.

Johar kept track of the days with tiny tick marks on the wall by the window, and I watched the marks spread. She and Alba explored the base, and mostly treated me as though nothing had changed.

But Gita watched me with a frown that grew more and more worried. It was hard to blame her; Aiz had refused to let her watch me fight. It was an order that infuriated my *Ekam* and left me privately, shamefully, relieved.

I played a good game on the surface most days, helping with the

Shen war effort. Offering advice when asked—sometimes even when not. I also withdrew, curling further into myself with every sunrise. The ghosts in my head grew louder, ever more demanding that I stand, that I fight, that I not dishonor them by quitting, until I was a broken, sobbing mess dying once more on the mat.

Worse, I had come to love the fights. The pain that seeped into my bones; the sharp, bright teeth of it when Aiz flooded me with his energy to bring me back to life. It was just and right, and I told myself I deserved it for failing those I loved.

I started to believe that nothing but the fight mattered.

"Why do you waste your time fighting me?"

Aiz blinked at my question, grinning when I followed it with a low spin-kick that would have broken his knee had he not dodged at the last second. "You think this is a waste?"

"You are so much better than me. The others, I stand a chance of beating them."

"You'll get there," Aiz replied. "You know as well as I do that the best way to get better is to fight someone you know you cannot possibly defeat in the training ring. You are a better fighter than most of the people here. It's impressive when you think about the age differences. Your instincts are so attuned. Your reaction time flawless."

I missed a block and doubled over from the force of his fist in my stomach. To my surprise, Aiz backed off a step, and when I straightened he was grinning again.

"Most of the time your reaction time is flawless. Hold the fight for a moment." The official call to pause a fight meant I could relax fully, and I went back to leaning my palms on my knees.

"This is the equivalent of me training a new recruit in the Indranan Royal Marines and you know it." I waved a hand at him. "I'm grateful for the experience, believe me."

"Are you really?"

"Shut up. I just want to know why."

"You are the Star of Indrana." Aiz gestured around the room at

78

the spectators. "These soldiers have heard of you their whole lives. Talos does a reasonably good job hiding his hero worship of you, Hail, but the others cannot possibly do what needs to be done here."

"You're telling me that you're the only one willing to kick my ass?"

"Basically. I am also the only one here who's actually killed some of these so-called gods. There is no one better to teach you how they fight and what to expect." He rolled his shoulders. "Are you ready?"

"Sure. Is that why you talk so much during a fight with me but not the others?" I asked as I ducked under Aiz's swing and elbowed him hard in the kidney—or at least where I assumed he'd have a kidney. I didn't know enough about Shen physiology to say for sure, but it was as good a guess as any.

"It helps separate your mind from your body, leaves your body free to do the work necessary to win the fight," he replied, and I watched his torso as we circled each other. "Your mind can be too much of a distraction. That's lesson two—these beings will lie to you, trick your eyes, do everything they can to gain the upper hand in a fight. You can't let them."

Aiz moved in on me. I blocked three punches, missed the fourth, and staggered away with a hand pressed to my left eye. I knew he was coming after me, so I put a bit more unsteadiness into my stagger than I was feeling and kept my back turned.

His footsteps were loud on the mat, and I leaned out of the way of the expected punch, catching his wrist with my right hand as I struck him in the armpit with my left elbow. His shoulder joint gave, but I didn't stop, kicking him in the right knee with as much force as I could muster. It cracked under the blow and he went down with a curse, rolling away from me and back onto his feet.

"Nice one." He limped a few steps, swore again, and then put his hands up. "Continue."

I shook out my arms and grinned. "So if I can't trust my eyes when I'm fighting, what can I trust?"

Aiz moved fast, grabbing me by the throat with his left hand and throwing me to the side with such force I blacked out when I connected with the wall.

I came to a second later, struggling to my feet just in time for not-Emmory to grab my throat and slam me into the wall a second time.

"You have failed us all. Over and over again. We threw ourselves onto your fire and not once did you honor our sacrifice."

I froze. Even knowing this wasn't Emmory, the words cut my heart out of my chest with vicious precision. Not-Emmory slammed my head into the wall a third time, and this time I saw stars. They were quickly accompanied by the warm trickle of my own blood down the back of my neck, and the pain I'd gotten so good at ignoring finally woke up.

"Damn it." Not-Emmory morphed back into Aiz. He dropped me to the ground and walked away, leaving me gasping for air in the silence of the room.

Talos took a knee at my side. "The irony there is if you'd been able to keep your guard up and attack him back, you might have been able to win that one. It's exactly what those Farian liars will do, Hail. They will try to trick you at a critical moment. You cannot let them. You have to be prepared to strike no matter what."

"No, hold still for a second," he said when I shifted. "I'm pretty sure he cracked your skull on that last shot, and trying to fix your brain would require someone with more skill than I have."

He slid his hand into my hair, into the pain radiating from the back of my head, and I dragged in a breath as it shrank down into nothing.

"And the rest of it."

"No, it's fine." I leaned away from his hand. "There's nothing major, it'll heal."

"Hail—" Talos stopped and cleared his throat. "Star of Indrana, it is not right to leave you injured."

"I said it was fine." I got to my feet, swallowing back the groan as it tried to surface, and slowly made my way across the room.

"The fights are not punishment." Even though his tone was gentle, the quiet statement slapped at me.

I grabbed a towel and wiped my face, wincing when my arms protested. "Who said they were?"

He leaned against the wall, watching me closely. "I've been where you are. I recognize it easily enough. Trying to hold the weight of the world on your shoulders and thinking that the pain somehow absolves you of the choices you had to make."

His words sank in like a precision laser strike, a piercing direct hit all the way to my soul, and I braced myself on the bench, refusing to look his way.

There's nothing to absolve you of the choices you've made, but the pain is a good start. The voice I couldn't identify, the ghost who refused to show their face had become my constant companion. They slipped in among the other ghosts with deft skill, weaving a poisonous story of my faults and my failures with unending relentless determination.

I threw the towel into the bin with a hiss of annoyance. "What do you know of it?"

"I left my whole family to the judgment of the Pedalion," Talos said, his smile weary. "It doesn't matter that my parents told me to go. Both they and my sisters were sent to atone for my defection to the Shen. It has been a very long time, but they are still there—serving my punishment." He sighed and looked up at the ceiling. "I am told if I turned myself in I could take their place. Do you know why I don't, Star of Indrana?"

"Why?"

Talos smiled again. "Because I know the Pedalion lies. They would kill me, or worse use me to try to get to the *Thinos*. It wouldn't save my family. The only thing that can do that is to win this war."

"At least you have a family to save." It was petty of me and such a cheap shot I felt instantly guilty, but Talos didn't rise to the bait; he merely smiled.

"The fights are not punishment, and the pain is not going to save you. Let me heal you, please. I won't do it without your permission."

"Good," I replied, heading for the door. "I'm not sure I have it in me for another fight."

Talos didn't follow me as I limped down the hallway, though I didn't doubt for a second he was on the com reporting me to Mia or Aiz—or both of them. I wasn't sure which I'd prefer at the moment, and instead of heading back to our rooms I found my feet taking me to one of the outside doors.

"Star of Indrana, are you all right?" The guard at the door gave me a once-over as she asked the question, and I waved her off.

"I'm fine, just going for a walk."

She frowned but held the door. "Don't go into the jungle, ma'am. It's dangerous in the dark."

I gave a noncommittal grunt and made my way into the cool night air. If Talos hadn't called someone, the guard at the door would for sure, so I limped to the edge of the circle of light surrounding the compound and lowered myself to the ground.

He's wrong, Hao said, settling down at my side.

"I know." I wrapped my arms around my knees and rested my cheek on them so I could see my brother's ghost. "I killed you all; I deserve whatever pain comes my way and more."

Hao shrugged. *You made a shitty call and we died for it. That's life, little sister.* His easy acceptance didn't take the sharpness out of his words. But that had been Hao—able to deliver a scathing rebuke or honest praise without ever changing his tone.

You've always been too trusting, he said, reaching a hand out to brush my hair from my face. *Even now, you believe everything the Shen tell you. How do you know they're not playing you, Hail?*

"I don't," I admitted. "Shit, I don't even know if you ghosts are playing with me. But what else am I supposed to do? I can't bring you all back, but maybe—"

You're fooling yourself if you try to say this is anything more than a suicide mission, sha zhu. Hao shook his head. *Whatever you're going to fight is going to step on you and keep on going. You can't win this.*

"Then I'll be dead and it won't fucking matter anymore, will it?" I turned my head and buried my face in my knees as the sobs broke free. "I just want it to end, Hao."

"Hail." The soft call of my name and the hand on my back belonged to Mia, not Hao's ghost, and I froze. She didn't say anything else, but I felt the soft, seeking pulse of her energy flowing from her hand and chasing the pain away.

"Talos said he wouldn't do that without my permission." I shifted away, annoyance rising to fill the emptiness.

"Talos won't do it because you are the Star of Indrana." Mia's laugh was barely an exhale. "Whereas I will precisely because of who you are."

"Do you ever get tired of talking in riddles?" Annoyance edged into anger and I heard the murmured response behind us. There were three guards, no, four, I amended as I heard another pair of boots scuff in the dirt.

"It comes with the territory," she replied. "Don't try to pick a fight with me, Hail; it won't go the way you think."

"I didn't ask you to come out here." I pushed to my feet, heard the scattering of the guards behind us. I'd always been good in a fight, but over the last few weeks, this hyperawareness of those around me and an almost instinctive cataloging of their fight potential had grown exponentially.

Mia was still the unknown quantity. Aiz had made it sound like she was a hell of a fighter, but I hadn't seen it. She still hadn't come to watch us fight and it was hard for me to believe she could be on the same level as Aiz if she didn't practice at all. Now I found myself wanting to know if the insinuations were true.

"I can practically see the wheels turning in your head. We're not fighting," Mia said as she rose. "Go get some sleep, Hail."

"I'm not a child. Don't try to order me around like one."

The guards moved forward but Mia made a shushing noise and they all backed off.

She could have easily countered with *You're behaving like one*, but it would have set me off. Though how she knew that, I had no idea.

"Your Majesty? Is everything all right?"

I closed my eyes as Alba's voice carried itself over the thundering of my heart. "It's fine. I was just headed inside." Shaking off the desperate desire to fight, I turned away from Mia and put my arm around Alba's shoulders, leaving her standing behind me at the edge of the light.

"How did you know where I was?" I asked as I ushered her back into the compound.

Alba smiled and tapped her head. "Still have these, ma'am. Plus Talos came by and mentioned you might not be feeling well. Gita and Johar were busy, I thought I'd come check."

I hugged her to my side, feeling the last of the fighting rage drain away and some semblance of normalcy returning.

"I found something, too, ma'am. It's strange. I thought you'd want to take a look at it."

"What is it?" I let Alba go so she could go through the doorway of our rooms first out of habit more than any sense that we needed to check the surroundings.

"Come look." She pointed at the blank wall, tossing up the images from her *smati* onto it. "I've been going through news reports—well, what reports I can get from the server here. It's limited access and we're so far away from Earth the only things available have been brought in by someone else on this base. The Shen are interested, though, which helps. But either time is seriously skewed on this planet or they're having trouble getting info because everything is out of date."

"Alba, the point?"

"Yes, sorry, ma'am. This is my point. I was digging in someone's private files and found this." She brought an image forward. It was dark and grainy, the figures blurred, but I recognized the set of the shoulders and my heart gave an awful little lurch.

"I know the image quality is awful," Alba said.

"It's Hao." I shook my head. "It's surveillance footage from before the embassy blew."

"It's not, though, Majesty, unless the dates on the report I pulled it from are totally wrong. This is surveillance footage from an hour after the embassy explosion. The rubble is—"

"It can't be. They're all dead." I tried to keep the heat out of my voice but fisted my hands with the effort. "You're wasting your time digging at this."

"Ma'am, I know what I saw—"

"You're chasing ghosts, Alba. Let it be." I didn't wait to see if she made another attempt at a reply, but turned on my heel and headed for the shower.

Chasing ghosts, you're funny.

I glared at Hao on my way by but didn't give him the satisfaction of a response.

The Shen didn't have any reason to lie about this. To hide surveillance footage like buried treasure.

Unless they do have a reason, that unidentified voice whispered in my head. *Unless they want you off-balance.*

The question there was why? What could they possibly be hiding from me?

85

11

I prowled the base the next day like a captive tiger, snarling and snapping at anyone who came near me. Distracted by the barest sliver of hope as well as the fear that being wrong would bring grief crashing right back down on me. I did the only thing I could.

I attempted to goad Aiz into a fight, but he just raised an eyebrow at me, then laughed and refused to rise to the bait, much like his sister had the night before in the face of my anger.

"No fighting today, Hail." He shook his head and went back to the book he was reading. "Sort your head out and then come see me."

"Might be a while."

"I can wait." His laughter followed me from the room and I glared at Hao's ghost, smirking at me by the doorway.

He held his hands up. *Don't get mad at me, little sister, you know I'd fight with you if I weren't dead.*

"That is not a comfort."

Hao chuckled. *You want comfort, go see Mia. I'm just here to remind you.*

"Of what, my failures?" I asked, but Hao's ghost vanished rather than answering.

"Majesty, where are you?"

"For Shiva's sake, not now, Fasé!" I muttered a curse and rubbed my hand over my face, letting my feet carry me through the base to Mia's room.

She smiled at me as I came in but didn't move away from the console in the far corner. Kag and two other Shen I didn't recognize were clustered around it, all of them studying the schematics hanging in the air.

I didn't join them, even though I knew I'd have been welcomed. I was still too restless to focus on anything, so I wandered to the corner where Mia's chessboard was set up.

I hadn't played the Earth game in years until we arrived on Sparkos, but Chaturanga was its predecessor and Gy, Hao's old partner, had loved to play chess. He'd taught me the rules shortly after I'd boarded Hao's ship.

I wondered who Mia played with. It didn't look like the board was just for show. The stone pieces were old, worn by handling, and the board was scuffed in places.

I picked up the queen, listening with half an ear as Mia spoke quietly with the other Shen before they left us alone in the room.

"I missed you this morning," she said, crossing over to stand next to me.

"You wouldn't have if I'd shown up." I rolled the queen between my palms. "I wasn't in the best of moods last night or this morning. I'm sorry."

"It's all right, Hail. I know this is hard on you." She smiled. "Do you want to talk about it?"

"You know the worst thing about hope?" I asked, tipping over a knight with the queen.

"What is that?"

"It's so fucking hard to kill." I held the queen up for a moment before I set her back on the board. "All you need is this little spark and it flares back to life again."

"That's a good thing, I would think."

"It's not. It's a distraction." One I couldn't afford, and I shoved it all into the back of my mind where I hoped it would die from neglect before it could bother me again. "How much longer are we going to hang around here?"

"Hail." Mia laughed as she picked up the knight and set it back in its spot. "You're not even remotely ready for the fight ahead. There's still so much I need to teach you."

"I know. I just—"

I am tired of all these ghosts.

"Who do you play with?"

"Aiz occasionally," she said, taking the conversation change in stride. "Vais is nearly to the point where she can beat me. Several others play when they pass through. Do you know how?"

"Sort of, I played with Hao's old partner on his ship when I was on his crew." I touched a finger to a pawn. "Gy was very good."

"Would you like to play?"

I pulled my hand back, surprised by the sudden ache and the tears gathering in my eyes. I shook my head, hoping the movement would hide them from Mia. "No. I—you're busy. I'll go."

"Sit." Mia caught me by the wrist, and though her smile was gentle there was no mistaking the command in her voice.

I sat. Mia didn't let me go but reached back and pulled the other chair around so she could sit without the table between us.

"What were you looking at?"

"Farian weapons. They were on the ship we stole, but I cannot— we have not been able to get them to work."

"If only you knew someone who knew a little something about guns." Mia laughed. "I forget sometimes. Even though that period of your life has so much to do with who you are now. I can send you the files, if you wish. The ship itself is not available."

"Afraid I'll steal it and run off?"

Her amusement slipped away. "A little. Though I think you wouldn't leave your people behind."

It was hard to know right now just what I would do, but on that she was probably correct.

"You asked me earlier how Aiz could heal with such limitless grace. The answer is one of the fundamental differences between us and the Farians." She changed the subject, turning my hand over so it was facing palm up. "Everything in the universe is moving. From the expansion of the universe itself down to the subatomic particles that make us all what we are. You humans figured out some of the most basic rules of the universe so quickly. It was amazing. But you missed this—how to harness the energy around you." She held up her free hand with a smile before I could protest.

"I'm not talking about the basic, rudimentary forms. I'm talking about this." She closed her free hand and opened it again, a blue ball of light gathering in the center. "You were focused on the energy outside you.

"By contrast, the Farians were, and are, told they can only use the energy that comes from within. That it is finite. It sets a limit on what a person can expend." She closed her hand around my wrist, the ball vanishing into my skin, and I felt my restlessness ease. "It is much the same as what humans are capable of doing to themselves when there is a need. You all have a limit, yes? Sometimes you can push yourselves past it, given the right circumstances, but too far and it will kill you."

"So it's not that the Farians can't use the energy outside themselves, but that they won't?"

"Precisely." Mia smiled. "The Farians throttle themselves. Their dogma teaches that they can only use the energy inside them, so they are drained by the smallest tasks, limited in what they can accomplish. We pull energy from the world around us. It means the whole universe is at our fingertips.

"Fasé did it when she brought your *Ekam* back from the dead. She didn't realize what she was doing, of course. It was instinct, an overriding of her conditioning in a moment of panic."

"It wasn't panic," I murmured, remembering Fasé's words about saving Emmory because of Zin. "It was love. Zin felt Emmory die, because they were bonded. Fasé told me that when Zin cried out, it forced her to act," I continued at Mia's curious look.

"Ah. That would make sense." Mia nodded and rubbed at the skin of my wrist for a moment before releasing me. "What happened, though, was that Fasé used most of her own energy before she tapped into the world around her. It was, not to be too blunt, lucky that she didn't kill herself or anyone else in the process."

"How long does it take for Farians to come back after they've been killed?"

Mia blinked, surprised by the question. "I am not sure. The Farians handle that differently from us. For Shen it is more random. You'd have to ask Aiz for a more detailed explanation."

"So there's no way to know when Fasé is coming back. No way to rescue her?"

"I'll be honest, it was not something we've considered. Fasé's faction may have held some of the same aims as us, but we were not allies."

It was my turn to be shocked. "You're just going to leave her with the Pedalion?"

"We are fighting a war of our own, Hail." Mia lifted her chin. "My people would not condone risking their lives to save a Farian. Besides, her people will be in a better position to rescue her, should it be necessary."

"I see." It was a painful reminder that whatever kindness and respect these Shen showed me, it didn't extend to my people.

What? Did you think they had your best interests at heart? Cire's voice was sharp in my head, like a splinter of glass.

"So," I said, pushing the thoughts and Cire's words to the back of my mind with all the other things I didn't want to think about. "Tell me about these weapons the Farians created."

"You said the future you showed me was different from the one Sybil saw?" I asked Mia a week and a half later as we sat in her room playing chess.

Things had settled somewhat. I was digging into the problem

of the Farian weapons, delighted to have something to occupy my time. Though the Farian on the schematics themselves was making comprehension difficult. Alba hadn't said anything more about the misdated image, and some of my restlessness had dissipated thanks to my fight with Aiz the day before.

The Shen had won a major victory that morning, in part because of battle strategies I'd suggested, at a small moon several thousand light-years away. It was the farthest they'd ever encroached on Farian territory, and the mood was now one of anticipation.

I'd been thinking about the future all morning, and now the questions were itching at the back of my throat to get free.

"It is connected in many ways. As I told you, I don't know if she didn't speak of it in the original telling or if the Pedalion censored it because of what it showed of the Shen." Mia smiled and lifted a shoulder as she toyed with her queen on the chessboard. "I even had a chance to ask Sybil about it directly during the negotiations. She was surprised, to say the least."

"They told us about the future, even if she didn't show us. Fasé was—" I choked back the grief that the thought of the Farian dragged out of my chest. I looked away from her and back down at the chessboard.

Mia and I had played a handful of times since our first conversation at the board, with every single game running into a dead draw despite my lack of practice.

This game looked to be headed in a similar direction as our previous matches. I had more pieces left than she did. Mia had an interesting habit of throwing all of hers into the fray, sacrificing more than half of them in her latest set of moves. But the pieces she had were currently boxing in my king, and I was going to be hard-pressed to keep him out of harm's way even with my superior numbers.

"We do not see these beings in the same light as the Pedalion and the majority of Farians do," she replied, releasing her queen without lifting the piece and instead moving her remaining bishop across the board, stealing my pawn and plucking it from the board. "They are oppressors. Holding the Farians down with their ridiculous prohibitions on this." She turned her hand palm up and wiggled her fingers with a smile. "As though it is their right to control something that the universe has provided."

"We all fight, we all die." I countered. "That's not a good thing for most of us."

"We surrender, we will die." Mia lifted a shoulder.

"So we're fucked no matter what I choose?"

"It's not a paradox, Hail. It just looks like one."

"Explain it to me, then. Because from where I'm sitting it sounds like this fight between the Farians and the Shen is what's leading us to ruin."

You said the opposite to Gita, the unknown ghost laughed bitterly in my ear. *Get your stories straight.*

Her surprised laugh bounced around us, distracting me from the ghost's rebuke. "This is why we need you, Hail. Someone with a clear eye to look at these eons of enmity and tell us we're all being fools."

"You don't think you're being fools," I replied, trying to ignore the warmth in my chest that had bloomed with her laugh.

"Of course I don't. I've been locked in this struggle my whole life. I know I'm biased about the outcome." She paused and stared at the board for a long moment. "I am . . . less attached, should we say, to the outcome than my brother is. Humans are meant to die." Looking up at me, she smiled softly. "Aiz would say that is my mother speaking, but I am part human, am I not? We are not meant to live forever."

There was a strange longing in her voice, and I looked down at the board, trying to collect my thoughts. The idea of Mia dying was astonishingly painful, like a knife to the lung, and the last thing I wanted to do was let that show on my face.

Whatever this fascination I had with her was, it was ultimately foolish. I didn't need to care for anyone else at this point.

Too late on that front. Why are you lying to yourself? Hao's ghost asked from the corner, and I shot him a look.

"What happened to your mother?"

"She grew old as humans do." Mia wiped at a tear that slipped free. "But she was loved and surrounded by love at the end. All of us could hope for such a death, right?"

None of my family had gotten that kind of peaceful end, and I doubted I would be any different. "I don't blame Aiz for his concern," I found myself saying, and cleared my throat. "It is hard to lose a sibling."

"I cannot imagine the pain. It was—" Mia paused, and I looked up as she continued. "Awful to watch. Especially hard to see you grieve for them."

"You saw?"

She nodded, a sad smile on her face. "I saw everything that happened, Hail."

"You knew they were all going to die." A sick feeling in my gut exploded to life only to be chased down and savaged by my fury. "All of you. Shen. Farians. It doesn't matter. You all saw this coming and did nothing to stop it. Did you see what was going to happen on Earth, too?"

"Yes."

I pressed my fingers between my eyes, all too aware of the sudden throbbing of my pulse in my head. They'd all known and none of them had cared.

"I am sorry." There were tears in Mia's eyes. Rain over storm clouds. She reached a hand out. "Hail, I know—"

"No," I snapped. "You don't know. None of you know what it feels like to be told so fucking calmly that you just stood by and watched my people die. That you did *nothing*." I reached out and tipped my king over. The clatter as it hit the board was loud in the silence.

"We couldn't interfere."

93

"Cowshit. All your preaching about my choices? You *chose* not to interfere. You chose not to help. You chose not to tell me. I could have saved them!" I got to my feet, pretending I didn't see her tears as I headed for the door.

Told you that you shouldn't trust them, Hao said.

I didn't see anyone on my way back to our rooms alone, which was probably a good thing. Fury was choking me, making it hard to breathe. Hao strode at my side, his face impassive.

"I'd rather be dead with you than keep doing this," I whispered.

He didn't reply, just shook his head and vanished.

Our rooms were empty. I closed the door and drove my fist into the wall next to it with all the force I could muster. The shock echoed up my arm, pain as bright as stars following after, and blood streaked over the gray surface. But I'd had nearly three months of fighting, three months of breathing through and surviving the kind of pain that would put most people on the floor.

I punched again, felt the remaining bones in my hand snap. Punched a third time and a fourth until my blood was dripping from my ruined hand.

Jiejie, stop. There were tears in Dailun's silvered eyes. Or maybe they were my own. It was so hard to tell. Sobs tore at my throat as I dropped to my knees and my tears mixed with my blood, spattering to the floor.

"Why should I?" It was a useless question. I knew what he would say as surely as I knew he was a ghost, and it didn't matter. I deserved all this pain and more for failing them. I deserved it for not listening to my gut and for trying too hard to be an empress when I should have just stayed a gunrunner.

The vision Fasé showed me of the world as it would be had I just cut Zin's throat and been done with it raced through my brain. Selfish of me, to wish I could die a drunk while the universe fell to ruin around me. Everyone would still be dead, but I wouldn't have known them. I wouldn't be mourning for them even now.

"Majesty, stop this." Fasé's voice was panicked in my head, over-riding everything else spinning around inside me.

"I can't. I'm sorry." I gasped the apology into the stillness, but there was no answer. There was no point in begging forgiveness from a ghost.

I cradled my shattered hand to my chest as I dragged in one breath and then another. In my lessons with Mia I'd healed myself plenty of times, but always with energy she'd given me.

Still it seemed easy, the sensation of water flowing through me and into my broken bones. The strange itch as they knit themselves back together. My breath caught, trapped in my chest as my vision blurred.

Then the blackness slammed into me.

12

I jerked awake, energy zinging through me like sticking my hand to the path of a Hessian 45 stun gun.

"That was fucking shit decision making, Hail," Aiz declared, his face hovering above mine.

I blinked up at him and then at Johar, who was cradling my head in her lap. I was still on the ground, Aiz at my side with his hand pressed to the middle of my chest. My hand was whole again, the pain gone. Gita and Alba looked on, their faces locked in twin expressions of horror.

"Punching the wall or trying to fix my hand?" I asked.

Aiz rolled his eyes at my sarcasm and pushed off my chest as he got to his feet. "Both of them. If you want to hit something when you're angry, find me."

"The last time I wanted to fight you when I was angry you told me to go away, remember?"

Aiz's jaw tightened and he stared at me for a long moment before he replied. "Don't ever try to heal yourself without supervision again; you stopped your own damn heart."

"That's a bad thing?" I snorted when he didn't respond, then rolled onto my side and tried to ignore Gita's wince as well as the tear that slipped out of the corner of Alba's eye.

Johar stood and crossed to Aiz, folding her hands together in a strangely formal gesture. "I'd like to come watch you fight, if I may."

Aiz studied her for a moment before he nodded. "You may. I think you can resist the temptation to intervene better than the empress's *Dve* can."

"Ekam." I murmured the correction. I didn't have to look up from where I was trying to get to my own feet to know that Gita was glaring in Aiz's direction, but I did manage to stifle the bubble of laughter in my throat. I had to stop laughing at things that weren't supposed to be funny.

"I'll keep my hands to myself," Johar replied.

"We'll see you tomorrow, then."

Gita and Alba confronted me the moment the door closed behind Aiz. "Majesty, this has to stop." Gita reached for me, but I dodged her hand. "Please stop. You can't keep doing this."

"I made a mistake. It happens." I crossed the room to the shower, but my legs gave out halfway there and I dropped to the floor. Johar watched from across the room, arms crossed over her chest and her mouth in a hard line as I struggled to my feet.

"Majesty, you don't have to kill yourself for the rest of the galaxy," Alba pleaded, tears still standing in her dark eyes.

"Who else is going to if not me?" I countered, pleased when I made it to the bathroom wall without falling over a second time. "And let's be honest. My useless life for the galaxy is a pretty good deal."

"People can fight their own battles, Hail," Johar said.

"Maybe." I shrugged a shoulder and looked up at the ceiling. "But this fight's mine. You are my responsibility. All of you."

"You're my responsibility, Hail." Gita's reply was soft, but the words hit me like a gut punch as she crossed to me. "That used to mean something to you."

"It does mean something. It means I'm not going to stand by and let you die for me like all the others have."

"It's my—"

"Don't you dare"—my voice cracked, and I stabbed a finger into her chest—"say it's your fucking job to die for me. Just don't. If I don't do this, everything burns, and I'd rather beat you to death myself if I'm going to be held responsible for it anyway."

Gita gasped as though I'd struck her, a hand flying to her mouth in horror. She backed away from me and for just a flash I wanted to apologize, but the words tangled themselves in my chest and refused to come out.

I never thought I'd say this, but Aiz might be right about her. Indula's ghost bumped shoulders with Iza's. *She is straight-up vicious.*

Like poking an angry viper. Iza agreed.

"Would you all be quiet?" I pressed both hands to my temples. The voices inside and outside my head were timed perfectly with the pounding of my blood through my skull.

Silence fell for a blessed moment.

Then Gita whispered something to Alba, who nodded and moved away. The ghosts of Iza and Indula vanished, but Johar and Gita remained. I slumped to the bathroom floor, still soaked in my own sweat, blood, and worse. Aiz had fixed me but everything still hurt.

I knew they were watching me as I cautiously got to my feet and sighed. "Out with it," I said. "Just don't shout. Please."

You're being an idiot, Hao's ghost said, and I shoved a hand at him, my palm passing through his face. The movement unbalanced me, and I caught myself on the towel rod with a muttered curse.

"Majesty, this is killing you."

My laugh sounded strange to my ears, jagged and uneven. "I only died once today; I think that's an improvement."

You killed yourself because you don't have a clue what you're doing. Or because you want to die. Either way it's disappointing as fuck. Hao crossed his arms over his chest and looked down his nose at me.

"Hao, shut up, would you?" I snapped my mouth closed, refusing to turn around and see the looks of concerned confusion Johar and my *Ekam* were likely sharing. Instead I reached in and turned on the shower, stripping out of my clothes and stepping under the spray.

The screaming panic that the water induced had become more and more welcome over the past few months, a grounding sort of pain that reminded me to keep going. A welcome echo to the memory of my skin splitting and bones cracking against the wall.

"I barely recognize you." Gita's lament was so quiet I almost didn't hear it over the water.

I finished washing off with a sigh and flipped off the shower. Grabbing for a towel, I wrapped it around myself, sitting down on the bench and staring at my knuckles. Somehow the old scars were there; Aiz never wiped them out when he was healing my new wounds, and I was grateful for the consideration.

"I am doing the best I can," I said. "If you no longer have any faith in me, then I can release you from my service." I offered up a bitter smile. "Maybe they will let you go back to Indrana, then, since you can't stand the sight of me."

"Majesty—"

I waved a hand. "Just go, Gita." I didn't look up but I was fairly sure Gita and Johar shared a look before she left us alone.

"Are you also tired of me?"

"That's not even remotely what she said." Jo sighed and rubbed a hand over her short black hair, making the ends stand up in little spikes. She sat next to me, started to put her hand on my leg, and sighed when I shied away, dropping her hand into her lap.

"Fuck, Hail. I told you months ago to be careful with Aiz," she said. "This was exactly what I was afraid of happening. He's using your guilt against you. He's using the deaths of the people you loved to get you to fight his battles for him."

"He's not using anything. I agreed to this, Jo."

"Why? Because Mia showed you some future that might happen? She's got you as tangled up as Aiz does, Hail, possibly worse."

"You think they've brainwashed me?"

"I know you're not acting like yourself. Oddly enough, though, I think they're worried about you, too. You freaked Aiz the fuck out with that stunt," she replied. "They wanted you here, but you're sliding off the deep end and I don't think that was part of their plans."

"You think I'm losing it?" I laughed.

Johar pinned me with a sharp look. "You're talking to ghosts, my friend, and you just killed yourself." She was the first person to actually call me on it, and I blinked at her in shock. "I think—" Johar paused and ran her tongue along her top teeth. "You want the punishment and the pain. You think you were responsible for what happened."

"Am I not?" I rubbed a hand over my eyes. "My ship. My crew. It's no different just because it's an empire instead."

Johar snorted. "In some ways I like the irony that the honor Hao drummed into you stuck so well, but really, Hail, you can't be responsible in the same way for an empire that you are for a crew of fifteen. You know that."

"They're all gone."

"I'm not going to argue with you about that." She shook her head. "You need to believe there's nothing left for you to do but to fight." She didn't look my way, smiling instead at the wall. "I happen to agree with Gita that this is not the way it should be, but I understand why it's the choice you've made. I just don't want it to kill you."

I couldn't stop the laugh. "It's hard to even see that as an ending now."

"I know, and that's what really scares me. We are mortal, Hail. Even me with all this." She gestured at herself and shook her head. "And the super cool things the Shen have taught us. We live, we die. There's no getting around that. We won't live forever. There's having a healthy fear of death and then there's thinking you're invincible. Aiz has beaten the latter into you, and Mia's made you think you can control it." She shook her head, waving a hand in the direction of the main room. "It's not a good thing."

"Maybe not," I admitted. "But what choice do I have?"

Johar sighed and got to her feet. "There are always choices, Hail. We just like to fool ourselves into thinking there aren't to justify making the shit ones."

I watched her follow Gita's path from the room and lay back on the bench, tears leaking out of my eyes and disappearing into my hair.

Don't listen to them. You dishonor us all if you quit now. Cire's ghost crouched at my side, smoothing a hand over my forehead. *We all died to put you here, sister; what becomes of that if you walk away and let the galaxy burn?*

Several days later I came to a stop in the corridor as the familiar sounds of strained voices wafted out of Mia's office toward me.

"I did not expect this recklessness, not from her," Aiz said. "And it is only getting worse."

"We can't stop now," Mia replied, though there was a hesitation in her voice. "It's not a surprise. Everything she's loved has been stripped away from her and then we push?" She exhaled and I heard the sound of footsteps pacing the floor. "The future holds for the moment. You need to find a way to reach her."

"I am the one out there snapping her bones!" Aiz's furious whisper surprised me, as did the strange grief clinging to the words.

"She trusts you more than you know, Aiz. We knew what this would cost. The scouts reported spotting a Farian ship in sector forty-seven. You know who it is. They will find us soon—"

The sound of footsteps behind me in the corridor forced me into movement and I wiped the expression from my face as I came in through the door of Mia's office.

I stopped, adopting a surprised look at the pair of Shen in the room, and then smiled. "I'm sorry, am I interrupting?"

"Not at all." If I hadn't heard the conversation I would have missed the forced smile as Mia turned around. "Aiz was just leaving."

He crossed the room, eyes on me, and inhaled as he passed as though he wanted to say something. I watched the indecision flash through his eyes and then it was gone. "Hail." He murmured my name, but nothing more as he left the room.

"Hail, I am sorry," Mia said with her hands outstretched in my direction. "You don't know how much."

"You'd think I'd get used to the idea that all of you sat around and watched my life implode like some cheap vid-drama."

The bitterness in my words was designed to cut like knives, but I got very little pleasure from watching Mia flinch.

"I understand it." I shrugged. "If anyone had come to me years ago and claimed to know how this was going to play out, I'd have laughed in their face and then probably shot them."

"Hail."

I dodged Mia when she came toward me. "Don't, please. Don't touch me. It still hurts. Don't you get it? Even knowing why you and Sybil kept all this to yourselves, it still hurts. I'm still angry." I spun on my heel, hooking my hands behind my neck as I walked to the far wall. "There is so much rage in me, you don't understand. I don't care about what happens to me, but there are a hell of a lot of people who are dead. People I loved. They didn't have to be tossed onto the fire."

"You think you could have stopped it?"

"I think it was my duty to stop it, to keep my sisters and brothers safe. To keep my people safe. Naraka, even to keep a galaxy's worth of strangers safe! Isn't that what you all want from me? To kill mighty beings and stop worse things from dropping in on this galaxy?"

"It's different, Hail."

"It's not!" I whirled around. "It's no different. Those were my people, my family. I owed it to them to keep them safe and I failed." I crossed the room to the console in the back, tapping it and bringing up a map of the surrounding space. "Now the Farians are closing in on us and I'm once again helpless to do anything about it."

Mia joined me at the console, none the wiser as she put a hand on my arm. "Hail, look at me. You didn't fail."

I lifted my head. My eyes were dry, but rage and misery battled it out in my chest as I met Mia's gaze.

"The hardest part of seeing the future is knowing that people are going to die and knowing you can't stop it." She attempted a smile, her lips only curving briefly before she gave up. "I had my first glimpse of the future when I was five. Too young to know what to make of it. Too young to realize that telling my father would result in a worse moment coming to pass. Too young to understand that some things are meant to be and they will play out no matter how many times we try to stop them.

"Your people didn't die because you failed at something. They died because we all die."

I laughed. "Mia, do you realize how that sounds given our entire plan is about ensuring your immortality?"

Mia shook her head. "Even the Farians. Even the Shen." She gestured around us. "This all ends someday. There's no escape from that."

"The abstract notion that the universe ends doesn't change things much." I rested my forearms on the console and went back to studying the map, my eyes seeking out section forty-seven. I found it and quickly cataloged the distance between Sparkos and the sector. It was strangely absent of any red-marked Farian forces, and I wondered again what Mia had meant by her words.

"I know," Mia said. "I was thirteen when my mother died, and during her funeral rites I saw a future of a young woman weeping over her dying father before she was dragged away by BodyGuards. The grief was a mirror of my own. Six months later I saw a future of a young woman with green hair facing down a man twice her size in a bar. It took me longer than I want to admit to figure out that it was the same person."

13

laughed and pushed upright. "I wouldn't feel too bad. In so many ways the person I was died there with my father. Cressen Stone and the princess Hailimi Bristol were two different people for a very long time."

Now it was pieces of Cressen who had died on the floor of my *Sophie* more than a year ago. Here I was, the Empress of Indrana, struggling to hold it all together in the face of my shifting fate. I wanted to ask Mia how it ended, or better yet to tell me what to choose to take this awful, yawning emptiness out of my chest. It didn't seem to matter that I knew I couldn't trust them; I wanted someone else to tell me what to do. "How much of my life have you seen?" I asked instead.

"A lot of it." Mia was smiling when I looked at her. "Some were of choices that weren't made, but mostly I've seen pieces of your life play out the way you've lived it, just a little in advance. I know this may make you uneasy, but I needed you to know."

"It doesn't." I shook my head. "That's strange, maybe, but it doesn't bother me."

"I feel like I know you, Hail, but it's hollow and more like a dream than anything. I'd like to change that." She tapped the edge of the console. "We are here, now, and I have been waiting for this moment my whole life. There was no way to change the things that happened up until now without bringing ruin to the galaxy. Your family still would have died, no matter the scenario. The only ones where they didn't, it all ended in disaster. I'm sorry."

Just like Cas. I rubbed a hand over my face as the thought intruded and couldn't bring myself to ask about Emmory and the others. "I could have made a difference, if you'd been willing to work at the negotiations."

Mia smiled. "I admire your determination, but you do not understand the depths to which the Pedalion will sink to keep their hold on power. We would have been willing if they had been."

"Aiz told me they tried to kill you when you were a girl."

Mia turned toward me and tugged the hem of her shirt upward. The rough knot of tissue ran in a jagged line just under her breast all the way to her side, as if someone had stuck a knife between her fifth and sixth ribs and tried to slice her open sideways. It was pale against the tan of her skin and made my stomach twist with both anger and horror.

"I was dying when Aiz got to me. He dragged every bit of energy from the room around him and almost everything from himself to save me."

"You were a child. How could they have—" I stopped myself just before my fingers made contact with her skin and pulled back, fisting my hand so tightly it hurt.

"The Farians are not your friends, Hail," Mia replied. "They are cold and methodical and ruthless in their devotion to the universe taking a path they believe is right. The path that placates their gods. The rest of us are nothing but pawns to be thrown away on an opening gambit." She dropped her shirt and stared past me.

I bit my tongue before I could make a joke about pawns; it hit too close to home given what I'd overheard. Pieces of my brain grappled—some wanting to go back to Gita and apologize for my stubbornness. We hadn't spoken since I'd suggested I should fire her. A larger part wanted to ask Mia about the conversation I'd overheard and demand answers.

You can't trust anyone, sha zhu. Hao appeared on the other side of the console, arms crossed and leaning against the wall.

"I am sorry for the pain you have gone through, and what you are still going through. It is a time of hard choices. The ones I have made helped you to be here, and I would make them again even knowing the pain. I understand what is at stake, not just the future of my people but of everyone in the galaxy. So do you. Your gut tells you the truth of this. You are the Star and people will wade through blood and fire for you."

I wanted to tell her I didn't trust my gut, that it was a seething mass of snakes all tangled in fury.

"Are we safe here?" I asked, pointing at the planet rotating above the console and then gesturing at the red-marked Farian forces.

"Safe enough," Mia replied, returning her gaze to the console. "The Farians have been seeking our planets for years with little success. We fight when we want to, not the other way around."

"Have you sent out feelers to Fasé's people? There have to be some Farians who don't want war with you."

"We have. They are in chaos because of what happened on Earth and we haven't gotten a response."

"As the Star of Indrana you'd think I'd have some pull with them? I knew Fasé. Her people may be open to an alliance."

"No, it's not safe." There was a curious hesitation in her voice.

"What's safe?" I laughed. "You trust me to help you plan troop movements but not this? Why?"

"Hail, this is not about a lack of trust, it's—"

"Mia, do you have a moment?"

She looked away from me to where Vais stood in the doorway; whatever she'd been about to say to me had been swallowed by the interruption, and she exhaled a frustrated sigh before leaving me alone.

"Majesty, where are you?" As if I'd summoned her, Fasé's voice

echoed in my head, distracting me with her volume. I looked away from the door reflexively.

Of all the ghosts she had become the most persistent, and at least once a day I would hear her voice. I couldn't, or didn't, answer her questions depending on my mood, and it seemed to frustrate her to no end.

"More damn walls. That does me no good."

"Fine," I murmured. "You want something. Here's something."

I looked down at the console and hoped that Mia would assume my absent hand-waving through the hologram of Sparkos was just me lost in thought.

My back hit the wall and before I could get a hand up to defend myself, Aiz locked his hand around my throat and squeezed. I heard Johar gasp from where she watched us and hoped to Shiva she wouldn't try to help me. Aiz would kill her. He'd already warned her as much the first time she'd watched us fight, and I knew it wasn't an empty threat.

I had been doing better, but the constant harassment from Fasé and the ghosts in my head were starting to wear me down. I could endure all manner of attacks from Aiz but couldn't seem to bring myself to make that last killing blow, and I knew that was frustrating him to no end.

I kicked at him. He blocked it easily, stepping in closer with a sigh and a shake of his head. The proximity kept my punches to his head from their full force, and I felt my larynx start to give under the pressure.

The movement in the corner of my vision called to me, and I spotted Mia in the doorway.

She tapped a finger to her eye, but my pain-soaked brain refused to cooperate, and my throat collapsed under Aiz's hand. Mia shook her head, tapped her eye again, and then suddenly the spark of comprehension flared through my brain, and I used what oxygen I had left to drive my thumb into his left eye.

Aiz staggered away, vicious curses and blood flying through the air as I slid to the floor in a dying heap.

I flopped around, my lungs desperately trying and failing to drag air in through my ruined trachea. It was automatic, instinctive, and useless.

"Oh, Hail." Mia laid her hand on my throat with a pained noise, and her energy flowed into me. I kept my eyes on hers as my throat was rebuilt and my lungs filled with air again. "Stay down," she whispered as she stood.

I doubted I could disobey her even if I'd wanted to. Mia had healed my throat, but the other injuries from the fight were all still present and reminded me of it with such force that I blacked out for a second.

When I came to, Johar was sitting with my head in her lap and her hands in my hair. I could hear Mia and Aiz's fierce discussion, but they were talking so fast it was hard to keep up, the bits of Shen I could understand making for a conversation as broken and disjointed as my body.

"Aiz, you push her *para skilira*—"

"*Para skilira?*"

"Beyond her skills," Johar whispered.

"I push because I have no choice. We are running out of time." Aiz shook his head. "She must be *prépei capaz na eínai de luchar* or die."

"Prepared to fight or die." Jo continued to translate at my murmured confusion.

"That's cheery," I muttered. "Not really a surprise, though."

"Don't move," Johar ordered when I tried to sit up. "You're fucked up. I'm not even going to try to help, I think I'd kill us both. Just turn your head."

Mia reached up, touching her fingers to Aiz's face, spitting a curse at him and grabbing the other side of his head when he tried to pull away.

"Hold still," she ordered, putting her hand over his ruined eye.

"You let your sympathies get over you," he said, leaning in and pressing his forehead to hers.

"Of course I'm worried. We walk on the edge of a knife's blade." Mia closed her eyes, smiled. "And I'm not the only soft heart in this place."

He pulled back, wincing. "Did you need something?"

"We got hit."

"Where?"

"Luasathia. I don't know how the Farians found us. Heckor got *la stóla* out, but not the civilians." Mia closed her eyes and swallowed. "We have to do something, Aiz. Before the Farians make more of those ships."

"I don't know *la stóla*," Johar said. "But I'd guess 'fleet' or something similar just from context."

Aiz dragged a hand through his hair and muttered something too low for me to hear before he scooped Mia into a brief hug. "Let me finish here and I will come see you after."

"She is getting better."

"She didn't die only because you helped."

"He's not wrong about that," Johar muttered.

"Hush." I glared up at Johar and she smiled, but there was worry in her ice-blue eyes.

Mia's laugh was a wash of warmth over my chilled bones. "We are stronger together, brother."

"She's not wrong about that." That comment earned me a raised eyebrow from Jo.

Before I could say anything else, Mia stopped and looked down at us with a smile. "Johar, if you'll come with me. I'll see you later, Hail. Watch out for him, he is angry. Also, he drops his left guard when he moves in."

"I'll remember that," I replied, rolling to my side and away from Johar with a groan. Aiz grabbed me under both arms before I could get to my feet and hauled me into the air.

Power surged where his bare skin touched mine, wiping away the pain, filling me with that delightful buzz I couldn't stop wanting. "We're not done."

"I gathered." Because I was expecting it, I was able to translate his shove into a forward roll and bounced to my feet, knocking aside his kick and ducking in to land a punch to his spine. "Farians giving you problems?"

"Your Shen is improving." He gave me a flat look.

"Your people talk a lot, and there's not much else for us to do," I lied with a shrug, shifting on the balls of my feet as I waited for him to move in again.

Instead he dropped his hands, shoulders slumping with the movement. I could have moved in. Part of me wanted to finally win a fight. I'd come close so many times in the last few days. But the look on his face stopped me.

"There were upwards of twenty thousand Shen on Luasathia, Hail. Men, women, children. My people. They are all dead. They are slaughtering us with that weapon of theirs and I am helpless to stop it."

My breath ghosted out, but Aiz didn't notice as he turned away, rubbing both hands over his face.

"How can I help?"

"You have no idea how much I appreciate the offer, but I don't know that you can." Aiz hooked his hands behind his head and stared up at the ceiling. "The Farians have these ships, Hail. We stole one, Mia and I, back before Father was killed. She was able to pull apart their technology, rebuild it into the ships that make up our fleet, but we never could get the weapon to work."

"I know. Mia sent me the files to look at."

"Did she?" Aiz gave me a thoughtful look. "Interesting."

"I understand the concept but can't make much sense of where things went wrong. Gun schematics are pretty universal, but the notes are all in Farian."

"I'll have someone translate them for you."

"You were telling me the truth about their colonies," I whispered, the memory of that awful beam of light cutting through the black and down to the planet. "They really killed their own people."

Your people, Hail. Zin's ghost whispered the reminder.

"They will kill us all to have their way." He turned, dark eyes haunted with grief. "We have taken down a handful of these ships. It's not enough. It costs too much to destroy them."

"It costs more to let them keep killing your people."

"We have been able to hide until now. I don't know how they discovered the planet's location." Aiz lifted a shoulder, let it fall, and offered up a genuine smile. "Now you see why I push the way I do. If we win, this will all be over."

I spotted Hao sitting against the far wall, shaking his head with sorrow etched on his face. "If I fail?"

"You won't." Aiz crossed to me, putting his hand against my chest. My heart thumped as though it were trying to break free of my rib cage to meet his fingers. "You are a warrior, Hail. You are the Star of Indrana. You won't quit. You won't lose."

I woke to the sound of Gita and Johar whispering in the dark, my nightmare fading into the background of my brain. The moons painted the wall by my feet with silvery light.

"I think we should do it."

"You know she won't come willingly." Gita's voice was heavy with frustration.

"Then I knock her out and we carry her ass." I could practically hear the nonchalant shrug Johar offered up. "What little I believe about the Farian abilities to see the future, you and I both know that the fucking emphasis was on Hail *not* fighting. That's what she's doing in there with Aiz and it's changing her, we can all see it. Shit, even the Shen are worried about it."

"Alba's located a shuttle depot about a hundred and fifteen klicks from here. We'll start making plans for it. I tried to hold out hope that the others were alive, Jo, but—"

"I know, it's been five and a half months here, which translates into who knows what as far as standard time goes. Either way it's been too fucking long for no sign of anyone."

"I'm never going to get to forgive that asshole. I know he's smirking at me from the afterlife," Gita whispered. There was a choked sob and the rustling of an embrace, then silence.

I rolled onto my side, coming face to face with Kisah. If she'd been alive my Guard wouldn't have fit on the bunk with me, but being a ghost meant you could break all the rules you wanted.

You know you can't let them take you out of here, ma'am, right?

I nodded.

Kisah smiled and pressed her forehead to mine. I squeezed my eyes shut, tears leaking into the pillowcase until sleep claimed me again.

14

"ail."

I blinked, my dry eyes telling me I'd been staring at my outstretched hand for far too long even before I looked at Mia.

She was watching me with a raised eyebrow and the beginning of a smile tugging on one corner of her mouth. "Are you all right? You've been extremely distracted today."

"I—" I closed my hand, extinguishing the sparks jumping across my palm. We were sitting side by side against the wall, my knees pulled up to my chest and my arm resting on top.

Tell her about Gita's plans, Muna said, but the words lodged themselves in my throat.

I shook my head. "I didn't sleep well."

Not so far gone you'd betray your own people yet. Hao was leaning against the far wall, legs crossed at the ankles. *I'm honestly kind of surprised.*

I made a face and gestured rudely at him when Mia's back was turned. Hao's ghost shook his head and vanished.

"We can pick this up again tomorrow?"

"No, I'm fine. Tell me again."

"You can't pull energy from yourself like you did with your broken hand. You have to focus outside yourself. It's the only way to keep from burning through your personal energy stores." Mia stuck a hand out and the air around her fingers rippled until it formed a ball of arcing blue light. She closed her hand into a fist and the ball vanished.

"Now you try."

I blew out a breath and extended my hand again.

"This isn't magic, Hail." Mia's voice was low against my ear. "There's energy in the air, atoms bouncing against each other."

"Like lightning."

"Exactly like lightning. All you have to do is take it. Think of how it feels when you're out in a storm just before the lightning hits."

I knew how it felt. The raw power of it singing through the air. When I'd lost Wilson's trail out in the black, I'd snuck out of the ship in the middle of the night on Falzour and screamed into the oncoming storm. The very air had been alive around me, and if Hao had caught me there would have been an epic ass kicking. As it was the storm had answered my rage with a lightning show that stole my breath and rained fire down around me as I'd stood stubbornly in the night, daring the gods to strike me down for my failures.

It rained here on Sparkos, but the lightning was blunted by the forest around us and I suspected I'd have a much harder time going outside to stand in the rain around here than I had on Hao's ship.

I dragged in a breath and exhaled again. I could feel what she was talking about, but it was trapped behind glass.

Or I was.

"Bugger me." I dropped my hand with a muttered curse. "What am I doing wrong?"

"Nothing specifically," Mia replied. "You are an extremely controlled person, Hail. This requires that you surrender. You can't control the energy until you've opened yourself up to it, and to do that you have to let go."

I turned to look at her, my speech about my control being the only thing keeping me from killing myself and everyone around me dying in my throat.

I'd forgotten how close her head was to mine. Mia's breath caught, and I watched her gray eyes darken with emotion.

I leaned forward to close the centimeters of space between her lips and mine. Then my heart gave a single, painful lurch as Mia leaned away.

"I can't," she said, pressing her fingers to my mouth. "It's not that I don't want to—" The blush appearing on her cheeks made my heart lurch again. "It wouldn't be fair to you, Hail. You are not here entirely of your own free will and I don't want you looking back on this thinking I coerced you into that choice."

"You're happy enough to have my help with this, coerced or not."

Mia smiled. "My brother would be furious to hear me say so, but the fight is less important than me getting this moment between us right." She dropped her hand and I felt the heat still tingling in my lips. Her exhalation was quiet. "It is selfish, I know, when weighed against the survival of my people and the galaxy, but I won't—" She fumbled and muttered a curse in Shen. "You matter for no other reason than the fact that you are you."

"I'm nothing special."

"You are everything that is special in this universe."

I wanted to push, to lean forward and kiss her anyway, but part of me knew she was right. I wasn't myself. I wasn't—all appearances to the contrary—in control of anything, let alone myself.

"Mia."

We jerked apart at the sound of Hamah's voice. Mia got to her feet and crossed to the doorway. I returned my focus to my hand. The rapid-fire conversation in Shen was beyond my abilities except for a few scattered words I recognized.

I didn't need to know what they were saying to understand the sudden snap in Mia's voice, and I lifted my gaze to the pair in the doorway.

Hamah's mouth was set in a thin line. Mia was shaking her head. He reached a hand out, but she danced backward.

I got to my feet. I could practically taste the fight brewing in the air. "Is there a problem?"

"Esai la muerte osa!"

"Hamah!"

I settled into my stance between one breath and the next, smiling as I lifted a hand. "If you have a problem, Hamah, I'm happy to oblige you."

"No." Mia held up a hand and gave Hamah a push toward the door with her other. "He's leaving."

Hamah left, but not without one last look over his shoulder at me, dark eyes filled with surprising hatred.

"What was that about?"

"Nothing." Mia lied so easily I almost missed the tightness around her mouth.

"You stole a fight from me; least you can do is be honest about why."

She raised a dark eyebrow. "I would have let you kill him, but I'm mad enough to consider not bringing him back."

The misery in her voice cut through my anger and had me spreading my arms wide. Mia crossed the distance, burying her face in my shoulder and holding on tight. There was no heat in the embrace, even though it had been sparking between us like a live wire only moments before. This was just comfort. I felt her choke down a sob and pressed my cheek to her hair. "What is it?"

"Old wounds. New arguments." Her voice was muffled. Then she pulled away and looked up at me with a smile. "You would understand. I have not been their leader for very long. Things shift, even when you try to keep them the same. You have to make choices and they are rarely the ones that make everyone happy."

"I do." I laughed, rubbed a hand over my face, and then dropped it to my side. "Those who are your companions are now your subordinates."

"And more." Mia nodded. She took another step away from me, slipping her hands into the pockets of her pants. "I am continuing

116

my father's work, this task that was set long before my birth. But Aiz and I have different ideas of how to accomplish it than our father did. Not everyone is happy about our choices."

"At the risk of sounding arrogant, I suspect I'm one of those choices that people are disagreeing with?"

"A small faction." Mia waved a hand. "Hamah does not agree with them, but he—"

"Doesn't like me very much." I grinned.

"He is concerned for me," Mia replied with a sigh. "We grew up together, though that was not his first childhood. It makes him overprotective."

"By all accounts you can take care of yourself, though I've yet to see it," I said, and held my hands up when Mia gave me a look. "I'm just teasing."

"I actually believe you this time." She smiled, and her shoulders relaxed. "Hamah is concerned about other things."

"What did he say to me? I couldn't quite understand it." I raised an eyebrow at Mia's hesitation.

"He said you will be the death of us all."

I couldn't think of a good response to that. "Why won't this work?" I asked instead, waving my hand in the air.

"You're not willing to let go," Mia replied. "Until you do, you're not going to be able to work with anything more than what Aiz or I could give you."

She didn't have to say it. I already knew that if we were hobbled with that limitation, there was no way Aiz and I would win the fight.

"Hamah had better watch his mouth, and so should you for repeating his nonsense. Aiz will step on both of you hard."

"I don't agree with him, Talos. I'm just telling you what he's saying."

I paused at the intersection. Several weeks had passed since the incident with Hamah in Mia's rooms and while I'd forgotten all about it, it appeared he hadn't.

"What he's saying is dangerously close to treachery. Mia has seen all this—the Star included. Hamah's personal issues are clouding his judgment."

Talos's and Vais's voices were clear in the quiet. Shen was slowly getting easier for me to understand. My choice to join my own people in the evenings as they practiced the language rather than take Aiz up on an offer to teach me was likely the reason. As an added bonus it seemed to have allayed Gita's concerns about my state of mind—at least for the moment—and I hadn't heard any more whispered conversations about knocking me over the head and making a run for it.

Being able to understand whispered conversations in hallways between Shen was a new experience and I leaned against the wall, careful not to make any noise.

"The point," Vais said with a heavy sigh, "is so you'll go talk to him. He'll listen to you. Maybe you can keep him from getting jarred."

I frowned. Jarred? I must have misunderstood that last word because it didn't make any sense. *Kivotio* was the verb for *kivo*, which was jar or vessel. I shook my head and made a note to ask Alba about it later. It must be slang of some sort.

"Fine. I'll try, but you know how he is and if he takes a swing at me I'm killing his ass and not bringing him back. Then you can explain to the *Thínos* why he's back with Jibun."

I tiptoed back a few steps and then headed down the corridor and around the corner. "Morning," I said with a bright smile.

Talos was better at hiding his discomfort than Vais, and his easy greeting almost seemed genuine. "Morning, Star of Indrana."

"One of these days I'm going to get you to call me Hail," I replied. "Are we sparring today?"

Talos shook his head. "I believe Aiz wanted to spar with you alone. Which, you should probably get a move on if you don't want to be late."

I grinned at him and headed down the corridor with a wave of my hand.

You going to tell Aiz what you overheard? Hao asked, catching up to me and matching my stride, his hands stuffed in his pockets.

You should tell Gita, Emmory said from the other side. *It's something you could use against them.*

She doesn't want to use it against them, Emmory. She's working with them.

Hao's words stung, but I couldn't argue with him. He was right after all.

"Do you two mind?" I closed my eyes, but not before I saw the flash of disappointment on my dead *Ekam*'s face. "It's necessary. I'm not going to tell anyone, though. Gita doesn't need to know, and it's Shen politics; they'll sort it out themselves."

The ghosts vanished without a reply and I continued on alone, trying to pretend like the disapproval of dead men didn't cut to the bone.

"You're late." Aiz didn't look up as I came into the gym.

"Kill me for it," I replied, rolling my shoulders in what felt like a futile attempt to release the tension from them. My tenuous grip on reality felt like it was slipping through my fingers with every passing second. I exhaled; the sound was louder than it should have been in the silence.

Now Aiz looked up, his eyes narrowing as he studied me. "What's the matter?"

"Nothing."

He caught me by the chin, raising an eyebrow when I didn't fight my way free. "Do me the courtesy of just saying you don't want to talk about it instead of lying, Hail. I can respect the former. The latter pisses me off."

"Fine," I said. "I don't want to talk about it."

"Was that so hard?" He released me with a smile that faded when I didn't respond. "Hail—" He caught himself and sighed. "I said I would respect your privacy, but I am here if you need to talk."

"I'd rather fight." I regretted the words as soon as they left my mouth. Aiz had a habit of recognizing when I was too eager for blood and denying me a sparring match until he felt I'd calmed down enough.

For a moment, his decision hung in the balance, but then Aiz shrugged and gestured. "Come on, then."

"You're doing well," Aiz said, sitting cross-legged by my side a little while later. "We're so close. I didn't expect you to progress this fast, but I suppose I shouldn't be surprised you took to this better than the healing."

I rolled over onto my back, the rush of coming back to life still scrambling my brain. There was something dangerous about the way Aiz's energy made me feel. Jo had spotted it that very first time. I knew I should be more cautious, but the cycle of pain, energy, pain was too strong for me to escape from. "How so?"

"Most recruits tap out a lot sooner, give in to the pain a lot quicker. You fight, Hail. The worse it gets, the more you fight, and the fact that you don't really know when to quit makes it all the more thrilling."

My head was spinning. The fight hadn't been as brutal today, but the ghosts were loud and Aiz had kept up his illusions until I wasn't sure which were ghosts and which were him.

He'd even morphed into Gita at one point and it had thrown me so badly that I'd completely missed the kick aimed at my head.

I'd woken up on the ground, the electricity singing through my skin the way it always did after Aiz healed me. Times like this I knew why everyone worried about me. I only felt alive when I was here—dying.

They were all right to be worried about me; I was coming unraveled before their very eyes.

"I really am going to beat you one of these days."

"I'm looking forward to it, Hail. I haven't been defeated in an age. It gets tiresome." Aiz stretched out next to me and held his hand up. "You and my sister are probably the only people alive who could accomplish such a victory, and she refuses to spar with me."

"You lied to me," I said, and was more than a little surprised by his laughter.

"You're going to have to be more specific about that. When?"

"During the negotiations. You dismissed the story about drinking the blood of the gods, but you were lying. Why?"

"It seemed easier at the time," Aiz said.

"So you did."

"Yes and no." He pressed his temple to my head until I turned to look at him. "It was a practical reason. There were genetic markers in their blood that contained the key we needed."

"Key?"

"The one that allowed us to have children. What we didn't realize at the time was that the markers were broken up among the gods, and by not killing them all we were missing part of the puzzle."

"The part that allows the Farians to reincarnate," I whispered, and Aiz nodded.

"Partially. We are able to circumvent the reincarnations of those who are Shen so they don't come back on Faria."

"Yes, Mia mentioned that."

"Good." Aiz sighed. "However, there is nothing I can do for those Shen gifted with humanity. All our children since the flight have been bound to one life and one life only. I lost my only child—a daughter—before I realized it and vowed not to have any more until we fixed what was broken."

"I'm sorry, it's horrible to lose people you love."

"I know you mean that and even more so that you understand it. It's one of the reasons I like you, Hail."

"You have a strange way of showing it." I reached a hand out, watching in drunken fascination as blue sparks leapt from his fingers to mine. "Why do you leave my old scars when you heal me?"

The scar from the failed bank job we'd tried to pull on Marrakesh still decorated my left forearm.

"I could take them away if you wanted," Aiz replied, tracing a finger along the scar. "But scars remind us where we've come from. It's rude to steal that from you without permission." He smiled when I turned my head to look at him. "I could fix everything, though, not just the scars. I could undo what happened to you on Candless."

"Hail," Emmory said, giving me the Look. "Your value as the Empress of Indrana is more than your ability to bear children. The empire needs you."

I pressed my right hand to my belly button and shook my head, clearing out the memory of my *Ekam* and his gentle reassurance that day in the palace. "No. No, thank you. I am not in need of fixing."

Aiz's grin was sharp as a broken bone. "Mia said you would refuse, but the offer stands regardless."

"Are you propositioning me, Aiz Cevalla?"

"Not me." He shook his head. "You are amazing, but I don't sleep with humans. Besides, my sister's wrath?" Aiz blew out a breath. "Not something I want to bring down on my head."

"You're not concerned about mine?"

Aiz made a laughing noise of dismissal. "You cannot make me miserable for eternity. When this is over, Mia will be able to."

I heard the words he wasn't saying. *She's not yours and she won't ever be.* That was what Hamah and the others missed in their concern about me. I would grow old and die no matter what we did here, while Mia would become like her brother. One way or another we would go our separate ways.

The thought of it made me sadder than I'd expected. "Like lightning, I am an expert at dying," I murmured. "Like lightning, this beauty has no language. It makes no difference whether I win or lose."

"I have not heard Rumi in a very long time," Aiz said.

"Hao had a real book of his poems; he let me borrow it once after a great deal of badgering on my part."

"Your relationship with Hao is a fascinating thing. I have misjudged it repeatedly."

"Most people do. I miss him with every beat of my heart," I whispered, rolling away from Aiz and getting to my feet so he wouldn't see my tears. I quickly wiped my face as Aiz got to his feet.

"Hail."

"It's fine." I waved him off, but Aiz grabbed my wrist and tugged until I turned around. "Useless to cry," I said. "I know."

"It's not useless, Hail. Our minds seek the comfort for a reason. There's no shame in it."

A soldier appeared in the doorway. "*Thíno* Aiz?"

"Yes?"

"*Thína* Mia needs to speak with you. She said it was important. She said she'd commed you directly, but you hadn't—"

"I was busy." The words cut through the air like one of the mysterious laser weapons, and the woman at the door braced. "Another attack?"

"Yes, sir. I am sorry, sir. It's important."

Aiz turned back to me. "I'm sorry to interrupt this."

"It's fine," I replied. "I'll go back to my rooms and clean up. Then join you?"

He nodded and we parted ways.

15

I wrapped my arms around my waist. The sudden grief over Hao was choking me, and I wondered if Aiz could be convinced to end this for me after the fight was over.

Ironic that you're assuming you'll survive. Or maybe not. You're the one who always makes it through alive, aren't you?

"Majesty!"

I froze, Gita's voice tangling with the voice in my head and my frayed nerves. *That's Gita,* the rational part of my brain reminded me as I came through the door. *You don't want to hit her.* I uncurled my fists with a great deal of effort.

"Majesty, they're alive." Her face was bright with hope. Alba was right behind her with a smile on her face.

"What?" I shook my head. "What are you talking about?"

"I got through," Alba said. "I know you said to drop it but I couldn't get that image of Hao out of my head. I realized early that it had been too easy to get into the Shen's systems. Almost like they wanted me in there so they could control what I was seeing. But that file I found didn't match with anything else. I've been trying to find my way around it for weeks. I couldn't get news or a line out. Nothing, it was like they were actively blocking me from the outside. But I did it. And I found this—"

I slapped her hand away before she could touch me. "What is going on?"

"Majesty?" Alba looked at Gita. "I just want to show you the news report. Fasé got everyone out; no one was killed in the embassy explosion. Everyone is alive. They are looking for us."

"No." *They are dead*, my brain screamed. "No one could have survived that explosion." I whirled on Johar. "You don't believe this, do you? You told me they were dead."

"I said I thought they were dead, Hail, in the face of overwhelming evidence." Johar shook her head. "The universe decided to prove me wrong and give us a miracle after all, and I am totally okay with being wrong here."

"Why are you—" I broke off with a strangled gasp. Was this a test? Or all part of the plan?

The last clinging thread of my sanity snapped.

Our minds seek the comfort for a reason. Aiz's parting words flooded back into my brain as the image of Emmory's face sliding away like water filled my vision.

The Shen could have replaced them all at any point, Hail. Cas's ghost pointed out the awful truth with a cheerful grin. *You have no way of knowing.*

How did I know this was Alba? That this was Gita. "Oh, Dark Mother, no."

This was the horror I'd been living in, and Aiz had practically thrown the clues in my face. I was truly alone. Everyone I cared for, down to the last person, was dead and gone. My heart cracked wide open, spilling onto the floor at my feet. I pressed a hand to my chest, fighting for a breath. Why I was forcing air into my lungs I didn't know, except that part of me had to stay alive.

"Hail?"

"Don't touch me." I backed away from Gita as Alba looked on in shock. "Just, don't. I don't know who you are."

"You don't—what is that supposed to mean? I'm your *Dve*, Majesty. We need to get out of here now."

"Gita is my *Ekam*, because Emmory is dead," I snarled.

"They're not dead!" she shouted back. "Aren't you listening? They're not dead, Hail."

"He could have replaced you. I don't know."

"Replaced us? What are you—"

"Don't touch me!" I grabbed Gita by the throat, propelling her across the room. She didn't fight me, and she hit the wall hard. There were tears in her brown eyes, but I stepped down on the sympathy.

That's lesson two—these beings will lie to you, trick your eyes, do everything they can to gain the upper hand in a fight. You can't let them.

"That's enough." Johar stepped between us, putting a hand in the middle of my chest and shoving me away.

I swung my elbow into her face without the slightest hesitation. Johar's head snapped back. I was already spinning to my left when Alba hit me from the side, and I sprawled face first on the floor several meters away. I was back on my feet in a flash, a hard lesson learned from the number of times Aiz had followed knocking me to the ground with a vicious kick.

"Majesty, stop this." Gita held her hand up, the other pulling Johar back by the arm.

"She's not going to," Johar murmured, wiping the blood from her mouth and cracking her neck. "Come on, Hail, you know me. You want to fight? Let's fight." She shook Gita off and put her hands up.

Two punches in, I knew two things for certain: It really was Johar and she was going to lose.

She let me slip out of an arm lock instead of pressing the last dozen centimeters to break my elbow like any Shen would have. I slithered free, kicking her in the face once, and was aiming for a second blow that would have snapped her neck when Gita's boot slammed into my ankle with such force that I felt the bones crack.

The door opened, and Shen rushed in.

"Stop this at once!"

They separated us. A pretty Shen with dark brown eyes whose

name I couldn't remember pointed his gun at me when I started to get up and shook his head.

"Stay down, Your Majesty. *Thíno* Aiz is on his way." His Indranan was surprisingly good.

Grinning at him, I settled back on my elbows and tipped my head back.

My ankle was throbbing in time with my heartbeat, pain shooting spikes up my right leg. It was glorious. I felt alive. I closed my eyes and hummed.

Aiz sighed heavily from the doorway. "Is everyone still breathing?"

"Yes, sir."

"Hail, look at me."

I lifted my head, smirking at Aiz for staying out of arm's reach, and swiped the blood from the corner of my mouth with my left hand, flicking it to the floor at his feet. "What?"

"What happened?"

"Did I pass your test?"

"What test?"

"They're not real." I gestured. "Well, Jo is, but not the others. It was a test, right?"

He frowned and approached me with the same caution one would use on a wounded animal, sliding a hand over my throat and up into my hair. The energy arced over my skin. The sound of Gita's choked rage pushed its way past my dulled senses, and the pain vanished.

The discontented noise crawled out of my mouth like a living thing. "I wanted that pain."

"Get them out of here," Aiz ordered.

"No! Shiva damn you, let me go. Hail—"

I didn't look away from Aiz when the sharp sound of a weapon meeting bone was followed by Johar's wordless snarl. The warning whine of a gun powering up ushered in a silence that my heartbeat easily filled.

"Hail, what are you talking about?"

"You told me," I murmured, unable to stop myself from leaning my head back into his hand, exposing my throat. "You said they weren't real. They claimed the others are alive."

"I said no such thing." Aiz blinked. "You think Gita and the others are Shen?"

"It makes sense. You said I can't trust my eyes. That our minds seek the comfort of believing the lie. You'd want every advantage, wouldn't you? Why not kill my people and replace them with yours from the beginning?"

"Oh, Hail." He sounded concerned, which made no sense at all to me. "They're your people. But I could have them removed, if you want."

His words were sharp, an ice-cold blade cutting into me. My strike knocked his hand off me. I rolled away from Aiz, coming up in a low crouch, my blood roaring so loud in my ears it drowned out everything else.

"Get out of here."

Aiz backed up, keeping his eyes on mine as he crossed over the threshold and the door slid shut. I collapsed onto the floor, wrapping my arms around my knees in a vain attempt to stop the shaking.

She's not completely lost.

I whirled around, scrambling back to my feet to find the threat. The ghosts of Emmory and Zin leaned against the far wall, shoulders touching as they studied me critically. My heart broke all over again at the sight of them together.

She's not. It's a surprise, I guess, Zin said. *I was expecting her to roll over for him, let him kill all three of them like she let him kill us. What do you suppose is keeping her here?*

Emmory pushed away from the wall. I tensed as he circled me slowly; that look of disdain on his face hadn't been aimed at me since our very first meeting. Now it hurt to see, and I squeezed my eyes shut, hoping they'd be gone when I opened them again.

I was not that lucky.

Are you waiting for something, Majesty? Emmory asked. *No one is coming to save you.*

"I never asked any of you to save me," I snarled at him. "I never asked for any of this!"

Cry me a fucking river, Hail, Zin snapped back. *We never asked for a spoiled brat to disrupt our lives, yet here we are. Or rather, here you are; we're dead.*

My reply died in my throat and I stared at Zin in horror until Emmory nudged me with his boot and crouched down so he was eye level with me.

You're losing focus. It leaves a nice warm glow around my heart that you feel so fucking guilty about us dying, but it pisses me off to see you playing Aiz's game. He tapped me on the forehead three times. *Wake the fuck up.*

I woke, Fasé's pale face filling my vision like a sad moon in a fall sky. *"Majesty, you're so much clearer now."*

"And you're still dead," I answered automatically. Odd that I could finally see her ghost when all I'd had before were her whispers. I swung a hand out, unsure if I was relieved or disappointed when it passed through her.

"I'm not dead." Her reply was startlingly peevish and I shook my head.

"I know. You'll be reborn on Faria, but that doesn't do me a whole lot of good, does it?"

The ghost's smile was filled with sorrow, and I swore I could feel her fingers on my cheek. *"Focus, Hail, it's so hard to reach you but it's been getting easier. Was the planet you touched the one you're on, do you know where?"*

"I haven't really left the compound. I don't know." I slipped from the bunk and padded across the floor to the window Johar had been trying to get loose. The moonlight shone down on the jungle beyond the compound. Fasé peeked over my shoulder and made a soft sound of frustration.

"There's a compound? What does it look like?"

I brought the map up on my *smati*. "I'm assuming since you're in my head you can see that. Though again I don't know what a ghost can do with the information. There are plants with tiny blue flowers around the camp. A jungle out there with big-leafed trees. They look like the ones on Si Ket and HiCrown, in the Thaimay system. I don't know what it matters, Fasé, you're all dead." I rested my forehead against the window. "I'm starting to think I'm dead, too, and I've been sent to Naraka."

"Hang on for us, Majesty. We're coming."

"No, you're not. No one is coming to save me."

"Majesty?"

I jerked away from the window. Fasé's ghost was, of course, gone, and Gita stood behind me, rubbing the sleep from her eyes.

"Majesty, what are you doing?"

"I was..." I looked back at the window, frowned. "It was just a dream."

"Come back to bed." Gita reached for my arm and tried unsuccessfully to hide the hurt in her eyes when I flinched away from her touch. Despite Aiz's assurances I wasn't wholly convinced she was real.

"What's going on?" Johar appeared behind Gita.

"Nothing. I was just restless," I said, avoiding contact with both of them as I slipped away from the window and went back to my bunk.

No one said a word about Emmory and the others being alive. It hung in the air with all the weight of the ghosts who still haunted me. I wrapped myself in the blanket, curling toward the wall.

"She was talking to Fasé," Gita whispered. "She's been talking to all of them, Jo, thinking they're dead. Whatever they're doing to her, it's killing her." Her voice broke. "We have to get out of here."

16

Several days later, I was lying on the floor, battered and dazed from the latest round with Aiz while he and Mia talked at the doorway.

I was swimming in a sea of pain, lost in the mists with nothing but ghosts to keep me company.

The fight had been close. Aiz was nearly as injured as I was, but he'd healed himself and then touched my bare shoulder before joining his sister. I could feel the energy rolling through my blood. I liked it when he left me to heal myself, liked being able to hold on to it and let the razor teeth of my pain shred just a little more of my soul.

Gita, if it was her, was right. I was a mess.

There was a small, conscious part of me that knew not using the energy to heal myself was wrong. It screamed, almost unheard in the back of my mind, getting weaker with every second that ticked by. It was the same voice that kept trying to get me to ask about Emmory and the others. That part wanted to believe they were alive.

The rest of me didn't want to deal. The pain was better.

I shifted, a broken rib stabbing into a lung with the movement, and the clean kiss of pain broke my drunken haze.

"Hail?"

I felt rather than heard their footsteps crossing the mat to me. Mia snapped something at her brother, too fast for me to comprehend.

"I did heal her," he replied in Indranan. "*Katadiki*—" His curse was in Shen, a word I didn't have a sense of beyond universal damnation. "I gave her energy to heal herself."

The mat shifted, and I cracked an eye open as Mia knelt by my head. "How can someone so intelligent be so foolish?"

My reply was cut off by the bubbling blood in my lung and Aiz muttered a second curse when I coughed, spraying blood across the mat.

It was a close call between his hand on my side or the energy jolting through me as to which hurt worse, but then Mia tightened her fingers against my scalp and murmured something to her brother. Electricity skittered down my spine and over my skin again. Now Mia's power felt cooler than Aiz's. It washed over me like a wave, sweeping away the pain.

"It's too much," she murmured, leaning in and pressing her lips to the crown of my head. "I am sorry, this is going to hurt."

Every cell caught on fire and I blacked out.

I woke a moment later, still on the floor, only now my head was in Mia's lap. "She's all right, Aiz," she murmured. "See. How do you feel?"

My breath caught in my chest and I locked my hands in my shirt before I gave in to the temptation of grabbing Mia by the face and kissing her.

"Better," I admitted. All my injuries were gone, along with the blood in my lung. But I felt like I was going to jump out of my skin and collapse from exhaustion all at the same time, and the ache remained. A longing for the pain I couldn't put words to even if someone had put a gun to my head.

I wish someone would put a gun to your head and save us all the trouble.

I winced away from the vicious, unidentifiable voice. Mia helped me sit up, rubbing circles on my back with one hand for a moment before she got to her feet.

"Why didn't you heal yourself?"

"I like the pain." The admission slipped out of me and I heard Aiz's ragged inhale. "It's better than feeling anything else."

Mia uttered a little wounded sound. "No, Hail, it's not."

Aiz muttered under his breath and got to his feet; whatever he'd said, it made Mia wince.

"Aiz—"

"No." He shook his head, a hand in the air as he headed for the door. "It is my fault. I was inattentive."

Mia followed him to the door and put a hand on his arm. I couldn't make out what they were saying, but the worried frowns creased across their faces were more than enough to give me a guess.

I got to my feet, swaying a little, and braced myself on the stack of mats Mia had been perched on during our fight. This was the first time she'd watched us fight and it had been distracting— painfully so—to say the least.

"How long have you been doing that?"

I didn't trust myself not to fall over if I turned my head to look at her, so I kept my eyes fixed on the mat in front of me. "I don't know, a month or so? Maybe more. I lose track."

"Your *smati* isn't on." Shock laced her words. "You've cut yourself off from your people?"

"I don't—"

Trust them, Hao said, boosting himself onto the mat next to me. *You don't trust them.*

"I don't trust myself," I snapped.

"Hail, will you look at me?"

I managed to turn and leaned against the stack, telling myself that it was just my imagination tricking me into feeling the vibrations from Hao tapping his heel as he swung his foot back and forth.

"Don't trust yourself with what?"

"To feel anything." I bit down hard on my lower lip and closed my eyes. "To know what's real anymore."

"You don't deserve to be in pain."

I froze at the feel of Mia's hand against my cheek and gripped the mats behind me to keep from reaching out and pulling her against me. The laugh that spilled out of my throat was brittle, snapping against the air.

"You don't know what I deserve."

"I know more than you want to admit. Open your eyes and look at me."

I did, digging my fingers so hard into the mats it made my bones ache.

The fear was clear in her gray eyes, and my skin burned when she took her hand away. "Aiz was trying to see how much energy you can take and hold, since you are having such a hard time accessing it from outside yourself. It is not as good as the alternative of you being able to pull energy to heal yourself, but it is better than nothing. When you refused to use it because you were determined to do penance for the crimes you think you've committed, you upset the balance."

"I seem to have a talent for that." I was surprised by the smile that took over my mouth.

"You do." Mia did not return the smile. "This is not a path I wanted you to go down, Hail. It worries me. You are slipping away."

It was starting to worry me, too, but there wasn't anything I could do. So instead I feigned nonchalance. "You want me to fight, I'll fight. There's not much else I can do for you."

"You are putting us all at risk!" The shove was surprising, knocking me back onto the mats, into Hao had he still been there. Instead my brother's ghost had appeared behind Mia, a look of impressed surprise on his face. "You're not a mindless brawler, Hail. You're an empress who should be wallowing a little less and thinking of her people a little more."

"Leave my people out of this. Most of them are dead. The rest—" I shook my head. "I wanted you to send them home and you refused!

Now I don't even know if they're real or not." I wanted with all my heart to take a swing at her and my hand closed into a fist, a move that didn't go unnoticed by Mia.

"Not everything is about the fight, Hail," she said. "You need to think more, *feel* more, and stop behaving as if you are the only one who has ever lost people that you love."

The words hit as intended. A well-placed strike to knock the wind from me. And that was the problem, wasn't it? I didn't want to feel what I was feeling. The paranoia, the loneliness, the fear. All my worst nightmares had come true with the deaths of nearly everyone I held dear. The pain of it made my response cruel.

"Says the woman committed to genocide simply so she can win a family argument."

Mia stared at me, her mouth open in shock, and I watched her own hand start to form a fist. However, she stopped, shook her hand as if shaking the anger from it, and smiled. "Not everything is about the fight," she repeated, and turned for the door.

Less violence, not more, honored sister, is always an option.

I didn't see Dailun's ghost, only felt the brush of air as the words were whispered in my ear.

None of it stopped me from charging at Mia's retreating back.

She moved faster than her brother, so fast I barely registered that she'd spun to the side in a move that would have made Zin insanely jealous. I realized too late she wasn't trying to avoid my strike and my palm connected to her shoulder.

Mia caught me by the hand, barely stepping back an inch as though the force didn't bother her at all. Then a wave of pain rocketed up my arm and slammed into me with all the force of a railgun.

I dropped to the floor.

By the time I was able to get my lungs to cooperate and rolled over onto my back, Mia was gone.

"Bugger me."

You always were horrible at flirting. Hao crouched at my side.

135

"Oh, fuck off."

Hao raised an eyebrow at me and then vanished. Ghost or not, the room felt emptier without him there.

Covering my face with my hands, I held my breath until the urge to scream had passed.

You are so fucked. The unidentified voice held a wealth of glee. *You've come completely apart at the seams. So much for the legendary Star of Indrana.*

"You can shut up, too, whoever you are. If you're not brave enough to show your face, just fuck off." I hissed the order as I dropped my hands and rolled onto my side so I could push my aching body to its feet.

I staggered out of the gym and down the hallways to our rooms. There was no one around, but I wasn't sure if it was a blessing or a curse. The silence made it hard to hold on to the world around me, and the voice started an endless litany of questions.

What if you're the one who's dead and everyone else is alive? Would you like to see how they're happily living their lives without you? What, you thought they'd mourn the loss of a worthless daughter?

Bile rose in my throat and I barely made it to the toilet before it spilled free. I clung to the edge as the shudders worsened and hot tears streaked down my face.

I'm serious, why are you still holding on here? There's nothing left for you. No great victory looming in the future. You're not special, Hail. You're just a fool who got everyone around you killed because you were too stubborn and arrogant to know when to give up.

"Stop. Please." The words were raw, scraping against my throat as they clawed their way out past the tears.

Baby. Portis's voice chased away the other, and I imagined his hand was gentle as he brushed my hair from my face. *Breathe.*

I dragged in a breath and threw myself into his arms. "I don't want to do this anymore."

You don't get to choose that option, he replied, his arms tightening around me. *Because you can do this. I know it's hard. I wish I could say it's going to get easier soon, but it's not. You're about to face even worse things and I need you to fight. The whole universe needs you to fight.*

"Why me?"

Portis pressed a kiss to my temple and then dragged me to my feet. *What do you want me to tell you? That it has to be you? That no one else will? You and I both know that's not true. Someone always steps up to take the place of the fallen; none of us are so special that we're irreplaceable. And yet—* He smiled. *Here you are and there is no one else in all the universes who will make the choices you make, Hail. There are people out there who love you and aren't giving up on you.*

He gave me a little shake. *Go get yourself cleaned up. Get some sleep and get up in the morning ready to fight again.*

I didn't have a chance to respond before he vanished, so I did the only thing left to me and that was follow Portis's orders.

17

I woke with Johar's shoulder in my stomach and the realization that my arms were bound together from wrist to elbow. All I could see was the dark brown dirt of the ground and the leaves slapping me in the head as we made our way through the jungle.

"Hey, she's awake," Johar said, her stride not slowing. "Fair warning, Hail, I will dump you right on that thick skull of yours if you try to hit me."

"Why are you carrying me? Why are my arms tied? And why does my mouth taste like I licked a morgue floor?"

"I don't even want to know how you can use that as a basis for comparison, Your Majesty," Gita said, her voice floating from somewhere ahead of us.

"It's a long story." I turned my head to the side, squinting in the dim light. We were out in the jungle and I guessed it was just before sundown.

"I'm carrying you because it works better than dragging," Johar said. "You know damn well why your arms are tied, and I found a plant out here in the jungle that is a reasonable approximation of *sapne* powder, which Gita said would not cause you any complications. So you're welcome for that."

"Explains why my head hurts," I muttered. The memory of Johar and the others returning after my shower and someone passing me a cup of tea as if nothing were wrong floated back into my aching brain.

"There were alternatives to knocking you out; however, this seemed safer," Johar replied cheerfully. "If I put you down, are you going to run from us, or are you going to listen to reason and help us get the fuck off this planet?"

"I don't know."

Johar sighed. "At least she's honest about it. Your ass is heavy, Hail, and I've carried you for two kilometers now. I'm putting you down. We stole a couple of guns from a patrol as we escaped, and I swear I will kneecap you with one if you take off. I'm good enough at this weird healing shit of the Shen's to stop the bleeding, and Fasé can fix your ass once we hook up again."

"That's fair." I bent my knees to absorb the impact when Johar dropped me on my feet and held my arms out.

She shook her head. "I feel like I'm less likely to have to shoot you if I leave those on. You'll manage." She took the Koros 201 from Alba and gestured. "Follow Gita, Hail. I'd like to get off this fucking planet and back to civilization. I miss room service."

I turned around to face the woman I hoped, but couldn't trust, was my *Ekam* despite Aiz's assurances to the contrary. She was also armed and watching me with a distressing mixture of concern and wariness. Gita looked past me, shared some unspoken thing with Johar, and then turned and slipped into the jungle.

I could have run. I could have fought. But both scenarios held unreasonable odds of success, so instead I followed her into the growing dark.

The jungle closed up around us, a suffocating mass of damp leaves and swinging vines. Every step kicked up the smell of earth thick with decay until it filled my head with memories of being trapped in tunnels.

"Careful, Majesty." Alba caught me just above the elbow when

I stumbled. Her smile held more worry than the others', possibly because Johar was behind us and we all knew she really would shoot me if I tried anything.

I didn't want to hurt them anyway. Either they were my people, or they were Shen, and I had to admit that I wasn't the best judge of what was real and what wasn't at the moment.

"Hail, are you okay?"

I kept the curse in my head; Johar must have seen me tense. "Specifically right now? I'm fine," I lied.

We continued through the jungle, the women helping me over massive tree trunks and slow running streams. Johar and Gita were ever cautious about keeping the weapons out of my reach. Even though I was bound, I was still a threat.

"It's a good sign things are quiet," Johar said to Gita in a low voice when we stopped for a rest. Slivers of moonlight filtered in through the trees, giving us just enough light to see by.

"No one saw us leave," she replied. "But they're going to come looking as soon as they realize we're gone or they find that patrol."

"Let them come," Johar said from ahead of us. "I once spent a month in the Dego jungles avoiding some hijackers who tried to take my ship." She snorted. "They were idiots. If they'd just taken my ship and run with it, it would have taken me a while to find them. Instead they chased me into the jungle when they realized there was a bounty on my head." She paused to pull back a curtain of vines heavy with purple luminescent blossoms and waved Alba through. "I picked them off one at a time while I circled back around to my ship."

Gita's laugh was soft. "I'm glad you're here, then."

"I'd rather be back in the hotel with room service and running water." Johar snorted, shooting me a glance. "And with everyone in command of their faculties."

"Emmory and the others will be here shortly."

"If Alba's message got through, sure. If not, we're shuttling out into the black with only a hope and a prayer."

Gita's reply was too low for me to make out, and Alba shifted on the log across from me, the noise drowning out any chance I had of overhearing her words.

"Majesty?" Alba's soft call further distracted me, and I looked up from my hands.

I wanted to believe it was her. She looked like my chamberlain, moved like her, spoke like her. But there was no way of knowing for sure. Aiz could have improved his imitations, had his people study mine for all the months we were here before replacing them.

Or worse, they'd replaced them from the beginning and I just couldn't tell the difference any longer.

You knew it was Johar when you fought her, Hao whispered in my ear.

"...I wish I knew how we could help you."

I blinked at Alba, realizing she'd been talking to me. "I'm fine, Alba."

"You're not, ma'am. We all know it. *You* know it." Alba shook her head. "I know it's hard to believe, but it was right there. Everyone's alive. You should be happy about it. It breaks my heart to see how you can't trust in anything, even your own eyes." A tear slid down her cheek and she impatiently wiped it away. "That's only going to make it worse. It's not going to fix what's broken."

"There's no fixing what's broken," I replied, looking down at my hands again. "All you can do is throw it away and start over. I wish you'd all left me when I told you to. This would have been easier." With a sigh, I dug my feet into the ground and stood. Gita and Johar's conversation stopped as they both reached for their guns. "I know you think what you've seen is real, but it's not. It's just one more trick. No one is coming, but if you all want to try to escape we should get moving."

We trekked through the night and well past sunrise, Gita and Johar stopping to rest every hour for a few minutes before pushing us onward.

I followed them, biding my time as my cooperation lulled them into enough complacency to allow for a chance to escape. One of two things was true—either these were Shen pretending to be my people, or they were my people. Both instances called for the same reaction from me: to escape and return to the compound, where I needed to be.

I hoped that if Gita and the others were real they would continue with their escape and leave me to my duty, but I knew the chances of that were as unlikely as Emmory and everyone else returning from the dead.

"This is awkward," I said to Jo as she tugged my pants back up after a bathroom break.

"Could be worse," she replied.

"Oh, really?"

"Your legs could be tied, too."

I laughed, hoping it didn't sound as forced as it felt, because it was necessary to convey the playfulness of my shoulder bumping into hers. I deliberately overbalanced, sending us both to the ground. "Shit, sorry."

Johar laughed as she untangled herself from me and hauled me upright. "Clumsy ass." She grabbed me by the back of the neck and pressed her forehead to mine. "It's good to see you more yourself, though. We'll get through this, Hail. Everything's going to be okay."

"Of course," I lied, hiding the knife I'd stolen off her in the palms of my hands. How Johar had gotten her weapons back I didn't know, but I wasn't going to question it.

I was just going to hope she didn't notice before I could get free.

We continued on through the jungle, stopping again several hours later for a meal. I'd managed to slip the knife into my pocket and was nibbling on a gray tuber that tasted fairly horrible even though Johar assured me it was safe to eat.

The real Johar's enhancements made her the perfect candidate to try out the local flora—we still hadn't seen any fauna besides a few birds flying overhead—without risking serious illness or death. But a Shen duplicate could easily pick out things to eat on the planet that would be safe for both of us.

Gita took a bite, gagged, and glared at Johar.

She grinned. "This one's not bad. It's got a decent mix of nutrients."

"I question your definition of 'not bad.'"

I couldn't stop my own chuckle, and the woman who was possibly not my *Ekam* transferred her glare my direction.

"Let me know if you're still laughing after you taste that," she said, but her mouth was curved in a grin.

"I already did." I bit into the tuber again and stepped hard on my gag reflex as I chewed and swallowed. The taste was somewhere between spinach that was about twenty minutes from going off and a rotten potato. "It's fine," I managed.

"Liar."

Gita's tease was an echo that slammed into my chest and lodged there, burning with all the strength of white phosphorous.

"Majesty?"

I shook my head, wordlessly dropping my food off and hauling myself to my feet with the aid of the branch above me. Grief was a fresh pain, meticulously cutting my heart into pieces and sewing it back together in a chaotic jumble. The tears flowed down my cheeks and I didn't try to stop them or hide them from my *Ekam*, who made a pained noise of protest at the sight.

If this wasn't Gita, she was doing a good job of pretending.

"Hail." Gita wrapped an arm around my shoulders and it took all my control not to stiffen at the contact.

"Did I ever tell you about the first time I met Emmory and Zin? Emmory called me a liar," I said instead. Real Gita or not, I needed to tell someone the story.

"To your face?"

"Twice." My words choked with tears. "I deserved it; I was lying to him, and his brother was dead in the hold of my ship."

"Majesty, why can't you believe they might still be alive?"

"Do you want the bullshit answer?"

"No."

"They're dead. Maybe not all of them; but Emmory and Zin. Hao—" My voice broke. "I saw that rubble. There was no sign of them on my *smati*. No sound on the coms. And this is my life, Gita. Everyone I love dies on me while I stand untouched among the flames."

She rested her head against mine. "I need you to have some hope, ma'am. I know it's hard. They're out there. I promise you. We're here and we'll get off this planet and back home. Whatever else happens. I promise you that much."

"I wish I could believe you." I forced myself to lean into her, to play the part until I could cut through my bonds and make my escape.

"Come on." Gita pulled on me gently, and I let her lead me back to the others. "We may as well get some rest."

"Aiz won't," Johar replied.

"I know, but he knows this jungle. Or at least we're better off assuming he does. We don't." Gita sighed and helped me to the ground next to Alba. "There's a very good chance he'll just circle around to the shuttle depot and wait for us there. I don't want to walk into a firefight unrested." She looked around. "We'll rest here for a few hours and then cover the last bit of ground. If we get there at dusk, we'll have a better advantage."

"The afternoon rains are going to be here in probably forty-five minutes, tops. But they shouldn't last too long and we've got several hours until nightfall." Alba looked up, squinting at the sky past the canopy. "This planet has a forty-standard-hour day, and I think is tilted in a similar fashion to Earth. We're in the northern hemisphere and it's summertime because we've had about twenty hours of daylight the last few days."

Well, that sounds like your chamberlain. Hao laughed, and I bit my tongue to keep from telling him to shut up. Instead, I stretched my legs out and pillowed my face in my hands.

I dozed, listening to Gita's and Johar's quiet murmurs and Alba's even breathing on my other side.

It was difficult to maneuver my arms into position to retrieve the knife from my pocket without moving to the point where I alerted the women on the other side of our little camp, but I managed, and stuck the base of the knife into the dirt. The sharp edge of Jo's knife cut easily through the bonds and they slid to the ground.

I lay still. Jo and Gita—or their duplicates, my brain insisted—had fallen into silence and I didn't dare move before checking to see where they were.

The jungle was quiet, only the wind and the rustling sounds of whatever wildlife inhabited it filling my ears. I eased my head up, spotting Johar with her eyes closed and her hands behind her head. Gita was gone.

Standing watch, most likely. The question was if she was watching me, or watching for Aiz.

It doesn't really matter, does it? It was Cas, not Hao, who smiled down at me. *Either way you need to go.*

There was a gap in the canopy, sunlight streaming down and illuminating the jungle to my left, showing me a spot under a downed tree I could slip through. I grabbed Jo's knife from the dirt and rolled under it, making my escape.

Sprinting through the jungle isn't the wisest course of action, but I heard shouting as I made my way down a hill and broke into a run.

The ground shifted under my feet and I narrowly saved myself from being impaled on a broken branch, though it raked a deep gash along my side as I threw myself to the right and landed heavily on my shoulder.

"Fuck." I got to my feet, left hand pressed to the wound and Johar's knife still in my right. There was no way to figure out where

I was going without turning my *smati* back on, but that would reveal my location to my pursuers.

Get some ground between you, baby, and then take a look. Portis was leaning against a tree ahead of me, and he tipped his head to the side.

"I know," I said, reaching out to pat his shoulder on the way by and feeling the rough bark of the tree instead. I looked up at the sky, spotting the sun briefly through the trees, and oriented myself in what I hoped was the right direction. Then I began picking my way across the jungle floor.

18

It was purely by accident I crashed into the patrol. My instincts were in better shape than my brain and I disarmed the startled woman I'd run into with ease, knocking her to the ground and powering up her weapon. Johar's knife fell into the dirt by my boot.

"Your Majesty?"

I blinked stupidly at the blonde who looked like Kisah, reminded myself she was dead, and then stiffened at the echo of other Hessian 45s powering up. "Don't move," I snarled when she started to get up.

More Shen, Hail. Aiz set this whole thing up. It's just another test after all. Don't trust them. Don't let your guard down. Hao's ghost rested a comforting hand on my shoulder.

"Shiva, it is her. Everyone, guns down."

"Majesty?"

I held the gun steady as I backed away. My brain screamed about the conflicting information that was colliding around me. "No. No no no."

"Hail." Not-Emmory had his hands up. "It's us."

"No. My *Ekam* is dead. I am not seeing this. I'm not falling for this again. Take one more step and I will shoot you."

"Little sister—"

I shot not-Hao before he finished his first step. He stumbled back, a hand pressed to his shoulder, with curses that the real Hao would have been proud of flying from his mouth.

"Next step in my direction and I shoot you in the head," I said. "Where's Aiz?"

"*Sha zhu*, I am going to kick your ass."

The pistol whined to life again in my hand. "You keep that name out of your fucking mouth. That is not your name to use."

"What is wrong with you?"

We stared at each other, his gold eyes locked on mine. My heart slowed in my chest and my muscles tensed as I prepared for a fight. For a moment I thought not-Hao was going to come at me, gun or no gun, but then the Shen wearing my *Ekam*'s face took charge.

"Hao, enough." Not-Emmory's voice was sharp. "Zin, take Hao back to the ship."

"Ah-ha." I waved my gun. "Nobody's going anywhere except for me."

"Hail." Not-Emmory blinked at me, his hands still up. "He's going to need medical care."

"You can move after I'm gone," I said.

"Please?" he asked. "I'd like to talk."

"Fine," I said finally, and the pair disappeared into the jungle. "You have one minute."

"Are you hurt?" Not-Emmory asked, his voice soft.

"I'll be fine." I smiled mirthlessly. "These are scratches compared to what I've been through the last few months."

The violence that ripped through not-Emmory's face startled me enough that I took several steps away from him. I clung to the words about not trusting my eyes, no matter how much my heart wanted this to be real.

Everyone was dead, lost to the flames, and I was the last woman standing.

"We could help you," he said, unaware of my inner turmoil. "Where are the others?"

I laughed. The wound on my side was still hot with pain and my shoulder ached, but I could get them both to heal without hurting myself further. "I'm fine. Time's up."

"I know." Now his smile was gentle.

I had a split second to regret letting not-Emmory have his victory, and then not-Zin crashed into me like a freight train. He hit me from the side, knocking us both over the downed tree, and I landed hard on my injured shoulder.

Not-Zin had a hand locked on my gun arm, fingers digging into my forearm until my hand went numb. I gasped, the gun dropping into the jungle undergrowth, and tried to kick at him. But he knocked my foot away with his own and then planted it into the back of my knee. My other leg was pinned against a log, not-Zin putting pressure on it with his thigh.

I slapped at him with the only thing I still had free, my left arm, even though the movement shot fire through me.

"Majesty, stop."

A hard hand grabbed my wrist and twisted my arm behind my back, but I only fought harder and the Shen surprisingly released me instead of letting my bones snap.

My captors were cursing in Indranan, which was also a surprise, but I was too far gone in the fighting rage Aiz had beaten into me to examine it for long. Not even the powering up of a Hessian 45 stun setting was enough to still my thrashing, and I almost got free of not-Zin's grip.

"Shiva's sake, Emmory, just do it before she gets free. I've survived worse."

The pain coursed through me, stiffening every muscle in my body for a screaming eternity. I felt not-Zin collapse on top of me as the same shock ripped through him, but before I could recover, someone rolled him off me and quickly cuffed my hands and my ankles.

The stunned silence settled heavily around us until I turned my head to the side to spit the loam out of my mouth, my laughter following after. "You bunch are going to get an earful from Aiz. No broken bones? You didn't even *try* to kill me! What is wrong with you?" I started to roll over, but someone's boot landed in my back.

"Majesty, I think it's best if you stay right there."

"That sounds like Indula." I craned my neck to get a peek at the Shen wearing my dead Guard's face. "He hated fireworks, loved harassing Iza, and was a horrible singer. Put that in your database."

"I'm hurt, Majesty. I thought you liked my singing." He grinned at me.

I spat blood at him. "You are not-Indula, because Indula's dead. Iza's dead. Emmory and Zin are dead. Hao is dead. They all died and left me behind. You are not-Indula. He is nothing but ashes and rubble back on Earth."

The Shen with Indula's pretty pale eyes stared at me, his smile sliding into a horrified look that twisted something buried inside my chest.

He looked away from me toward not-Emmory. "Sir?"

"We'll handle it. Let's get her up, we're going to have to carry her back to the ship. I don't trust her not to run if we take those cuffs off her legs."

"Smart man," I said, smiling into the dirt.

"Emmory, what the fu— What did they *do* to her?" Not-Zin was breathing hard when he hissed the question.

"I don't know, but I'm going to be asking our prisoner that question."

They lifted me up, hands sliding under my armpits. I turned my head and closed my teeth on exposed fingers. Not-Indula swore and dropped me. I crashed into the Shen on my other side and tried to roll away, but she grabbed me, wrapping her arms and legs around my torso.

"Dark Mother, Emmory, she bit me!"

Not-Emmory crouched at my side with a sigh. He grabbed me by the chin with one gloved hand, holding me still as he released a cloud of *sapne* with the other. I tried to hold my breath, but the flare of pain as his fingers tightened on my bruised face made me gasp, and I inhaled the foul lavender smoke.

As the world dropped away, the last things I saw were the sad brown eyes of my dead *Ekam*.

I sat quietly on the floor of an unfamiliar medical bay, my arms locked together behind my back while the Shen stared down at me wearing the face of my dead *Ekam*. My demands to speak to Mia or Aiz had been ignored, or rather, met with stunned confusion that had to be faked. It made the optimistic part of my brain whisper things I wanted to ignore.

My people were not alive. They were dead and I was alone.

My jaw ached from where not-Emmory had punched me during my third escape attempt since they'd taken me prisoner. It had been a wicked strike, not enough to knock me out completely but enough to put me down so they could restrain me again.

"Majesty." He crouched a distance away, even though my legs were shackled at the ankles. There was a frustration in those dark eyes. "I need you to stop doing that."

"I need you to let me go, so I guess we're both going to be disappointed." I shook off the creeping desire to believe that the man in front of me was truly my dead *Ekam*. Emmory and all the others were gone, and no amount of fanciful dreaming could change that fact.

What if you're wrong, though?

"Where is Aiz?" I demanded before not-Emmory could say anything else. "What is going on? Are you Farians? Or are you part of Hamah's little faction of Shen who don't seem to like me much? I haven't had the pleasure of meeting you if that's the case. Either way, I wish you'd wipe those faces off. It's not fooling me."

Not-Emmory heaved a sigh and pushed to his feet. I watched him cross to the doorway of the medical bay where not-Zin stood, and the pair stood in silence.

You're in a pickle, aren't you, ma'am? Willimet asked.

I leaned my head back against the wall, keeping one eye on the two men at the door. "I'll get free," I replied. "It's only a matter of time. They'll drop their guard. I'll get a chance and I'll take it."

What about Gita and the others?

My breath lodged in my chest at the ghost's quiet reminder, and I squeezed my eyes shut at the sudden pain. I didn't know where they were. I didn't know if they were alive or if they'd joined the growing ranks of the army of ghosts at my back.

You don't even know if they're actually your people. That hadn't come from Will but the spiteful unknown voice.

"I don't know, I'll find out."

"Majesty?"

I opened my eyes. Not-Emmory and Zin were both just out of reach watching me curiously. "What?"

"Who are you talking to?" not-Emmory asked.

"Willimet," I replied, and was surprised for a moment when he flinched before my brain reminded me that the Shen would know who she was and how she'd died.

"If I take those leg cuffs off you so you can walk, are you going to give me a reason to regret it?"

"Most likely."

Not-Zin chuckled under his breath, and the Hessian 45 in his hand made a whining noise as he powered it up. "You know the stun function hurts, Majesty. We don't want it to go down like this and I suspect you don't want to spend the next hour on the cold floor."

"It's not so bad down here." I smiled. "Let's just save ourselves the trouble, shall we?"

"Have it your way." Not-Emmory crossed his arms over his chest and leaned against the examination table. Not-Zin followed suit, putting his gun back in its holster. "You want to tell me why you think we're dead?"

"Because you are. Same as Will here. Difference is she's a ghost." I jerked my head toward her, but she was gone.

I closed my eyes and leaned my head back against the wall again. "You all are whatever, Shen I'm assuming. Or maybe Farians, it's so hard to tell at this point if you won't fess up. Aiz said you both could do this." I rubbed at my cheek with the back of my hand, cuffs clattering with the movement.

"Do what?"

"Make yourself look like other people," I replied. "It's how Aiz got past my BodyGuards in the deli on Pashati. We'd all assumed it was a masking program of Hao's, but it wasn't."

"That explains a lot," not-Zin murmured.

"Right? We were all so focused on Hao's betrayal we never really followed up on just how Aiz accomplished it. Either way, my Emmory and Zin are dead and gone. I'd say buried but there probably wasn't enough left of you after the embassy exploded. Alba seemed to think there was news to the contrary, but I don't believe it. Everyone I love dies, it's just a fact."

One of the men made a noise like I'd kicked him.

"You didn't see us die," not-Emmory said, his voice full of quiet pain. "Alba could be right."

"I'm not even sure Alba's alive, to be honest." I cracked an eye open and watched the shock dance across his face. "Gita, Johar, Alba, and I escaped but then ran into Rai. He was working for Aiz. I should have fucking seen that one coming. But hey, whatever. Anyway, there's been some recent debate about if the three of them even got off Earth alive. My vote's on no, just because that's about how things have been shaking out for me."

I watched the men share a concerned look that morphed into an unspoken conversation. Not-Emmory sighed and looked back at me. "We're—"

"Look, I saw the wreckage and there was nothing on the coms, no life signs, no contact. They were gone. I can't trust a lot of what's going on with me, but I know that truth—" I choked on a swell of unexpected sadness and had to clear my throat before I could continue. "If they'd been alive they would have come for me, not left us here to rot for six months."

"Hail—"

"Don't," I snapped, my cuffs rattling as I held my hands up. "Don't talk to me like you know me. Don't talk to me like you're my friend. He's dead."

"What do you want us to do?"

I opened my eyes all the way, meeting not-Emmory's gaze squarely. "Let me go. Or if you won't, put a blast through my head. Portis says I should keep fighting, but Dark Mother, I am tired. I won't complain if you make this stop. The galaxy can save itself for once."

"Majesty—"

"I'm serious. I was going to help Aiz and Mia, but if you won't let me go, there's little point in me being alive. Gita and the others are probably dead, too. I've spent these last six months learning how to fight up to the end of my life and beyond. I just want to finish this one way or the other because I am tired of holding the pieces of me together." My voice cracked. "Just kill me and be done with it. Or let me go so I can kill the fucking Farian gods and then find a quiet place to drink myself to death."

"Dark Mother, Hail. What did they do to you?" Not-Zin's shaky curse almost sounded real and the expression of horror on his face dug at the wound in my chest, magnifying the pain I'd thought was already dialed up to eleven.

"They didn't do anything. I made a choice! It was the only choice I had, but it was still mine to make." I clenched my jaw shut against the desire to tell them everything and glared.

Not-Emmory was silent, and I couldn't guess at what was going on behind that expressionless mask. He tapped not-Zin on the arm and headed for the door. Only after it had slid shut behind them did I let the tears loose.

19

I don't know how long I dozed, slumped awkwardly against the wall, but when I woke Hao was sitting on the examination table.

No. Not-Hao. "Ghost or Shen?" My voice was rough, still clogged with tears and sleep.

Pragmatic as always, ghost-Hao smiled and stuck his arm in the table. It passed through like a knife dipped in ghee and he wiggled his fingers at me from the underside before removing it and hopping down.

What kind of shit are you in, little sister? he asked, settling onto the floor next to me. I knew I was imagining the heat, the warmth. I knew if I leaned against him I'd fall the rest of the way to the floor. I did it anyway, and pretended that there was something solid for me to touch.

"I don't know," I murmured. "I don't know who these people are or why they're playing this game. I don't know what they want."

How are you going to get out of it?

"I don't know. I'd rather they just kill me."

If I could smack you right now, I would, he said, the tone in his voice chipping away at my self-pity.

"I wish you could."

Get up, Hail.

I snapped awake at the sound of voices outside the open door.

"Are you okay?"

Not-Emmory's quiet sigh came on the heels of not-Zin's question. "I just finished debriefing Gita. They—she's shaken, Zin. Hail's apparently been training for some big showdown with the Farian gods. Aiz killed her, beat her to death over and over again. Messed with her mind. Hail's been seeing ghosts, acting erratically. Helping the Shen. They all thought we died in the explosion on Earth."

"No wonder she thinks we're not real." Zin exhaled. "You probably don't want Hao to find out about what Aiz did."

"Yeah." Not-Emmory sighed again. "We're going to have enough trouble corralling Hail and figuring out how to convince her we're real. I don't want to add pissed-off Hao with a vendetta to the list."

"I don't like to admit it, Emmory, but I might help him with it."

"Me, too," Not-Emmory replied. "Go tell Gita and the others to keep it to themselves for now. I need to deal with Hail."

I closed my eyes, pretending to be asleep as Not-Emmory came into the room. He reached down and hauled me to my feet, leaning out of the way of my awkward attempt to slam my head into his nose. His gloved hand tightened on my upper arm to keep me from falling forward, and the cuffs at my ankles lengthened from an unspoken command just enough to allow me to take short, shuffling steps on bare feet out the door. Not-Zin was nowhere to be found.

The ship we were on was unfamiliar. Dark gray walls and a curving corridor that seemed to extend upward forever. I could hear voices above us, echoing through the air, but otherwise the ship was silent.

"Are we still on the ground?" If the ship wasn't running, it meant we weren't in space, which meant I still had a chance of escape.

Not-Emmory shot me a sideways glance before he answered. "For the moment."

"Where are we going when the moment's up?"

He didn't answer.

We came around a bend and I spotted a familiar silhouette in the hallway ahead. Portis's smile faded a bit as he looked me up and down.

You look rough, baby.

"Shut it, Portis. I've had a bad day."

"What?" Not-Emmory asked, and I shook my head.

"Nothing," I said. "Just talking to myself."

We continued in silence, Portis following behind, not-Emmory stopping outside a doorway that slid open silently at his touch. The interior room was mostly empty, obviously stripped of anything that could be used as a weapon or in an escape attempt.

"Shower, clean clothes, sleep," he said. "There's no surveillance, but I'm right outside that door. Don't try to escape, Majesty. Just clean yourself up and get some rest."

The cuffs at my feet fell away, followed by the ones at my wrists. I spun, ignoring the screaming pain in my shoulders, and took a swing. Not-Emmory was ready for me and ducked under it, hitting me in chest with the palm of his hand. The perfect blow knocked me backward and drove the air from my lungs. Pain wouldn't stop me, but lack of air was a surprisingly effective stalling measure. I went down on a knee, gasping for air that wouldn't come. By the time I recovered I was alone in the room.

I didn't head straight for the shower—though I both desperately wanted to and was terrified of it at the same time—and instead prowled the room to see if they'd missed anything.

Get some sleep, Portis said. He was sitting cross-legged on the bed. *It's been a while. You'll do better if you're rested.*

I rubbed both hands over my face. Every bone in my body hurt, and exhaustion was dragging me down toward unconsciousness. Exhaling a shaky breath, I headed for the bathroom, cataloging my injuries as I stripped out of my filthy clothes. The cut on my side was hot and red but healing. My body seemed to be winning the fight against whatever possible infection there was. I left it. I knew I couldn't risk trying to heal it myself as exhausted as I was.

Dark bruises bloomed over my right shoulder. The fresh wounds from my tangle with not-Zin were tender to the touch, and the red

157

mark on my sternum from not-Emmory's hand would definitely bruise.

I turned on the water, wincing at the sound of it falling against the floor of the shower. The expected panic didn't surge up into my throat, and instead growled from the corner of my brain like a trapped cat. Desperate for a distraction, I powered up my *smati*, but there was nothing except static on the coms, and the array of chips in my brain refused to connect to whatever computer this ship had, so I turned it off again.

The water was hot and felt good even as I sank to the floor, my arms wrapped around my head to hide the tears just in case someone was watching. After several minutes I stepped hard on my misery, forcing myself back to my feet and scrubbing away my time in the forest with a determined focus. The dirt and debris swirled down the drain, taking with it some of my grief and fury.

The clothes they'd left for me were of Farian make: underwear, a soft gray tunic with long sleeves, and matching pants. I dried off my hair as much as I could before pulling them on and staggered back out into the other room.

Portis was gone.

"Lights off." I crawled into the bed, curled into a ball, and let the exhaustion take me.

I woke up and knew immediately I'd made a mistake letting my guard down. The familiar hum of a spaceship in flight vibrated the bed, the wall, and the floor beneath my feet. Spitting a string of vicious curses into the darkness, I slid from the bed to the floor and felt my way across the room to the doorway.

The control pad was on the left.

No, the right. I corrected myself, shaking away the disorientation plaguing me.

I didn't have anything to pry it off with, but maybe there was something in the bathroom.

My fingers brushed the edge of the control panel and the shock ripped through me, an all-too-familiar jolt of electricity that dropped me faster than an atmo-based ship losing its thrusters at thirty-three kilometers up.

The door slid open and light spilled in from the hallway, illuminating a pair of boots in my vision. Emmory's boots. No, not-Emmory's boots. Who would have thought I'd get sentimental over footwear; but then who'd have thought the Shen would have put so much effort into this charade as to get a pair of so obviously broken-in Tracker boots to wear?

"Lights up," he said, crouching down out of reach, a Hessian 45 hanging loosely in his hand.

I wondered if I could move fast enough to grab it. First, I had to convince my limbs to start working again.

"I told you to just get some sleep, Hail. Why don't you listen?"

"I slept some. Besides, if you were really Emmory you'd already know the answer to that." Laughing was painful, but I did it anyway. "We're in space."

"I realize it didn't stop you from trying last time, but it does make my job slightly easier." He smiled, a slow curving of his lips that made my heart ache. "Hail, what's it going to take to get some cooperation from you? I'd like to get you some food, but if you're going to fight me every step of the way, I'll knock you out and hook you up to the auto-feed."

I looked up at not-Emmory from my spot on the floor; the familiarity was so on point for him it made my heart ache. The worst of the shock had dissipated, but I kept a wary eye on the Hessian 45 in his hand as I got to my feet. My stomach growled, making the decision for me. "I'll behave."

"I have your oath? Don't hurt anyone. Don't try to escape."

"For the next hour, I give you my word I won't hurt anyone, and I won't try to escape," I replied.

The smile that flickered to life on not-Emmory's face was so much like my *Ekam*'s it broke my heart. "Done."

I held out my wrists but not-Emmory shook his head. "I trust you to keep your word."

"You shouldn't. Aiz could tell you how many times I've broken it."

"Oaths to your captors don't count. We all know that."

"Aren't you my captor?"

Not-Emmory shook his head again. "I am your *Ekam*, Majesty."

I looked at him with a sad smile. "I wish I could believe you were. But my *Ekam* is dead."

The pain that flashed across his face shouldn't have been so easy to replicate, and for an instant I wanted to break my oath and tear out his throat for daring to show me such an expression.

Be better, Haili, Cire whispered in my ear, and I turned my head to look the ghost of my sister in the eye. *Just because they are liars and deceivers doesn't mean you have to be.*

I straightened my shoulders, spotted the way my not-*Ekam*'s hand tightened on his gun, and smiled. "Well, if you're going to feed me let's be about it, your hour is running out."

He stepped aside and gestured at the door, leaving me no choice but to head out into the corridor. We walked in silence, the ship around us eerily quiet except for that telltale hum of spaceflight.

"The Shen ship didn't look anything like this."

"This is Farian, Majesty. It was the only way we could get here fast enough."

The news that we were on a Farian ship threw me. One more missing piece in this puzzle my addled brain couldn't seem to wrap itself around.

Focus on the details, Haili, my mother ordered.

"Six months isn't fast," I said with a bitter laugh.

"It took us that long to find you."

"You couldn't just track me?"

"You were a long way away, Majesty. Besides, your *smati* is off."

"Oh, right," I replied, and switched it back on again, unsurprised when it registered the person in front of me as Emmory. A trick of light, Aiz had said, enough to fool even the tech.

"What did you do? Kick over every rock in the galaxy first?"

"We kicked a few rocks over, Majesty," he replied with a slight smile. "But mostly it was Fasé."

Her ghost's insistent questions echoed in my head, but I shook them away. "Is that why I haven't seen her? Why she hasn't fixed this hole in my side or the bruises all over me?"

An expression I couldn't quite name flickered over not-Emmory's face, and I snorted a laugh. "Don't sweat it, you were bound to screw something up. Though I'll give you points, yours is much more convincing. Even Aiz didn't get it right on the first try."

"How so?"

"Aiz's Emmory was—" I looked up, my eyes following the curve of the gray wall, and I reached a hand out to touch it as I searched for the words. "His Emmory was what he thought Emmory was to me—my *Ekam*, my loyal BodyGuard—all duty and formalities. He didn't realize there was more to it than that." Foolish tears sprang into my eyes and I flicked them away even though I knew not-Emmory had probably seen them.

"Anyway, you know I'm going to get out of here, right? I've got places to be, powerful beings to kill. Or Farians, whatever, at this point I'm less than picky. You know they might be the ones who paid Jamison to blow you all up?"

"Food first, Majesty." Not-Emmory stopped and gestured at the open door across the hall.

I poked my head in, and my stomach grew more insistent at the smells weaving their way around my head. There were a pair of trays sitting alone in an otherwise deserted mess and Portis was sitting on the tabletop, his boots propped up on the seat.

You could probably get to the table before him, knock him out with one of the trays, he suggested.

It was tempting, but I shook my head. "I need to eat."

"That's why we're here, Majesty," not-Emmory said from behind me, a thread of confusion in his voice.

"Not you," I replied, waving a hand at Portis. "I was talking to—" The words stuck in my throat and I dropped onto the bench with a frown. "Nothing, never mind."

Are you worried you're going to offend him by telling him you're talking to his dead brother? Portis asked, nudging me with his foot. *That's not Emmory, baby. Come on.*

"Hush," I muttered, then snatched up a piece of roti and crammed it into my mouth.

Not-Emmory didn't comment, eating his food slower and with a decorum that suggested his meal was there more to make me feel comfortable than because he needed it. But he ate like an Indranan, bunching up labra with a bit of roti between his thumb and fingers.

"Is there no silverware because you don't want me stabbing you with a fork again?" I asked around a mouthful of food.

Not-Emmory chewed and swallowed, studying me for a long moment before he answered. "You've never stabbed me with a utensil, Majesty, fork or otherwise. But Zin thought it would be safer this way given the circumstances."

I swallowed, hating the dangerous sliver of hope jabbing itself into my brain, and wiped my hand off on the napkin next to my tray before I crossed my arms over my chest.

"Who are you and what do you want?"

"I'm your *Ekam*, Majesty."

"My *Ekam* is dead!" I shoved my tray across the table at him and got to my feet. Hope had turned into anger and it burned in my throat. "He was murdered back on Earth. My friends were murdered back on Earth and I'm tired of seeing you wear his face like you own it. Your hour is up. Take me back to my room or let me go."

Not-Emmory sighed. "We're in space, Majesty, so obviously the second option isn't happening."

"Majesty."

I turned as not-Zin came through the door, Gita in front of him. *It's not her, Hail. You were right before. They replaced everyone.*

I wasn't even sure whose ghost was whispering that into my ear because I was too busy backing away from the trio who were watching me with pity written so clearly across their faces.

"Hail, everyone's ali—" Not-Gita stuck a hand out, but I slapped it away. Tears appeared in her eyes.

"I am done with this farce." I jabbed a finger through the air in not-Emmory's direction. He'd gotten to his feet, a resigned look on his face and his hand on his gun.

"She's not going to believe us," he said, shaking out a pair of cuffs with his other hand. "Turn around, Majesty."

"An oath to a liar," I replied with a smirk. "You want cuffs back on me, you're going to have to work for it."

"I've never lied to you, Majesty."

I rushed him and got a face full of *sapne* for my trouble. Not-Emmory hadn't pulled his Hessian 45 but instead lifted his hand to release a cloud of the foul lavender smoke directly into my path.

The floor surged up to meet me, followed just as quickly by a blanket of darkness dragging me down into the depths of unconsciousness.

20

The voices filtered in through my pounding head.

"We should have sent Johar instead. Not me. She hasn't trusted me for weeks."

"Gita, it's not your fault. We knew it was a risky play." Not-Emmory's reply was sympathetic.

"I don't understand why Fasé can't fix this," not-Gita said.

"I don't either, but she says she can't. There are limits, and Hail's so deep in this delusion it's too big a risk for Fasé to interfere."

"What about Mia? She said she thought she could help, and as much as I hate to admit it, Hail trusts her."

"I've already said no, Gita." Not-Emmory's voice was hard. "I'm not letting that Shen put a hand on her. I wouldn't have before and I'm especially not in the mood now."

"I know you're awake," Hao's ghost whispered in Cheng next to my ear.

I cracked an eye. "How did you know that?" I was strapped down to the table in the medical bay again and for a moment wasn't sure if I'd imagined the last few hours, but I was in the same Farian clothes I'd put on after my shower and wasn't hungry. Turning my head slowly, I met my dead brother's metallic gaze.

"Your breathing shifted." Hao smiled, tapping a finger to his temple. "Besides, I know you well enough to recognize the difference."

"Pity you're just a ghost, you could help me get loose."

"I could," he conceded after a glance at the pair in the doorway. "Why is it so hard for you to believe they're real?"

"They can't be real."

"Why?"

"You know why. Because you all died, Hao," I hissed the reply. "I sent you into the embassy and you all died."

"If we're not all dead, then what? You didn't fuck up and kill us? I would think that's a good thing. Putting aside the fact that you had no idea Jamison would blow up the embassy, you're not responsible for keeping us alive. We're all adults here."

"You know as well as I do that's a nice fantasy but it's not the case. We're *always* responsible for our crew. I was listening to you when you lectured me, you know."

"I never lectured you."

I gave my brother's ghost a flat look. "You lectured me every chance you got, and you know it. What's the point of this thought experiment?"

Hao smiled. "Just trying to get you to follow your logic through to the end because you're stuck in a loop at the moment. Why would they keep up the pretense even after you've called them on it? Where's Aiz? Or Adora?" He gestured around him. "Why go to all this trouble just to convince you we're still alive? What do they get out of it?"

"I don't know, okay? I don't know anything anymore, it's all a mess. I'm a mess. You all died, and it destroyed me." I blinked back the tears. "I'm not nearly as strong as everyone liked to pretend."

"You are, *sha zhu*."

"No. Aiz spend almost six months kicking my ass, killing me, and bringing me back to life, fucking with my head the whole time. Don't act so surprised, *gege*," I said when the murderous look slid over his face. "You sat and watched it happen."

"I know," he said finally, smiling a sad smile. "It's still hard to hear."

"I liked it." The words were raw in my throat. "I am so tired and there is still so much left to do. Always more fighting. You were lucky, you got to get out early. I am stuck here, trapped again between a duty and my own desires." I forced a smile. "But I'll fight and maybe we will win and then I can join you."

"Oh, little sister. It hurts to see you like this."

"It's all right."

Hao shook his head. "What you need to do now is figure out what's real. We're alive or we're not, which makes more sense?"

"I don't know."

"You think about it and let me know when you decide, okay?"

"You're just a ghost, what can you do?"

"You'd be surprised." Hao smiled at me as he got to his feet. "Don't let this beat you, Hail. Your heart knows the truth; stop being so scared of what it's telling you."

I squeezed my eyes shut, could have sworn I felt a brush of his fingertips over my cheek, but when I opened them Hao was gone and not-Emmory was looking down at me.

"How are we going to get through this, Majesty? What do I need to do to prove to you we're real?" He looked weary, a sheen of exhaustion in his brown eyes. They'd replicated the look of the Tracker augmentations, too, so that silver chased through his irises.

"Go get some sleep, not-Emmory," I replied, closing my eyes. "You look like you need it. Pretending to be someone else is exhausting enough, but Emmory is relentless. I'm going to hang out here for a while. Maybe when we both wake up we'll be in the mood to compromise."

His exhale was quiet, and I couldn't stop the flinch when he put a gloved hand down on my hand and squeezed. "Sleep well, Majesty."

He turned the lights down on his way out, leaving me alone in the dimly lit med bay. Hao's words spun around in my head; try as I might to ignore them, they kept resurfacing. They were buoyed by that last shred of hope that just wouldn't burn to ash no matter how many fires were lit with it.

What if Emmory and the others were alive? They couldn't be; it was impossible. What would be the point of Aiz or any other faction of Shen pretending to be them when I already knew he could pull off this trick?

These people, whoever they are, Hail, have Mia prisoner. Which means they're not Aiz's. They're the enemy.

That thought slammed into me with the same force as not-Emmory's palm strike.

The restraints holding me down were standard medical ones, and I was able to get myself free with a minimum amount of fuss and padded on bare feet to the doorway.

I steeled myself for the shock as I tapped the pad by the door, but it slid open without protest and without putting me on the floor.

The hallway was empty, except for Hao's ghost, who leaned against the curved wall, one leg crossed over the other. "We getting out of here?"

"I need to find Mia," I replied.

His smile curved upward. "Of course you do. Lucky for you I know where she is."

The corridors were silent, only the hum of a spaceship in flight to give away the fact that we were still out in the black.

"I don't suppose you know where we're going?"

"You wanted to bust Mia out?"

"Oh, no, I meant where is the ship going?"

Hao's ghost laughed. "I don't, *sha zhu*, sadly. Could probably find out for you. Or you could just ask Emmory."

"Not-Emmory," I corrected absently.

"Right," he said. "Not-Emmory." Hao stopped at a doorway. "Door is probably locked, but if you pop the panel you should be able to short it."

"Thanks." I bent to the task; the panel came loose easily and a few twisted wires later the door slid open. "Hey, are you—"

Hao was gone.

"Mia?"

"Hail?" Mia scrambled to her feet, her hands gloved and in complicated-looking shackles. "What are you doing?"

"Getting us out of here." I closed my hand around her upper arm. "Are these Farians? Or that opposition faction you told me about? I don't know how they found us, but we need to go."

"Hail." My name was an exhale laced with sadness, and I frowned at Mia when she resisted my pull toward the door. "They aren't Farians. These are your people."

Her words were a hammer to my throat. "My people are dead!" I hissed.

"Majesty, let her go and step away."

I glanced over my shoulder at not-Emmory and muttered a curse.

Mia stepped in close, pressing her cheek to mine, her lips brushing my ear. I heard not-Emmory's warning behind us and the sound of Hessian 45s powering up. "Sleep, Hail," she whispered, and I did.

When I woke again, I was curled up on the bed in the room not-Emmory had put me in originally. For a moment I let myself pretend that I was back on the *Hailimi*, safe and surrounded by the people I loved.

"Majesty, I know you're awake."

I rolled over, spotted someone who looked like Fasé perched in a chair and not-Emmory standing by the door. The lights were dim, throwing shadows around, and I sat up, folding my hands in my lap.

"That's a new low," I said. "When Fasé comes back and grows up she's going to kick your ass for wearing her old face."

Not-Fasé smiled, a perfect replica of the look she used to give me when she knew more than I did but wasn't telling. "Why is it so hard for you to believe we're alive, Majesty?"

Her words were an echo of Hao's and I wondered for a moment if the ghost I'd seen was really a ghost. It was the kind of sneaky, reckless thing my Hao would do.

Except if it wasn't a ghost it wasn't your Hao, you idiot, my brain screamed at me. *None of these people are who they say they are.*

"Nothing adds up," I replied. "Besides, I heard not-Emmory there. Even if you were Fasé and I were someone who needed to be fixed, she couldn't do it."

Fasé winced. "It's a wonder you don't have a splitting headache, because I think I just got one trying to follow that logic."

"This would go a lot smoother if you'd all just stop with this charade and show me your real faces. Tell me what you want."

Fasé dipped her head and unfolded her legs from the chair. "How about if I show you what really happened on Earth?"

"I saw what happened," I snarled. "You all died and left me alone."

Not-Emmory's face was impassive, but I saw his hand shift to his gun as not-Fasé approached me. I scooted away from her until my back was pressed to the wall.

"And the Cevallas didn't tell you differently, so you just went with it because of course you would expect your worst fears to come true."

The memory of Aiz's words floated back to the forefront of my brain. *"At this point would you believe any answer I gave you besides yes?"*

"There wasn't—" I cleared my throat. "There wasn't an answer they could give me that I would have believed. I already knew you were all dead."

Fasé held a hand out. "Let me show you otherwise."

I reached for her hand before I let my brain come up with a thousand reasons not to.

"Move, move, move." Fasé's breath was high in her throat as she pushed the others toward the exit. Sybil was at the front of the pack, just behind

the Marines as they hit the door. Gunfire echoed in the night air and Fasé felt Stasia's hand tighten in hers.

No one had argued about her sudden order to evacuate the building. It was still going to be close.

"Move!" she shouted, releasing Stasia's hand to gesture for the only other cover in the compound, a low-slung aircar garage ten meters away.

She spotted Emmory and the others, gave Stasia a shove toward Sybil, and sprinted across the yard, tackling the BodyGuard as the embassy exploded behind them.

I jerked away, pressing my hands to my eyes, but it didn't block out the image I'd just seen. "You're lying," I said.

"Hail—"

"No! Six months!" I pushed her off my bed with a foot and not-Emmory came away from the wall as she fell to the floor. "If any of this were true, why did it take you six Shiva-damned months to find me?"

"Because you were so damned set on us being dead you wouldn't fucking cooperate with me!" she shouted back. "I tried, Hail! I tried to find you. I tried to get you to tell me where you were."

All the questions I thought had been from Fasé's ghost suddenly flashed through my head, and my breath lodged in my throat. "No," I whispered. "You were too far away. I—my *smati* was off a good chunk of the time."

"I know." Fasé's anger seemed to dissipate. "It is not something we normally do with outsiders, Hail, but it was the only way to reach you."

It's a trick. I froze at the voice in my head.

"Get. Out. Of. Here."

Not-Fasé put a hand on not-Emmory's chest before he could respond. "I told you it might not work," she said to him. "We need to leave her be for a while."

He backed for the door, not taking his eyes off me even though I hadn't budged from the bed. There was sorrow and frustration twisted among the silver threads of his eyes. "Majesty, please come back to us," he said, dipping his head at me as the door slid open and they went through.

I held his gaze until it was gone and then buried my face in my hands and wept.

21

My captors didn't leave me alone for long. Not-Emmory probably figured that would lead to trouble from me.

He wasn't wrong.

So the steady stream of familiar dead faces kept me company—Emmory and Zin, Iza and Indula, even Gita and Hao. Which was an odd pairing given they were supposed to be mad at each other. I noted the absent faces more than the present ones. Johar and Alba, Fasé and Sybil. Though those pairs weren't a surprise given that my companions were supposed to be guarding me. Johar was the only one of the four who could possibly keep up with me in a fight.

Though I doubted it.

I glanced toward the open doorway. Not-Hao and not-Gita stood too close together, their murmured conversation only reaching my ears in bits and pieces.

"No, I get it. I'm not happy about why you didn't tell me. It would have been easier than hearing her say it, though." Not-Hao's sigh was tinged with curious violence.

"What I hate is the idea that we might have to work with them, even after all this." Not-Gita shifted against the door frame and I felt, rather than saw, her gaze shift to me. Her voice dropped, despite my indifferent posture stretched out on my bed. "...trust the Farians."

"You know my feelings on that," not-Hao replied.

"All too well."

I watched out of the corner of my eye as not-Gita reached out, tangling her fingers briefly with not-Hao's.

"You know," I said, sitting up and swinging my legs to the floor, watching as the pair tensed at my movement. "I hate to keep giving you pointers on how to impersonate dead people, but you two are supposed to be mad at each other?"

Not-Hao looked at me, his lips fighting off a grin. "You know there's this thing called apologizing and forgiveness, little sister?"

I paused, at a loss for how to respond, and instead raised my eyebrow in acknowledgment. "Just like that? My Gita was rather adamant about not accepting an apology."

"You mean when she almost shot me?"

Shiva, for just a second I wanted to believe it was my brother replying to me. The amusement in his golden eyes, the tone of his voice. Everything was fucking spot-on.

"Hao." Not-Gita said his name like a warning, and my longing vanished.

"I know what you're doing," I said.

"If you mean not walking around you like you're made of glass, then yes," not-Hao replied, shoving his hands into the pockets of the black jacket he was wearing. I knew that coat, had been there when we pulled the real one out of a pile of laundry on a frantic race through the streets of Paritz Vala to cover Hao's tattoos up.

Tattoos he'd removed. For me.

I swallowed and stood. I'd seen the edge of the Bristol crest on his hand before he covered it. Their attention to detail had gotten better. "I'm fine," I said.

"Well, yes and no." Hao shook his head. "Really wish you'd pull your head out of your ass so we can get on with this."

"Go fuck yourself."

"That's enough," not-Gita said, giving not-Hao a shove out of the door and holding out a hand. "Sit back down, Majesty, please."

I calculated the distance between us, decided I didn't want to get stunned today, and sat back down. "Can I get a few minutes alone?"

Not-Gita studied me for a moment and then nodded. "Don't make me regret it?"

"I'm too tired to try to escape right now." I offered up a smile that wasn't returned. The door closed and I lay back down with a sigh and stared at my hand. I wasn't lying; a bone-deep exhaustion from always being on guard had settled in. I couldn't sleep for more than a few hours at a time, and couldn't do anything but restlessly prowl this prison.

The ghosts had abandoned me, except for Hao, who kept vigil from the corner in the rare moments I was alone. I lifted my head, spotted him sitting there, and laughed. He was dressed in the same clothes as not-Hao and I wasn't sure if the morphing physical presence was my own brain messing with me or something else. There were times when I was sure he wasn't a ghost but the man wearing my dead brother's face.

I didn't think they would pull something that risky, especially after deliberately challenging me, and part of me really didn't want the confirmation so I was content to let the charade go.

"He's a bit of an asshole, isn't he?"

"Almost as much of one as you were," I replied, rolling onto my side. "I do wish you'd gotten a chance to apologize to Gita, *gege*, and that she could have accepted it. It doesn't seem fair."

"Life's not fair," he said with a shrug.

"Isn't that the fucking truth?" I replied, and went back to focusing on my hand.

I'd spent some of my downtime constructing a program on my *smati* to mask my bios from my captors, and I flipped it on so I could make another attempt at trying to break through the wall barring me from drawing on the energy outside of me.

If this was about control, as Mia had said, I had to give up what little control I still had in order to do it. The question was—was it worth it? Was the loss of the one thing still left to me worth this ability?

I didn't know. I rolled from my bed to pace while my brother's ghost watched me with his golden eyes. The ship shuddered under my feet and I glanced across the room, but Hao seemed unconcerned. I dropped onto my bed and stuck my hand out, palm up.

Think of lightning, Hail.

I thought of Mia. The way my breath stuttered and my skin lit up whenever she touched me.

I could feel the difference between the energy in my hand and the air around it—heat versus cold—and blew out a breath.

Let go of it.

The space around my hand rippled and I felt an energy I'd never touched before seep beneath my skin. It slid like silk over raw nerves and my wounded heart before it settled, as content as Mother's cats in my chest.

Swallowing down the crow of triumph, I grabbed my pinky and bent it back; the crack of the bone breaking was loud in the silence.

Hao didn't blink, didn't even shift from where he was sprawled in the corner. "You do that again and not-Emmory's going to come into the room."

"Maybe." I shrugged. Ghost or not, I wasn't about to tell him about the program. "It's not just for fun, though."

"Your ideas of fun were always a bit skewed, *sha zhu*, but this is pushing it."

I tossed a pillow in his direction with my uninjured hand, smiling when he caught it.

"I'd wondered if you'd start to question it." He was smiling and still as relaxed as he had been a moment ago.

"I've been questioning it for a while, or at least I suspected. You are quite good at being Hao, but not a replacement."

"That hurts a little," not-Hao replied. "But given the circumstances I'm letting it slide."

"How did you get in?"

"Masking program," he said with a smile. "I never left the room and you were too busy watching Gita to notice."

I smiled again, returning my focus to my throbbing pinky. Just like the real Hao, not-Hao seemed to understand that I needed the silence and he didn't speak, though he did tilt his head and raise a curious eyebrow.

The silken feeling unfurled and flooded my finger, wrapping around it and extinguishing the fire burning within the broken bone. I took a breath and smiled. "There, all better," I said, wiggling my now-healed finger at not-Hao.

Not-Hao was impressed, but it was quickly overtaken by something else. Concern? Disapproval? "Hail, what have they done to you?"

"Why does everyone keep asking that? Nothing," I said. "They've done nothing. I did it myself. I made the choice."

"You made the choice to let Aiz beat you to death?"

"You don't get to care about that."

"The fuck I don't." He still hadn't moved, and I couldn't bring myself to cross the space between us and shut him up.

Suddenly restless and angry at myself for wanting approval from a dead man, I slipped off the bed and walked to the far wall. I pressed my hand to the cool metal surface instead of punching it before I turned around to look at him. "I don't expect you to understand; even if you were Hao, I feel like he'd be just as disappointed in me."

"Is that so?"

I shrugged. "I failed you all and then I stopped caring about anything but the pain. That's interesting."

"What is?"

"That flicker of violence in your eyes." I smiled, leaning a shoulder against the wall. "What are you angry about?"

"What a question." Hao moved slowly, sitting up and bracing

his forearms on his knees as he answered me. "The thought of you fighting and dying over and over, alone and grief-stricken, thinking you were the last woman standing while that butcher beat you to death, makes me very angry, little sister. There are people in this universe who deserve that; you are not one of them."

I studied him. There was no lie there, no hesitation in his answer. Not-Hao was very angry, but it couldn't possibly be about me.

Unless it is Hao, in which case he'd have every right to be furious.

I brushed away the thought. "It's not impressive, though. The healing thing." I waved my hand in the air. "It's not nearly enough for what I need."

"What do you need it for?"

"To fight gods." I smiled again, as this time the disbelief was clear in his arched eyebrow. "Or something powerful enough that it's convinced the Farians of its godhood. That seems to be a matter of contention."

The ship shook again and the door slid open; not-Emmory came through with a grim look on his face. "They're here. Fasé says we're out of time. It has to be now, or it's never going to happen."

"Well, fuck," Hao muttered, getting to his feet and watching me closely. "Hail, we're at a crossroads here and there's no going back— if your Farian fortune-teller is to be believed. This is it, little sister. Time for you to make a choice. You come back to us or stay gone forever."

"I'm not your sister." I mirrored his movement, my triumph over healing myself vanishing in a haze of adrenaline as I recognized the beginning of a fight and put my back to a wall.

Both men were tense, not-Emmory's hand on his gun, and not-Hao was taking those loose, rolling steps that he'd always done just before jobs.

What if it is them, Hail? What then? What if Alba was right and they survived? What if Fasé showed you the truth of it?

I shook my head at the unknown voice. I couldn't take the

heartbreak if I hoped and was wrong again. I couldn't believe, and yet I was so tired of fighting.

"I wish with all my heart that you were real." I slid down the wall, all the strength leaching out of my body. "But you're not. None of you are because I couldn't keep you safe."

"Hail." Not-Hao crossed to me, crouching by my side. His fingers were trembling when he reached for me. It was fear that made them shake, but not of me.

For me?

"How do I make you believe that this is me? Tell me what to do and I'll do it. Anything you ask."

"You can't." I didn't resist when he took my face in his hands, hoping it was a Shen and they could just stop my heart. But he didn't and the tears spilled from my eyes. "You're gone. I have been dead for so long, and like a collapsing star in the black, there won't be anything left of me soon."

"No," he whispered, pressing his forehead to mine. "I won't let you go. Not like this. You can't leave me here al—" Not-Hao broke off. "Emmory, give me your gun."

"Hao—"

Hao released me with his left hand, keeping the right and his forehead pressed to me, his eyes never leaving mine. "Just do it. We're out of options and out of time."

I tracked not-Emmory as he crossed the room and put the Hessian 45 into Hao's hand.

"Little sister, look at me," he said, his voice low.

"You. Are. Not. My. Brother." I gritted the words out, hating that even as I said them I wished they were wrong, that it really was Hao in front of me, that the last six months had been a lie.

He smiled, a sad curving of his lips. "Do you remember, *sha zhu*, what I said to you, while you were lying in that piss-poor excuse for a hospital on Candless, all shot to shit? We were all alone. There was no one else to hear it."

178

"I remember. I remember everything we ever said to each other," I whispered back. "I won't tell you any of it."

Not-Hao smiled and put the gun in my hand. It was cold and not nearly the comfort I'd expected it to be. "You don't have to. I never told another soul what passed between us there. No one knows but me and you. You know the Shen and the Farians can only look like other people. They can't become them. They don't have their memories."

"Hao, she'll kill you."

I glanced down at the gun, then back up at those shimmering metallic eyes, which were filled with a kindness he'd only ever shown to me. How they could duplicate such emotion I didn't know. I hated them for it.

"I'll tell you what I said and if I'm wrong, I want you to pull that trigger. But if I tell you what I said and it's right, you need to believe that I'm real. There are no other options."

"You aren't Hao." I was begging at this point, pressed so hard against the wall with no escape.

"It's all right, little sister," not-Hao whispered. "Do you remember?"

22

I was swimming in a sea of pain, but the cool brush of lips on my burning skin anchored me to the shore. "You can't leave me here alone, little sister."

"And why is that, Cheng Hao?" I whispered the question past my cracked lips and felt him start in surprise.

"Because I will be inconsolable at the loss of the brightest star in the black."

"I guess I shouldn't die, then, huh?"

I felt his lips curve against my forehead and his fingers tighten around mine. "I guess not."

Hao let go of the gun, cupping my face in both hands and looking straight into my eyes. "You can't leave me here alone, little sister."

"And why is that, Cheng Hao?" The question slipped out automatically and his fingers tightened on my head in response. An ember, long thought dead, glowed in the darkness.

"Because I will be inconsolable at the loss of the brightest star in the black," he replied, and I suddenly wasn't sure if the tears were in my eyes or his.

That struggling spark of hope caught flame in my chest, painfully bright, and I fought the sob trying to claw its way free as the wall around me cracked.

There was no way, no possible way that anyone in all the universe but Hao could know those words. Everything crashed down around me, drowning me like waves tossed against the shore. Fasé's vision of what had truly happened at the embassy flashed in front of my eyes and I dragged in a breath, the exhalation releasing my pain as I cried his name.

"Hao?"

"I am here," Hao murmured, pressing his cheek to mine. "I am not dead. We are not dead. Believe me when I say that I am real. Please, little sister, don't leave me here alone in the black."

My sob burst out, raking through the air. I collapsed against Hao, the gun falling to the floor; he caught me in his arms, holding me close against his chest as I wept.

"I thought I'd killed all of you. I thought I sent you into the embassy and when it exploded—"

"That's enough. We're not dead, Hail. It's okay. You're okay." He murmured the comfort over and over as I sobbed. "I'm sorry it took us so long to get to you." Hao pressed a kiss to my hair. "So sorry for everything you've gone through. I love you. I swear I'll never let you get hurt again." His arms tightened around me.

The ship jolted, and this time alarms sounded. I swallowed back the rest of my tears and let Hao pull me to my feet. "What's going on?"

"Reasonably sure we're being shot at." Hao looked past me, and I turned to see my *Ekam* standing behind me.

"Emmory." I pressed fingers to my mouth in an effort to hold in the tears. I wanted to believe it was him.

"Hail." Emmory put a gloved hand on my hair, moving with such care that my eyes filled again. I tried not to tense, but I couldn't help myself and he paused, his look gutting me. "We are not the enemy here, Highness. I swear."

It was the *Highness* that did it. The otherwise useless platitude jerked me back to a moment when this had all started. When it had just been the three of us—me, Emmory, and Zin alone in my room

181

on the *Para Sahi*. Two Trackers and a runaway princess unsure who to trust. That moment where I'd had to choose to trust Emmory and he'd never given me reason to doubt since.

I stepped into his embrace, feeling the solid safety of his arms wrapping around me. "I'm sorry."

"No, don't apologize," he murmured against my ear. "Never for that. I'm sorry I couldn't keep you safe. I promised you never again and I broke that promise."

"It's all right. You couldn't have stopped this, I know that now," I whispered back, the sobs catching in my throat again, spilling into the air in a staccato mess.

"Emmory, why aren't you answering your com? We've—" Zin broke off, skidding to a halt in the doorway. "Hail?" The hope in his voice almost set me crying again as Emmory released me.

I nodded, holding a hand out. Zin took a step into the room and my treacherous brain whispered, *Are you really sure it's him?*

Zin saw my flinch and froze. His easy smile almost hid the sorrow as he folded his hands together and bowed. "Majesty, it is good to have you back. Emmory, they need you on the bridge."

"Stay here." Whether Emmory's words were for me or Hao and Zin, I remained rooted to the floor. I wanted to follow, but my feet refused to carry me forward.

"What's going on?"

"The Shen, Majesty." Zin had backed up and was by the open doorway; the movement was meant to give me space, but part of me just felt lost again.

"Is Mia—" I had to pause and unknot my thoughts. "Bear with me, please. Did I imagine that Mia was here?"

"No, you didn't imagine it," Hao replied. "You tried to bust her out."

"That was you, wasn't it? Not your ghost."

"It's never been a ghost, Hail." Hao's voice was gentle even as the words stung. "Just your brain telling you what you wanted to hear, but to answer your question, yes that was me."

"I need to talk to her," I said. "If the Shen are shooting at us they need to know she's on the ship and they'll only believe her, or me, maybe. It depends on if it's Aiz."

"Majesty, Emmory said to stay here."

"Since when have I ever listened to him?"

A smile flickered to life on Zin's face. "You do occasionally, ma'am."

"Fair point." I smiled back. "How long has it been?"

Hao figured out the nature of my question before Zin did, and he touched a hand to my elbow. "A year, *sha zhu*. Standard. About eight months back on Indrana."

Time was a funny thing out in the black, almost inconsequential except when you were planetside and trying to ground yourself. If it had been a standard year, that meant the time on Sparkos had been only slightly longer back home on Pashati.

I wanted to ask about home, but the words refused to form. Whatever it was, I had to hold out hope that Alice and Taz and the others were handling it.

I was in no position to be empress. Not right now, possibly not ever again.

I looked between the two men and straightened my spine. Hao was safe. I knew that. Trusted it more than I trusted anything else at the moment.

Zin was, if not exactly safe, not unsafe. I knew he was real, had to trust it in the general scheme of things or I'd probably lose my new tenuous grasp on reality altogether.

I wanted that certainty, needed it as much as oxygen, but I couldn't find the words, and I ruthlessly told myself that if Hao trusted them and I trusted him, it was good enough. It seemed awful to demand that these people who'd fought so long and hard to find me prove they were who they said they were.

I rubbed at my face. "Things have been rough, and I may not be capable of rational thought right now, but I do know Aiz will stop at nothing to rescue his sister."

"You're capable, Majesty, crown or not," Zin said.

It is him.

I squeezed my eyes shut at the sharp burst of relief in my chest as a conversation at the bottom of a canyon on Guizhou came to life in my head. "You pick words from one of the few times we've shouted at each other, Starzin? It's a risk to use something so out of character for you to prove to me you're real."

"It seemed appropriate." He held his hand out and this time I took it, pulling him into a hug.

Zin exhaled, pressing his cheek to mine. "We are still here, with you, and will remain so to the end."

"I don't deserve any of you." I clung to him and felt the muscles in his arms shift as he hugged me closer.

"You deserve it, and you have us. Welcome back."

"Not all the way." My exhalation was shaky, but I managed a smile as I pulled free. "But closer, I think. Let's go to the bridge before Aiz—I'm assuming that's Aiz shooting at us—blows us out of the black."

We headed out into the gray corridor, following the curve around to a set of stairs and another, longer hallway that dead-ended with doors that slid open when Zin pressed his palm to the panel on the side.

I prepared myself for the onslaught of greetings as we walked onto the bridge, but someone had passed on a requirement that everyone give me space and act like I'd only been gone for a few minutes instead of a year. Sergeant Nidha Sathi, the Royal Marine who'd been part of the team on Earth fighting with us during our flight from the embassy, stood near the door. She met my gaze and gave me a nod that I returned.

Kisah offered a smile, and I spied her fingers reaching for me before she stopped herself and shoved them back into the pocket of her pants.

Emmory greeted me with an eyebrow. "I thought I said to stay in your room, Majesty."

"You did. But you need me here." I leaned against a console. "Nice ship, where'd you get it?"

"Stole it," Fasé replied without looking up. "There wasn't any way to fit all your people into my ship, and taking a *Vajrayana* would have made the trip take a little longer than any of us were happy with."

"Took you long enough as it was," I muttered, and Fasé slanted a gold-eyed stare my way.

"If you'd been a shade more cooperative we could have found you sooner."

"I'm sorry, I was busy thinking you were all dead."

"Yes, I'm well aware," she snapped; her earlier gentleness had been tossed aside and this new angry Fasé was a stranger to me. "I expected less wallowing from you."

"Fasé Terass!" Sybil stood up from what I assumed was the captain's seat to stare at us.

"What?"

"You will not speak to the Star of Indrana like that."

Fasé waved a hand, dismissing Sybil's words. "Tell me it's not true. Between her and the Cevallas, they've likely killed us all with their stupidity. I think I'm allowed to be peevish when I'm scrambling to fix the mess."

Sybil's reply was garbled and it was only then that I realized they were shouting at each other in Farian and I'd understood all of it up to that point.

The ship shook, more alarms blared, and my temper hit the end of its tether. "Someone give me coms," I ordered.

"Right here, ma'am," Iza said, lifting her hand in the air across the bridge.

"Bring them up." I crossed the room to her, putting a hand on the back of her seat at the last second instead of her shoulder. The majority of the people on the bridge were Indranan, mostly my BodyGuards, though I spotted a few naval uniforms in the mix. Along with a few Farians, all of whom were staring at me. "Is there more than one ship?"

"Three, ma'am. Com's live."

I nodded, wishing my answering smile to her weren't so forced, or that the voice in my brain weren't babbling a list of reasons why it couldn't be Iza sitting next to me.

Would you fuck off for five minutes and let me handle this? I thought.

Fine, if you want to put yourself at risk.

"Hey, Aiz, you want to stop shooting at us? I'm reasonably sure you don't want to kill your sister or me."

"Hail." Aiz appeared on the screen in front of us, and I whistled at the dark circles under his eyes.

"You look like shit."

"Back at you. Where is my sister?"

"She's fine," I lied, but Emmory nodded in the corner of my vision as a confirmation.

"Give her back."

"We should talk," I replied, shaking my head. "You and I both know that being at opposite ends of the table isn't where either of us wants to be. We're going to keep at this, though, until someone comes to their senses."

"And you think that should be me?"

"You're older," I said, and watched his mouth twitch as he fought to hold in his amusement. "More experienced, more familiar with the Farians and this whole mess."

"Flattery, Hail?"

I lifted a shoulder with a tiny smile. "You're too far away for me to punch in the throat."

Aiz's laughter made several people, Iza included, jerk in surprise. "Very well. We have a base not too far from here. We can't jump to it, the Farians will spot the energy signatures. So stay in regular drive. I'll send you coordinates and see you in a few days. We can talk then."

The screen went blank. I looked down at Iza. "Received coordinates, ma'am."

"Good. Who's flying this thing?"

A Farian with red hair split into two braids smiled and raised her hand. "I am, Your Majesty. Teslina Agne."

"You're one of Fasé's converts?"

"Yes, ma'am. Though I was serving on the *Pedalion's Favor* before the *Mardis* and your people—appropriated it."

"You can say *stole*," I replied, unable to stop the smile from spreading.

"Yes, ma'am."

"Let's be on the way."

23

"Majesty." Emmory cleared his throat and I turned to look at him. "We should go home."

"Not a conversation to have in public, *Ekam*," I said, looking around. "Aiz will chase his sister across the galaxy if necessary, so the first step is returning her. Iza, give Teslina those coordinates so she can get us under way."

I ignored how her eyes flickered to Emmory and my *Ekam* gave a tiny nod of approval before she answered me. "Yes, Majesty."

"Is there a ready room on this ship?"

"Behind you, *sha zhu*," Hao said just before he touched my arm. My instinctive jerk was small, but I know he felt it nonetheless. "It's over there."

"Someone bring Mia up here. You with me." I reached up and squeezed Hao's fingers on my arm. "Fasé and Sybil, you two come with us."

"You go," Sybil said to Fasé. "I will fetch Mia."

"Emmory and Gita." My *Dve* was standing by the door to the ready room with her arms crossed over her chest, and I forced myself to pat her on the shoulder even though the motion was stilted and made us both flinch.

I noticed Hao's fingers tangling briefly with hers as we went through the door, and some of the screaming in my brain stopped. If he trusted that she was real, I should be able to also.

Shiva, this dance was going to be exhausting. I struggled to wrap what composure I had around myself like armor, shoring up the broken bits of me into something resembling the empress I knew they all expected.

"Majesty, we need to take you home."

Six months and a hundred deaths coupled with the images of the future Mia had shown me had burned a certainty into my soul. Going home would only result in disaster at this point. I had a feeling if I set foot on Pashati again before this was over I would never leave and the galaxy would burn around us before the fires consumed us, too.

"I can't do anything for Indrana from Pashati, *Ekam*." I shook my head at Emmory.

"I cannot keep you safe here. Not with one ship and a handful of BodyGuards."

I held his gaze, knowing I was seeing the concern and frustration only because he was letting it show, and then offered a gentle smile.

"I know." I looked at Gita and Hao before I leaned both palms on the table in the middle of the room. The ready room was a decent size but the closed door made me edgy, and I struggled to keep those feelings at bay as I dealt with the issue in front of me. "Gita told you what happened on Sparkos?"

"I received her report."

I couldn't stop the chuckle and gestured in Hao's direction. My brother's entire body had tensed at my question. "His reaction makes more sense."

Emmory didn't respond. I looked to where Fasé sat in the corner farthest from the door.

"Did you see it?"

"I did not."

"Interesting." I nodded, mulling over my next words before I allowed them to leave my mouth. "I would ask you all for a favor that I will in return owe you."

I had Emmory and Hao's interest now; they recognized the importance of my words. Gita and Fasé didn't, though they were still curious thanks to my formal tone.

"The events of Sparkos are violent, there is no doubt of that. I died—repeatedly. It was not mindless, though. It was for a purpose and it was something I agreed to."

Gita closed her eyes. Emmory swallowed. Fasé and Hao watched me, the pair of them with their golden eyes that were so similar. They had always been at odds, more so after Cas's death, but they were more alike than either wanted to admit.

"I do not doubt that the events Gita relayed to you happened as she remembers them, as she was shown by the Cevallas. I, however, carry something different." I lifted a hand off the table and pressed it to my heart. "The favor is this—meet me halfway, despite any misgivings you may have. Do not seek vengeance against the Cevallas for the choice I made. I don't ask you to trust them. I ask you to trust me."

"Done, Majesty," Emmory said without hesitation, and Gita was surprisingly only half a second behind him in her agreement.

"That was three favors," Hao said, but he smiled and dipped his head. "But I will agree to meet you halfway, and I will always trust you."

I shook my head. "I need you to agree to all of it or none of it."

"I am not sure I can do that, little sister."

"What chaos reigns when the pair of us agree," Fasé said, glancing over without a hint of a smile at Hao. "I need no favors from you, Your Majesty, and my trust in you has been shaken by the company you now keep."

"Fair," I replied. "My trust in you was shaken when you sent Cas to his death, but I got over it, didn't I?"

The other humans in the room sucked in startled breaths at my sharp words. Fasé still just looked pissed.

"Anyway." I took a deep breath and pushed away from the table. "You two are welcome to change your minds; just let me know. Emmory, Gita, I appreciate your understanding."

The door opened, and Sybil walked in, one hand wrapped around Mia's covered arm and Zin behind them. Mia's hands were curiously no longer bound or covered, and I wondered whose decision that had been.

Sybil stopped at Emmory's gesture and directed Mia into a seat on the opposite side of the room from me. The Shen sat, her gray eyes finding mine first before she looked around the room at the others.

She held Fasé's gaze the longest, and I bit the inside of my cheek at the Farian's glare. Whatever composure Fasé had carried prior to my disappearance seemed to have vanished.

I shared a glance with Emmory, giving a tiny shake of my head as I crossed my arms over my chest, content to let this contest play out.

"Something on your mind, *Mardis*?" Mia wasn't at all concerned by Fasé's glare, and she asked the question in Indranan, not Farian. I quirked an eyebrow up, watching as Fasé's eyes narrowed even further.

"You knew!" she shouted, shoving herself out of her chair and pointing at Mia. "You knew we were alive and didn't tell her. You pushed her down this path, Mia, knowing what it will bring down on our heads!"

I wasn't the least bit surprised by this news, though Fasé's obvious anger was interesting. Now that my head was clearer, I could see all the clues both Mia and Aiz had dropped—either consciously or not. Or even Talos, when he'd called Gita my *Dve*. Aiz had done it, too. I should have caught that. Should have known the Shen would know the difference between my BodyGuards. It was obvious to me now that I hadn't wanted to believe anything other than my deepest fears.

In some ways, Fasé had been right: I had been wallowing. That was a bitter pill to swallow.

"Fasé."

She ignored the warning I turned her name into. "You have twisted this—twisted her—to your own ends. Did you think for a moment about the consequences?"

"You are so new at this," Mia replied with a tiny shake of her head. It seemed a strange comment, coming from her, but Fasé didn't react with more than a snort of derision. "I understand your anger, but there is nothing else that will stop what is coming, Fasé, except to kill those things the Pedalion insists are gods. Don't pretend you don't want them dead as much as we do. We did what was necessary to give Hail the tools to win in a fight." Mia got to her feet, frustration rolling off her in waves. "But she made the choice, we didn't force her into it. You're foolish if you fall into the same trap as the Pedalion and think you can somehow control the Star!"

"I should have known better than to trust you."

"Your problem was the assumption that we were in agreement on everything," Mia replied coolly. "I agree with some of what you are proposing, Fasé, but I have no interest in what happens to Faria. My concern has always been and will always be my people. This path is the one that will bring them home."

"And you think it's just a happy coincidence that the very thing you want is also what the future says the Star will choose?"

"I think that you all have been trying to control Hail for far longer than I've been in the picture. I showed her what was coming. I gave her a choice."

"You let me believe everyone was dead," I said.

Mia looked to me. There was sorrow in her gray eyes, but also the same determination that had been there from the beginning. "We did—I did, yes."

"Were you responsible for the attack on Earth?"

"No," she said. "I told you the truth about Jamison." She drew in a deep breath. "But I knew it was coming and I didn't warn you. They could have all died, were it not for Fasé."

"Why?"

"You needed to make the right choice, Hail, and that required extreme measures."

"Not the right choice," Fasé said, crossing the space between them. "Your choice. Your obsession with revenge could mean the death of us all."

I caught Hao's eye and shook my head at the question in his eyes, pleased when he pulled his hand back from his gun.

"My obsession?" Mia laughed. "The Farian obsession with an endless life is what put us here in the first place, Fasé. Don't try to suddenly pretend you're okay with that. You're fighting against it the same as we are, and you're just as willing to sacrifice people"— Mia pointed at me—"for your fucking cause, so don't preach at me like you're a saint."

"How dare you."

"Enough." I came around the table, catching Fasé's wrist before she could strike Mia and dragging her back several steps. "That's enough, Fasé."

"Are you going to forgive her for this?" Her golden eyes went wide with shock. "You've already forgiven her."

I smiled, glancing at Mia for a moment before looking down at Fasé; the memory of the destruction I'd seen was heavy on my tongue. "There are worse things coming. You know this. I know this. I made my choices. You could make an argument about incomplete information, but the truth is every choice we make is based on what we know at the time and nothing more."

"You cannot get involved, Hail."

"I *am* involved. Don't you get that, Fasé? I tried to stay out of this fight. It didn't work. We tried it your way and everyone almost died. I won't take that chance again."

"How can you forgive her for this?"

"How did I forgive you?" I let her wrist go and cupped her face with both hands. "How do any of us forgive for the horrible things we do to each other? We make the choice. It can't be coerced or bought. It just happens like the sun rising for one more morning. I don't fully understand what is going on, both out there and in here." I let her go briefly and tapped my chest. "But there's no backing out of it now. We move forward and we have to go together."

Fasé's frown deepened and I tightened my grip when she started to pull away. "I need you to listen to me," I said. "You're the one who said the future isn't set, so stop acting as though it is just because things didn't go the way you wanted them to go."

Sybil's shoulders jerked as she unsuccessfully choked back her laughter, but Fasé didn't look away from me. "This is not about me not getting my way. You are walking a dark and dangerous path, Hail. I grieve for the pain it will cause you."

"I've already been in pain and spent a lifetime grieving. I thought you were gone—all of you—and it destroyed me. Don't you realize that?" I replied, leaning down and pressing my forehead to hers. "You all sat and watched as my family was killed. You did it because I had to be here. Well, I am still here. What the Cevallas did is no more or less right than what you've done, so you don't get to take the moral high ground here. Mia is right, nobody gets to control me."

Fasé closed her eyes, visibly collecting herself before she opened them again. "I never quite know what to make of you, Hail Bristol."

"You're not alone in that, believe me." I let her go and dragged in a breath, feeling a bit like I'd just run a hundred-meter sprint.

"I hope you are prepared for what is coming." That was directed at Mia, who dipped her head in acknowledgment to the Farian.

"We are not the same side, *Mardis*, but we can be," she said. "We would be stronger together."

Fasé shook her head, wrestling privately with something. "I need to think on this," she said at last, and headed out the door.

Sybil followed her, laying a cool hand on my bare arm. "Watch out for the riptides, Your Majesty."

The breath I dragged in was a shaky half sob, and Sybil smiled.

"You have passed through the fire. It may not feel like it now, but you are whole, Majesty, and stronger than your fears." She reached down, smiling at Mia as she helped the Shen to her feet.

"Don't touch her," Emmory ordered as Mia reached out to me.

"*Ekam,*" she said, a patient smile playing over her mouth. "I couldn't kill Hail even if I wanted to." She spread her fingers wide and wiggled them. "The moment Aiz brought her back from the dead he made that impossible."

I blinked. "What?"

Hao groaned. "Please don't tell me she's immortal. She's hard enough to live with as it is."

I choked on my laughter, but Sybil's laugh flew free and even Emmory let a reluctant smile curve the corner of his mouth, though he didn't move from Mia's path.

"She is not," Mia said. "But she is protected from the power we and the Farians have. We can still heal her, can still bring her back, but we can't use the energy to kill her. I couldn't kill you either, *Ekam.*"

"Because of Fasé," I murmured as everything clicked into place, and Mia nodded. I looked to Emmory, reaching a hand out and putting it on his forearm. "That's why you didn't die when I shot that assassin at the party. Even though he was touching you."

"So you're safe?" Hao asked.

"I wouldn't go that far." Mia's eyes were on mine when she answered, and I had to fight to keep from pressing a hand to my stomach where a riot had taken up residence. "But Hail's safe with me. Any human who's been brought back is safe from that particular threat." She looked away from me at Emmory. "Besides, I like your empress, and I swear on my mother's grave I will not hurt her. Hail." Mia stopped, staring past me as she considered her words before she met my eyes. "I am sorry for not telling you that your people were alive. I know it caused you pain."

It had, there was no denying that, and I knew it looked odd that I wasn't angrier about the betrayal—if I could even call it that. I understood in my gut why Aiz and Mia had hidden the truth from me, hidden me away. It was like rubbing dirt off a window until I could finally see through it to the other side. The future Mia had shown me was growing clearer with every day that passed, and I knew down in my soul that the only way to prevent what I'd seen was to forge ahead and fight.

"You would do it again, given the chance."

This time she met my gaze. "I would do anything for my people."

I couldn't stop the smile from spreading. "I know. That's why I forgive you."

She dropped her lashes down over her eyes for just a heartbeat before looking up at me again, and my blood hummed in response. "You don't need an assurance from me that I am myself?"

"I don't. I know you." I leaned in. "I need—"

Emmory cleared his throat and I snapped backward, refusing to look around. I knew my people were staring at me. Sybil was watching us with a curious half smile curving her mouth.

"We'll leave you alone, Majesty," she said, tugging on Mia's arm until the woman turned from me and followed her from the room.

"Bugger me," I muttered, closing my eyes briefly and opening them as I turned. Gita was frowning. Hao had an eyebrow raised. My *Ekam*'s face was perfectly blank. Zin wore his worry for the whole room to see. I sat in the chair Mia had vacated and stared at my hands.

"Majesty." Emmory crouched at my side. "We can't trust the Shen."

"It is, ironically, not about trust. I—" I curled my fingers inward, nails biting into the skin. The pain grounded me some, and I exhaled. "We don't need her captive and we don't want to be on

Aiz's bad side, trust me on that one. This will be hard enough as it is. We'll meet with Aiz, and I'll try to get him to see that we need to work together." I took a deep breath and looked his way.

The silence in the room was tantamount to a bomb going off, and I rolled my eyes. "Can we please not do this? We're going to have to be on the same side as them no matter what happens; it would be easier if you all didn't think I was—" I broke off, frustrated at the words that wouldn't cooperate.

"What, Hail?" Hao asked with a smile that was sharp. "Obsessed with that Shen?"

I gave him a flat look. "Not the word I would have picked."

"I would have." Gita's mutter was only just audible.

I gave her a look even as I knew they were right and rubbed both hands over my eyes with a groan. "Yes, I know. All of you are concerned."

"For good reason, Hail," Zin said. "We've seen this kind of reaction in hostages before."

"You are the Empress of Indrana, Majesty," Emmory said. "There is concern to be had."

I shook my head. "I am not, Emmory. I heard you say 'Empress Alice'; moreover, I know how the laws of succession work. This may be a strange situation, but it's not out of the realm of things the government is prepared to deal with."

I watched the frowns as the four of them tried to keep up with my subject change, even though I knew it would only buy me a little space from the issue of Mia.

"It's been close to eight months on Pashati since I disappeared. Alice would have been crowned by what had better have been a unanimous vote of the councils after the second month had passed. Indrana couldn't afford to be leaderless. Not on the heels of a civil war. The council's first priority would have been to secure the throne. Did that happen?"

"Yes, ma'am."

I smiled in relief that something had gone right in this whole mess.

"It will be reversed, Majesty," Emmory said, and though his tone was soft, the words hit like a sledgehammer to my gut. "I've already sent word home of your rescue."

"Did you include the bit where I was out of my mind?" I waved a hand. "Am still kinda hanging on to sanity by my fingertips, if we're all going to be painfully honest with each other."

The muscles in Emmory's jaw tightened.

"I haven't even kissed Mia," I said, turning away and rubbing at my forehead with the palm of my hand. "I won't lie. I want to. Do I have to have a reason for it? And I feel like you all should know she very deliberately did not respond when I pushed the issue because she recognized the imbalance of power between us."

"You only have to be careful, Majesty. Especially if you want to pursue an alliance with the Shen. The Farians will jump on any reason to say you are being coerced."

"She's dangerous, Hail." That was from Hao, and I muttered a curse.

"I know, you've already said as much." I squeezed my eyes shut at his look of confusion. That hadn't been this Hao, but the ghost in my head. "Sorry, wrong Hao. So am I, damn it. I'm not some lovesick schoolgirl."

"We're not saying you are."

"Then what are you saying?" I couldn't keep the snap out of my words, no matter how unfair it might be.

"That you need to be careful," Hao replied.

"Careful is a matter up for debate." I shook my head and put a hand up. "Drop it for now, *gege*. I hear the protests. I promise to keep it in my pants. How are things at home?"

"Stable, at the moment," Emmory replied after closing his eyes at

Zin's choked laughter. "I told Empress Alice we would com them as soon as you were feeling better."

"I can't." I hated how the words stuck in my throat and shook my head again. "Not right now."

"She will press, ma'am."

"Let her press! I'm not—" I shoved out of my seat, anger rolling in my chest as I paced the length of the room and back again.

What was I? If not empress, was I a citizen of Indrana still? I didn't know for sure if I was even me. Right now it certainly didn't feel like it.

"I need some time and to focus on one looming catastrophe before going to the next. We have things to do here now. Alice can hold the empire together for a little longer. Mia said she didn't hire Jamison because she knew I hated him," I said, changing the subject so abruptly again it was surprising no one got whiplash. "She didn't know if the Farians had or if he was after Hao."

"Rai claimed the same thing." Hao's voice was quiet, but it made every muscle in my body tense.

"You talked to Rai?"

"At great length." Hao's gold eyes were filled with simmering violence. "He's still alive, though, *sha zhu*."

"Good." I held on to the spark of answering fury I felt. "He's on the list. So is Jamison, but I can't deal with either of them at the moment."

Hao looked as though he wanted to say something, but he shook his head with a tiny frown at my raised eyebrow.

"We assumed the money was coming from the Cevallas," Zin replied. "But I bet you a hundred credits if we looked at it again we'd find something we missed."

"The money was—" Hao snapped his fingers and moved to the wall. Data from his *smati* appeared on the surface. "It wasn't. Gita, do you remember when we were looking at the sources and Jamison's had one extra—"

"Yes." She joined him at the wall. "We discounted it at the time, assuming it was extra security on his part."

"I should have known better. He's not that careful." Hao shook his head, then reached a hand out and tapped a finger against the list of figures. "Here. Someone slotted that in to make it look like it was coming from the same source as the other payments."

"We'll have to do some digging," Gita replied, her shoulder just brushing his as she leaned in to examine the accounts. "I don't believe the Farians would be so foolish as to let the money trail lead straight back to them, but it may give us something we can use."

"They really did make up?" I murmured under my breath to Emmory and watched as a smile appeared at the corner of my *Ekam's* mouth.

"Yes, Majesty."

"Are you going to stop calling me that?"

"No, Majesty."

"You know nobody else is going to stop calling me that unless you do?"

"I know." His smile flickered. He reached down and closed his fingers around mine, squeezing them once before he let go. "You are the empress, Majesty. Time or distance does not change that fact. We swore an oath to the Star." He reached up and tapped a finger to the tattoo on his cheek. "You are the shining stars in the blackness of space. The hope of the lost and forsaken. The spark that must not be extinguished."

"I don't know about that."

"I do."

That pulled a smile from me, though it vanished just as quickly. "Emmory, there's something awful coming and I think—I know this sounds arrogant but—I think I'm the only one who can stop it."

"I heard Mia say that, too," he said. "Show me."

I held my hand out and Emmory took it, frowning at me before he tightened his fingers on mine. I exhaled and cued up the playback of the images I'd seen when Mia had shown me the future.

They'd gotten clearer the more I'd watched them. Scenes of flame and fire transformed into soldiers in white marching through deserted streets. Their faces were still obscured, but I could see the weapons clearly enough and there was nothing like what they carried in this entire galaxy.

We saw Earth in ruins. Indrana destroyed. Graveyards of ships stretching through the black. I felt Emmory jerk at the sight of his corpse and was surprised that this time my own eyes were dry.

24

ark Mother," Emmory breathed, bracing himself on the table after he turned away, Zin's hand on his back.

"What's going on?" Gita and Hao had turned from their conversation and were watching us.

"I showed him what's coming."

There was silence, then a low gasp from Zin. I started to reach for him, but Emmory turned and pulled him into an embrace. "Have you two seen this?" Zin asked.

Gita and Hao both shook their heads. Emmory murmured something that made Zin straighten and leave the room.

"No," Gita said. "Her Majesty told us about it on Sparkos, but I didn't—"

"Want to see it," I finished, my voice sharper than it should have been, and Gita flinched.

"We're not meant to see the future, ma'am. It's not right."

"What's not right is running headlong into a battle without the slightest clue who we're fighting or what they're capable of." I waved a hand at the window in the ready room, the space beyond as calm as an undisturbed pool, and the chaos we'd just watched was laid over it, so that the black was filled with dying ships and stars. "What's not right is not using every advantage to stop what's coming. That means me, with Aiz, fighting gods."

"Gita, you need to see it," Emmory said, holding up a hand

before she could protest again. "I'm not saying believe it. I'm saying watch it. We need to know what's driving the Shen the same way we've needed to see what's driving the Farians."

I held my hand out to Hao, watched his eyes narrow. "Are you going to argue with me twice in under an hour?"

"I'm considering it."

"It will help you understand why I am so willing to trust them." I wiggled my fingers. "I need that understanding from you. I don't have the energy to fight you every step of the way."

"You want to die, *sha zhu*; I feel like fighting you on that is sort of my place."

"Oh." I smiled and shook my head. "I'm—no, not anymore." I didn't know how to explain the tangled emotions that had knotted in my chest when I thought they were all dead. "I told Aiz I would fight with him if the Farian gods wouldn't listen, but I want the chance to talk to them. To try to convince them. I promise to you I won't throw my life away."

Gita's sharply indrawn breath dragged Hao's eyes away from me, and he muttered several curses before crossing to me in three steps and grabbing my hand.

He closed his eyes against the onslaught, fingers tight on mine, and I held his hand as he rode through the shock wave even though I didn't need to.

What he did next surprised me.

Hao leaned in and kissed my forehead. "I need to speak with Dailun," he said, and left the ready room without another word.

"Emmory, I'd like to speak with Gita alone," I subvocalized over our private com.

"Yes, ma'am. I'll wait outside." He tapped Zin on the arm and gestured for the door. The pair left and I walked around the table to where Gita was braced, palms flat on the top and head hanging down.

"I owe you an apology, Gita."

To my shock, she dropped to her knees, her eyes locked on the floor. "You don't. I'm sorry. This is all my fault. I failed you. I didn't keep you from harm's way, Majesty. Worse, I left you blank with grief and then alone to rage at the universe because it felt like my world had ended, too, and I didn't have the strength to grieve with you."

"Gita." I stared at her bent head, her words echoing back at me from a quiet moment in my palace rooms. They weren't verbatim, but they didn't need to be when the emotion behind them was so fucking clear.

Tears dropped to the floor, the moisture gleaming against the gray surface. "No," I said, crouching down next to her and reaching out to cup her face in my hands. "Shiva, you didn't fail me. Look at me, Gita."

"You carried that vision in your head for how long? All alone," she whispered.

"I won't feed you some cowshit line about how this was all meant to happen," I replied. "I'm not that messed up, and Dark Mother knows that I'd much rather it had gone down in a manner that was less painful than what we had to endure. I needed you when it was happening, and you tried. I am sorry I pushed you away."

She wrapped her arms around me, holding me tight, and everything in me uncoiled, the tension sliding away as I hugged her back.

"Any failures were mine and mine alone," I whispered. "I'm so sorry that I went down a path you couldn't follow." I couldn't find the words to say I would do it again if presented the choice, but I think she knew as I sat back and met her gaze. "I'm sorry that I was so cruel to you. It was uncalled for, no matter what I was going through. I need you now, at my side with your critical eye and your ability to see the problems before they happen. It's going to take all of us to keep the empire—to keep all of humanity safe."

Gita reached out with shaking fingers to touch my face. "I'm afraid, Hail. Not just because of what Emmory showed me. We lost you back on Sparkos. I don't think you're fully back, are you?"

I wasn't, but I smiled. I could fake it well enough, and maybe that would get me where I needed to be. "I am finding my way." That was honest at least. "I don't think it's possible for me to go back to who I was, but that's life, isn't it?" I took her hands, pulling her to her feet and into a hug. "Everything is going to be okay, Gita."

"I don't trust Mia," she whispered against my hair. "Please be careful, she's dangerous."

"So Hao just said," I replied. "But so am I."

Gita left me alone, the door closing behind her, and I broke two fingers on my left hand before the pain registered, sinking down onto a chair with a shaking exhalation.

The sharp tendrils of pain wove their way up my wrist and into my forearm as I murmured the words of the Aparadha Stotram. "O Lord Shiva who is all compassionate, please forgive me. You are the Lord of all deities and one whose nature is to bless all."

The words and the pain filled me as I curled into myself for a long moment. I didn't try to escape them but let them crawl under my skin and into my bones until I had the strength to stand once more.

It was early the next day when the knock sounded on my door. I looked away from the weapon schematics Aiz had translated for me to where Emmory stood.

He had, surprisingly, deferred to my desire to stay in the original room they'd put me in. It was smaller, safer as far as my still paranoid brain was concerned. There wasn't a lot of space in this ship to begin with, and moving me just for the sake of my position seemed ridiculous.

"Majesty? Mia would like to speak with you."

I hadn't pushed about keeping Mia under guard, even though I had a feeling that anyone other than Sybil wouldn't be able to actually stop her if she decided she wanted out. It seemed a better course of action to wait to speak with her, especially if I wanted to avoid any more accusations of obsession from my people.

What surprised me was Emmory taking the cuffs off Mia and waving her into the room at my nod. He planted himself by the doorway, dark eyes unreadable.

"It appears your *Ekam* took my promise of not hurting you seriously," she murmured as she sat in the chair on the other side of the desk.

I suspected it was more he believed the bit about her not being able to kill either of us with just a touch. What I wasn't sure was if Emmory thought Mia not a threat because of it, which seemed strange for him. Of course, I hadn't told him about how she'd put me on my knees with just a touch of her hand either.

"I think he's just in a good mood," I murmured back, and was pleased by the smile it earned me. "What did you need?"

"I would like to speak with my brother if you will allow it."

The realization of the complete shift in the power balance between us hit me like a railgun in the chest, and I stared at her for so long Mia frowned.

"Hail?"

"Sorry, of course you can. I—"

"Majesty."

I looked away from Mia to Emmory. He hadn't moved except to raise an eyebrow in silent question. "We can do it here. You understand, yes?"

"Of course." If Mia was thrown by the situation, she was doing a much better job at hiding it than I was.

She didn't lose everything and have a breakdown because of it, that voice in the back of my head reminded me. I rubbed at the bridge of my nose, muffling a sigh and sending the com request through on my desk.

"Hail." Aiz appeared on the screen on the wall, smiled at his sister, and then his eyes flicked to Emmory, visible in the background.

"Good morning, to what do I owe the pleasure of this com?" he asked in Shen.

"Don't be rude," Mia replied in Indranan. "I wanted to speak with you, and Hail was gracious enough to allow it."

"Given that you are her prisoner."

Mia held up her hands and shook her head. "You're being petty. We knew this would happen. It's fine."

"We knew this *could* happen," Aiz replied. "There is a difference, though you seem to be unharmed and I don't need to win this argument so badly as to pursue it."

"He's just saying that because he lost," Mia murmured to me, and I grinned.

"I'm hanging up now."

"Aiz." She held up her hand. "It's time. Tell the fleet to meet us at Encubier."

"You are sure?"

I held my breath. I couldn't understand the significance of what was happening, only that my gut knew something had been set in motion and now there was no turning back from it.

"I am sure," Mia said. "It is time to go home, to Faria."

Aiz was at a loss for words, and he blew out a breath before giving us both a brilliant smile. "Well, I will spread the news and see you both on Encubier, then. Hail, I hope you're prepared to decide which of us will be in charge." His wink said all too clearly that the decision would likely not come as a result of a polite conversation.

"I am." How, exactly, I was going to accomplish that when we both knew I hadn't yet beaten him in a fight was something I was going to have to figure out and quickly.

"We'll see." He nodded and cut the connection.

"I take it you've seen all this." I waved a hand in the air.

"Not all, Hail, you know that." Mia got to her feet with a smile. "But I've seen enough. I will go back to my quarters, *Ekam*, unless you feel the need to have someone escort me?"

"No, *Thína*, I think I trust you enough to go where you should. I will tell Sybil to expect you."

I saw in the slight hesitation between one step and the next how Emmory's use of her title had surprised her, and I pressed fingers to my lips in a poor attempt to hide my smile. Mia disappeared around the corner and there was silence for a moment before Emmory spoke again.

"Are you up for another visitor?"

"I'm not made of glass," I replied. "You don't have to keep filtering people in."

He gave me the Look, and the burst of relief in my chest was painful. "Stasia brought you chai, Majesty. Would you like to see her?"

"Yes." I fumbled, pushing out of my chair with more force than was necessary in my haste. The familiar smell of blue chai wafted on the air, and tears filled my eyes as my maid came into the room.

"Your Majesty." Stasia set the tray on the table and dropped into a curtsy. "I am so glad to see you again."

"Up." I tried to make my command as gentle as possible, then tried and failed to keep my hands from trembling as I reached for her.

Stasia stepped willingly into my embrace and repeated the words I'd once said to her in that quiet, calm voice of hers, " 'You are not *just* anything, Stasia Vintik, and certainly not just my maid. You are my friend. Don't ever let anyone tell you differently.' "

I pulled her close and buried my face in her gold curls.

"I am so sorry, ma'am," she whispered as her arms tightened around me. "Sorry we didn't keep you safe. Sorry we couldn't get to you faster and keep you from this pain."

"It's not your fault. You have always been there for me." I pulled back, cupping her face in my hands and pressing a kiss to her forehead. "Thank you."

"Of course. We would all wade through blood and fire for you."

Coming from anyone else, that could have been dismissed as bravado. But from my maid the declaration simply rang pure, echoing

Mia's earlier words. I didn't know why it didn't scare me, but the voices in my head were silent for now and I would take what stillness I could get.

"You brought me tea." Tears filled my eyes a second time; Stasia's answering smile was kind.

"I talked Hao into getting some for when we found you because I knew you'd be missing it."

"Thank you." I took the steaming cup from her and something broke, or healed, inside me. The pain had blurred together so long ago I couldn't tell the difference. I clapped my free hand to my mouth, not quite stopping the sob that broke the air and nearly spilled the tea all over both of us.

I fumbled to set the cup down on the nearby table, and it rattled against the surface before Emmory reached down to still it, taking me by the arm with his other hand.

"I'm okay."

Stasia sniffed away her tears. "Do you need anything else, ma'am?"

"One more hug," I said, tucking her against my side for a moment before I let her go. I picked up the mug, closed my eyes and inhaled, letting the pepper and star anise sink into my lungs before I took a sip.

Little did Stasia know that the chai would have been a perfect proof all on its own. There was no one else who could make it this way, just the right side of sharp spice and hot enough to burn an unwary tongue.

When I opened my eyes, Emmory was watching me. "Better, Majesty?"

"Momentarily." I mustered up a smile he didn't answer. "What is it?"

"How?"

"You're going to have to be a little more specific."

"You treat them like friends." He hesitated, closing his eyes for just a moment. "Johar showed me what Aiz did, Hail—"

"Oh, I wish she hadn't done that." I didn't consider that Jo would have logged some of the fights she watched, but I should have. "What *I* chose, Emmory, not what Aiz did." I rose to my feet, cup in hand, and turned my back on him so I couldn't see the expected flinch. "I chose this. Stop trying to make Aiz the villain."

"He beat you to death."

Well. There was that.

There was a wealth of violence in Emmory's voice, and for a shameful moment that thing squatting in my chest came to life, snapping and snarling with a dreadful desire to answer his violence with my own.

"I *chose* this!" I kept my hands wrapped around the cup and tried to steady my voice. "I understand your need to protect me. But this was my choice." I put my cup down, fisted a hand, and hit myself in the chest hard enough to bruise as I turned to him. "Please don't take this away from me."

"All right." Emmory held up a hand in surrender. "I don't—Hail, I get it. I don't like it, but I hear what you're saying. Now I need you to listen to what I'm saying; all of us who love you know what happened, and every single one of us from Hao to me and down the chain to Stasia wants revenge on Aiz." He pointed at the open doorway. "And on Mia. Choices aside. They hurt you. It would take a thousand years to see vengeance served. A truce with them is even more ambitious than peace between the Farians and the Shen."

The fight drained out of me, chased away by the love that clung to every word Emmory had just uttered.

"I'm sorry," I whispered, my words choked with tears, and sank back into my seat.

I'd been so lost in my own misery I hadn't stopped to think for a moment that those who loved me were also fighting their way back to what we'd had before.

It was a long road ahead for all of us.

"Don't apologize." Emmory went to a knee at my side, his gloved hand resting lightly on the back of my head. "I understand. I really do. I just needed you to see the other side, too. We will follow you through blood and fire but not without question or hesitation, Hail, because looking after you is what we are supposed to do. We need you to trust in us."

I grabbed for his other hand. "I hate that I am terrified of losing you all over again, and that is the only part of this I would change. Nothing else—not the fights with Aiz, not my time with Mia—none of it broke me. You all being dead broke me, and I don't know if I'll ever recover from it."

He pulled me into a hug, cradling my head like a child's as I clung to him.

"I missed you, Emmy. Every Shiva-damned day."

"I know." He released me and sat down, bracing his forearms on his knees. "Tell me what happened."

I took a deep breath and told him everything.

25

The rest of my people filtered by in the following days, offering unprompted assurances of their validity in a way that I neither asked for nor deserved. Alba was easier than expected, but we'd had so many quiet moments together before Earth and I desperately wanted her to be real.

Dailun handed me back kindness I had shown to him with a tenderness that I didn't deserve. Kisah reminded me of the space I'd given her to grieve for Willimet's death while on Hao's ship. It was a moment shared between the two of us during that desperate flight from Red Cliff.

Iza and Indula came to me with their fingers linked. "Family, ma'am," Indula said with tears in his pale blue eyes. "Found is just as blessed by the gods as those who share blood. You gave me a little sister."

"You gave me an older brother." Iza reached a hand out to me and I took it. "Please, for Shiva's sake take him back."

My laughter dissolved into a second round of tears and I pulled them both into a hug as the memory of a rainy afternoon at the beach overflowed and wrapped around my heart.

Johar, of course, picked the most obnoxious way to verify herself short of punching me in the face. "Am I interrupting?" she asked, poking her head into the ready room later that afternoon when I was talking with Emmory, Zin, and Hao about Shen fleet locations.

"No," I said, pleased that I not only didn't flinch, but I didn't have to look across the room at Hao for reassurance. Plus Emmory and Zin were by the door and Jo wasn't visibly armed as she strolled into the room.

"You need to know I'm me, right?" She smiled and spread her hands wide. "That's an easy thing to prove. Though I'm certain you'd rather I not say this out loud for everyone to hear—" Johar leaned in when I raised an eyebrow at her, still grinning, and whispered in my ear, "You make the cutest noise when you—"

"Uff!" I slapped a hand over her mouth before she could finish the sentence, even though I was reasonably sure no one else had heard her.

Hao laughed out loud. Emmory raised an eyebrow and I closed my eyes as embarrassment and amusement went to war in my head. "You are awful," I declared, finally opening my eyes again and letting her go.

Jo grinned. "I think I won that contest."

"It wasn't a contest."

"You know it's me, though, right?" Her amusement fled, and she slipped her hand around the back of my neck, pulling me in until our foreheads touched.

"I do." I blinked back the tears. "Thank you for always looking out for me. Especially there."

"It's what I'm here for, though holy shit you owe me for being stuck on that damn planet for six months. Don't scare me like that again, okay?" She released me with a smile.

"I promise." Clearing my throat, I looked at the three men, who were all grinning.

"Not a word, *Ekam*."

"I wouldn't dream of it, Majesty."

"Emmory. Jagana? Riddhi and Sahil?" I hadn't seen the newer guards, and the fear of the answer had kept the question in place for the better part of a day.

"They are fine. I had them wait for Captain Saito to pass along what little information we had. Sahil had a minor injury from the explosion but the other two were uninjured. Everyone, in fact, survived the explosion of the embassy, even Ambassador Zellin and all her staff."

"Everyone?"

Emmory smiled. "As improbable as it sounds, yes. Fasé got us all out in time."

"Good." I lapsed back into silence for a moment, the relief overwhelming. "I was afraid—well, you know."

"I do. Are you going to talk about it?"

"I don't know." I squeezed my hands into fists. I'd fixed my fingers, telling myself that the injuries were good practice, knowing somewhere deep down that was at least partially a lie. "What else is there to say?"

We sped through the black, Aiz's escort of ships around us, and as the hours rolled by things settled into a new normality. Still, there was a rhythm to the ship, and to my people, and I was out of sync. It was as painful as a heart beating at the wrong moment, slamming up against bruised ribs with a desperate force.

I missed fighting. The sudden absence of the pain and the adrenaline rush that had been an almost daily part of my life for six months was a sharp needle in my brain, distracting me from my attempts to catch up on everything I'd missed while on Sparkos.

The worst part of it was I couldn't confide in anyone. I knew how bad it sounded—to want to feel that connection of fist to flesh—and I didn't have the words to translate it into something that sounded less masochistic than it was.

The knife I'd sweet-talked from Johar was heavy in my pocket. It would be quiet but messy to cut myself open. Still, part of me wanted to head for the privacy of the bathroom so I could do it. That pain grounded me. Brought me back to reality when the world started to spin out of control. And it was far easier to access than the pain I could get from fighting.

"Majesty, Empress Alice—"

"Not going to talk to her."

Emmory gave me the Look. "Received a message from the Farians. They heard about your rescue, not a surprise given we didn't try to keep it quiet. But now they're insisting on speaking with you."

I wanted to talk with Adora even less than I wanted to talk to Alice, but I blew out a breath, sat back down, and made my reply as diplomatic as possible. "Tell Alice she's the empress and she doesn't have to do a Shiva-damned thing for the Farians."

"We are still technically allied with the Farians, Majesty," Zin said from the other side of the door. "And until we have some actual proof that they were involved in anything that happened on Earth, that's not going to change."

"We could go to Faria and I could beat a confession out of Adora. Before or after the fight with the gods, I'm good either way."

"You want to talk about this?" Emmory asked, settling a hip on the desk near me.

"Talk about what?"

"This 'I'm spoiling for a fight' attitude."

"Not particularly," I replied.

"Hail." Emmory shared a look with Zin. "You don't have to fight anyone."

I hummed the denial in my throat and forced a smile at my Trackers, standing so solemn and concerned in front of me. "The future says otherwise, and even if I did want to talk this out we saw how that went down on Earth." I waved a hand in the air. "Anyhow, we just had this conversation, Emmory, and I thought we resolved it."

"I told you we would question it." He sighed and headed for the door.

"Every step of the way?"

"Right up until you are set to face these gods if it means I might save your life," he replied, and he and Zin left me alone.

I was left staring at the door, the words hitting me like a ship dropping out of atmo. Scarcely a heartbeat later Mia came through.

"Are you all right?" She gestured behind her. "I saw Emmory in the hallway and he suggested I speak to you."

That was interesting. Emmory seemed fine with allowing Mia to wander without a guard, and she now had access to the coms so she could speak with Aiz. But for him to actually suggest she speak to me and let her do it in private? That was a new leap of faith for him.

"Fine," I said automatically. "My *Ekam* thinks I'm trying to kill myself."

"You disagree?" She perched against the very spot Emmory had vacated and tucked a strand of hair behind her ear.

"I don't have a death wish, if that's what you're asking." I pushed out of my chair with a hiss of annoyance. "I'm just prepared to do whatever necessary."

"Does breaking your own fingers and cutting yourself fall under what's necessary?"

The question stopped me in my tracks, and I muttered a particularly vicious curse under my breath. "Yes," I said finally, not turning around to look at Mia. "It keeps me here. Reminds me this is real."

Reminds me everything I feared could happen again if I let my guard down.

"Oh, Hail, are you still afraid this is all a trick?"

"Wouldn't you be?" As badly as I wanted to reach into my pocket for the knife there, I knew if I came out of this room with blood on me Mia would be the one who paid the price.

"Possibly." She moved with that lightning-fast speed again, closing her hand over mine before I could yank my finger back. "No. Just stay here, Hail, sit with the pain instead of trying to distract yourself."

I don't want to hovered on my lips, but I caught the words at the last second, all too aware of how childish and petty they sounded.

"It hurts." That wasn't much better, but Mia smiled softly.

"I know. Just breathe, Hail."

Breathe. That I could do. In theory, anyway.

"What hurts?"

I squeezed my eyes shut. "Everything."

"Be more specific." There was kindness in her words, but it was bolstered by steel.

Pressing my free hand to my eyes as I sank into the chair, I whispered, "Fires of Naraka, I am not good enough for this. You deserve better. My people deserve better. The whole buggered galaxy deserves better than me. I'm just a gunrunner, Mia. A princess who ran away from home, from all her responsibilities, and ended up with a throne because she was all they had left—"

"Stop."

I was reasonably sure Mia could get anyone to obey her when she used that commanding voice.

"You have led your people and your empire through fire, Hail. Look at me."

I dropped my hand and opened my eyes, but I couldn't keep my gaze on Mia's for long without drowning in those gray depths. Instead I fixed my eyes on the wall behind her head, and after a moment she sighed and continued.

"The deaths hurt, they always do. And I would think so much less of you than I do now if you were able to brush that off and keep going without the least bit of remorse. We can't lead with the fear of those we'll lose at the forefront of our minds, Hail. You are living through what that does to you.

"If the light comes, we will all have to fight and you will have to say good-bye to people you love." She stopped, swallowed, and continued. "What hurts?"

"They think I am throwing my life away. Emmory and the

others, I can—" I shook my head and pulled away from her hands. "I can see the concern in their eyes and I know why they feel that way."

"Do you really?" Mia tilted her head to study me. "They love you, Hail."

"They shouldn't." And that, I realized suddenly, was what hurt. Pressing a fist to my heart, I stared at her. It was all too easy to call up the looks from everyone in my mind. All too easy to see the faces of those who'd already given their lives for me. "Oh Shiva, they shouldn't love me. They shouldn't put themselves at risk for me. I have done nothing to deserve this devotion."

"Love isn't about what we deserve," Mia said, kneeling by my side and putting a hand over my fist. "Your people love you because of who you are. All of it, not just the good."

I wasn't sure I believed her, but then, I loved Hao—didn't I? Hadn't I forgiven him for his fuckups, his betrayal? Hadn't I known, somehow, from the very first moment that he was holding a piece of me in his hands? The same thing was true of Gita, of Emmory and Zin and all the others. I loved Johar without hesitation and yet I didn't think I was worthy?

"There it is," Mia said with a smile, squeezing my hand once before letting me go and getting to her feet. "That's better, isn't it?"

"How do you do that?" I blinked up at her, unclenching my fist and rubbing at the space above my heart.

"We cannot turn away from the love in our hearts, Hail. No matter the fire burning around us and the anger clamoring for attention. If we give in to that, if we turn our backs on the love? Everything we are dies."

"Mia, I can't fight and keep this." The confession came out in a whisper, and for a moment I thought she hadn't heard me.

She stopped by the door, her back to me as she replied. "You can. I've seen you do it." She tapped the panel by the door and slipped through the opening, leaving me alone in the room.

26

The ping of the incoming call on my *smati* the next morning startled me so much that I answered it without thinking and then blinked when Alice's face appeared on the wall of my room.

"You hang up on me, Hail, and I will fly across the galaxy to kick your ass myself."

I blinked again at the unexpected threat, but the tears that appeared in Alice's eyes stilled any response I could have come up with.

"I was so afraid," she whispered. "Not about all this here at home. Though I should have known something like this would happen with your Shiva-damned luck. I was so afraid for you."

"I'm sorry."

"Why are you apologizing? For trying to ignore me?" She smiled. "I'll accept it, then, but you didn't really think that was going to work, did you? You taught me how not to take no for an answer. Then you up and made me empress." She shook her head. "Which, by the way, I'm signing documents today to put that crown right back on your head."

"Alice—"

"You don't get to argue with me, Hail. I'm empress, remember?" Her smile softened. "At least for another hour. I wish I could hug you. Caspel passed on Emmory's report about what happened. I know I don't fully understand, I'm not sure any of us could, but I'm here for you."

I glanced away from the wall as Emmory came into the room. He spotted Alice, raised an eyebrow at me, and then did a half-assed job muffling a smile when I shrugged helplessly.

"Good morning, Emmory," Alice said. "I hope you don't mind I took matters into my own hands here."

"You are allowed to do that as empress, I'm told," he replied.

"I was just telling Hail that. Also, that I'm only empress for the next fifty-seven Indranan minutes, so you'll want to be prepared." She smiled. "What's the plan after that, Hail?"

"You're not going to like it," I said, finally finding my voice.

"That's entirely possible," Alice replied, surprising me again. "But you're in charge and I trust you to do what's right for the empire."

"Even if that means putting our alliance with Faria at risk?"

Alice didn't even flinch. "Even then. The Farians were less than helpful after your disappearance, Hail." She took a deep breath. "You know we can't afford to go to war, but that doesn't mean we should continue to roll over for the Farians, and I know all too well about the fracture between Fasé's group and the Pedalion. Faria is no longer unified in word or deed."

I remembered seeing a report from Caspel about a rise in support for Fasé since Earth. "The increase in support for Fasé has grown, hasn't it?"

"Yes. They've been more vocal and their numbers are increasing both here and back on Faria from what I've been told. Caspel has, unofficially, reached out to them with Fasé's permission. There have been some clashes between—I don't even know what we should call them. Regular Farians? Pedalion supporters?"

"I would lean toward the second one myself," I admitted, and she smiled.

"There have been clashes. We've managed them as best as we can. Thankfully no one on Faria has demanded we turn over any of Fasé's supporters. I think it's because they've been far too distracted by what happened to you." Alice's laugh was strained. "That and the fact that all the Shen and Farian forces seem to have pulled out of the human sectors is the only good news we've had lately. Besides your return, that is."

I felt a little burst of relief that my insistence back on Sparkos had resulted in tangible results. "So no more fighting?"

"Not near any human targets, and as far as I can tell the mercenaries are minding their own business."

"You're welcome." I laughed at the look Alice gave me.

"I should have known you'd have something to do with it."

"I convinced Mia and Aiz that pulling back here was a better plan of action since it seemed clear the Farians were trying to provoke the rest of us into going to war with the Shen by deliberately causing human casualties."

"I shouldn't be surprised," Alice replied with a shake of her head. "Adora wanted us to declare war on the Shen after you were taken. I told her no and also that her time would be better spent looking for you rather than trying to tell me how to run my empire."

I didn't bother to hide the grin that spread over my face at the thought of how frustrated Adora must be right now with Alice, who'd defied her wishes not once but twice. Then I sobered. I was going to have to get my thoughts in order on this whole situation and fast.

"Alice, if Adora coms you again, tell her I am safe and will speak with her about resuming the negotiations as soon as possible."

"You're, but I thought—" She fumbled. "Emmory said you were going to Faria to fight gods."

"Not if I can help it," I said. "Yes, we're going to Faria. But to resume the negotiations, I'm just planning on bypassing the Pedalion entirely. Though obviously Adora doesn't need to know that. These gods of theirs are the ones in charge and they are the ones I need to speak with." I lifted a shoulder in a gesture that looked more nonchalant than it truly was. "If they won't listen to me, well that's a whole other bridge to cross."

Alice nodded. "Very well, Majesty. I will continue to handle things here and I wish you all the blessings of the gods in this task."

I accepted the formality and the blessing with a nod of my own. "I'll speak to you again soon. Thank you, Alice." I looked to Emmory after I ended the call. "What's that look for?"

"No concern?"

"For what? Oh." I glanced back at the wall and shrugged. "That she's not who she says she is?" I shook my head. "Alice didn't die, unless I missed some catastrophic event on Pashati while I was gone, and the feed code was real."

"Ah." He smiled. "How are you?"

"I had a breakdown about the shower this morning. So, back to normal?"

"You're being very honest with me about all this, Majesty."

"It seems like a good idea?" I replied, reaching for my now cold chai.

"It makes me wonder what you're not sharing."

"Ouch." I held his gaze over the rim of the cup. "I'm reasonably sure you don't want a running tally of my thoughts, *Ekam*. That wouldn't do either of us much good."

"Fair enough. Do you want me to tell the others about you resuming the throne or would you rather do it?"

"I'll do it. We should probably all be on the same page as to what the plan is before we meet up with Aiz tomorrow."

"What is the plan?"

"Convince Aiz to come with us to Faria. Somehow get in to see these so-called gods and negotiate some kind of peace between three warring factions of aliens?"

"And the bit about what's coming if you and Aiz don't kill these gods?"

"I don't know." I made a face. "In all honesty I think it's going to end up in a fight no matter what I try, Emmy. In which case the plan is kill the gods, which should stop the bad things from killing us all."

Emmory gave me the Look. "I was hoping for a little more detail."

"I have had little time to plan." I lifted my shoulders. "I don't think convincing Aiz of the first part of my plan will be that hard, but deciding who's going to be in charge will. I'll probably have to fight him to get him to come with us. And I don't know if I can beat him."

I don't want you to watch me fight.

Those words hovered in my throat and I looked away from Emmory, sliding my hand free of his grip to wrap my arms around my waist.

"I could just shoot him."

The suggestion was so very like Emmory, and the laugh that erupted out of my throat startled us both.

"I'm not going to lie," I managed, still laughing. "The look on his face would be priceless. But, no, as tempting as that is, it wouldn't solve anything. This is a fight for dominance and you can't interfere. I have to be the one to fight and to win. Two rival crews trying to work a job together. The politics of that—"

"Get messy. We interrupting?" Hao asked from the doorway.

Emmory got to his feet. "No. Just talking. I'm going to go find Zin. Start thinking of an actual plan, Majesty. We need one."

"I don't want any complaints then if the plan turns out something like Canafey."

Emmory chuckled on his way out the door but didn't reply. I smiled at his retreating back before turning my gaze to the trio who'd come in the room.

Alba smiled and I took the hand she offered between mine. "How are you?"

"I'm all right." It was startling to realize it was mostly true despite my rough start this morning. I felt somewhat settled for the first time since we'd left Sparkos.

"Jiejie." Dailun pressed his cheek to mine for a brief moment.

Hao closed a hand around my arm, landing right on the spot

where I'd drawn three precise lines with the tip of a knife just after my shower, and I swallowed down the gasp of pain that almost escaped.

"What are you three up to?" I asked, deftly slipping out of Hao's grasp and using Dailun as a shield against the pain that had to be crawling across my expression.

"Came by to say hi," Hao said, dropping into a chair. "And to let you know Gita and I finally tracked down where that money originated. We found the skip, and the false back-dated entries to make it look as though the money was all coming from the same place. I can't believe I missed it the first time."

"We all saw what we wanted to see. Well?" I prompted when he didn't say anything more.

"We traced it through half a dozen ghost companies; whoever was trying to make it look like the Shen were paying him did a really good job. But the original source was a Farian tech company based in the Solarian Conglomerate, ironically named Star Optics. Their headquarters are actually on Earth."

I muttered several curses in Cheng, stopping only when Hao lifted a hand.

"You want to know my theory?" At my nod, Hao continued. "Someone, Adora let's say, thought that they could get out of the negotiations if they hired someone to disrupt things. All the big players are off the table—you and me obviously."

I grinned at him.

"Rai, Po-Sin, the Barton boys, Lacy and O'Brien and more than a dozen of the smaller outfits got swept up in this Shen payday. But you know who didn't get an offer?"

"Jamison," I murmured. "Mia said it was because I didn't like him. She was building a crew of mercs who'd work with me in charge."

"She knew her shit, I'll give her that much. With the exception of Po-Sin but that's only because of, you know." He waved a hand.

"Anyway, the pool of contenders was not the cleanest, and on top of that the Farians were pretending the payment was for coming after my ass, which further wiped out some of the options."

"So they fucking hired him because he was basically the only one left?" I laughed. "Oh, he's going to be pissed for all of two seconds when I tell him that."

"Only two seconds?" Alba asked.

"He'll be dead after that," Hao replied. "So the Farians hired Jamison, not having any clue about the history there or his impressive way of turning the simplest job into a violent clusterfuck, and it unsurprisingly blew up in their faces. Fucking amateurs."

"That makes a terrifying amount of sense," I said. "We don't have any proof of it, though?"

"Beyond the money coming from a Farian company? No." Hao shook his head. "So it's a wash as far as leverage goes, but it at least clears up the mystery. You could always ask Adora about Star Optics when you see her. She doesn't have a great poker face."

"No, she does not." I filed the information away for later use. One more check mark against the Farians, one more for Jamison—though his fate was already sealed.

"You okay?" Hao asked.

"I'm fine. Why?"

"You seem a little more bloodthirsty than normal."

"It's been a long six months." I met his golden gaze calmly. "It never used to bother you."

"You'd be surprised, but back then you had Portis to keep you level so I didn't worry much." He studied me, frowning at whatever he saw on my face. "Are you going to declare war on Rai, Hail?"

"I might." My smile had no warmth. "I suppose if the universe burns I won't need to bother with it."

"He wasn't responsible for what happened."

"He could have taken us to safety. Instead he took us prisoner.

225

Are you defending him?" My voice rose and the quiet conversation between Alba and Dailun across the room cut off. I muttered a curse. "He helped the Shen kidnap me."

"I know and believe me I had some words with him about that. You've forgiven the Shen for that easily enough. I'm just wondering why Rai's not getting the same consideration," Hao replied. "To be fair, Mia's a whole lot prettier than Rai, but don't tell him I said that."

I gaped at him. "You are the worst."

"You love me." He stretched in his chair. "These two have something for you."

"Dailun more than me, Majesty," Alba said with a smile.

I looked between them and waved a hand. Dailun sat on the edge of the bed at my gesture, elbows braced on his knees and his fingers linked loosely together. There was a solemnness about the pink-haired pilot I'd never seen before. "I have been studying the future Mia showed you," he said, staring at the floor. He was choosing his words with care. "My honored cousin came to me after you showed him. We have spoken a lot about my people and he saw something that he thought was familiar to my people's memory."

Dailun's father was Cheng, but his mother had been Svatir. The Svatir were as alien as they came. A reclusive race who only ever interacted with humans during their Travelings. They had a collective memory, all the experiences of their people shared among them. I couldn't even begin to fathom how jumbled and chaotic that must be, but Dailun didn't seem bothered by it, even though he was half human.

"I didn't realize that was something that could be shared with non-Svatir?"

"It is complicated," Dailun said. "Since Hao and I are related he has a right to certain family memories." He gave me a look, eyes chased with silver lights, and then smiled boyishly. "I may have bent the rules somewhat, but I was young and Hao is the closest thing to a father I have."

It was obvious from Hao's reaction that Dailun hadn't ever said that out loud in his hearing. My brother sat up in the chair with a shocked look racing across his face.

"Vybiramai srdce kterah vybiramai," I murmured, and watched the lights flare in Dailun's eyes.

"Yes, precisely. Where did you hear that, *jiejie*?"

27

A story for another time," I said. "But it had to do with him, too." I pointed at Hao.

"Is someone going to tell me what that means?" he asked.

"No," I replied after a shared smile with Dailun.

"I am sorry it took me so long to find what I was looking for." Dailun lifted a hand and I realized how weary he sounded. "I had to go far back in our memory to find what I sought. It is an exhausting process."

"I'll bet. So what did Hao see that triggered this?"

"Those creatures you saw in the future. They are known to the Svatir. We call them the *hiervet sveta* in our language."

"Monsters of light?"

Dailun nodded at my translation but still didn't look at me. "We were not always pacifists, sister. Long ago we fought among ourselves as much as humans do now. We gloried in it. Developed newer and more awesome ways to send someone to their dreams. We were very, very good at war."

I glanced Hao's way and he gave the slightest nod of confirmation. What was interesting was Alba had also nodded, and I raised a curious eyebrow.

"I had a Svatir nanny as a child, Majesty. She went to her dreaming while she was with us, and her family came to thank us for the memories." Alba looked at Dailun with a soft smile that had my eyebrow lifting a little higher.

"It was a distant branch of my family," he said. "But it was a delight to realize who Alba was when we met on the ship."

"And you didn't tell anyone?"

"Emmory knew," Alba replied.

"Emmory knows everything." I sighed.

"I don't know that I'd go that far, Majesty."

I looked at my *Ekam* in the doorway, Zin just behind him, and waved a hand. "Come in. Dailun was about to tell me something important, I think, but we got sidetracked." I waited a beat. "So these monsters of light that we all saw in Mia's future. You know them."

"The Hiervet came from outside the disc. They looked like us, only better." A bitter smile curved Dailun's lips up. "By design, no doubt. They can shift their appearance much like the Shen and Farians can."

"Oh, that's lovely," I murmured.

"They taught us a different way to live; a better way, they said. It was only later that we realized the cost of their lessons. We were nearly enslaved, would have been ground under the Hiervet's bootheels had the braver among us not risen up to fight."

"You defeated them?"

Dailun smiled again, this time turning his head to look at me. "We were well versed in war, sister, with generations of memory at our backs. We drove them out of the disc. It cost us so much. Generations gone. So many sent to their dreaming early. So much potential lost. We returned home, and those who had led the rebellion announced they would fight no longer. That less violence, not more, was always an option. They spent their lives seeding peace among our people and we were all so grateful for their sacrifices, so weary from the battle, that we agreed to lay down our arms and never raise them again."

"That's why the Svatir are pacifists?" I asked.

"It is, and though I have sent word home warning them of this future you saw, I do not think it will change anything for the Svatir." Dailun shook his head. "We will not fight again, Hail, not even for the Star of Indrana."

"They may not have a choice."

This time it was Fasé in the doorway, Mia and Sybil behind her.

"We're throwing a party, I suppose," I said, and Fasé's mouth twitched as she suppressed a smile. "Come on in, find a seat somewhere." I got up as the others shuffled around for available seats, and leaned against the wall by the door, giving a quick recap of what Dailun had just told us.

Sybil seemed unsurprised by the news from Dailun. "I remember a similar story many years later when we first made contact with the Svatir." She nodded after a moment's thought. "We never investigated it further. It happened many years after your family was killed—after the incident."

Mia nodded. "Aiz told me of how the Shen met the Svatir shortly after we left Faria. I do recall something about it, though the ones we met were hesitant to go into much detail for some reason." She looked at me. "Now you see, Hail, why this mission is important not only to the Shen but to every living thing in this galaxy."

"Yeah." I ran my tongue over my teeth. I saw it. I didn't like it much, but I saw it coming like a charging Hagidon.

I'd never been to Nugwa XIII, and I'd only heard stories of the massive beasts. If you were in a vehicle it was a simple matter of outrunning the deadly bulk and sharp tusks. If you weren't, bravado was your only option because running would get you trampled.

Could I stand my ground? Not fight the gods and hope that the future we saw with the Hiervet coming was something we could still avoid?

Or was I fooling myself, and was fighting the only way through this mess?

"Hey." Mia snapped her fingers in front of my face and I jerked backward, hands flying up to defend myself. She blocked my strike, dancing out of reach with her own hands up. "We lost you there."

"I was thinking." Feeling foolish, I dropped my hands and tried to ignore the hammering of my heart as I lowered myself onto the edge of the desk.

"This news doesn't change anything," Mia said softly. She lowered her own hands with a smile. "The Farians are on friendly terms with the Svatir, but they've seen this light coming the same as we have."

"True." Sybil frowned. "Our foil for it has always been the Star."

I looked at her. "I can't believe you would put your very survival into the hands of one person. When you saw this, Indrana didn't exist. I didn't exist. Why?"

"It was the clearest, most consistent future," Sybil replied. "Things change over the years. Empires rise and fall. People die—both deliberately and accidentally. The future isn't static." She pinned me with a fierce look. "But this one, it has remained largely unchanged for all these years."

I swallowed, feeling the weight of it all in my chest. "You're not going to actually show it to me, though, are you?"

"You don't need to see it, Hail. You know what you need to do. You've always known." Sybil smiled. "I don't want you to get hung up on the future when it's the choices you make that matter."

"Now you sound like Fasé." I shared a look with Hao as I got back up to pace.

"She is right about some things," Sybil replied. "As is Mia. As are you." Her smile vanished. "I am not the linchpin here, Hail. You are."

Fasé, Mia . . . and me.

I stopped, looked across the room at Fasé and then to Mia.

"Oh." I breathed as it all suddenly made sense. I dragged a hand through my hair. "Mia. Fasé. Me. We're it." The pieces fit so neatly into place in my head. "Trust the heart of the star and the sides that will collapse without each other to lean on."

"Quoting prophecy now?" Hao raised an eyebrow.

"It's appropriate, given the direction we're headed in," Fasé said.

"Which is?" I asked.

"Disaster, probably. We shall see," Fasé replied, and Mia rolled her eyes.

"Fasé and I have come to an agreement, one I hope my brother will also find benefits us. Though I can make no promises, and if he decides it does not I will have to go with him."

"Why the change of heart?" Hao asked.

"Because Hail is right, there are the futures we see, which are shifting and changing with every choice that is made, and then there is the future Sybil saw, which stays more constant and immutable than anything in this universe." Fasé shook her head. "I was reminded I am young, as is Mia. But of the two of us she has more experience interpreting the things she has seen with a greater degree of accuracy."

Mia looked around the room. "We are the sides that will collapse— Farian, Shen, and human. We need each other. We need to find some way to work together. To find a way to trust that our common enemy is not each other, but the gods who stand in the way and bring the light down on us all."

I released the breath I'd been holding when Emmory finally nodded. "I'm not entirely convinced," he said. "But I'm willing to consider all the options because I trust her." He pointed at me. "And that future I saw is not going to happen. Not while I'm around to stop it."

"Same," Hao said. "Though I have a question first. Little sister, why did you make this choice?"

"The choice?" I frowned at him.

"Your choice." He glanced at Gita and then back at me. "You kept saying it, over and over, that it was your choice to do what the Shen asked of you. Why?"

"Why what?"

Hao smiled. "Why did you choose it?"

Mia's little gasp was loud in the quiet. Hao didn't look away from me but instead waited patiently for an answer.

I wrapped my arms around my waist and stared at him as responses crashed around my brain. Aiz's words from our very first fight came back to me.

"You are the person who will put herself between the chaos and all she loves. You will stand against the tide. Sacrifice everything to see the galaxy safe. You have always made that choice and you always will."

"I couldn't, *I can't* stand by and watch my people burn. I can't watch humanity burn. Not if there's a chance I can stop it."

Hao's smile rivaled the sun. "There's my little sister," he replied. "So fucking noble it's a wonder you survived as a gunrunner for as long as you did. You give so much more than the universe deserves. Than any of us deserve," he added quietly. "Sacrificing yourself to save the universe because you'd rather die than see the rest of us hurt.

"You made the choice. It wasn't the best of circumstances." He shot Mia a sharp-edged look as he got to his feet. "But you made it and I won't take it away from you by treating you like a victim." Hao shook his head. "But by that same token, little sister, you need to own your choice and use it. If you run from it, try to deny it, it will ruin you."

"Spoken like a man who's made that mistake."

"You know I have." Hao's grin was quick. "You also know that I won't stand in your way, but I'll be damned if I'm going to let you do this alone. You have that favor you wanted, all of it."

I took the hand he held out, squeezing it once before I released him.

"Same, Majesty," Gita said. "You're stuck with us on this and anything following. Empress or not, doesn't matter. You can't make us go."

I grabbed her by the back of the neck and pressed my forehead to hers as the tears I'd thought were dried up started fresh in my eyes.

I felt Hao's hand slide over my back and his cheek against the top of my head.

"Gita speaks for all of us," Emmory said as we separated. "We're in this to the end. Whatever happens."

I had to clear my throat of emotion before I could get the words out. "That's settled, then. We'll meet with Aiz and see what he says. How are you going to convince him?"

Mia shook her head. "I won't. You will."

I stared at her. "Me?"

"I understand him, of course; he's my brother." Mia glanced Emmory's way before stepping closer to me and putting a hand on my cheek. "But you speak to him in the only language he understands and one I no longer can find the voice for. He listens to you, Hail, even better he respects you. It may be that which saves us all in the end."

"Less than three standard days with those two and you're talking in riddles," I replied.

Mia's grin flashed like an orbital bombardment. "If I am committed to this fight, there are concessions to be made. This is one of them." She trailed her fingers along my cheek, just brushing my lips as she dropped her hand.

"I really hope that's not another one," I murmured, unable to stop myself.

"It's not, but I think later is probably better." She stepped away. "I'm testing your BodyGuards' patience as it is and things are still unbalanced."

"Mia, I'm still set on finding a way to end this without bloodshed."

"You are welcome to, Hail. That is the part that is uncertain."

I glanced past her, and the seer from the Council of Eyes lifted her hands from her lap. "She is right, Majesty. Mia is the only one who has seen a fight. The rest of us have seen nothing but blackness."

"Hai Ram." I rubbed a hand over my face. "Well, fine. It's still plan B, though, since there are no major objections about it."

"What's plan A, Hail?" Hao asked.

"It's not done yet. I do have the start of one, though."

"That makes me nervous," Hao replied, pointing a finger at me. "The Hail I know plans everything out. My job got far easier once I brought you on board because you were always four steps ahead of me in the strategy department."

"I thought you said I made your life harder?"

Hao snickered. "You did that, too. But my point is, this isn't like storming a station. Though I'll grant you Canafey was a bold move. If you get Aiz on your side—"

"When."

"When you get Aiz on your side." Hao gave me a look as he continued. "You know damn well you're not going to be sneaking onto Faria with him."

"Why not?"

"Because both of you operate better by kicking doors open and strolling in like you own the place."

Dailun's laugh spilled out into the open air and I couldn't stop myself from joining him. "You're not wrong," I managed, still laughing.

"You can't do it," Hao said, abruptly serious.

"I'm the Empress of Indrana," I countered, spreading my hands wide and bowing to him. "And a state visit to Faria is hardly kicking in a door, but it is loads better than trying to sneak in the back."

28

The meeting broke up and I stayed by the door as everyone filed out.

"We'll see you later." Dailun gave me a quick hug and stepped into the corridor.

"I would recommend, ma'am, coming at Aiz like a gunrunner rather than an empress," Alba said with a smile. She squeezed my upper arm and followed Dailun from the room.

I watched her go, her words tangling with Emmory's earlier offer, and snorted with laughter.

"You okay?"

I looked around; everyone else had left except for Hao, who'd gotten to his feet and joined me at the door. "I just figured something out about Aiz." I shook my head. "No, don't ask me, I'd rather hold on to it for the moment."

"Okay." He dragged the word out. "Can I ask you something else?"

"Sure."

"You want to tell me why you keep cutting on yourself and not healing it?"

The question was unexpected, throwing me off my easy stride across the room. "What?"

Hao smiled at my side, but his golden eyes were filled with sorrow. "You think I don't notice, Hail? The others might not. I can guarantee Emmory has no matter what masking program you've tagged onto your *smati* to try to hide the bios." He caught me by the arm again before I could dance away. "Don't you think about it," he said, holding up his other hand. "You hit me, and we rumble here. We're not supposed to fight you, but I'll do it. Emmory will probably shock my ass, too, and I'm not in the mood."

It was tempting to take a swing anyway, but I forced myself to drop my arm and unclench my fist. Hao tugged my sleeve up, revealing the narrow lines of cuts running up my forearm.

"Little sister," he murmured. "Why?"

"You all died."

Hao closed his eyes for a moment and then opened them again. They were filled with tears so that the gold shimmered like the sunrise over the waters of Balhim Bay. "No, we didn't."

"Part of me still swears you did. That none of this is real. I'm trying, I really am, but this—" I pulled my arm out of his grip and waved it in his face. "This keeps me here, where all of you are alive. There's so much I have to do. Everyone is depending on me to hold it together. It's a small price to pay, and less than I deserve."

"It's not." Hao sighed, looking up at the ceiling. "Not on either count. You're breaking my heart, little sister. If anyone in this universe has earned a lifetime respite from pain, it's you."

I leaned in, pressing my forehead to his. "I love you, *gege*. I don't believe the universe gives a shit about me, but I am grateful you still do."

"Until the heat death of the universe, Hail." Hao smiled. Then he smacked me in the back of the head. "Stop hurting yourself, little sister. That's an order."

"You're not my captain anymore." Even as I protested, I knew it didn't matter. Hao was, and would always be, someone I could put my trust in and whose orders I would consider.

He shrugged. "And you're the Empress of Indrana. Some things change, some things don't."

"I will try." I had to force the words out, but once they were in the air part of the weight holding me down seemed to vanish, and Hao nodded once in approval before he turned and left me alone.

I only hoped I could live up to his expectations.

"Hail, you got a minute?" Johar had her hands in the pockets of her black pants as she sauntered down the corridor toward me with Gita at her side. Her black tank top made her tattoos stand out in even sharper relief against her pale skin.

I paused in the corridor. It was late evening and Mia's words had been rolling in my head all day. "Sure, I'm headed to the gym. Walk with me," I said, and the pair fell into step easily.

Johar was uncharacteristically quiet as we headed through the ship, but I didn't push her. Jo didn't like wasted words. Whatever she needed to say to me could wait until she had the words right. And Gita seemed content to walk along with us without saying anything.

"It's no secret we're all a bit worried about you, yeah?"

I chuckled and scratched at my cheek. "You two draw the short straw?" At her blank look, I continued. "Emmory said he was going to keep trying to talk me out of this right up to the end. I didn't think he meant he'd get everyone else to do it, too."

"Oh. No, just me." Jo shook her head. "I'm actually not here to talk you out of it."

"Me either," Gita said.

I stopped outside the gym and studied the pair. "I'd ask if you want to spar, but I don't know how to dial it down—"

Jo shook her head again with a laugh. "Naw, I'm good. I like my spine where it is."

"Did Emmory really tell everyone not to spar with me?"

Johar shrugged. "Mia told him it would end badly. His concerns about her aside, he's not an idiot. He saw the vids. Standing order is for us to say no to you. But I'll run you through some paces if you want."

"Sure." I hadn't had a plan when I headed out of my room other than to work off some of this restlessness rolling around in my gut and to try to make some sense of the tangled path in front of me. I pressed a hand to the panel. "So you're not trying to stop me from fighting gods?"

"I would really prefer you didn't, Majesty," Gita said. "But we all know you'll do what you want."

"Does it help that I would prefer not to? Prophecy or no, the idea of going up against something that is potentially so far above my level no matter what Aiz thinks we're capable of is frankly a little terrifying."

"Eh, prophecies." Jo pulled a hand free from her pocket and wiggled it. "I confess I'm not a hundred percent convinced that's happening, but you are going to have to fight Aiz—and you're going to have to beat him."

"Is that so?"

"You know it is." Jo tilted her head. "It's the only thing the Shen respond to and him especially. You can't talk your way in charge. You have to show them you're worthy of leading. I want to help."

"I very much doubt he'll let you fight with me." My gut twisted a little at the thought of Jo trying to go up against Aiz—even though she probably had better odds than anyone else, he'd kill her in an instant.

"Dear sweet crispy noodles, no." Jo laughed. "I don't want to fight him. Dying isn't my idea of a good way to pass an afternoon, and even though we're apparently at 'bring people back from the dead like it's a normal Tuesday' level? I don't know what that'll do to my extra bits." She made a sweeping gesture at herself. "And I like them, so no, for once no fighting for me. But I can help you see what you need to do to beat him, and potentially others if it comes to that."

I didn't tell them that I had a plan for beating Aiz; I'd discussed it with Emmory and he agreed that the fewer people who knew about it the better.

However, Jo had forgotten more about fighting than most people I knew, so it was worth it to listen and take whatever advice she was willing to give.

"So, this prophecy thing," Johar said carefully as I pulled off my jacket and tossed it to the side. "Do you actually believe it, or are you just going along with it because you don't see any way out?"

I stutter-stepped on my way to the corner and didn't answer her until after I'd finished stretching and cued up the heavy bag. I normally hated these illusions, but the one benefit they had was I could destroy them repeatedly and a new one would always take its place.

I threw a few punches at the bag, feeling the impact rock up my arms, before I answered Johar. "I don't know. I hate that I keep saying that and I hate that it's the truth. My life used to be simpler, Jo, and some days I really miss it."

"Tell me about it." She laughed and even though it wasn't necessary moved around to brace the hologram of the punching bag so she could look at me.

I ran through a routine pulled off my *smati*, no thoughts, just throwing punches as the instructions came up. Jo stayed silent until I paused to drag in a breath, taking the water Gita handed me with a nod of gratitude.

"Tell me something, if I came to you before all this and said I had a job for us. If I gave you the details as I believed them, but warned you there was going to be a certain margin for error—would you take the job?"

"You know I would," I replied without hesitation.

"Why?"

"Because I know you. I trust you."

"Why?" Johar spread her hands with a grin. "I'm a scoundrel. We all know it."

"Because I know you," I replied, more than a little confused by where this was going. "We've worked jobs together, we've—"

"You trusted me the moment you met me." Johar cut me off and shook her head. "Sized me up in an instant. I saw the wheels in her head turning," she said to Gita, who was watching the conversation with her head tilted curiously to the side. "And just like that, this green-haired titan decided the suspicious-looking man across from her was worth trusting. No questions asked."

I blinked at her, my brain crawling back through memories to find the truth of what she said. "Jo, what's your point?"

"You read people, Hail," she replied. "It's what you do and you're damn good at it. I'm not saying you're infallible, because no one is, but you've been right more than you've been wrong about who you can trust."

"Okay."

"Why do you trust Mia?"

I froze. Fires of Naraka, that was a question. I flicked my eyes to Gita, but her face remained expressionless. Whatever her feelings on the matter, my *Dve* wasn't about to let me see them.

"Give me a minute," I said, and turned back to the bag.

I laid into the bag as I untangled my feelings. Despite Hao's commentary earlier about being obsessed with Mia, I knew that wasn't the case. I was attracted to her, but that wasn't why I trusted her.

Was it truly that simple? That I trusted her because I knew in my gut I could? That I could recognize the echoes of myself there—her dedication to her people, her loyalty, even ironically her honesty?

I thought of Fasé, who I'd trusted the same way when I'd agreed to let her touch me that very first meeting. It had been different, a shift from mistrust to trust borne of the circumstances we'd been in, but in many ways it was the same as with any of the people around me.

I trusted them initially because my gut had told me I could.

I leaned my forehead on the bag, the energy of the hologram

pulsing against my skin before I pushed away and wiped the sweat from my eyes with my forearm. "My gut, Jo."

She smiled, not the least bit surprised by my answer.

"Did you have some input on this?" I asked Gita.

Gita looked at Johar. "I think she actually brought me with her to teach me a lesson."

"Hey, your job is to keep her safe and you're damn good at it. Don't argue with me." Johar held up a finger and Gita closed her mouth on whatever protest had been forming. "You're supposed to be suspicious of people like Mia and Aiz. Especially when they've proven to you they're willing to hurt her to get what they want."

"I'm not a hundred percent clear on what this has to do with the prophecy," I admitted.

"Right now your gut is saying what needs to happen is talking, not fighting. Even though that's in some pretty direct opposition to the future everyone's seen, right?"

"They said the fight will happen regardless."

"You don't believe that," she replied with a grin, and reached out to poke me in the stomach. "Because your gut says otherwise. But if you need harder evidence than that, you know the real problem— the conflict between the Shen and the Farians—isn't prophecy. It's happening, right now, and we need to put a stop to it. As much as we'd all like to wade in there and knock heads together, we know that won't fix anything. You're focusing on the negotiations, just like you should be."

"So you're telling me that the way to deal with this potentially galaxy-destroying problem is to just trust my gut?"

Johar shrugged. "Little bit, yeah."

"Shiva help us," Gita muttered, staring at the ceiling, and I laughed.

Encubier was desolate, a barren swath of red-brown rock with a barely breathable atmosphere. The hangar for the underground base was hidden within an outcropping of boulders that sloped up into an impressive mountain range.

I straightened my spine, ignoring the pressing feeling of the hangar and the rocks above my head as we came down the ramp of Fasé's stolen ship.

Aiz stood with a handful of his people behind him; all of them except for Aiz were armed. And tense, though I couldn't blame them for that given the circumstances.

"Mia, you are all right?" he asked in Shen as we approached.

I rolled my eyes and gently nudged her with a shoulder in his direction. "You think so little of me?" I countered. "I wouldn't have let any harm come to her."

"I trained you. I know you," he replied, wrapping his arms around his sister and pressing a kiss to her forehead. He murmured something too low for me to catch, and she answered him with a reassurance that made the tension in his shoulders vanish. Then he looked at me and continued in Indranan. "But it was your people I was more worried about. How are you, Star of Indrana?"

"Ready for a talk," I said, stopping a meter away from him with Emmory next to me. Like Aiz's people, he was armed, his Hessian 45 in a thigh holster instead of his usual shoulder one.

"So talk." He smiled.

"You know we need to be on the same side, but that means my people need to be with us also."

"We do." He nodded at me. "However, we're going to need a consensus on who's in charge."

"I would think you'd be used to the co-leadership thing." I shoved my hands into my pockets and scuffed the toe of my boot in the red dirt that had blown in through the hangar door.

This scene was so familiar from my gunrunning days: two groups with no reason to trust each other besides a common goal and the leaders of both trying to figure out how best to get the score and not die in the process. Only difference was I actually trusted Aiz a little more. I knew he wouldn't shoot me full of holes like the Bolthouse gang had.

"My sister is an exception and always will be. With you and me, we need a clear leader here." Aiz studied me for a long moment and I remained motionless under the scrutiny. "Best two out of three, Hail?"

I kept my smile easy, even though my heart was pounding in my chest. I had one shot at this and if I fucked it up we had to leave everything to chance. "We're a bit pressed for time. How about just a single round, last one standing wins."

"Wins what?" A grin spread over Aiz's face and I had to keep mine from widening to match. I had him, now I just had to finish it without raising suspicion.

"The right to make the choice. Be the one in charge. If you win, I'll join your crew, fight gods and monsters and whatever else you want. If I win?" I gave a lazy smile. "I admit I'll probably still fight gods and monsters with you. But you go with me to talk to the Farians and I get to call the shots."

Aiz's answering smile was slow. "Very well, with one adjustment."

"Which is what?"

"Last one standing? No." He shook his head. "First death is cleaner, and you did say we were on a schedule." I watched as Aiz's gaze flickered to Emmory and then back to me, felt Emmory tighten beside me like a panther about to spring. Aiz's smile grew. "Yes, first death will be perfect."

Mia stepped away from him and the other Shen started moving at her signal. Emmory waved a hand and my people mimicked the motion until they'd formed a circle around us.

"You ready?" Aiz asked.

"Sure." I dipped my head in agreement.

Aiz echoed the gesture, and as he came up, I pulled Emmory's Hessian from his holster and fired. The building noise of the crowd silenced abruptly as Aiz dropped to a knee, a look of surprise on his face.

He slumped sideways and for a moment nobody moved.

"Everyone, hold." Mia ordered in Shen, and her people froze in the act of reaching for their weapons.

I had my own empty hand up and didn't look to see if my people were obeying the silent command. I knew they would. "You probably want to bring him back," I said to Mia, handing the Hessian back to Emmory.

"He is going to be so pissed at you," she managed to say through her laughter as she knelt at his side. I joined her and helped roll him over, hearing Emmory's muttered appreciation for my single shot through Aiz's heart. Mia gave Emmory a heated look and then pressed her hands to her brother's chest.

Aiz came back to life with a gasping inhale. "Really?"

"You didn't specify how first death needed to occur, only that we were fighting." I spread my hands wide and grinned. "You should have been prepared. Gunrunner, remember?"

"Well played, Star of Indrana." Aiz chuckled as Mia helped him to his feet and stuck his hand out. "You won that one."

I clasped his forearm. "Welcome to my crew, Aiz Cevalla."

29

I leaned on the railing of the upper level of the hangar, a booted foot propped up on the rail, and watched as humans, Shen, and Farians moved around below unloading gear and supplies. We'd survived the first few hours of this tentative—did I dare call it an alliance—without bloodshed and I was feeling the most settled I had in months.

"Ekam."

I didn't turn at Aiz's greeting to Emmory, trusting that my Body-Guard would either shoot the Shen and get it out of his system or let Aiz pass.

"Evening," I said without looking away from the sun setting on the far horizon. The rays were streaking in through the open door of the hangar, dust motes dancing in the still air.

"I'm still waiting for one of your people to shoot me in the back," Aiz said, leaning on the railing next to me.

"Consequences of your choices," I replied with a small smile. "To be fair, most of them would look you in the eye when they did it."

"That is the kind of people you surround yourself with, isn't it? Not only loyal to a fault but honorable."

"I like knowing who I can trust." I saw his grin flash out of the corner of my eye and turned to look at him.

"Is this the point where I'm supposed to ask you if you trust me?"

"I trust you to think of your sister first and everything else second," I replied, and the surprise flickered across his face before he could stop it. "I trust you to tell me the truth when it suits you and lie to me just as easily in the same manner." I rubbed a hand over my arm, smoothing out the matte black of the BodyGuard uniform Stasia had modified for me. "And I trust you enough to fight with you at my back should the occasion arise."

"Well," Aiz said, his amusement fading into something I'd only seen once or twice on his face. The Shen's respect wasn't something he gave easily, but I was seeing it now.

"The better question, Aiz Cevalla, is do you trust me?" I gestured at the people below us. "There are a lot of lives at stake here. Do you trust that I can find a solution that will keep all of them safe—not just my people—but yours and Fasé's and all the rest of this galaxy? If your sister and Sybil are right about what's coming for us and we can't stop it, I need to know you're on my side for that fight." I pushed upright and took a step closer. "Are you capable of that?"

He stared at me for a long moment, then leaned forward so that his forehead touched mine. A smile curved his mouth just before he spoke. "I am, Star of Indrana. I will stay at your side through fire and blood. You have my word."

"Good. Though." I stepped back, shook my head. "Everyone keeps talking about fire and blood to me; can we do peace and a decent glass of whiskey instead? It sounds so much more appealing."

Aiz's laugh rang through the hangar, and I knew more than a few pairs of eyes turned toward us. "Perhaps after, Hail."

"I hope so." I leaned on the railing again. "I'm told the fight with these so-called gods is going to happen no matter what I do, but you understand I have to make the attempt?"

"I do." His easy agreement was surprising and it must have shown on my face because Aiz chuckled and bumped his shoulder into mine when he rejoined me. "You are not the only one who has changed in the last six months, Hail. When I started this I was convinced the fight was all that mattered. I threw myself into training you because it was important, even though it drew the ire and concern of many of my people. There are those who feel the war against the Farians has taken a turn for the worse because of what Mia and I chose to do on Sparkos."

"I wondered how you could spend so much time with me," I replied. "Though from my possibly unreliable vantage point it seemed as though you both had things well in hand." The memory of Talos's conversation with Vais floated back into my head and I frowned. "Aiz, speaking of Sparkos, I heard a conversation—"

"Let me guess, about what a horrible influence you are?" he asked, glancing up at the ceiling with a smile.

"I suppose. Come to think of it I didn't have a lot of context. It was concern for Hamah and something to do with me, but I don't know for sure." I laughed. "Beyond the fact that he doesn't like me."

"He doesn't," Aiz confirmed. "And I know about it. Mia and I had a conversation just before your people showed up and I need to confront Hamah, though I confess I am afraid it will not end well. Some of our people think your influence will cause us to back down from this fight we have been preparing for all these years." He sighed. "What they don't understand is only a fool ignores the changing of things and continues to barrel headlong into a conflict. I don't deny I want vengeance, but only a madman turns away from a chance to end things without bloodshed." He shot me a wink. "See, I am not so obsessed with revenge as you may think."

"I have always liked this scene."

I looked over my shoulder to find Sybil smiling at us. The Farian spread her hands briefly, then pressed them together and bowed. "Star of Indrana. Aiz Cevalla."

Aiz crossed to her, folded his own hands together, and bowed. "I did not get to do this on Earth," he said, and pulled Sybil into a hug. "You have grown so much."

"It has been a very long time, but I've seen you in my mind; it was almost the same." Sybil hugged him back with genuine warmth in her pale silver eyes.

It no longer surprised me, this feeling of having skipped an important page in a book and having no idea of what had suddenly shifted between one moment and the next.

"If you tell me you two have been working together this whole time I just might shoot the both of you," I said, and Sybil laughed.

"No, Majesty. At least not in the way you might think." She held a hand out to me, smiling when I took it, and I noticed she'd kept hold of Aiz's left hand. "The thing about living forever is that you all know each other."

"Whether you want to or not," Aiz murmured.

"True," she replied. "And I am in a unique position because of what I have seen. Faults aside, I like Aiz, and at least in some respect support what he is trying to do. I want our people whole again."

"There is no whole, Sybil. There is Farian and Shen and there always will be."

"Will you say that in a thousand years?" she asked Aiz.

He took a deep breath, then laughed, letting go of her hand and lifting both of his in surrender. "Do not argue with this one, Hail; she thinks she knows everything."

"Maybe not everything." Sybil winked. "But enough. Come, both of you, we need to talk."

We shared a look. Aiz shrugged. "I try not to argue with the future-seers."

"I think Mia would call you a liar," I replied, waving a hand to Emmory and following Sybil into the corridor.

The setup of this underground base was similar to the one on Sparkos, though the hallways were cut right from the rock, giving us smooth red walls instead of the grayish concrete.

The room Sybil led us to was a large area with a handful of consoles laid out in a row from one end to the other. A group of people were clustered around one side. Mia and Fasé had their heads bent close together in conversation. Fasé's cousins sat nearby, trying to pretend like they weren't watching Vais and Talos, who were in turn trying to pretend like they weren't watching Hao and Gita.

Zin was there also and he smiled at me as I followed Emmory through the doorway. I reached out and Zin took my hand. The strength of his grip grounded me like Gita's had, like Emmory's did. I was discovering I could face down the panic in my chest with them to anchor me, but I didn't want to cling and it was still so hard to ask for help.

I was, at least, not injuring myself at the moment, so I figured that was progress.

"This is cheery," I said with a wink at Talos. He tried and failed to keep his smile under control. "Nothing like a group of people who all want to kill each other trying to work together."

Aiz stepped up to my side. "This is necessary," he said, looking around the room. "If there are issues, I expect everyone to bring it to us—meaning me or Mia, Fasé, or Hail. It will be dealt with accordingly. Now is not the time for vendettas, not with the fate of all our people hanging in the balance."

I nodded in agreement. "Sybil, what did you want to talk about?"

"Our gods." Sybil reconsidered her words at Aiz's snort and Mia's raised eyebrow, then gestured at herself and Fasé. "Farian gods, I suppose. I know you have questions."

"I do." I rubbed a hand over my face and leaned against Zin's chair. "I'm lacking in details about this whole situation, and frankly your gods seem to be at the center of it all. What can you tell us about them?"

I had a file crammed full of things about the gods already. Bits and pieces I'd picked up back on Sparkos. Things that Mia or Aiz had said. What little information from Indrana I could find in our archives. It was all a jumbled mess I hadn't had a chance to sort through. I'd spent six months gearing up for the fight of my life, but now I was resistant in ways I couldn't articulate.

I wanted to fight and I didn't. I wondered if this was how Mia had felt, what she'd been referring to when she said she didn't like what it had turned her into. If Aiz wrestled with the same thing, given his admission that he was willing to walk away from the revenge he'd been after his whole life for a chance at peace.

Sybil tapped a finger on her lips. "That's an extremely general question. I could tell you quite a bit, but it's easier if I know what you want to know."

I didn't know what I was looking for, that was the whole problem. I wanted to know how they connected to the light that was coming. How their deaths could possibly stop it, especially if that seemed like the one thing we were speeding toward with reckless abandon.

"Have you met them?"

"I was nine years old in my very first life when the gods arrived on Faria." Sybil smiled. "We weren't much further along than you humans are now, and behind in some ways. We hadn't figured out faster-than-light travel and we were so isolated. This galaxy is so old and most moved on long before you or even I were born into existence.

"When the seven landed on our planet it was terrifying and exciting all at once. These amazing beings who towered over us and glowed with power but were filled with such peace. It was like looking at a better version of ourselves. We had no idea then how everything would change. Practically overnight. They told us they were travelers, voyagers seeking out knowledge. They told us they had knowledge of their own to share. They showed us how to manipulate the energy in our bodies to heal our wounds, to live longer, to be born again."

"Could you see the future before they came?"

"Yes." Sybil dipped her head. "But it was unreliable and hard to grasp. Some of us had always had the talent for it, but the gods showed us how to make the images clearer, how to separate ourselves from the visions."

"Sybil, you call them gods in one breath, but in another you admit they just showed up on your planet. Aiz and the others have repeatedly said they're not gods." I gestured at him, and he nodded with a frown on his face. "We didn't think you were gods when we first met you. Doesn't the disconnect bother you?"

"It would, if it were a disconnect for us. The Farian word for them is *evergieti*, which means 'benefactor.' When we first met your people there was some difficulty getting the scope of that across, but 'gods' you seemed to understand and so that is the term that stuck." She sighed. "You have to understand, Hail. They are not gods like yours. They are real. They gave us life—everlasting life—and if that's not worthy of godhood I'm not sure what is. We've been worshipping at their feet for millennia. There is no other human term that covers the scope of that kind of devotion."

I resisted the urge to debate with her on whether the Indranan gods were real, but oddly enough her casual dismissal rankled. "You've met them, can you tell me about the three who are still alive?"

"They are the youngest of the seven. Adaran, Priam, and Thyra are the ones you know as the Tuesday, Thursday, and Sunday gods." Her mouth twitched. "I never will get over your human need to label and categorize things into boxes."

"Human nature," I replied with a shrug. "Someone thought it was a good idea. You didn't want to give us their names, and we couldn't very well call them one through seven, could we?"

Sybil laughed. "No, I suppose not. Though that would have been equally amusing."

"Sybil, what did the gods want with you?" I asked, and Mia unsuccessfully muffled a snort of laughter.

"Want?" Sybil shot Mia a flat look and I bit the inside of my cheek to keep my own laughter from joining hers. It was, I thought, the first time I'd seen the Farian the least bit ruffled.

"Did they ever tell you why they came?" I waved a hand. "Beyond that public relations line of being explorers and wanting to share their knowledge." I didn't say out loud how very close that was to what the Farians had told us when they first made contact.

"They didn't, Hail." Sybil seemed surprised by the question and frowned in thought. "All these years and we never thought to press that point."

"Some did," I replied, tipping my head toward Aiz and Fasé.

"True. Some have, I suppose. Especially the Cevallas. Javez never was very happy about the arrival of the seven. He protested it from the beginning. Aiz was just a teen, not much older than I was. Adora was among the first to greet them, and she broke from her family in her wholehearted acceptance of the gods."

"That's a nice way of saying she betrayed them for power." Mia pushed out of her chair and paced toward the wall.

This time Sybil's look in Mia's direction was sharp, though it vanished so quickly I thought for a moment I'd imagined it. It appeared things were not quite as cohesive between the three of them as I'd been told.

Fasé hadn't said a word and was still staring at the wall. She looked tired, the skin under her golden eyes bruised to the color of Indrana blackberries, just the lightest shade of purple under the surface.

I crossed the room, slipped my hand over Fasé's shoulder as I leaned against the wall near her. "Are you all right?" I murmured.

"I didn't sleep well." She whispered the reply.

"I also welcomed them," Sybil continued. "Because I had seen their arrival and the stability they brought." She sighed. "Because I wasn't old enough or wise enough to look beyond any of that."

"Sybil, the healing ability. We were always told that it was necessary for you to come heal humans. That you would burn up if you didn't expel that gift, but that's not true, is it?" Zin asked.

I swallowed with the realization that truly everything the Farians had told my people when they first arrived was at best a dodge of the truth and at worst a bald-faced lie.

253

"The Shen have no problem with holding it, even taking in more than I've seen regular Farians use. I've done it myself. So has Johar." I held up a hand before Mia could comment. "Let Sybil answer, you can have a turn after."

"It is a fabrication, of sorts, though to be fair every Farian who told you that believed it." Sybil looked down at her hands for a long moment and I moved away from Zin, crossing the room and leaning against the wall next to Mia, letting Sybil collect her thoughts.

"When the gods gave us that gift, it was heavily controlled. The proscriptions and rules are many, the punishments for violation swift and harsh. Final death, the violators killed, and their souls given to the gods."

I put my hand on Mia's forearm, felt the muscle tense under my palm, and smiled when she finally relaxed.

Sybil sighed and rubbed a hand over her face. "But if I am being honest, it is a measure of control for reasons I do not yet know. This is why I helped Fasé escape, Hail, and why I help you now with information we were forbidden from ever sharing with not just humans but Indranans specifically."

I was going to have to call cowshit on that, I thought, but not right now in front of this crowd. Everyone was more tense than they had been at the start of this conversation, and despite my and Aiz's warning I didn't think bloodshed could be avoided if things went sideways.

"It all comes back to that, doesn't it?" I wasn't the least bit surprised by my own frustrations. "My people, leading to me because of this future. We were dragged into some galactic conspiracy thousands of years ago. More than anything, Sybil, I want the answer to that question. Why me? Why my people? What do your damn gods want with us?"

"For that, you're going to have to ask them directly, Hail." Sybil spread her hands wide as she lifted them from her lap. "I don't have those answers."

"You've seen so much of this happen, haven't you?" I asked. "All three of you." It was hard to keep the bitterness out of my words. Mia winced. Sybil had the grace to look slightly ashamed. Fasé finally looked at me again, but her expression was neutral, unchanging from how she'd been staring at the wall. "But you never have the answers when we need them."

"Hail."

I shook my head at Emmory as I pushed away from the wall. "No, I'm perfectly calm. I'm angry, but I'm not going to start throwing punches or"—I looked down at my guns and crossed to him, holding my hands up—"shooting people, but take those just in case. Because I'm in the mood to hammer this out."

Emmory pulled the Glocks free and put them on the table behind him. I saw a smile flicker over Fasé's face and found myself equally grateful and infuriated by the sudden reaction.

I looked to Aiz, hoping he was going to back me up. "I want everyone out. Aiz and Mia, stay. Emmory, you and Zin. Fasé and Sybil." Hao looked like he wanted to protest, but I shook my head. "There's too many variables right now and this is too important to risk being interrupted by people shouting at each other."

There was surprisingly little argument and I waited until the door closed behind the last person before I turned and pointed at Fasé. "We'll start with you."

30

will remain endlessly grateful to you for saving these two." I pointed behind me at Emmory and Zin. "And for Admiral Hassan's life as well as everything else you've done for me and my empire. But you're still new to this, Fasé, and kicking yourself for things not going the way you thought they would isn't going to do us any good."

She tilted her head curiously. "How did you know?"

"I recognize the look," I said. "What happened on Sparkos was, I don't know, maybe it was the way things were supposed to go. We'll never know and it doesn't matter anyway because it's done."

"Fair enough." Fasé's easy agreement startled me. "Would you have listened if I could have gotten through to you?"

"Probably not," I replied. "But I'll own it, I made my choice."

"You made the choice she wanted you to make." Fasé's gold eyes flicked toward Mia.

"We're getting to that," I said.

"Hail."

I turned and smiled at Mia. "There's no point in trying to sugarcoat it, Mia. You lied to me, Aiz lied to me. You both had a very specific reason for wanting me there, and it served your purpose for me to think most of my people were dead." I scrubbed at the back of my head. "It makes a lot more sense why you didn't want to send Gita and the others away now."

"It was easier to get you to see right there on the edge," Mia whispered, looking at her hands.

"Nearly fucked it up, though, didn't you? You both were worried about me—for good reason." I smiled at her startled look. "I may have been eavesdropping on some conversations. You know the messed-up part of it all?" I asked. "I would have agreed to help you anyway." I gestured at Emmory and Zin. "These guys would have protested, but I would have convinced them in the end."

"As much as I hate to admit it, she's right," Emmory said, and I winked at him.

"Which brings me to you, Seer of the Council of Eyes." I pointed at Sybil. "I have a sneaking suspicion you knew how this was going to play out from the beginning. That you know what's going to happen in the next minute, the next hour, the next day. You've had years with the future, thousands of them if not more because damned if I can get a handle on how long you've actually been around. I don't buy for one second that you haven't seen the same things Mia has."

"That's mildly insulting, Hail."

I shrugged. "That's life. Given what the stakes are, I'm done with being led around by the nose, so how about you tell me what you saw in that future that made you agree when the Pedalion ordered you to help Fasé escape?"

"It is not just about that future, Hail. It is also—" Sybil broke off and stared at me. "You knew? How?"

"Gunrunners who believe in happy coincidences don't live for very long." I smiled and lifted a shoulder.

Fasé was looking at Sybil in horror, her careful façade of indifference shattered by the news. Mia and Aiz, on the other hand, were muttering curses in Shen I knew all too well, and I really hoped they didn't try anything before I was finished.

Emmory was giving me the Look.

"I'll be honest, it was in large part a guess. But Fasé was on lockdown in Faria and though they were letting her talk with Stasia—likely to keep me from getting suspicious—there wasn't much of a chance of her getting out of there on her own. You haven't seemed the least bit surprised by anything that's happened. Except you told me back on Pashati that you didn't peek at the future for day-to-day things. Which means you'd already watched this all play out before you ever hooked up with us." I tapped a hand on the holster strapped to my thigh and knew without looking that Emmory and Zin both had their guns in their hands. "I am curious if you saw this part, but if you didn't I bet you are wondering why I've let you go on for so long."

"Star of Indrana, I—"

"You're not sold on Adora and the Pedalion, are you?" I cut her off with a smile. "There's something you've seen. Something else you know. I see it in your body language, how you're holding something in. I can hear it in what you're not saying and the way you've said the things you did choose to share.

"So tell me, Sybil, do you finally share it? Or do I have Emmory send your soul back to the Pedalion? We'll muddle along fine without you, I promise."

"I—" She pressed shaking fingers to her lips, dropping her gaze to her lap for several heartbeats before she looked at me again. "Star of Indrana, I hope you know it is not empty flattery when I say that you are the most amazing human I have ever met. The things you see, the secrets you keep, the way you have lost yourself and then found it all again. Even the company you hold close to you is amazing beyond belief.

"You cannot imagine the reputation that preceded you, though it was no fault of your own that my expectations were so high." Sybil smiled when I snorted. "I was given a task along with the vision I saw so long ago. It is not something I have ever shared with another beyond my sisters in the council until this moment, and it is words meant for you, no one else."

"No." I shook my head. "We're done with secrets. We're in this together, and together is how this goes down. You'll tell me now and you'll tell me in front of those who need to hear it just as much as I do." I raised an eyebrow and made a motion for her to continue. Sybil pressed her palms together and bowed her head briefly.

"I have seen the possible future Mia told you of, and it is terrible indeed. I was also told that the gods want to meet you, Hail. The Pedalion has known of this since the beginning. What is not known is what will happen once you are there." She shook her head and gestured at Mia. "It could be as she sees and you will kill our gods. Or you will simply speak with them, though to what end I do not know. I have not seen it—no one has seen it. And that uncertainty scares the Pedalion more than you can know."

"I'm not surprised." I tapped my fingers against my holster. For a race so dependent on their future-seers, the black wash of an unknown future had to be terrifying. "What about Fasé?"

Sybil smiled. "For all that I have not seen, I know this. It is imperative that Fasé and the Cevallas are at your side when you meet the gods, but the Pedalion cannot know that this is our plan. If they know, they will do everything in their power to stop you, and this is the one thing that must come to pass if any of us are to survive the light that is bearing down on us. All other paths lead to chaos."

"That's rather been the plan from the beginning," I said. "I'm fully intending to meet with your gods."

"I know." Sybil let out the shaky breath she'd just dragged in. "And that is where I have the most fear, Hail. I do not want to see you fight my gods. It is true that everything dies, that everything needs to end. I would be lying if I said I wanted you to kill my gods, but you must meet them and I do not know how to reconcile this paradox."

"It's not yours to reconcile, Sybil," I said, and looked over at Aiz. He'd composed himself somewhat, but I suspected the only thing keeping his hand off the gun at his hip was my BodyGuards. "Aiz and I have already come to the agreement that we will talk first and fight only if we need to, which I hope you realize is a huge concession from him. If they will not listen, we will fight. And make no mistake, we will win that fight."

"I know," Sybil whispered. "I have seen that, too, and wept for the loss of everything I hold dear."

"I can sympathize. It's been a long few years. I know realistically I can't stop all wars, but if I can stop this one? I want my people safe. I want your people to have the freedom to leave home and live their lives. I want Aiz's people to be reborn if they choose. I want everyone to have the choice to die if that is what they wish. If we have to fight some mysterious force invading our galaxy in exchange for that?" I blew out a breath and smiled. "So be it. It'll be a lot easier to do if I have some gods on my side."

"You really think you can make it happen?"

"I think I got my miracle already." I glanced Emmory's way and smiled. "But we do this, or die trying. Are you willing to make that kind of sacrifice?"

Sybil looked at me, eyes shining, then nodded. "Yes, Star of Indrana, I am."

"That's what I was hoping you were going to say." I smiled. "We're not going to tell the Pedalion about this little chat, because you're a wild card I'd like to keep hidden just in case."

"Of course." Sybil got to her feet. "If it is all right, I would like to go and lie down for a while?"

"I'll take her back to her room," Aiz said after sharing a look with me. Mia offered up a sympathetic smile at Fasé and followed her brother out the door.

"You're just going to trust her, Hail?" Fasé asked. "My people are at risk." She waved a hand at the empty doorway. "Sybil was instrumental in setting up the network on Faria; if she has betrayed us they are all dead."

"I don't think we need to worry, but you might want to tell them to do what they need to in order to keep themselves safe. I'm assuming she knows what'll happen if she's lying to me," I replied, then reached for the Farian's hand and gave it a reassuring squeeze. It had to hurt Fasé, to shake her faith even further to know she hadn't swayed Sybil to her side with the strength of her words. "Your message is no less valid for this," I murmured. "If anything, remember that you won her over the hard way."

"I'm not sure that helps."

Because she still looked so lost I bent down and pressed a kiss to her forehead. "Then console yourself with the fact that the Star of Indrana believes in you and that when the dust settles on all of this you'll have what you're seeking for your people."

I strode back to Emmory and held my hands out for my guns. He put them in my palms and I holstered them, amused to note that my hands were shaking.

"That went well," Zin murmured.

"Everyone is going to have to get on board with the idea that this is going to bring a shit-ton of trouble down on our heads."

"We already are, Hail. Your side is the side we'll always be on," Emmory replied.

"I can tell you it's a fucked-up universe where I'm the one who's expected to be the peacemaker."

"You're better at it than you think."

"I hope you're right."

The water I splashed on my face was warm, and I hung on to the edge of the sink, trying to stop the tremors that were crawling under my skin.

Emmory stood just outside the doorway of the bathroom. Three steps away. Two if I really pushed off from where I was standing. The former wasn't enough to get to him before he pulled his Hessian and shot me with the stun function.

But if you really try, we could see what happens, the wicked voice in my brain whispered, and I shook my head so hard the room spun.

I didn't want to fight him. Flashbacks and sudden awful impulses notwithstanding, I liked my *Ekam* and I did not want to kill him.

If I repeated it enough I would start to believe it.

Emmory seemed to understand my struggle and didn't say a word, didn't do anything to draw attention to himself. He just stood there, a hand on his gun and sorrow in his eyes.

I pressed my fingers to my eyes and dragged in a breath, blowing it out slowly as I coaxed my legs to support me. Dropping my hands, I met Emmory's eyes in the mirror. "That was unexpected. I'm sorry."

The urge to fight had come out of nowhere, scaring me with its intensity, and I was grateful Emmory was the only person in the room with me when it had happened.

"I know. It's all right."

"It's not, though." I pushed away from the sink, could practically feel his flinch on the air. He backed up as I came out of the bathroom, but the need to fight had passed and instead I knelt to gather the shattered bits of the mug I'd thrown at the wall. "It's not all right," I said. "Shiva, that was so unlike me I don't even know how to process it. I thought I was okay, but I am apparently barely keeping it together."

"Majesty, we'll get someone to clean that up."

"I'll clean up my own damned messes." I waved a hand and dumped the shattered pieces of the mug, sticky with chai, onto the tray Stasia had delivered and cursed myself for wasting it.

Emmory was silent as I rinsed my hands off in the sink and came back out with a wet towel.

"Mia warned us this might happen," he said finally as I tossed the towel onto the tray. "And Gita chewed my ass yesterday about putting too much on you."

"She what?"

Emmory's smile was sheepish, a look I hadn't ever seen on him before. He leaned in the doorway of my room. We were on board the Farian ship where I'd retreated to try to deal with this unexpected desire to put my fist through something during a com with Alice first thing that morning.

"She said we needed to be careful about asking you for too much. That you weren't, despite appearances, back to normal."

"Well, she wasn't wrong." I gestured at the ruined mug and sighed. "I hate feeling this way, Emmory, like a gun with a malfunctioning trigger." I dropped onto my bed and buried my face in my hands. "You know, the worst part is I'm not sure I'll ever be back to normal."

"Hail." The bed shifted as Emmory sat on the edge, and I heard him tugging off his gloves before he curled bare fingers around my wrists. "Look at me."

I did and the care shining at me from his eyes was a balm on my rough edges and shattered nerves.

"I know you chose this," Emmory said. "But it's okay to be afraid and overwhelmed." He shook his head before I could find the words to protest. "The universe will rise and fall on its own. You're not responsible for what's coming, and you're not responsible for saving everyone. You're the one who keeps saying we move forward, not back. So why aren't you giving yourself the same permission?"

I flung my arms around his neck, hugging him tightly. "Thank you," I whispered.

"For what?" Emmory smoothed a hand over my hair as we separated.

"Coming to get me?" My smile was watery. "I haven't said that yet, but I am grateful."

"It seemed like you were pretty close to getting out yourself."

"No." I shook my head. "I was pretty close to being lost for good." I held my hand out, curling my fingers around Emmory's when he took it. "So thanks."

"Of course. I'll always come for you." He smiled. "Better?"

263

I rubbed my free hand over my chest, surprised that the worst of it had faded away. "Yes."

"Good. Now, at the risk of stepping on toes, I'm going to handle the morning briefings with Alice for a while. If for no other reason than you've got plenty to do with Aiz and the others."

"Caterina's going to love that." I mustered up a small smile. "Though I guess she's just going to have to get used to the empress surrounding herself with gunrunners and alien outlaws. Having my *Ekam* handling briefings is a minor infraction comparatively."

"She'll deal with it. If they all haven't figured out by now that you're not a typical empress and things aren't going to go the way they're used to, I'm not sure what we can do to help them."

31

What is it you're objecting to?"

"I object on general principle to the idea of walking right into Faria." Aiz waved a hand at the console in front of us. "Diplomatic mission or not, the second Adora realizes that we are on board the trouble will start."

"Are you being contrary already?" I demanded. "Because we're just getting things sorted here and if I have to remind you I'm in charge every step of the way—"

"Then you're not really in charge," Aiz finished, bumping me with his shoulder.

We stood next to each other leaning over the console in the main war room of the base. Sybil and Mia were in the corner, deep in discussion once more, and I wondered just what the pair were getting up to. Fasé paced, occasionally throwing in a comment or two in Farian I couldn't follow.

The three of them seemed to have recovered from Sybil's revelation. We'd had a hard talk about just who else to tell, and at present it was limited to the people in this room.

Hao had accepted it with a shrug. Gita had been less casual about it but deferred to Emmory's judgment. Talos had been equally sanguine, though I suspected the reason for that was his trust in Mia. It did not escape my notice that Aiz chose not to tell any of the rest of his people.

"I could shoot you again; would that help lay the matter to rest?" I asked.

"You two bicker like siblings," Hao said from the other side of the console. He and Emmory stood shoulder to shoulder, and the sight of it brought me a surprising measure of peace.

"Watch it, I'll shoot you again, too." I warned with a look.

Hao lifted his hands and grinned. "I'm just saying."

Our wary truce had solidified. It was born of necessity, but also following the example both Aiz and I were trying to set. Fasé and Hao had dug in and gotten to work, which had also smoothed over the tension that lingered among my people and the newer Farians on Fasé's side.

"I'm not just saying it to poke at you, Hail," Aiz replied. He pointed across the table at Sybil. "The Farians will know the truth of why we're coming. Trying to pretend it's for negotiations is pointless."

"Fair point." I was annoyed I hadn't thought of a way around it.

Sybil looked up with a shrug. "To the best of my knowledge, no one else on the Council of Eyes has seen the vision I did of you all meeting with the gods. The problem is there's no way to be certain. If they have someone focused on the possible futures it's bound to come up, but the negotiations aren't the lie, just who's going to be involved."

"Is there any reason for us to think they wouldn't have some-one paying attention?" I wasn't about to underestimate the Farians. They'd proven their willingness to use the ability to see the future against us; there was no reason to think they wouldn't do so now.

"I would do it," Mia replied. "Before you ask, no, we can't figure out which choice will be best and run with it. You have to make the choice, Hail."

I was reasonably sure that Sybil had something to do with Mia's sudden reluctance to share information with me, but I could do little about it besides mutter a curse.

There was movement in the corner of my eye. I reacted on instinct, knocking the strike Aiz threw at me out of the way with my left hand. I grabbed him by the back of the neck with my right hand and kicked his left leg out from under him, stopping just short of slamming his face into the console.

The entire room froze, but Aiz chuckled even though his nose was a centimeter from the polished surface. "The restraint is new. Who'd you kill?"

I let him go and shook my head. "Nobody."

"Really?" Aiz whistled. "I'm impressed." His brown eyes were locked on mine. I could see the amusement in them. I knew what he was doing and couldn't stop myself from curling my hands into fists. I didn't want to fight. Not here. Not in front of everyone. If we were going to do it I'd rather it be somewhere private.

Just throw the fucking punch, Hail.

"You keep taunting her like that, you're going to have trouble on your hands." Hao's warning broke through the staring contest and put out the flame of anger licking at my heart with the ease of a heavy blanket.

Aiz smiled. "Perhaps. It's close, but she's not quite at the point where I think she'd beat me in a straight fight."

"He's not talking about her," Emmory said, and it was then I noticed both men had their hands on their weapons and their eyes locked on Aiz. A glance at Zin and Gita by the door showed they also had their hands on their Hessians.

Mia, Fasé, and Sybil stopped their conversation and watched us with nearly identical smiles hovering on their mouths.

Aiz lifted his hands in surrender and winked at me. "Now you see why we had to separate you from your people, Hail. No matter what you say. They would never have stood by and let you make your choice."

"Maybe," I said with a shrug. "Maybe not. We'll never know because you stole that choice from us." I pointed at him. "I'll warn

267

you now that if you choose to poke at them, the reaction will be on your head."

"Fair enough. Now, about this current problem?"

"Which is what?" I asked.

"You are trusting in the Farians when you shouldn't be."

"Oh, the irony of that statement coming from you."

Aiz gave me a narrow look, then sighed. "I realize it. But this plan fails rather spectacularly if Adora decides to blow your ship up and claim it was an accident."

I leaned a hip on the console. "Do you really think she will? As scared as they are of anything that's coming, I would think that they will stick to the path they've always kept—try to somehow get me to cooperate."

"I have learned never to underestimate the depths of my sister's horrific choices." Aiz took a deep breath and shook his head. "Do I think she would kill the Star simply for a chance to remove me, Fasé, and Sybil from the equation, even temporarily? Possibly. Especially if she feels backed into a corner." He poked at the ever-growing mass of Shen ships clustered around the marker for this base. "We're bringing the entire Shen fleet to Faria. It is a rather aggressive opening move for negotiations."

"Aggressive keeps people off balance. What?"

"We should probably spar soon and get some of that out of your system."

I kept my expression neutral even as my excitement soared. "Probably, just tell me when."

Aiz studied me for a moment more before he looked back down at the console. "If you are set on this plan? The Farians have pulled back all but a handful of ships from the Solarian Conglomerate and another handful from your empire. Those ships are all at Faria and they will wipe us out if things dissolve into a fight."

"So how do we disable those ships?" I had a sudden, desperate urge to com home to talk with now Warrant Officer Ragini

Triskan, a computer genius who'd been working on the *Vajrayana* ships at Canafey and saved our asses more times than I could count during the battle to retake my throne.

"I don't know," Aiz admitted. "We've been over them dozens of times but haven't found a way into the systems that doesn't involve being on the ships."

My reply was cut off by the blaring alarm that suddenly filled the air. Aiz stabbed at the console, and the image of main control appeared. "Report."

"A contingent of Farian ships just dropped into the system, *Thíno.*"

"How many?"

"Three dozen, but it's all smaller—" She broke off, frowned. "Sir, there's an Indranan ship with them."

"What?" My exclamation echoed with Aiz's.

"They got it to work!"

I gave Fasé a look that had to make Emmory proud.

Royal decorum be damned. I sprinted across the hangar as Admiral Inana Hassan descended the ramp of the *Hailimi Bristol*, the *Vajrayana* I had taken from Pashati what seemed like a lifetime ago, and wrapped my arms around her in a bruising hug.

"Sorry I'm late, Majesty."

"Shut up and hug me back."

She did, chuckling softly before she untangled herself from my embrace and straightened into a formal salute. "Your Majesty, the Heir sends her regards. She thought a ship of your own would help with the mission."

"How?" I looked sideways at Fasé, who was grinning.

"You have some very intelligent people, Majesty," she replied. "Who were able, with a little assistance, to retrofit a Farian drive into a *Vajrayana.*"

"They started working on it not long after Earth. Took us almost a year to do it," Inana said. "Would have been longer if these two hadn't been working day and night on it." She gestured behind her and I spotted Ragini standing on the ramp as though I'd conjured her with thought alone. And next to her was now Senior Tech Yama Hunkaar, the other of the trio who'd helped us at Canafey. Their friend, Hasa Julsen, had died in the fight for Pashati.

"I hope you two got some sleep, because I have a new problem for you." I crossed to them both and pulled the startled naval techs into a hug. "Aiz, who's been working on your weapon problem?"

"I'll have someone find them, Hail," he replied from behind me.

"Good." I smiled at the women. "You're gonna love this, I promise."

"Majesty."

I turned back around to Inana, spotting the curious smile my admiral was wearing. "Come with me. We have so much to catch up on."

"Obviously. I have read Emmory's reports, but—" She glanced at Aiz, who'd fallen in step as I led her across the hangar. Emmory and Zin were behind me. "Are you all right, Hail?"

"I am managing." I waved a hand. "Don't apologize, Inana. You didn't have anything to do with it and you couldn't have done anything if you'd even been in the same system. We've got bigger problems to tackle."

"Like what, Majesty?"

"Oh, you know, ending a major war and preventing the destruction of the galaxy." I grinned. "The usual."

"I guess I got here just in time, then."

Inana caught me up on the situation in the empire while we walked. They'd left two days ago. The Farians and the techs had felt better about two short jumps than coming straight to this base with the new engine.

"Are we going to be able to put them in the other *Vajrayanas*?" The idea of a fleet of ships that could jump the same way the Farians and Shen could was immensely appealing.

"It depends," Inana replied with a lifted shoulder.

"On?"

"If the Farians will give us the components. They're hard to source."

I glanced Mia's way as we entered. She and Sybil had stayed behind in the war room, but she got to her feet with a smile. "Admiral Hassan, it is good to see you."

"Mia Cevalla," I said at Inana's confused frown. "You haven't met, but she apparently knew you were coming."

Mia tipped her head in acknowledgment. "How was your trip?"

"Uneventful. The engine performed perfectly."

"You know," I said with a look at Mia, "the Farians aren't the only ones with that drive tech. We've been hammering the terms of an alliance out over the last several days. Should I add that to the list of Indrana's demands?"

"I think maybe we can come to an arrangement. I have some people back in your sector who could get what you need."

"Do you? Send me contact info. I have a friend I could com who'd be able to facilitate things." I smiled slowly. "What's it going to cost me?"

"Why don't we call them a gift?" Mia's lips curved, and then she nodded to Inana and went back to Sybil's side. I watched her go, all too aware that the admiral was watching me.

"You under orders to report back to Caspel about me?" I asked, and received a flat brown stare in response.

"I am the admiral of your fleet, Majesty."

I gave her a flat look and she sighed. "There have been some concerns over Emmory's reports, and I know he was picking his words carefully because of his loyalty to you. But the only ones who've read them are me, Caspel, and Alice."

"I'll bet Caterina isn't happy about that." I waved Inana into a chair at a desk away from everyone else and then sat opposite her.

"There were some loud discussions. It would help matters if you would consider speaking with her the next time you talk to Alice.

What I can tell you is I'll be reporting back that you are of sound mind, under no duress, and doing the best you can with a shitty situation."

I reached a hand across the desk. "I appreciate it, Inana. Truly."

"It's the truth, Hail. You've weathered this storm far better than anyone else could and your focus is still on the preservation of our empire. I may disagree at times with your methods or allies, but I will never doubt your heart." She glanced around the room. "There is a lot going on."

"There is." I gestured to the trio in the corner. "Fasé, Sybil, and Mia are hammering out several millennia of disputes between their factions in the hopes we'll have a better platform to start with on Faria. Aiz and Talos there have been working with Hao and Gita to come up with plans for getting us to Faria and fighting the Farian forces when we show up. Though that's a plan B no one wants to actually do."

"And you, Majesty?"

"Oh, I got the fun job," I replied, hooking an arm over the back of the chair. "I'm trying to figure out what to say to a trio of gods that won't get us all killed."

"That's why you're the empress," Inana replied with a smile.

"Life was easier when I was a gunrunner." I waved to Alba when she came in the door. "Alba, where's Emmory?"

"Just outside," she replied.

"Thank you. Will you get Admiral Hassan settled? I need to go take care of this."

"Of course, ma'am. Admiral?"

I left the pair, tapping Emmory on the arm as I left the war room. He fell into step with me with little more than a curious eyebrow in my direction.

"I want you to meet someone," I said, heading down the corridor to a smaller office. Emmory followed me through the doorway, shutting the door behind him. I tapped into the base's com, waited a beat, and then smiled as the screen lit up.

"Cressen! Long time no talk." The silver-haired man on the screen clapped his hands in delight.

"Hey, Barry, this is Emmory, he's a friend of mine. I'm calling in a few favors." I wasn't even going to ask if Bartholomew Uhin knew about what had happened to me. He'd likely called me by my old name out of habit, though it could have been preference also. Self-described *entrepreneur pour l'univers*, Barry was the guy who got you what you needed, when you needed it, with no questions asked and no details disclosed—provided your credits were good.

"Absolutely, my girl." He looked at Emmory with a beaming smile. "Nice to meet you. Cressen's a good friend to have. She saved my life, you know. I was all set to go to the crusher. Got herself favors for life."

"It was an accident," I subvocalized to Emmory over our private com link. *"I thought he was someone else. Turned out handy, though. Barry's the go-to guy for all your payback needs. Among other things."*

"Who are we paying back, Majesty?"

I grinned at Emmory and then looked back at the screen. "Barry, I need a few favors. And I want you to cause some trouble for Bakara Rai."

"You being a shit again, Cress?"

I smiled. "Maybe, but he deserves it. No blowback on you, I promise."

"All right." He rubbed his hands together. "Property damage? Loss of life and limb?"

"Just property damage and a few sleepless nights."

"I can do that." He snapped his fingers. "Easy peasy. What else do you need?"

32

"You are a hard woman to track down these days."

I looked away from the hangar and smiled at Mia. "You've been busy yourself. How's the fleet?"

"Anxious." Mia leaned a hip on the railing. "We haven't told them precisely why we're mobilizing, but you can imagine that the rumors are we're finally going to Faria to do battle."

"Is it going to be a problem when we don't?"

"No." There was no hesitation in Mia's reply. "I won't lie that there aren't some of my people who are spoiling for a fight, but the majority just want an end to this war, Hail. They want a home."

"How much longer before we're ready?"

"Another few days, I'd say, but we should tell everyone today. The last of the ships come in this evening. Your admiral has been most helpful with the battle plans. I don't know why I was surprised."

"She's been doing that longer than either of us have been alive," I replied with a grin. "Well, me at least. I'm not sure about you."

Mia gave me an innocent smile but didn't say anything.

My com with Alice this morning had included Caterina and Caspel and more than an hour of me trying to assure everyone that the plans we were about to put into motion were going to play out the way we hoped they would.

I was lying to them, but I think they all felt better about it by the time we'd wrapped up.

"I'm going to have to put in a com to Adora, then," I muttered with a sigh, and Mia laughed.

"I don't envy much of what you have to do, Hail, and that is one of the more unpleasant tasks." Her smile faded. "Things are going to move so fast once we leave here; I worry, for all of us, what the coming days hold." She stared past me, lost in thought, and even though I knew Emmory and Gita were watching us from several meters away I reached out and slid my hand into her hair.

Her eyes snapped back to mine, darkening into storm clouds as I leaned in, stopping before my mouth touched hers.

"I had wondered if this was a product of my grief, if I did us both a disservice by clinging to you because I felt like everything else had been taken from me. If you were just manipulating me into these feelings so I would do what you needed. If we had nothing to build upon."

"And now?" The trembling in her question wasn't all from the way I tugged her closer to me, but it was the lion's share. I felt her fingers curling into my belt and let my smile lift the corner of my mouth.

"Now I am grateful you waited, because while I wanted you before this started and I wanted you during—you were right about the timing. Thank you."

"Hail—"

I kissed her, felt rather than heard her indrawn breath, and grappled with my own control as Mia surrendered. Her lips were soft under mine in a way I'd imagined a thousand times but never gotten quite right, and I sank deeper into the kiss for just a heartbeat before I made myself pull away.

"Six months of wanting," I murmured, stepping back completely. The shudder that shook her when I dragged my fingers along her jawline delighted me. "Worth it."

"Yes." She blinked at me. "I should go." Mia walked away, nearly staggering into Emmory as she passed my BodyGuards, and he raised an eyebrow at me. I smiled, lifting my shoulders slightly as I turned back around.

"Pleased with yourself, Majesty?" It was Gita, not Emmory, who joined me at the railing.

"A little," I admitted.

"She's starstruck by you."

The comment was so unexpected I stared at her for several beats before I could get the words to finish forming in my head and come out of my mouth. "What do you mean, 'starstruck'?"

"You are the Star of Indrana," she replied. "I was concerned for you on Sparkos for so many reasons, but that was a big one." She smiled out at the activity below us. "I'll be honest. I don't know now if that concern was warranted."

"It was," I admitted. "She was thankfully more in control than I was, and not willing to use it against me."

"It's shifted again," Gita said, and looked at me. "Maybe it's different for you, but when she's speaking to me or Emmory or the others, there is awe in her voice, in her eyes. Whatever secrets she's keeping, and I'm sure there are many, she cannot keep that one hidden. I know the Shen claim not to have gods, but whatever she has seen of your future puts you up there in her estimation."

"No pressure."

Gita shook her head. "I'm telling you this so you understand why we're not nearly as vigilant about her as your BodyGuards should be. I like her, though; all things considered I probably shouldn't, but I do."

"Gita Desai, are you matchmaking?"

Gita's smile was so slight if I hadn't been staring at her I'd have missed it. "I'm just observing, ma'am." The smile vanished. "And cautioning you to be careful of your choices and to make sure that she sees the whole of you, not just the Star of Indrana."

"Well." I cleared my throat and looked around at the assembled group that afternoon. I was standing at the front of the mess hall with Mia, Aiz, and Fasé by my side. "Here we are again with me giving speeches about impossible odds. I am, however, game for making my score two-nothing, if the rest of you want to come along for this ride."

The laughter eased my nerves.

"Star of Indrana." Emmory's voice was crisp, cutting through the air. My people came to attention as one. The Farians and Shen all lowered their heads in our direction.

"Our happy little alliance seems to have survived the first several days. I'd like to take this opportunity to remind everyone to play nice or you'll answer to us." I gestured at the others. "We're leaving in a few days. Our next stop is Faria. What I'm about to tell you may mean this is your last stop, and we are fine with that if you choose to depart."

Aiz straightened at his sister's side and looked out at the assembled crews. There wasn't room for all the Shen, so our address was also being broadcast to the ships above the planet, a whole armada breathlessly waiting for word of an attack that wasn't going to come. "My people," he said. "We have fought long and hard for this day. I thought I knew what the future held, that our paths were set on one final conflict to determine our fates."

Mia picked up after only a moment of pause, and I wondered if they had rehearsed this, or it was just timing borne of their closeness. "The future is not set and I appreciate the help of our Farian allies in helping me see clearly. We value your lives and will not throw them away in a needless campaign."

"Lives are easily spent, *Thínos*. We will give them again and again!" Hamah called, and the resounding cheer echoed through the room.

I saw the flicker of annoyance in Mia's gray eyes as she held up a hand.

"A wise woman said to me, less violence, not more, is always an option. You have all fought for so long and fought so hard. You've done this for us, for a chance for all our people to live. We want you to have that chance. My brother and I will honor that loyalty and go to Faria to put an end to this conflict once and for all."

I'd kept from staring at her when she spoke Dailun's words into the open air, but I saw the Svatir standing off to the side with a smile on his face.

Aiz continued speaking before the murmured confusion could grow in volume. "We have learned much these last few months with the Star of Indrana and even more with Fasé these last few weeks. We trust the Star as we trust all of you. If there is a way to make a home for our people without bloodshed, she is the one who will find it, and it is the greatest gift that could be given. One we do not deserve." He pressed a hand over his heart with a smile.

I saw the flash of hatred on Hamah's face, felt the disappointment surge in my chest. Aiz's talk with him had apparently not swayed the Shen's judgment of me in the slightest. But he stayed silent and it was just as well, for Aiz's passionate words pulled a cheer from the crowd louder than the previous one.

Fasé took a tiny step forward as the cheers tapered off. "As the Star said, if you are in disagreement with our plan, you are welcome to depart and we will hold you no ill will. Those who stay may still be called upon to fight and die. What we seek to do here is bigger than all of us and serves a greater purpose than just Farian or Shen or Indranan. We hold the fate of the galaxy in our hands; do not hesitate in your choice. Make it and go forward."

"Ship captains, the meeting for your battle assignments will be at oh six hundred hours tomorrow with Admiral Hassan and me," Mia said. "Briefing packets should be in your inboxes now; I will expect you all to have read them. Dismissed."

I took a step back as the crowd broke up, watching the people disperse. The few humans in the mix were spread evenly through the room, and I saw Iza and Indula joking with a pair of Shen.

Three Farians exchanged a good-bye with Talos, and I arched an eyebrow in surprise when they clasped hands, their smiles genuine.

"You've built something here, Hail," Mia murmured at my side.

"We've built something," I replied. "Here's hoping it survives."

"It will." Aiz tapped me on the shoulder and tipped his head at the door. "Let's go spar. I want to see how well you can keep that new restraint of yours in the middle of a fight rather than the start of it."

My heart leapt, or maybe it was just the desire to hit something that I'd managed to lock down so completely lunging on its chain. Either way, I had to make a choice, and making the best of it seemed to be the way to go. "Sure."

"Can we watch?" The question was from Hao, and Aiz paused at the doorway.

"It's up to her," he said, pointing at me.

I swallowed down the thousand protests. They'd all seen me fight already, or at least seen the recording of me and Hao. Even I'd watched it, despite Jo's push for me not to. This was what I was now; I couldn't keep hiding from it and fighting against it.

I caught Emmory's eye, and he gave me the barest of nods, his voice gentle over our private com link. *Your people love you, Hail; watching you fight isn't going to change that.*

That was the scary part that Emmory so easily put into words. I was different than the Hail they knew, but I wasn't a wild animal. I could control this, control myself.

I exhaled and smiled at Hao. "That's fine. I suppose it will be good to get used to fighting for an audience."

There were some chuckles in reply.

The news spread through the room and the base like wildfire, and a crowd waited for us at the door of the gym. Aiz had grabbed Hamah and Talos as he passed them in the mess hall, leaning in and whispering in their ears. They'd followed us to the gym and I raised a curious eyebrow at Aiz.

"You'll fight them," he said with a grin. "I want to watch, and it's impossible to do while fending you off."

I took a slow breath. We'd practiced with multiple opponents—sometimes me against Aiz and another Shen, or me and Aiz back to back against what had felt like a horde. This wasn't anything new, and I apparently had fewer problems with killing Aiz's people than I did my own.

We moved to the center of the gym, the walls already ringed with spectators. I spotted Dailun standing next to Hao, worry in his eyes and his hands shoved deep into his pockets. I crossed to them.

"You okay?"

Dailun blinked his silvered eyes. "Yes, sorry, *jiejie*. I am looking for another memory."

"Something important?" I asked.

"Maybe." He shook his head. "I will stop for now, though; the break will do me good and I want to watch you fight."

"What happened to less violence, not more?" I teased.

"It is still the better option, but I would honor your skills by watching even as I wish they were not necessary."

I gave him an impulsive hug, squeezing tight. "Thank you."

"Do you want advice?" Hao asked as I pulled away from Dailun.

"I'll always take it from you."

He snorted. "Watch the taller one."

I glanced back at the pair of Shen. "Talos has a mean right hook."

"I'm sure he does, but his posture changed when Aiz spoke to him just now, so keep an eye out. They've got something planned."

"Duly noted." I tapped his outstretched fist. Whatever had shifted inside me, Hao was a constant, and I would trust his read on things better than my own in most cases.

Gita gave me a nod and a smile that didn't quite erase the fear clinging to her eyes. I stepped in, pressing my forehead to hers but not saying anything. There wasn't a need for words from my *Dve*; I knew her concerns, I shared them. This was territory as unfamiliar as it was familiar. Everyone here was about to see what I was capable of doing in real time. It would change how they thought of me—for good or ill. There wasn't time to worry about it. All I could do was fight.

"Relax into it, Hail," Johar said as she took Gita's place. Thumping me in the chest when we separated. "Make them work."

I nodded, exchanging a nod with Zin and then Emmory as I turned to face Aiz. He was leaning against the wall next to Mia, propping one foot up on a nearby seat.

"What's the plan?" I asked.

Aiz smiled. "They're going to be trying to kill you. Stop them. Don't kill them."

Relief and disappointment blossomed in my chest.

I nodded once, shaking my arms out as Hamah and Talos split and circled me. The noise level in the gym dropped off with the precision of a silencer nuke. I had fought Talos, who was the taller of the pair, on a number of occasions, but the only fighting interaction I'd had with Hamah had been the two times I kicked his ass.

That, coupled with the anger I was sure he was feeling over Mia's announcement just now, meant he'd be looking for payback.

I turned my back on Talos, trusting that he wouldn't be reckless enough to charge me at the insult and gestured at Hamah with a wicked smile. He complied, rushing at me, and I saw Aiz roll his eyes to the ceiling with a shake of his head.

33

I dropped low when Hamah was a step from me, planting my shoulder into his diaphragm and flipping him up and over my back.

Talos, sadly, was too alert for his own good and dodged Hamah's falling body. I blocked his first punch, landed one in return to his side, grabbed him by the neck, and slammed my knee into his crotch. The sympathetic groans from some of the crowd broke the stillness. I grinned, adrenaline and the unadulterated rush of pleasure at finally getting to fight rushing through me.

I shoved Talos away, my focus on Hamah as he scrambled to his feet. Straight into my kick.

I dared a glance at Aiz. He was laughing and shaking his head.

"Drop." Hao's order echoed in my head over our com link and I obeyed without question. Talos's kick sailed over my head. I rolled in the opposite direction, bouncing to my feet with my hands up.

Talos had recovered from the miss and grinned at me. "You got a warning on that kick," he said. Hamah was still on the floor, but not unconscious, and Talos blocked me from going after his downed companion again.

"You think?" I threw an easy punch that Talos blocked, dancing back a step before he could get a grip on my arm. "Maybe I'm just that good." I kept one eye on Hamah as he struggled to his feet. I didn't want him up, but there wasn't a way to circle around without engaging Talos, so I surged forward.

Talos chuckled, blocking my punch as expected. I collapsed my arm, clipping him in the ear with my elbow as I caught his right hand with my left. We tangled briefly, nothing but the sound of our breaths filling the air, until I was forced back a step. I took the loss, bending a knee and deliberately giving way so I could get loose of his grip.

The bright flash of hot pain rolled along my side as we separated and the hand I reached back came away wet with blood. "Bugger me."

Talos winked.

My *smati* wasn't screaming alarms at me, just flashing an injury warning in the corner of my vision, so it wasn't a fatal wound, but I felt the blood running down my back, and, worse, I couldn't see the weapon he'd used on me.

Hamah was on his feet, if still unsteady, and my BodyGuards had all gotten the notification of my injury when it happened. The shift in their mood was almost immediate, furious silence falling once again as I backed away from both Shen, giving my *smati* time to tell me that Talos had opened a gash about fifteen centimeters long and six deep along the left side of my back. He'd missed my spine, which was probably what he'd been aiming for, but not by much.

"Hail, use the injury, make them think you're hurt worse than you are." That was from Zin, his voice steady and soothing on the com link.

I smiled, trying to inject as much worry into it as could be faked, and took more breaths than I needed, stumbling a little as I continued to move to the side.

Hamah once again took the bait, though this time there was some coordination in their attack and Talos was right on his heels.

Gotcha, I thought, and held in the smile that would give me away.

I moved at the last second, ruining the angle of their attack, and caught Hamah by the throat.

I couldn't crush his throat, couldn't snap his neck. The answer

283

came to me as he landed a brutal punch in my injured side and the pain snarled to life. Rather than try to control it, I instinctively took the lesson Mia had taught me about the energy around us, and it was unbelievably easy to grab onto that pain in the same manner. Only this time I used it like a weapon. I dragged it up through my arm, forcing it through my hand into Hamah's throat.

He dropped like a rock, startling Talos enough to give me the space to grab his punch and twist his arm behind his back. I drove him toward the wall where Aiz was, people scattering out of the way as I bounced his head off the surface, and then dropped him at Aiz's feet.

"A knife? Really?" I said, stepping on Talos's wrist until he groaned.

The voice in my head wanted more, but I shook it off, standing still until the urge to fight ebbed, then faded as I took a deep breath. I closed my eyes for a moment when the room gave a slow spin around me. I opened them again; Aiz was grinning at me.

"Low-tech seemed the way to go. Did you crush Hamah's throat? That's technically going to kill him."

"He's fine." As I said it, I heard the Shen roll over with a loud curse. "I just"—I grinned—"gave him a bit of the pain I was feeling from his punch."

Aiz's eyebrows shot to the ceiling while Mia gaped, and as a pair they crossed the gym to where Hamah was lying still, gasping for breath.

I bent and helped Talos to his feet. He smiled down at me. "A good fight, Star of Indrana."

"You'd have done better if Hamah weren't so damned reckless."

"Possibly, but I knew that was a risk going in." His dark eyes sparkled with humor and he touched his forehead to mine. "Turn around and let me look at that."

I did, coming face to face with Emmory and Zin, the former catching me by the arm when I wobbled. "It was a good fight," my *Ekam* said, and the pride in his eyes made my heart swell.

"Thanks." I hissed when Talos pressed his hand to the cut on my back, but the pain vanished almost instantly, and the warmth flowed through me, easing away the remnants of the fight.

"Good as new," Talos said.

"It's appreciated. Make sure someone looks at you, I'm probably not in any shape to—" I gestured vaguely, the words escaping me.

"It's an honor to carry bruises from you." He grinned and winked. "I should go check on Hamah."

"A concussion is not an honor." I rolled my eyes and called out after him, "Get fixed, or I'll tell Mia to look for you specifically when we need someone to scrub the bathrooms."

I tightened my grip on Emmory's arm when he started to move away. "Give me another minute to get my feet under me."

Sybil slipped through the crowd and I looked down at the Farian when she put a hand to my side, tilting her head and closing her eyes. I felt the smallest surge of energy, easing the loss of adrenaline.

"Thank you," I murmured.

She opened her eyes, winked, and moved away.

"I take it you don't know what that was about any more than I do," Emmory murmured, and I snorted.

"I'm flying as blind here as the rest of you." I reached my free hand out to Hao. "Thanks for the assist."

"That kick would have broken your neck," he replied, bumping his fist to mine. "Glad I could help."

"You all helped." I looked around at them. "I can't do this without you. Thank you for being here."

"You fight—" Hao whistled. "We could make some serious credits in the cage matches on Mars."

I thumped him in the kidney and he yelped. Gita rolled her eyes and Emmory sighed. But the tease broke through the last of my fading adrenaline and their worry like sunlight after a vicious storm.

"Where did you learn to do that?"

"Do what?" I looked over my shoulder at Aiz. Talos and Mia

were helping Hamah limp out of the gym. "He really needs to learn some control," I said. "It's going to get him killed for real one of these days."

"Hail." Aiz grabbed me by the upper arm and the people around us stiffened. "You should not have been able to do that. You struggle with the easiest healing, with gathering energy from outside of you."

I lifted my free hand and Hao relaxed, the others following suit. "I don't know what to tell you. I just took the pain and tossed it back at him."

Aiz frowned but released me, shaking his head. "Mia is the only one I know who can do that. You shouldn't be able to do it. Even I can't—"

"I know how to inflict pain, Aiz." My laugh was sharp. "Human lives may be short, but we're very good at hurting each other."

"So I am learning." He patted me on the shoulder, but his look was still wary. "It was a good fight. You did well. Even if you did cheat." He said the last bit looking in Hao's direction.

My brother met it with an innocent look.

"I don't know what you're talking about," I replied, my expression blank.

"I understand what makes Po-Sin so nervous about the pair of you together," Aiz replied with a shake of his head. "I suppose I should be grateful you're on my side."

"You're on mine," I said.

Aiz hummed in his throat and walked away, a small frown still marring his face, and I wondered just what it was about my strike on Hamah that bothered him.

The days passed without further incident, and the last day before we headed for Faria dawned much the same as the others and slid quietly through its paces without much fanfare.

I'd insisted Emmory and the others take the night off since I hadn't any plans to go anywhere, and I sat in my room on base late that evening composing a letter to send to Adora while Mia spoke

via com to several of the captains of the Shen fleet and what few Farians from Fasé's contingent were joining us in the space above Faria.

"I want the 3rd and 4th Fleets with engines hot and ready to jump
the moment we get to Faria. The 1st and 2nd Fleets will follow us
in but break off just shy of sensor range." Mia highlighted the cutoff
point with a sweep of her arm. "Aiz and I may be out of contact, but
if you don't hear anything else from us after we land, then you stick
to the plan and hurt them as much as you can. Understood?"

"Yes, *Thína*." The woman on the other end of the com nodded
sharply.

"Good." Mia smiled and tapped the back of her index finger to
her forehead twice. "It is time. May the stars light your way home,
Marcela. I hope we see each other again soon."

"The same to you."

Mia disconnected and looked over at me. "Are you done pretending not to eavesdrop?"

I set my tablet down and grinned at her as I got to my feet.
"Technically this is my room. If you didn't want me listening you
should have had that conversation elsewhere. Besides, we're allies,
aren't we? I should probably know what your fleets are up to."

Mia didn't move when I boxed her in against the desk, the smile
peeking through just before I kissed her.

"Allies, is that what we're calling this?" She murmured against
my mouth, her fingers digging into my hips and tugging me closer.

"I don't know what to call this, to be honest," I confessed, pressing my forehead to hers.

"It doesn't need a name, does it?" she asked, staring up at me.
The lights in my room reflected in her eyes, and Gita's warning was
an unwelcome thought in my head.

Starstruck.

Damned if I didn't suddenly feel guilty.

"Hail?" Mia caught me by the hand as I pulled away. "What is it?
What's the matter?"

"I don't know." I shook my head, forced the words out. "I feel like I'm taking advantage of you."

She laughed, then stopped and stared. "Oh, you're serious. Why?"

I dragged both hands through my hair when she let me go. "I am more than just the Star of Indrana."

"Have I ever suggested otherwise?" There wasn't any bite to her words but I flinched from them all the same. "Hail, I know you. What I feel for you doesn't have anything to do with you being the Star. I know who you are."

You're the person they all keep dying for.

The voice in my head had been quiet since just after Aiz came on board, so the sudden and vengeful appearance of it was enough to make me curse out loud.

"Hail." Mia grabbed for me and pressed me down into the chair. "You are scaring me."

"I can't be the one who gets you killed." I blinked, scattering the tears that had gathered on my lashes.

"What are you talking about?" She cupped my face in her hands. "Look at me. You are not getting anyone killed, least of all me."

"I wish I could—"

"Star of Indrana, your brother sent me to fetch you. He wanted to speak with you about the ships. He's in the hangar."

Mia let me go with a frustrated noise at the unfamiliar Farian who poked his head into the room. "We are busy," she said.

"No." I pushed to my feet. "I'll go see what he wants."

"Hail, he could wait."

He could, Hao would have understood, but I was being a coward and running. "I'll be back."

"I'll come with you."

The Farian made a noise of protest even as I shook my head. "No," I repeated, holding up a hand and backing for the door. "Just wait here, I'll be right back."

I followed the Farian down the corridor and forced a smile when he stopped at the stairs leading down into the hangar. The whole area was quiet, everyone resting before we headed out for this final fight.

"I'm sorry for interrupting you, ma'am."

"It's fine." I nodded at the gesture for me to go first and started down the stairs. I was going to have to face up to Mia, I knew that. She'd wait for me and all the words in my head were inevitably going to spill out because I could only manage—

The hot pain radiated outward in a spiral as the knife drove deep into my back. My *smati* started in with the screaming warnings, but I didn't need them to know I was in trouble and that my distraction had cost me. The Farian kicked me in the knee and sent me crashing down the steps, knocking the wind from my intact lung. I hit the ground and rolled to my feet, stumbling sideways before a hand grabbed me by the shirt.

The Farian was gone; in his place Hamah grimly swung the knife down and the second blow landed in my upper right shoulder. He wrenched the knife out and swung again. My right arm refused to work and I barely got my left in the way of the knife, the blade slicing through flesh and scraping along bone.

"Hamah, what—" I choked on the blood flooding my right lung.

34

You are an *avedélcion*," he snarled in Shen. "You have corrupted our fight, infested our leaders with your division. They will not find you in time to bring you back." He jerked the knife free with a gloved hand, dodged my kick, and grabbed me by the shirt again.

I tried to brace myself, but he spun me around and slammed me into the wall of the secluded stairwell. It was the perfect attack point and I'd dropped my fucking guard for just long enough to give him the opening.

I attempted another kick through the pain, heard him grunt, and felt another hot kiss of pain as he stabbed me in the back again.

"I'm going to cut your throat, leave you down here. By the time they realize what's happened it'll be too late. You will be dead and gone and things will go back to the way they should be."

Somehow, I got my left hand up again and grabbed the knife, felt the blade bite into it as Hamah tried to drag it across my throat. I kicked behind me, connecting with something as I fought with the desperation of a doomed soul.

Shouting flooded past my panic, and then the pressure on my throat vanished. I collapsed, facedown against the hangar floor, and for a moment the memory of cradling Portis's bleeding body in my own ship flashed in front of my eyes.

"Two stab wounds in her back. Left kidney is compromised.

Lacerated right lung. Right brachial plexus is severed. Stab wound, left forearm—through and through. Left hand—no, Hail, come on—" Emmory's voice started to fade as the world grayed out around me. "Hail, stay with me," he murmured in my ear. "I'm turning you over, Fasé is almost here."

I wished I'd blacked out from the pain, but sadly my training with Aiz had lifted that threshold a lot higher and so I was awake for every excruciating second of Emmory carefully rolling me onto my back.

I tried to say something comforting, but the blood still pouring into my lung made it impossible and I felt Emmory's hands in my hair as he turned my head so the blood sprayed to the side as it left my mouth.

"Are you tired of being drenched in blood yet?" Fasé demanded when she lowered herself to my side. I managed to flip her off with my blood-coated left hand and felt Emmory's hands tense against my head.

"Just fix her, Fasé, save the commentary for later," he ordered.

Fasé pressed one hand to my chest and the other to my stomach. It had been a while since she'd healed me. The feeling was distinctly different from the Shen, but I suspected if I had a different Farian put their hands on me I wouldn't feel that same tinge of wildness. Still, it was so much gentler than I was used to, a soothing wave wiping out the worst of the pain in one pass.

"What the fuck happened?" Aiz demanded, and Zin gave an indistinct reply.

"Hail!" Mia dropped down next to us but didn't touch me; instead she put a hand on Fasé's and closed her eyes. Fasé shuddered, the energy inside me changed, and I squeezed my eyes shut as I dragged in a full breath.

There was more shouting as Hao, Gita, and Johar clattered down the stairs, more voices added to the cacophony in my head.

"Don't move just yet," Fasé murmured when I tried to sit up.

Mia reached across Fasé with her other hand, touching my throat with the tips of her fingers. "Good, Fasé. You got the blood out of her lungs, too. You're getting better."

"How do you do that?"

Mia smiled. "I'll explain it to you later when you're not lying bloodied on the floor." She glanced over her shoulder, and her smile vanished. "Where is the Farian who—"

"It was Hamah." I hated the pain in her eyes.

"Hamah did this?"

"Yes. He was ranting about me corrupting you, diverting the cause."

Mia hissed a curse in Shen and got to her feet. Gita took her place and I closed my fingers around her outstretched hand.

"I'm all right." I met Hao's look over Gita's shoulder and he gave me a sharp nod. "Help me up." I patted Emmory's arm. He nodded and with Gita's help got me on my feet. She slipped easily against my side, her arm wrapped around my waist.

"What happened?" Johar asked.

"Hamah led her down here and attacked her," Emmory said. "If the warnings on her bios hadn't gone off—" He cut himself off, shaking his head when I looked at him with a frown.

Hao snarled a curse in the air and put his hand on his gun. I lunged, snagging him by the arm, and would have fallen with the movement had Gita and Emmory not caught me. "No, Hao. It's not our place. Let Aiz handle it."

Hamah was on the floor, his hands bound behind his back and his head hanging low. Aiz whispered furiously with Mia, both Shen wearing dark looks. Zin stood with his gun in his hand, pointed at Hamah's head. He looked briefly away, caught my eye, and raised an eyebrow in silent question.

I nodded, leaning on Gita, still holding on to Hao, who'd stepped closer to my side. My legs weren't quite interested in supporting me yet, it seemed.

"Hail." Aiz broke away from the conversation with Mia and touched my shoulder.

"I'm all right."

He frowned in response and slid his fingers through the quickly cooling blood. The curse he spat out was in Shen, the same words I couldn't understand from Mia. "Mia, this ends here. I'm sorry."

Mia's eyes widened when Aiz crossed to Hamah, grabbing him by the chin with his clean hand and drawing three bloody stripes across the Shen's cheek.

"The depths of this betrayal, Hamah. You attacked the Star. For what?" Aiz fisted his hand, looking for all the world like he wanted to strike out and was only stopped by a thin thread of sanity. "Are you *kataespier?*"

"No. I am not a spy for the Farians. I am loyal to the cause," Hamah replied with defiance in his eyes. "She brought chaos to us, Aiz. You have been blinded to it, to the damage she does. She puts everything you have worked for in danger, but you refuse to see! She has corrupted Mia, made her doubt the righteousness of our course. She's corrupted you! You have lost your conviction. You are willing to sit with those bastard Farians and negotiate." He spit the word into the air. "They will betray us all and it will be the end of everything we have worked for all these long years."

"You assume so much, Hamah. How dare you?" Mia hissed, and Aiz held up a hand, stopping her when she advanced on Hamah.

"What do you know of the future that my sister does not?" Aiz's mouth thinned when Hamah blinked at him in shock. "Nothing. You don't have the gift of sight, Hamah, and you cannot protect her from the end of this. None of us can, only the Star. Mia and I will do what we have always done—make the best decision for our people that we can. What we may feel personally has little bearing on those decisions. You attacked the Star. Do you realize what would have happened if you had killed her? You almost brought ruin down on us all with your arrogance."

"Aiz—"

"Enough." The snap of Aiz's command cut into the air. "How many others believe as you do?"

"None."

"You could have at least given me that truth." Aiz sighed in disgust. "I once would have trusted you with my life; now I can't trust a single word you say." Aiz held out his hand, and Talos moved in, handing over an empty hourglass. It was no larger than a handgun, the surface etched with something, and I saw the fear chase itself across Hamah's face when he read the inscription.

"For this, you have thrown everything away." Aiz shook his head. "You will not see our triumph. You will likely see nothing ever again."

Hamah's face crumpled. "I am sorry. Mia, please don't. I will—"

Aiz slapped a hand to his mouth. "Enough. You are done. You are undone. No death. Only an eternity locked in here." He waved the hourglass in Hamah's eyeline. "It was your choice. Your consequence."

Aiz pulled his hand away, making a fist as he did, and a pale smoke came with it. It wasn't quite silver, and was filled with lights much like the fireflies of Hagan dancing over the summer fields of gray wheat.

I realized with gut-clenching terror that it was Hamah's soul.

"Holy Shiva, protect us," Emmory whispered, his arm tightening around me. Zin watched from the other side of Hamah, his graygreen eyes wide with shock.

Aiz wrapped the smoke around his fist. Hamah convulsed, his eyes rolling back in his head until the last thread came loose, and his body fell to the floor. Aiz put the base of the hourglass into his palm, closing his fingers around it, and the smoke dissolved into it, pulsing frantically.

"Talos, pitch that detritus out into the desert," Aiz said, nudging the body with his boot. He looked me over, jaw tight. "How did he get the drop on you?"

"I was distracted. And I let my damn guard down." I shot Aiz a rueful smile. "Thought I was among friends, or at least people who weren't going to kill me. First stab hit me in the lung. It went downhill after that."

"You should be more careful. We will be in my room, mourning our friend. Then we will see if he was telling the truth about the others." With that parting shot, he turned on his heel and headed for the stairs with Mia, the other Shen trailing after them.

"Let's get you cleaned up," Emmory said. "Fasé, have you got this?"

"Go. We'll have someone come down and clean it out," she replied with a wave of her hand. Gita and Jo were in quiet conversation as we left. Hao released me and joined them, staring at the pool of blood on the floor with a hand over his mouth.

Zin closed a hand around my upper arm as we headed across the bay, and I smiled at him. "Sorry I interrupted your night off. Thanks for saving my ass."

"Any time." He pointed at his husband. "You know we're never really off duty, Hail."

"What in the fires of Naraka did Aiz mean by 'no one can protect Mia'?" I muttered as we made our way up the stairs.

"I don't know," Emmory replied. "That's a question you're going to have to ask her."

"I guess so." I sighed and leaned on him. "Shiva, I'm tired."

"Please stop getting killed, Hail. It's hard on my blood pressure."

"I swear I'm not doing it intentionally," I said, looking down at my blood-soaked clothes with a sigh when we reached my room. "Fasé wasn't wrong, you know? I'm getting pretty tired of this, too."

"I wish I could tell you we're done with it." Zin let me go at the bathroom door.

"Yeah, me, too." I patted his face, slipped out of Emmory's grasp, and closed the door behind me.

35

Fasé was in my room, equally clean, when I emerged from the bathroom fifteen minutes later. Emmory and Zin were standing at the doorway and I knew we were back to guards on my door full time whether I liked it or not.

"Fasé." I gave her a nod as I finished squeezing the water out of my hair into the towel.

"We need to talk." Fasé folded her hands and shook them at me. "I am sorry about earlier, Hail. And about everything."

I blinked at her, too stunned to even say anything sarcastic.

"Sorry for what you went through. Sorry my words weren't better when you rejoined us. I could blame my inexperience on my reaction, but we both know the truth is I am as uncompromising as you. That's what got us into this mess in the first place, after all."

The apology threw me, but I knew how much it had taken Fasé to make it in the first place, so I dipped my head in acknowledgment. "I am sorry, too. For not listening to you better."

"Are you ready to listen now?"

"Yes. Why, though? Why are you apologizing now?"

Fasé went silent for a long moment, staring down at her lap as she collected her thoughts. "We almost lost you. I did not see this. I don't know if Sybil did, or Mia, but I didn't. Had Emmory not—"

"Been himself?" I finished with a half smile and a glance at his back. I knew he was listening.

"Things are shifting too fast to see. Sybil warned me this might happen. The closer we get to the blank spot, the more things will be in flux. The choices that are made not only by you but by others will have impacts like boulders thrown into a stream.

"Whatever my disagreements with the Pedalion, there is a reason the Council of Eyes don't share the futures they see with the general public. There is a reason that even the futures they do share are heavily filtered and carefully worded." She looked me in the eyes as she reached for my hands.

"What we see isn't clear; it's still filtered through our perceptions. Through our own fears and knowledge. We must be careful with what we share and how." She smiled; it was the first genuine smile I'd seen from her since before Earth. "Here is where I disagree with Sybil, because I do think we need to share. I think there are things you need to know."

"You just think you should control them, rather than letting me decide for myself what's important."

She released me and leaned back in her chair with a sigh. "I suppose I should be grateful you are so uncompromising."

"You sure you don't mean aggravating?"

"Possibly." Fasé laughed, the sound ringing out into the air. She tapped a hand on the desktop as her mirth subsided. "You're not wrong, Hail. Though I have since learned there is no controlling the Star of Indrana. You do what you want, what you feel is right, regardless of what the rest of us think."

"That's not entirely true," I murmured. "I do occasionally listen."

"The point here," Fasé replied with a sharp grin, "is that you need to realize that what you have seen—what Mia has shown you—is filtered not only through her perception of the future but through your own, Hail. Your fears. Your concerns. That's why you see Indrana when you see what's in ruins and not some random town on some Solarian planet.

"It is the same with Mia. It is the same with me. It is even the same with Sybil. When she was separated from the world it was a cleaner vision, but now that she's out and interacting with you? Things change, there's no way around it. It's important you recognize this. It's important because there's no other way for you to handle what I show you, what you will see when we reach Faria. You have to know this so you can truly make decisions without being influenced by not only your fears but the fears of those around you."

"I'm up to here with ominous shit, Fasé, no lie." I held my hand above my head. "I'm just trying to keep all of you safe; beyond that?" I sighed and gave a weary shrug. "I don't know. Emmory's right. I'm not the savior of the universe, the Star of Indrana, whatever. I'm just me."

"I know." She smiled, getting to her feet and crossing the room. "I see you clinging to hope, though, when it is all so close to despair." Fasé reached up and touched my cheek. "You lost it once, never again. I know your concerns about fighting. I know you're unsure this is the best road to take. How can I help?"

My exhale was short and sharp as relief flooded through me. There wasn't a word for the absence this break with Fasé had created in me, and I didn't even know how to explain how it felt now except that a yawning void in my battered heart had just sealed itself up as easily as Mia healing a cut without leaving so much as a scar.

"Fasé, tell me if you think I am right that there has to be a better way than more death, isn't there?"

Fasé was silent for so long I thought I wasn't going to get an answer, but then she sighed. "I don't want to tell you."

"Please."

Emmory had turned in the doorway and was watching us closely. Fasé sighed again, tugged on a red curl, and then looked up at me. Her golden eyes glowed with a sudden light.

"You will have to make a choice, Star of Indrana. I can't tell you exactly what the choice is, only that it will not be what you think.

You cannot let this paralyze you with fear of making the wrong choice, because there is no wrong choice. People will die, that is the way of things. You hold the fate of the galaxy in the balance. Do not disrupt it."

"Fasé?"

She slumped forward and I lunged out of my chair to catch her before she fell. Emmory moved at the same moment and helped me put her back upright.

"You with us?" I asked when her eyes fluttered open.

"I was—" She broke off and rubbed her eyes. "Yes, I'm all right. That was draining."

I smiled and pressed my hand to her cheek for a moment before I got to my feet. "I need you to do something for me, Fasé."

"Anything."

"Back me up. No matter what. Against Sybil or Hao or anyone. You back me. Things can go sideways on Faria really quickly, we all know it. I need to know that you trust me enough to make the right decisions." I dragged in a breath, let it out as the rushing sound of the stars spinning through the universe filled my ears. "I know I haven't been—"

"I trust you, and I'll be there when you need me." She got up and wrapped her arms around me in a hug. I returned it, pressing my cheek to the top of her head and exhaling as a great weight lifted off my shoulders for the first time since I'd woken up on the floor of my ship so very long ago.

News of Hamah's attack spread like a shipboard fire and by the next morning two ships had bolted and Aiz had performed that horrifying ritual a handful more times. My people and Fasé's understood the gravity of it without having to be told, and I decided we'd stay at the base until things had settled down.

"Another day, maybe two," I said to Inana as we headed down the corridor toward the war room.

"Do you think the Farians know we're coming?"

"I do." I sighed. "If the news hasn't gotten out that they've got a mass of Shen ships less than fifteen thousand light-years from their home planet, then Adora will figure it out when she gets my letter this morning."

"You're being very sanguine about the fact that someone almost slit your throat yesterday evening, Majesty."

"Would you believe it's not the worst thing that's happened to me in the last six months?" I laughed at her frown. "Well, at the time I was concerned, but it's over." I nodded in greeting to the Shen we passed. "And I think Aiz and Mia have things in hand. We were expecting something. Not quite to that level, I grant you, but that's been an issue for them since I arrived on Sparkos."

"They certainly have a way of dealing with dissenters," Inana murmured.

I thought of watching my cousin fight for her last breaths during her execution. "Not all that different from ours."

"True. Good morning, Alba, Dailun."

My chamberlain and pilot were standing at the doorway of the war room, shoulders touching, fingers just a hairsbreadth from being intertwined, and I raised a curious eyebrow. Alba had been working with Dailun on gathering as much intel about the Hiervet as they could over the last several weeks. We were all hoping it was information we wouldn't need.

"Majesty, Admiral." Alba smiled. "It's good to see you, ma'am."

"Good morning, *jiejie*." Dailun leaned in and touched his cheek to mine. "May I speak with you in private?"

I caught Alba's eye as I pulled away and on cue, she gestured at the door. "Admiral, Mia is already here if you wanted to join her. There will be some adjustments to make with the loss of the two ships from last night."

Slipping my arm through Dailun's, I walked us farther down the corridor to an empty office and leaned against the desk. Dailun shoved a hand into his pink hair and I marveled for a moment how much this young man had grown up in front of my eyes since the first time I met him on the bridge of Hao's ship.

"I have found more information in my hunting. Alba has been an invaluable help. *Jiejie*," he sighed. "Do not."

"What?" I couldn't stop the grin I'd tried to muffle before.

"You look exactly like Hao when you do that."

"Odd considering we're not actually related."

"I know, but the facial expressions." He waved his hand in front of his face and rolled his eyes. "We are getting off track, which is exactly what I didn't want."

"I like that you're happy," I said. "That's all."

He smiled. "Information."

"Right. Focus." I rubbed my hands together as I leaned against the nearby desk.

"What I'm about to tell you I would ask you not share with any-one else. I know that is a strange request, but it was the only way I could obtain permission to share it with you in the first place."

"Now you have my attention, and my promise." I smiled and gestured with one hand. "Go on."

"When the Svatir laid down their arms and walked away from war, we did so willingly. Our weapons were destroyed, the designs erased; our warriors turned their lives away from war. This is the memory that is carried by all Svatir." He took a deep breath. "It is a memory that is not entirely true."

I kept my mouth shut through sheer force of will.

"The Istrevitel were the best of us. The elite warriors in a race of warriors. After we defeated the Hiervet, our leaders decided to lay down their weapons, and they also decided that the Istrevitel would vanish from our memory."

"Why?"

"So the Istrevitel could stay vigilant for threats. And the rest of us could walk away from war." Dailun's smile flickered. "They were all too aware of the dangers and while they wanted our people to know peace, they were also willing to sacrifice some of us to prepare for an unknown war."

"You're angry about this?"

"Of course I'm angry," he snapped, and then lowered his head. "I'm sorry."

"Don't be." I pushed away from the desk and wrapped my arms around him. "I get it. Do you know why they chose to do this?"

"Fear?" Dailun sighed and shrugged, dragging his hands through his hair again after he stepped away from me. "Justified or not, what else drives people to break the oaths they made to step away from war forever?"

"What does this mean for us?" I asked. "I can't tell anyone about their existence. It doesn't seem like it's changed things."

"I suspect the Istrevitel will reveal themselves when, or if, it is necessary. I received a message from someone shortly after the memories were given to me. It only said: *We will speak with the Star if the time comes. Pray it does not.*"

I let that spin around in my brain for a breath or two. The meaning was clear enough given everything else we'd been dealing with. If the Hiervet came, we would need all the help we could get, and I sure as shit wasn't turning down some mysterious force of Svatir who'd beaten the pants off them the first time around.

"Well." I blew out a breath. "That's something. I'm not quite sure what, Dailun, but I guess let's all hope we don't ever talk to them."

"I cannot lie, sister. Part of me would love to see these legends, but I agree with you." He cleared his throat. "The other thing I have for you is something that can be shared with the others. I found a curious memory that happened at the end of the war. A Svatir officer questioning some Hiervet prisoners who were apparently part of a crew attempting to round up deserters." He held his hand out. "It is a violent memory, but I can show it to you if you wish."

I took his hand.

*   *   *

The screams echoed around the room, stopping only to devolve into sobs between one heartbeat and the next.

"The war is over. Your people were supposed to retreat. Tell me why you are still here." The speaker had the familiar silver-chased eyes of a Svatir, their sharply angled face and dark skin standing out in the harsh light of the interrogation room.

"We—we are looking for someone." The pale blond hair of the Hiervet on the table was soaked with blood. "Deserters. Please. They are criminals. You have to let me go."

"I don't have to do anything. You're in violation of the treaty."

"You don't understand—" The Hiervet broke off with another scream.

"If there are still Hiervet in our sector. I will find them and they will meet the same fate as you."

I gasped and doubled over, feeling Dailun's hands on my sides as he helped me over to the chair.

"I am sorry for that, sister. I know it was horrible."

"It was certainly intense." I rubbed the back of my hand over my mouth, swallowing down the bile because there was nowhere to spit it. "How could I understand them?"

"I tweaked the memory so it was all in Indranan." He smiled. "It would have been far too cumbersome for me to translate the whole thing while you watched so it was easier to do it beforehand."

"So there were still Hiervet in the galaxy after the war?"

"Not long after, and that's the only recorded incident I could find." Dailun shook his head. "I don't know if it means anything or not, but I thought it was worth bringing to your attention."

"I appreciate it." Taking a deep breath, I stood, smiling when Dailun reached a hand out to steady me. "I'm assuming Alba has this in the file with all the other things you two have collected?"

"Yes."

"Good work." I patted him on the shoulder as the ping of an

incoming message went off in my head. "Oh, it's Adora, this should be good."

Dailun grinned. "I'll let you take this one in private, *jiejie*. That's beyond my pay grade."

"You're getting paid?" I teased, and he laughed as he left me alone in the room.

36

Good morning, *Itegas* Notaras," I said when I answered the com link. My polite, practiced empress smile was on my face, and it seemed to confuse her for a moment before she dipped her head to me.

"Your Majesty—"

"Given the circumstances, Star of Indrana is probably a more appropriate title." I smiled. "I think it's a bit pretentious, but I'm not the one who chose it."

"Star of Indrana, then." Adora dipped her head a second time. "We are very glad you are safe. Where are you?"

"Somewhere." I glanced sideways and shrugged. "We'll be on our way to you soon."

Adora couldn't quite keep her eyes from starting to narrow in disbelief, even though she corrected it and dipped her head again in agreement. "Of course. I received your letter. We would be more than delighted to receive you. You must be exhausted after your ordeal."

Aiz appeared in the doorway. Without looking away from the screen, I slipped my left hand out of my pocket and waved it at him out of the camera's view. He stopped, the curious frown melting into realization at my next words.

"I am, Adora, and I'm looking forward to wrapping this up."

"Yes, the negotiations." Her face twisted as if the word were unpleasant in her mouth. "That did not go so well on Earth."

"It didn't, did it?" The smile I let slip was cold, deliberate, and Adora shifted away despite the fact that I wasn't physically near her. I desperately wanted to spit out the accusation about her involvement with Jamison, but I stayed silent. As Hao had said, we had no real proof and I didn't want to give her any time to concoct a story to cover her ass. "These things happen and despite our brief recess I'm ready to get back to work."

"You're serious." Adora's voice squeaked a little and I had to fight to keep my composure.

"Of course I'm serious. We're talking about a conflict that has killed far too many people, Adora, my own included. It's time to end it."

"But the Cevallas kidnapped you. They blew up your embassy! It was a miracle no one was hurt."

"It was because of Fasé no one was hurt," I replied. "And in light of other events I have forgiven the Cevallas for their actions on Earth."

"They blew up—"

"They did not." I let her chew on that one without any further explanation. "Adora, I am at the end of my patience with a fleet of ships capable of doing a lot more damage than shooting a chandelier out of a ceiling. If the Pedalion will not agree to these negotiations and let us land on Faria, I will not hesitate to bring those ships to bear on your planet."

"You would not."

I stared at her. "You are welcome to see if I am bluffing."

There was a long silence.

"I—I am afraid I have underestimated you again." Adora had somehow gone even paler than normal for a Farian when she finally spoke. "Very well. Your ship will be cleared to land and I promise no harm will come to anyone you choose to bring with you for as long as the negotiations are proceeding."

"Excellent." I smiled. "I'd recommend warning your fleet admirals about what's coming. The bulk of my fleet will stay back from your planet, but if someone gets nervous and starts shooting it wouldn't be a very good day for any of us, would it?"

"Of course." Adora disconnected, but not before I saw the troubled frown slip over her face.

I chuckled. Aiz raised an eyebrow. "Mia said you were with Dailun."

"I was. He had some information for me."

"What was all that?"

"Got us a clear path to Faria. For the *Vajrayana*, anyway." I made a face. "Which means we're all going to need to ride on the same ship. We'll figure out who's necessary and who can be shifted to another ship."

"I'm starting to regret all the times I bounced your head off the wall. You threatened Adora with war if she didn't agree to the negotiations. With *your* fleet?"

"The best part of that is she doesn't know if I'm lying or not." I grinned and winked at him. "Reputations are so fucking handy."

"That was cold," he replied. "If I didn't know any better, I'd have believed you."

"I know I'm a good liar," I said. "What bothers me is Adora."

"Adora bothers everyone. It's her talent."

"As old as she is, you'd think she'd have more practice at lying."

Aiz choked on a laugh, but it died when I didn't join him. "You think she's hiding something else?"

"*Hai Ram*, I certainly don't think she's just going to agree to these negotiations. Not after trying to kill us all in the last one."

Aiz blinked at me. "What?"

"Oh, you weren't there for that conversation. We don't have

proof but it's extremely likely that a Farian hired Jamison to attack the party." I held a finger up. "And before you swear some oath of vengeance—he's mine."

"Fair enough." He smiled. "Can I help?"

"With that?" I shrugged. "It's on my list of things to worry about if we make it out of this alive, but sure. Anyhow, something's off there with Adora. I liked my life better when I wasn't dealing with people who could see the future."

"That's not true."

I thought of Mia and smiled. "You're right, it's not. Adora's hiding something. The Farians have always been good at seeding lies with truth. Tell an obvious lie, the listener thinks they know what's going on. They don't bother to look for the bigger lie hiding behind everything else."

"You're afraid that's what she's doing?"

"I don't know her as well as you do." I transferred the file over. "Take a look at the recording and tell me what you think." I leaned against the wall and watched him as he reviewed the conversation.

"She's off her stride from the beginning. Do you always make her so unsettled?" Aiz exhaled in surprise. "You know, I assumed her behavior at the negotiations was all due to me, but my dear sister is scared of you."

"She should be, especially if I get proof she had anything to do with Jamison."

"You're right about her not being sure if you're telling the truth or not. It's good. It keeps her off balance. She's hiding something; see this?" He tossed the video back onto the screen. "That tic in her jaw. She's poking at a molar with her tongue. I knocked it out when we were children. Father made her go without it for a month before he regrew it, and she developed this habit of messing with it when she's planning something."

"So she's planning something, but there's no way of telling just what it is." I pushed away from the wall, taking an absentminded swing at Aiz. He blocked it with his right. I took the punch to my side, collapsing with it, stealing the power from him with a hold Zin had taught me months ago. Aiz fumbled, barely stopping my elbow from hitting his head, and I watched the frown flit over his face at the unexpected move. "I want to talk to Fasé's people. Get a backup plan in play for when things go to shit. And then there's the big question. How do we get to the gods?"

"I have an idea for that."

"Are you going to share that idea with me? Or just keep it all to yourself?"

"We should go find the others. It would be easier to only go through it once."

I grinned; the pace of our fight was easy, without any of the heat and anger that normally swamped my brain. Still, I knew I had him on the defensive with my almost-lazy style, and I pressed my advantage in the small space.

"So we'll go to Faria, talk with some gods, convince them to cooperate, and be home in time for tea."

"You know it's not going to work out like that." Aiz threw a punch. I blocked it, stepping in and sweeping his leg. He avoided it at the last second, but the chairs were in his way and I laughed when he stumbled into one of them.

"I know, but a girl can dream." I sighed. "Besides, we've got the whole saving-the-galaxy portion of events to deal with, too." I glanced over my shoulder, spotting Emmory and Mia standing shoulder to shoulder in the doorway. "Morning."

"The gym might be a better place for a fight, Hail," Emmory said.

"I know, we were just—" I fumbled, dropped my hands. "It helps me think."

Mia laughed, but there was a soft look in her gray eyes. The memory of her mouth underneath mine flooded my brain, stealing my breath.

Aiz's punch to my kidney put me on my knees, finishing the job. I folded over, palms flat to the floor, and dragged in a breath, tasting blood in my mouth.

"You can't afford to get distracted," he whispered, his voice amused as he hauled me to my feet.

"Too late for that." It was meant to be light, but Aiz frowned, leaning in until his forehead was pressed to mine.

"I have come to care for you, Star of Indrana. I told myself I shouldn't, that it would complicate things. But I have." He offered up a smile. "I know you agreed to this; however, I would not see you dead for the sake of my people."

"You should care a little more for your own life," I murmured back.

"I have had a long one, filled with violence unending and far too little love." His smile was forced as he pulled away.

"We will finish this, then, for my people and yours." I caught his hand, squeezed it once before letting it go.

"At times I almost believe you could make that happen," he replied. "But that is not the reality you and I know. Is it?"

It made my heart ache, but I knew he was right.

"Adora has been informed we're coming for a second go at the negotiations." I gestured at Aiz with my mug ten minutes later in the war room. "How do we get in to see the gods once we're there?"

"Fasé and I will invoke the right of *ilios porthmeios*."

Mia gasped. "Aiz, you cannot."

Fasé looked impressed. I frowned. The words were Farian, but they meant nothing to me. "What does that mean?"

Sybil's mouth dropped open in surprise, and then she laughed. "I can't believe I didn't think of that."

"Someone want to clue the rest of us in on what that is?"

"It is the ritual ending. A challenge of sorts. We use their own laws against them." Sybil was practically bouncing in her chair.

"The Pedalion grants special privilege to those looking to end their lives."

"I'm assuming you mean permanently."

"Aiz, no," Mia repeated, pressing a hand to her mouth. "You can't risk it."

"I will," he replied. "This is always where it was headed. I fight the gods and win, or I lose, and this is over for good."

"Adora's never going to believe you want to end your life," I said. "And I'm reasonably sure I don't qualify for this given that I'm neither Farian nor Shen."

"My sister will jump at the chance to approve my petition even if she doesn't believe me, and I suspect the Pedalion would be glad to see Fasé follow me to the same fate." Aiz's smile was bitter. "It's not about if I actually want to, Hail. It's about what will happen. Their arrogance will lead them to assume I can't possibly win and they'll gladly send me to what they think is my doom."

I had some thoughts of my own about arrogance, but I kept them close. Setting the cup down and resting my chin on my hand, I gave him a level look. "What about me and Mia? All four of us need to be there."

"I make the challenge. The Pedalion will hear it and deliberate, finally making a decision on my petition. I will go through the trials to face the gods. I will fight them. I will finish them. So we can finally be free."

"What. About. Me?"

Aiz grinned. "I get a plus-one to the party, Star of Indrana. Fancy a dance?"

I laughed at him. "I'm not even going to get dinner out of it, am I?"

"I could, if you really need it."

Dhatt. I picked up my chai again and smiled at him over the rim of the mug. "I see where you're going with this, though. If you and Fasé both issue the challenge, you'd each get to take someone with you. It could work."

"Can we back up a few steps here?" Hao asked. "If your people want to truly die, they have to fight their gods for it?"

"It is a ritual challenge," Sybil replied. "Some fight, most don't. It's seen as an honorable death either way. It is the ritual that's important. When the gods kill a Farian, or Shen"—she looked in Aiz's direction—"they consume their souls; there is no coming back from that."

"Can they do that to her?" Hao gestured at me, and I raised an eyebrow in surprise. Of all the people to be concerned for my immortal soul, my atheist brother was the last one I'd have picked.

"Unlikely." Sybil smiled. "Star of Indrana she is, but Hail is still human. They'd have no need of her soul."

Hao was unimpressed by the answer. "You're talking to someone who has spent a great deal of his life taking things he had no need of, Sybil. That's not very reassuring."

"I'll be dead, Hao; it won't matter anyway."

"It does," Zin said. "You matter, Hail, and what happens after matters."

I wasn't about to get into a theological discussion with Zin in the middle of all this, so I simply nodded. His eyes narrowed and I mouthed *What?* at him.

"You know damn well what, this is—"

"Focus, people," Emmory said. "We've already committed to the idea of Her Majesty and Aiz facing down the gods; there's no backing away from it at this point. So deal with the problems as they come up, and stop worrying about step eight."

His sharp order stunned the room into silence, and I watched Zin bite down the rest of whatever he'd been about to say to me. Hao was staring with a look in his eyes I knew all too well meant I'd get an earful as soon as he could get me alone.

"I like it," Fasé announced with a finality no one seemed to want to argue with. Mia still looked troubled, but she nodded in agreement.

"So we go in under the pretense of negotiations, drop this challenge on them, and go to meet the gods instead." I lifted hands. "Beyond the obvious dangers, can anyone see a problem with this plan?"

"Beyond the potential mortality of it all?" Aiz grinned. "It'll be a stroll through a supernova."

37

W e've started with the retrofits on the other *Vajrayana* engines, Majesty, thanks to your contacts. Caspel?" Inana gestured in to Caspel, who was on the screen in front of us.

"At your request, I spoke with Prime Minister Toropov. He was appreciative of the information. You were right that there was some growing concern that it looked like we were mobilizing for war again. They haven't finalized negotiations with the Farians yet, and he's going to come up with some way to stall until there's an outcome on your end. He said to tell you that Saxony is Indrana's friend and ally first."

I blew out a breath. That was a big risk on the Saxons' part and one that Toropov or the king didn't have to take. The fact that they were willing to do so said a great deal about just how committed to keeping the peace between our people they were.

I shouldn't have worried about it. Toropov was canny enough to realize just how fast things would go to shit if Earth was attacked and our two nations were left to fend for ourselves in our arm of the galaxy.

"Tell Toropov if there's a way for us to figure out how to get this tech to work with some of his ships, we'll do it." I saw Caterina's frown form a second before her question.

"Is that wise, Majesty? This tech could give us a big advantage. If something were to—"

"We're not going back to war with the Saxons, Caterina, and

King Samuel was gracious enough to offer up the *Likho* tech as part of the reparations."

"Yes, because they owe us for the war. You're basically handing them something that's worth a thousand times over what their warp technology is worth."

"Possibly because I recognize that we won't get paid back anything if war comes and the Saxons fall, Caterina. Beyond that, think for a minute about how this could improve the shipping interests of both the Indranans and the Saxons. We'll have tech that the Solarians won't and the ability to ship things almost instantaneously between our arm of the galaxy and theirs."

"I—" Caterina blinked and closed her mouth, shaking her head. "I apologize, Your Majesty. You have obviously thought this through. I shouldn't have assumed otherwise."

"Apology accepted, Caterina. I want to be done with war. I want the peace with the Saxons to open up a new era of prosperity for our people."

Alice cleared her throat with a smile.

"I received a very concerned message from Adora," she said. "About you suggesting you had a fleet that would fire upon the Farian forces should she refuse the negotiations."

I was glad I'd thought to bring Alice in on the loop immediately after that conversation with Adora. Otherwise I'd probably be fending off her and Caterina on this call.

"I told her that yes, that was the case, and that moreover not only Indrana but the rest of the governments in the human sectors were in full agreement about putting a stop to the war. I'd spoken with President Hudson shortly before that, and he will be passing on the same ultimatum to the Farians. Humanity is united on this idea of peace between the Farians and the Shen."

"Good. We'll be sure not to waste it." I wondered if they would all be as united if they knew the real plan, and looked around. "Is there anything else?"

"No, Majesty. Just be careful," Alice said.

I nodded in acknowledgment. "I'll do my best. Same to all of you, keep an eye out."

Caspel nodded at my parting words and then I disconnected the call, sharing a look with Gita as I got to my feet.

"Under normal circumstances, Matriarch Saito would have a point, ma'am," Inana said. "While I agree with your plan for our shipping consortiums, we also could gain an advantage over Saxony with that tech."

"We got the tech from Fasé, which means it was illegal in the first place. Then we got more components because one of the leaders of the Shen gave it to me as a gift." I shook my head. "We wouldn't even be here if this were normal circumstances, Inana." I rubbed a hand over my face. "I want to be done with war after this. I want to trust our neighbors. I know there's always a chance Saxony will turn around and use that on us at some point down the road, or worse that the Solarians and others will pitch a fit when they catch wind of it. But we need the advantage right now, and I'm willing to bank on Toropov knowing that staying on my good side benefits his people more than the other option."

"I hope we don't need it," Inana replied. "Which really is the bigger issue." She gestured at where the screen had been. "Those three are going to be furious when they find out we didn't tell them about your backup plan."

"Yeah, well." I grinned and shrugged. "There's nothing they can do about it from Pashati, and the more people we tell the greater the risk is that it'll get back to the Pedalion. And I'm not taking any chances on that." My amusement fled and I met Gita's grim look. "I'd like to at least get us down onto Faria before I have to start worrying about whether the Pedalion is going to try to have us killed."

"I'm in agreement with you," Inana said, getting to her feet. "Just warning you. I'm going to go make sure Captain Saito and her crew are ready for departure."

Isabelle Saito was the captain of the *Hailimi Bristol* ever since we'd stolen the ships from Canafey. The tall, broad-shouldered woman and her crew were all familiar to me, and I knew that had been the major reason Admiral Hassan had decided to bring them with her in the first place.

I settled back down on the bunk in my room as Gita walked with Inana to the door. Everything was as sorted as we could get it. I'd ruthlessly compartmentalized all the problems for after our show-down with the gods and shoved them into a box in the back corner of my *smati*.

I'll deal with it later wasn't very imperial, I knew, but it was going to have to work for now.

"Majesty?" Gita stuck her head back in the door. "Do you have a moment for Sybil?"

"Sure." I rolled from my bed and got up with a smile. "Have a seat, what can I do for you?"

"You are looking for something?" she asked with a smile, gesturing at the mess of information I had projected onto the wall.

"The link," I replied. "There has to be something that binds all this together. Something that links your gods to the Hiervet and the light coming."

"You won't believe it's all just random?"

"Recognizing patterns is what we do." I crossed my arms and stared at the wall. "It's there, I just can't quite put my finger on it yet. You don't believe there is? Even having seen all the possibilities?"

Sybil joined me with a shrug of a shoulder. "There are some eternal patterns. Honestly, the rest of it is just you all trying to make sense of chaos instead of embracing the uncertainty."

"Uncertainty gets you killed," I replied automatically, waving Emmory and Zin into the room when they appeared in the door-way. "I have questions about the *ilios porthmeios*."

"What kind of questions?"

"The basics—how does it work? What are we looking at if the

Pedalion approves it?" I leaned against the desk next to Zin, smiling at his murmured greeting.

"The petitioner can be of any bodily age, but their soul age has to be at least a hundred," Sybil said.

"As if it takes someone a hundred years to know if they want to die," Mia said from the door. Aiz was at her side and the pair moved into the room, taking up the last free spots.

"It is admittedly an arbitrary cutoff point."

"It makes a certain amount of sense, all things considered," I said. "That was a decent life span before longevity meds. You wouldn't get to experience everything, but you could make a good showing of it."

"I suspect that is the reason for the ruling." Sybil nodded. "There is no limit, as I said, on the age of the body the Farian is in, given that it is really just a way for us to move through the world. Though I'd expect it would have an impact on those who were hearing the petition maybe if the petitioner were younger. I can think of only one instance where a Farian you would consider a teenager was granted *ilios porthmeios* and they were very old indeed."

Intellectually I knew the teen Sybil referred to hadn't really been a teen, but it was a still a hard thing to wrap my head around. I glanced at Mia; she had her arms wrapped around her waist and a lost look in her eyes, but when she looked up at me she mustered a smile.

"So is it just the Pedalion who hears the petition?" I asked, and Sybil nodded.

"The petition is heard by the Pedalion; they make the determination over the course of seven of our days."

"A day on Faria is thirty-four standard hours," Aiz supplied, and I blinked.

"That's a hell of a long time to be in potentially hostile territory," Emmory said with a frown. "They're not going to be happy once they realize the negotiations were just a ruse for the petitions."

He wasn't wrong. The length of the Farian day meant we were looking at close to ten standard days while the Pedalion deliberated. "We'll have the ship," I said, tapping a finger against my lower lip. "If I could get the Pedalion to agree to it being Indranan territory, it would give us somewhere safe to stay."

"You mean like an embassy?" Aiz made a little face at my nod. "It could work; you'd have to trust them to keep their word. Though the Farians have always been desperate to stay on your good side. But with this, I honestly don't know how they're going to react."

"Eh." I waved a hand. "It'll be fine. Sybil, continue."

"The petitioner is allowed to witness the final deliberations and the vote, but they cannot argue for themselves. All arguments must be put into the original petition and it is this, along with the record of the petitioner's life, that the Pedalion uses to make their judgment.

"They and they alone decide if the petitioner is worthy to face the gods and have the blessing of the *ilios porthmeios*."

"What happens if they deny the challenge?"

"Normally, nothing," Sybil replied. "There's no shame in the challenge, at least not overtly. I'm sure there are many who don't understand why someone would willingly choose to end an immortal life. But there's no punishment from the Pedalion. There is a ten-year waiting period that must be endured before they can issue the challenge again."

"Two problems," I said. "We certainly don't have ten years and it's probably unlikely they'll let us walk if they deny Fasé and Aiz's challenge," I muttered. "What happens if the Pedalion grants the challenge?"

"The petitioner is sent through the entrance to the *kai pethaménon psychón*—the well of dying souls. Which is located in the Pedalion chamber and it is only opened when the challenge is accepted."

"Or for a punishment," Aiz said.

319

"True," Sybil admitted. "On extremely rare occasions Farians have been sent through to the well to face the gods as a punishment. The petitioner will undergo a series of trials with their witness. They are designed to show the passage of life, to test the resolve of the petitioner, and so the gods can judge if they are worthy of *ilios porthmeios*. If they succeed, they meet the gods, and their end."

"And everyone who has passed through the trials has died?"

"Every one of them, but they were going to their deaths willingly. I suspect the four of you will have a much better chance."

Except we hadn't planned on Mia and Fasé fighting. I pressed my fingers to my eyes in an effort to relieve the building pressure. Something was nagging at the back of my brain, but every time I focused on the itch it vanished. "What about the trials?"

"I can't tell you about the trials; I've never seen them, and they change from petitioner to petitioner. It's said the gods are the ones who create them." She shook her head. "The final meeting with the gods is also private, but some witnesses have spoken of it."

"So we're going into this blind with a possible fight against three gods at the end of it." I shared a look with Emmory. "I know I'm supposed to be reckless and shit, but I like this plan less and less."

Mia's muttered "Finally" echoed in the silence that followed. Aiz didn't look at his sister.

I hooked my hands at the back of my neck and faced her. "The problem is, we don't have a better one. I can't march in there and demand to see the gods. We can't sneak in because the only way to get to them is through the well of dying souls.

"If we sit around and wait, those things you saw—whatever they are—come crawling into this galaxy and start killing everyone. *Hai Ram*, I've half a mind to land on Faria and slap the Pedalion around until they come to their senses. It seems like an easier solution." Dropping my hands, I shrugged helplessly. "I'm open to suggestions, people, but I don't think we have any other options."

Sybil was frowning, but she remained silent as did everyone else, and I voiced the concern that had been rolling around in my brain for days. "You don't think the Pedalion will grant Aiz's request, do you, Sybil?"

"I do not. Fasé's possibly, because they will jump at the chance to remove her voice. But Aiz—" She shook her head. "I feel as though it is more likely Adora will try to kill you herself than let you have the honor of dying by her gods' hands."

"Why?"

"The depth of Adora's hatred for what she considers her family's greatest betrayal is unfathomable. She knows Aiz is capable of killing them; she will not risk allowing him anywhere near the gods."

"Have you seen her vote no?" Aiz pressed, and Sybil shook her head again.

"I have not. This is too tangled with everything else about the choice the Star must make. I am going off of what I know of Adora, but that, I think, is enough."

38

"So you think she'll vote no to keep Aiz away from the gods and we'll all end up trapped in the Pedalion chamber? Bugger me."

"I don't agree with you," Aiz countered. "Adora will see me dead by her gods' hands. That is the best outcome she could imagine."

Sybil wasn't bothered in the least by his disagreement. "You are welcome to believe otherwise, Aiz; however, I have spent a great deal more time with your sister than you have."

I held up a hand before Aiz could reply. "Do you have another idea for getting us in to see the gods, Sybil?"

"No," she admitted. "Short of us sneaking into the Pedalion chambers in the middle of the night, me opening up the entrance, and you jumping in?"

"Okay." I laughed and blew out a breath. "I mean, I'll take it if that's our only other option, but I guess for now we'll have to run with this one."

The group broke, Aiz giving me a look like he wanted to talk before Sybil touched him by the arm and said something I didn't catch. He nodded and the pair left the room deep in discussion.

"It's going to be okay," I said to Mia as I put a hand on her shoulder. There was so much pain seething under the surface of her skin that I couldn't stop myself from reaching out and taking it.

The shock almost put me on my knees, and Mia swore as Zin grabbed for me.

"Sorry." I patted him awkwardly on the arm. "I've got it, it's fine."

"It's not fine," Mia said. "How are you doing that?"

"What just happened?" Emmory's question cut through the air and I squeezed my eyes shut for a second, wishing I could disappear.

"Chair," Mia ordered, and to my surprise Zin deposited me into the seat she'd just vacated without a word of protest. "She took my pain away. When she was fighting Hamah and Talos, she threw her own pain back at Hamah. He said it was like nothing he'd ever felt before." She dragged a hand through her dark hair, disheveling it, and my fingers itched to bury themselves in the suddenly loose curls.

"Before anyone asks, I don't know how I'm doing it," I said.

"You struggled for months to control the healing. You can't pull the energy from outside yourself—"

"Actually, I did finally figure that part out," I volunteered with a smile. "We haven't had a chance to talk about that with everything else going on."

Mia pinched the bridge of her nose with a sigh, and Emmory's chuckle almost hid his murmured "Welcome to my life."

"I don't understand what you're doing, Hail," Mia said finally. "And it scares me a little."

"You were hurting," I whispered. "I just wanted to make it go away."

Zin bent down and pressed a kiss to the top of my head, smiling as he straightened. "I'm surprised you haven't figured that out, Mia," he said, slipping an arm around Emmory's waist and heading for the door.

"Figured what out?"

"That one would cut off her own arm if it meant the people she cared about were spared the pain." His smile was tinged with sorrow. "And you've apparently taught her how to do it without even having to pick up a knife."

I pressed my fingers to my mouth at the look of utter shock

on Mia's face as the men left us alone. I was reasonably sure she wouldn't appreciate it if I laughed.

"Hail, why?"

I dropped my hand and met her curious gaze with a smile and a shrug. "When I was little and I'd get in trouble for hurting my sister Cire, I'd ask my father what was the point of getting mad at me? That there was a life before this one and a life after, so what was the point? Why should I be good in this life?" Now I did laugh and rubbed at my throat.

"I don't remember this, I think I was six, but he would tell this story all the time. My father, no doubt fed up with my shit, grabbed me by the face and said, 'Haili, listen to me. Before and after don't matter. Now matters. You cannot help the people you love before and after, you can only choose to cause them pain or take on their pain now.'

"I have caused a lot of pain in my life," I said, holding up a hand to her. Mia took it and I tugged her forward until she was standing between my knees. "I would think you of all people would understand that I don't want to do it anymore. And Zin, as much as I hate to admit it, is right. I will always stand in the way of whatever is trying to hurt the people I care about. You are included in that." I skimmed my hands up her arms to cup her face.

"I know what you're doing," Mia murmured, sliding her fingers over my cheek and into my hair.

"What am I doing?"

"Trying to distract me. It won't work."

"Should I come back later?" Hao asked.

Mia pulled away and I contemplated, for just a moment, pulling one of my Glocks and shooting my brother in his smug face.

"What do you want?"

Hao's grin grew and he winked at me as he came into the room and leaned against the desk. "Mia, what are your plans for the mercs?"

"Nothing yet, why?"

"No real reason." He blocked the lazy punch I threw his way as I got to my feet, and I was surprised at the lack of seething rage in my gut. Nothing reacted at all, but I didn't push my luck and wandered away from Hao, pulling up a star chart on the wall with my *smati*.

"He's planning ahead for when things go to shit," I said to Mia without turning around. "Do we know if these mysterious foes of ours have the same warp capabilities as you and the Farians?"

"We don't, I'm sorry," she replied. "I would say it's likely."

"There's no way for us to cover the distance without the tech," I said to Hao. "Barry met up with some of Mia's contacts to get what we would need for the remaining *Vajrayanas*, but there's bound to be a limited supply there. It's going to be every sector for themselves."

"I can send the mercenaries to protect Indrana."

I looked over my shoulder with a low laugh. "Po-Sin would rather set himself on fire than defend my empire now. No, don't push him on it," I said when Mia opened her mouth to protest. "He really will return your money and hole up somewhere to ride it out."

"Maybe," Hao said with a shrug. "He's not vindictive past the point of logic. If he knows for sure something's coming, he'll do what needs doing."

"We don't have proof."

"Don't worry about it for now. I'll handle my uncle when the time comes."

"When?" Mia asked. "You don't think my brother and Hail can win?"

Hao shrugged. "I have a great deal of faith in her. I'm still deciding on the rest of you."

Mia smiled. "It's good you have faith in her; you'll need it. We all will." She smiled mysteriously and moved across the room, leaving us to stare after her.

"The prophet thing is unsettling no matter who's doing it," Hao murmured.

I bumped my shoulder into his. "Tell me about it. Hey, let's give Rai a call."

"Why?"

"I just want to talk to him," I said when he shot me a look.

"You could have just called him without involving me in it." Hao tossed the com up onto the blank wall, wiping out the star map I'd been looking at.

"Yeah, but I like making you feel useful." I dropped the smile when Rai appeared on the wall. "Hey, Rai, you look like shit."

"Hail." He rubbed a hand over his face, the brown skin under his eyes tinged with purple bruising. "You still mad at me?"

"Maybe." I dragged the word out, letting the smile play over my mouth.

"Almost all my crew on that job took off after your threat, you know. I lost some good people."

"Good. They can stay gone and hope I never see them again. How've you been?"

"Did you need something? I've got slightly more pressing matters to—" He broke off, his eyes narrowing. "Are you responsible for these damned riots, Hail?"

Hao was staring at me, openmouthed.

"I haven't slept for a week, Hail," Rai snarled. "What the fuck did you—"

"Six months," I said; the tone of my voice was deadly quiet, and Rai shut up. "You could have helped me get Gita to safety. You could have reunited me with Emmory and the others if you'd only taken me to the rubble of my embassy instead of onto Aiz's ship."

"Hail," he protested. "I took a contract."

"I don't fucking care; at some point loyalty should count for more than money. Don't bitch at me about a week of no sleep, Bakara Rai, when I spent six months thinking my brother was dead. That was part of my payback. At the moment I've decided to let you live; don't make me change my mind by running your mouth."

The fight went out of him and he rubbed at his face again. "Fair enough. What do you want, Hail?"

"I want someone over there to be prepared for the very real possibility that the shit is going to hit the proverbial fan without worrying about the details of it all. Get yourself ready for war, Rai, a big winner-take-all conflict. There's no money in this, only survival, and I'll tell you right now you're either on my side or the losing side. Be ready for our call." I smiled a tiny smile. "Since Mia still owns you, this one is not my favor. That loyalty I mentioned? It's the difference between your people alive or dead. I'll see about those riots for you. You still owe me, big-time."

"Thanks," he said.

"Don't thank me. I might kill you after this is all over."

He sighed and raked a hand through his dreads. "I'll get it done, Hail. Whatever you need."

"Good."

"Is—is Jo still mad at me?"

"Oh." I sucked air in through my teeth. "You have no idea."

Rai winced. "I was afraid of that. The first message I got from her was a graphic description of what she was going to do to me when you were finished. It was unpleasant."

"You'll want to apologize a few million times, especially right now with a galaxy between you." I smiled. "Oh, and Rai, don't tell Po-Sin this was my idea; tell him it came from the Cevallas."

"I was planning on doing that already." He smirked. "As mad as Jo is at me? That's a flash in the pan. Po-Sin's temper burns long and low. I hope you're prepared."

I knew that comment was directed at Hao, but I didn't look his way until the com link was disconnected. Hao met my concerned gaze and passed a hand over his hair with a shrug.

"We'll deal with it later," he said. "No point in worrying about it now." Reaching out and patting me on the shoulder, he winked and headed for the door, leaving me alone with Mia.

I smiled softly. She was curled in the chair in the corner, and judging from her eyes she was reading something directly from her *smati*. I realized I hadn't heard the Shen word for *smati* in the whole time we'd been on Sparkos and wondered what it was.

I tossed the star chart back on the wall and leaned against my desk. I had no clue where our mysterious opponents would come from, or even if I'd be alive to help stop them when they came.

"What is it?" Mia asked when I laughed.

"I don't even know where we are."

"It bothers you, not knowing where you are." She unfolded herself from the chair and crossed to me. "Here, approximately." She ran a slender finger along the Perseus arm of the galaxy up and past the galactic center. "Technically still home for you, just a lot farther away."

"And with a massive black hole in between."

"The Svatir live out here." Mia traced along the outer edge of the Sagittarius arm. "Away from the rest of us."

"Are there others?"

Mia shook her head, smiling at the chart. "Not here. This is an old, wild galaxy. We've been mostly forgotten by the rest of the universe, which is probably a good thing."

"Why is that?"

"Humans are so young," she whispered. "You need the space to grow without being overwhelmed by the rest of us."

"You're part human, too, remember?"

Mia laughed softly. "I do forget at times."

"What do you call this?" I tapped at my head. "Our *smati*."

"Ah." Mia reached up and pressed a finger to my temple and then to hers. "*Enlaci*. It means—"

"Connection," I murmured, and forced myself to look back at the chart.

"Do you believe this will work?" she asked.

"I have to," I replied, still studying the stars and telling myself I wouldn't look at her again until my heart stopped its erratic beat. "So many lives at stake—"

She leaned up, kissing me so quickly I was half convinced I imagined it as she turned for the door. I caught her by the wrist and pulled her back, staring down at her as my heart thundered in my chest.

"Since I can't see the future. Give me this just in case," I murmured, and lowered my mouth to hers.

39

Hail, are you up?" Hao's quiet question over our com link woke me, and I rolled over. *"I didn't want to barge in there again and embarrass you."* There was laughter in his voice.

"You're going to be as smug about this as you were with Portis, aren't you?"

"Yes."

"I hate you. Yes, I'm up. Give me five minutes and I'll meet you in the mess hall." I slid from the bed, trailing a hand over Mia's bare back with a smile. "Don't get up," I said at her sleepy murmur. "It's early. I'm going to go see what Hao wants."

She settled back to sleep with a soft sigh. My heart twisted and I blinked away the tears as I headed into the bathroom. When Portis had died, I'd been so sure I would never feel that way again. Even through the chaos of my return home and all the ensuing madness, my love for him—my grief for him—had remained a constant.

"I'm going to miss you forever," I whispered to his ghost. "But it's time to let go."

I know. I love you, baby.

What I felt for Mia wasn't the same, I already knew that, just like I'd known I couldn't ever love another man as Portis had breathed his last in my arms. But there was something in my heart, and it wasn't a painful tangle of sharp-edged wire but a sun-warmed afternoon on the beach. Still and peaceful. Like coming home.

The mess hall was mostly empty, a few scattered groups of sur-prisingly mixed Shen and Farians getting in one last breakfast before we headed for Faria. Hao looked up and a smile spread across his face.

I braced myself for the inevitable lecture, but all my brother did was gesture for me to bend down. He reached up and cupped my face in his hands, pulling me down and kissing my forehead.

"'Rare are the moments of happiness, blown away like cherry blossoms in a breeze.'"

I hugged him, tears pricking at my eyelids. "You're getting all sappy, quoting poetry at me," I said as I stepped back.

"It's good to see some light back in your eyes." He waved at the table. "I made us breakfast. I wanted to talk."

"That sounds ominous." I swung a leg over the bench and sat.

Hao grinned. "No more so than what we've been dealing with." He grabbed for his fork.

"This seems decidedly un-Farian." Breakfast was eggs over rice with a spice I couldn't identify. "Did you cook?"

"I was restless this morning, you know how it is. I made Emmory stop for supplies before we left the Solarian Conglomerate space. It's where Stasia found your tea. The kitchen was stocked well enough, but—" He made a face. "Some of what the Farians and Shen eat is questionable and when you multiply that by space-travel rations I wasn't interested in spending however long it took to get to you without some familiar foods."

"What's on your mind?"

"I don't like this plan," he said, taking a bite and chewing, then swallowing before he continued. "It's got a high risk of death and a low payoff."

"I don't either, but it's the only plan we have."

"You and I know that's never a good enough excuse."

I sighed and pointed my fork at him. "We're not talking about some job, Hao. We're talking about the safety of the galaxy."

"It's no different." He shook his head. "You keep your crew safe, always. If you can't, you don't do the job. All of us marching in there together is too damn risky. I don't trust the Farians and neither do you."

"Do you have a better idea?" I asked. He stared at me, an eyebrow raised; I ignored it and continued. "Because I don't and I'm trying to keep my crew safe, Hao. It's all I've ever done. It's just gotten a bit bigger over the last few months."

"Beo-max," he said, and resumed eating.

I blinked at him in confusion. "What?"

"Do you remember when we busted Kasai out of Beo-max?"

I leaned back in my seat and frowned at him. Tall, willowy Kasai was a master thief and an old friend of Hao's. She'd gotten scooped up on an unrelated charge by the Suvani government and sent to Beo-max, a maximum-security prison on Mars thanks to an extradition treaty with the Solarians.

We'd busted her out.

Or, more accurately, Portis and I had gone in through the front posing as lawyers for Johnquin Stronge, a notorious hatchet man for some of the worst crime families in the Solarian Conglomerate.

What Hao hadn't told me was that Johnquin was exceedingly suspicious of new faces—a prudent trait among someone who could have easily spilled enough trash to put most of the mob bosses on death row. When two new lawyers had shown up without any warning, he lost his shit.

During the ensuing chaos, Hao had slipped in through the guard entrance and back out again with Kasai in tow.

"I almost got killed." I pointed at him. "*You* almost got killed. I had to talk Portis down from going after you every day for a month, and you know how hard it was to get him that angry."

"He was pretty pissed." Hao chuckled. "I slept with a gun for weeks hoping I wasn't going to have to shoot him because I knew you'd never forgive me." He laid his fork down and looked at me. "I'm serious, though. I want a backup plan for when things go inevitably to shit, and you don't need me there for the negotiations. We've all been caught up in choosing between sneaking in and kicking in the door—why not both?

"You and Fasé and the Cevallas go in the front and distract them. Sybil and I, maybe Talos, too—I like him. We go in the back and poke around a bit, rally Fasé's supporters while you're distracting them with these negotiations and the challenge to their gods. Then when things go sideways we're in a position to cause as much of a domestic disturbance as we can."

I laughed. "You always did like the go-in-and-blow-things-up plan."

"It gets attention where it needs to be." Hao shrugged. "We'll stay aboard the ship and disembark after you've led the greeting party away. It'll allow us to move freely and see what we can learn. Fasé can do her whole 'I've returned' recruitment drive ahead of time and introduce us to her people so that we can do our work while you're doing your diplomat thing."

I snorted with laughter. "You and the Shen are going to be rather conspicuous on Faria."

"We wouldn't make it three meters if any of us looked like ourselves. We've got that handled."

"And you're okay about going in with Sybil?" I asked Hao.

"If she's telling the truth about being on our side, it could work in our favor," he replied. "We'll have her throw the Pedalion a few false leads and keep them out of our hair even further."

"If she's not?"

Hao's look was one I'd seen only a handful of times before. "I'll kill her, Hail. I know it won't be permanent but it'll buy us some time."

"Fine." I blew out a breath. "It's not a bad idea, and for what it's worth you're right. Splitting up is safer. Since you lot won't let me go in on my own."

"Never again if I can help it." He held a hand out and I slid my fingers over his palm. He closed his hand on my forearm, squeezed once. "Does she make you happy?"

Tears pricked at my eyelids again. "It was unexpected. You know that feeling when you get back to your ship after being away for too long?"

His lips twitched as he tried to hold in a smile. "I would suggest not using that line on her."

"You are such a brat." I laughed. "She makes me happy."

"Good." He squeezed my arm once more and then got to his feet. "Finish your breakfast, *sha zhu*."

I shot him a dirty look, but smiled when he grinned back and leaned down to kiss the top of my head. "I love you."

"Same goes."

"Hey, Hao?" He paused by the dish return and I picked up my fork again. "I don't think I've said it yet, but I'm glad you and Gita made up."

"Now who's a brat?" His laughter lingered in the air after he'd left the room.

I finished my breakfast. Not because I was actually hungry but because it gave me something to do as I sifted through the information Barry had sent me.

Jamison's crew was off Earth, which wasn't a surprise. Even if the Solarian officials didn't know who was responsible for the attack on not one but two protected areas, someone was bound to figure that out. They wouldn't find him. If Jamison was good at anything, it was running away and hiding until the smoke cleared.

"Hail?"

I looked up, my heart doing a funny little dance at the sight of Mia in the doorway. "Good morning."

"I thought you were with Hao?"

"I was, he just left." I caught Mia by the wrist, tugged her down next to me. "How did you sleep?"

She hummed, leaning into me, and I didn't see a reason to resist the opportunity to kiss her again.

"I haven't had a chance to ask you this, but are you all right? What happened with Hamah was hard."

"Isn't that supposed to be my line?" she asked, looking up at me with a smile. The warmth of it was like stepping onto a planet after a month in space and feeling real air and sunlight on my skin. "I'm sorry he hurt you."

"He was your friend. I'm sorry he betrayed you."

Mia dragged in a breath; it hitched as she fought with the tears I could see gathering in her eyes. "He did not understand that this is the way things must be. I thought it was settled long ago. I thought he believed in the cause, not just in me. And maybe he did. But he lost his way. Worse still, he tried to blame you for it when you have never given him cause to do so."

"I gave him plenty of cause," I whispered. "Haven't I said over and over I don't think we should do this?"

Mia smiled. "And yet here we are, and when the time comes you will do what is necessary, what is right."

It was a relief to know that our definitions of what was right happened to circle around the same things. I didn't know how long that was going to last, but I wanted it for as long as the universe would allow it.

"Can I ask you something?"

"Of course."

"What did Aiz mean when he said Hamah couldn't protect you from the end of this? That no one could but me?"

She looked away, eyes darting around the mess hall.

"Mia." I made her name into a warning and saw the flash of determination in her eyes that rose to answer it.

"This is a difficult path for all of us, Hail. I am not exempt from that."

"What is going to happen? What have you seen?"

Mia closed her eyes for a moment before she turned her head back to me. "This I will not share, Hail. You have so much to carry already; I swore to myself at the beginning of all this I would do what I could to not add to it."

"But if I—"

"No." She cut me off with fingers on my lips. "You need to go into this without the knowledge, because it won't help you. It will only make the choice more difficult."

I stared at her for a long moment, but it was clear Mia wasn't going to budge and I finally caved with a sigh. "Fine. One other thing?"

"Go on."

"I caught most of what Hamah said while he was attacking me, but he called me *avedélcion*, and I don't know what that means."

Mia frowned, reaching for my hand. "It means 'abomination.' I'm sorry, I don't know why—"

"Don't worry about it." I squeezed her fingers and lifted a shoulder. "He was angry, it's an easy word to use." Even as I brushed it off, that itch in the back of my head continued to bother me.

"I wish I were less worried about all this," Mia whispered.

I leaned in, pressing my forehead to hers with a smile. "The worry is a good thing. Trust me. The last thing you ever want to do is go into a job thinking everything is already wrapped up in a bow for you. That's how people die."

This close I could see the darker gray shards of color in her eyes and a thousand things rolled through my head, discarded unsaid until I could find the words important enough to give life to them.

"Because I know things will get chaotic and I might not get a chance to say this: Please stay safe," I whispered, cupping her face in my hands. "I am not sure I would survive the loss of you."

Mia reached up, wrapping her fingers around my wrists. "Whatever happens, know I would have made these same choices a million times over." She kissed me and the world outside us ceased to exist.

I wanted to stay there forever. Away from the impending fight. With no trace of the catastrophes bearing down on us. But as Aiz had said, that wasn't our lives, and somewhere deep in my gut I knew we were headed for a fight.

336

40

Emmory found us in the mess hall and walked with us back to my rooms. I was as awkward as a schoolgirl with a crush walking with my *Ekam* on one side and Mia on the other. "Emmory, Hao and I talked over another idea I think you need to hear."

"He discussed it with me and Fasé yesterday."

I frowned at him. "Without me?"

There wasn't a trace of expression on Emmory's face. "You were occupied."

Bugger me, I'd walked right into that one. Slanting a glance at Mia, who was smiling, I picked a noncommittal noise as a response and crossed over the threshold of my room. Mia stopped where she was and leaned against the jamb.

"I agree with Hao, for what it's worth," Emmory continued. "Splitting up will make things easier and hopefully keep both groups a little safer. Sybil will be able to navigate Faria better, and rallying Fasé's people to our side could be helpful."

"Someone talk to you also, or do I need to fill you in on this?" I asked Mia.

Mia's smile didn't waver. "I missed the meeting last night."

Emmory snorted in amusement. I closed my eyes, feeling my cheeks heat, and dropped into a chair. "Hao thinks it will be a good idea to have a small force sync up with Fasé's people just in case. He suggested Talos." I looked at Emmory. "Gita should go also, to help keep Hao out of trouble."

"And the point of this?" Mia asked.

"The general plan is to rally Fasé's people and see if they can't find some leverage for us just in case we need it. I'm leaving the specifics of this up to him. We're hoping the Farians will be so distracted by our arrival they won't see them coming."

"It's a good idea." Mia nodded. "I'll go find Talos and speak with him."

I thought she was going to kiss me and was surprised how disappointed I was when she didn't. I watched her leave the room, and dared a glance in Emmory's direction.

"You don't need my approval, Hail."

"I know." I rubbed my hands over my face, so the response was muffled. "I know." Dropping my hands, I looked up at the ceiling and then back down. "Emmory, what am I doing?"

"If you mean about her, you'll have to ask Zin." He pointed at the door. "That's not my department. But if you mean all of this?" He leaned a hip on the desk. "If everyone's to be believed, you're fulfilling your destiny. No one's come right out and put it that way, but the writing is clear enough. The better question is, what do you want to be doing?"

The laugh hurt and I caught myself rubbing at my chest wishing for a knife for the first time in a while. "I wanted to stay away, but Portis died and you made me go home. I wanted to keep my empire out of the hands of a madman, and I guess I succeeded at that?"

"You did." Emmory's rare smile eased the ache in my chest.

"Everywhere I turn it feels like violence is just around the corner. I can't get clear. I can't walk away. I meant what I said to Caterina. I want this to be done and for us to go live in peace afterward." I blew out a breath and hooked my hands behind my head as I looked up at him. "Between you and me, I know fighting the gods is the best option to stop what's coming. But the cost? I'm afraid, Emmory."

"Of what?"

"Of what that fight will do to me." I swallowed, surprised by the tears suddenly clogging my throat. "When I fight, it's like tearing off little pieces of myself. I can't stop doing it. When I thought you all were dead, I didn't mind. I didn't want to be me anymore."

"Hail—"

"I can't quit, though, can I?" I dropped my hands, frustration overtaking me, and I pushed out of my chair with a hiss. "*Hai Ram.* I can't be so fucking selfish as to condemn the galaxy just because I don't want to have a fistfight with a god!"

"The irony is that you try to downplay it, like having a fight with a god is just an ordinary afternoon for you." It wasn't Emmory who responded, but Zin, and I spun on my heel to face him. He was standing in the doorway but reached out and tapped the panel, closing it behind him. "I could hear you down the corridor and I suspect you don't want our Shen friends to catch wind of your indecision."

"I think you'd be surprised," I replied with a shrug. "Aiz and Mia both seem like they're hoping for a nonviolent resolution to this. Anyway, it's not indecision."

He gave me the Look and I blinked at him.

"You've been practicing, or I've really gone completely off the deep end. Fine, it *is* indecision, at least in part. I am tired of fighting."

"I don't blame you," Zin said. He reached out and took my hands, pulling me into a hug. "I don't blame you, Hail. And it's not selfish, whatever you think."

"If I don't, something even worse happens?" I hugged him back and then stepped away. "I'm reasonably sure that's the definition of selfish."

"Hail, fighting the gods isn't going to fix the problem. What happens to the Farians if you kill their remaining gods? What does that do to them?" He shook his head. "It doesn't improve Indrana's relationship with them, that's for sure."

"I can't say I think that leaving them in the care of these gods is any better, Zin." I lifted my hands. "Fasé, for all her inconsistencies, is a good leader. If I had to back anyone for taking over in the wake of the kind of instability we're about to bring, it would be her."

"And what would you do if you didn't know what the future held?" It was a quiet, simple question. The kind that only Zin would think to ask, and it stopped me in my tracks.

What would I do? I sympathized with Mia and Aiz, the plight of the Shen who couldn't be reborn with their people. The pain of families split apart by that injustice ate at me.

But I wouldn't condemn all Farians based on the actions of the Pedalion. I knew there were those who sided with Fasé, or who were just trying to live their lives with no clue of the atrocities their government committed.

Who was I to be their judge and executioner?

Less violence, not more, is always an option.

I sank back into my chair with my head in my hands as Dailun's words rang in my ears. "I don't know. Go back to square one? Figure out some way to make peace between the Farians and the Shen?" When I looked back up they were both watching me with sympathetic smiles. "That's still an option, even with all this gods-and-monsters cowshit we're rolling around in."

"When are you going to stop second-guessing yourself?" That question from Zin hurt.

"When we go back to the world where my arrogance didn't get you all killed."

"Damn it, Hail. You didn't." Zin looked like he wanted to say more, but Emmory stopped him with a hand on his arm.

"Your arrogance didn't have anything to do with it," he said. "That confidence makes you who you are. The gunrunner. The empress. Even the Star of Indrana. When you own who you are, there's nothing that can stand in your way. Stop hiding from it."

"I don't know what I did to deserve you two," I whispered, blinking back the tears in my eyes.

Emmory held out a hand and tugged me to my feet, pressing his forehead to mine for a moment before he leaned back and brought his hands up to cup my face. "I saw you during that fight with the Shen. Like it or not, you're in your element there. Treat it like a tool, Hail. Learn to control it instead of letting it control you."

The pain that had been tormenting me since Earth eased, the slivers of uncertainty and fear slipping free. The wounds they left behind healed as easily as one under a Shen's touch. "That was better than Zin's bathroom 'be the empress' speech," I teased.

"Hey, I was pressed for time," Zin protested with a grin.

"I know. It did the job, though, didn't it?" I remembered being crammed into the shuttle bathroom with Zin as he ordered me to pull myself together for my people and be not only the empress I was born to be but the gunrunner I was.

It had done the job, just like this had.

"We'll proceed as planned, but I'll think of something." I had to think of something. The only alternative was a fight I was becoming more and more worried Aiz and I couldn't win.

I showered and changed into the pair of black pants and BodyGuard top that Stasia had tailored to fit me. "Welcome back," I murmured to my reflection as I twisted my hair up into a knot at the base of my neck, startled by how familiar and yet strange I appeared. My holsters had vanished with the embassy back on Earth, but the pair of thigh holsters someone had found me were now worn in and holding the pair of the newest model of Glocks from Hao.

The fleet had jumped from the base to just outside the Farian home system, and then the *Hailimi* had made the two-hour trek in-system all by herself while the other ships waited to see what the Farians would do.

Gita and Johar were standing by the door of my old room as I came out of the bathroom. The familiar trappings of the Indranan ship had eased some of my nerves. It felt more like home again.

I was keeping things as compartmentalized as I could. Hamah's betrayal still made me uneasy, and despite my assurances to the others I couldn't be completely sure of anyone's loyalty but my people's.

However, I also knew I couldn't control any of it. I wanted to give Hao, Sybil, and the others the chance to deal with things as they came up on Faria. I'd be wholly distracted by my part of the plan anyway and needed all my focus to be on Adora and the Pedalion.

Everything was coming together, but it could all go horribly wrong, and to make things even worse I still had no idea if I was going to be able to follow through with this fight or what Fasé had meant by her message about my choice. Despite what everyone had tried to tell me, the fate of the galaxy really was on my shoulders. I was determined not to let everyone down.

"Would you prefer I go with Hao or come with you?" Johar smiled, a quick flash of teeth, at my surprised look. "I don't know that it matters either way. But I figured I would ask."

Emmory and I had split the groups as evenly as we could. I'd lost the argument about keeping Kisah, Iza, and Indula behind with the ship, and my BodyGuards would be at my side. We were back to the Empress of Indrana.

I did at least manage to keep Admiral Hassan on board with the directive to hold our way off Faria for as long as physically possible and find us a new form of transportation if it came to that.

Dailun and Alba would also stay on the ship; Dailun was still in contact with his family, and staying put would give him the time he needed to get all the information on the Hiervet that he could.

Privately I could admit I wanted them out of danger, and the ship seemed the safest place for them.

Emmory and Zin would be with me. Gita was going with Hao, not because I didn't want her by my side, but because I knew my brother did and would be too stubborn to ask. The look he'd given me at Gita's laughter had been worth it.

For a moment I considered telling Jo she'd be better off with them, but something stopped the words in my mouth. "I'd love the company," I said instead with a smile. "It'll be fun to see Adora's reaction on top of dealing with her brother and Fasé."

Johar grinned as we headed out of my room and toward the bridge. "Not to mention, think of the story I'll get to tell once we're home. I won't ever have to pay for a single drink ever again."

I burst into laughter, not caring about the looks it drew from the crew members we passed. Johar could always be counted on to break the tension, and I wrapped an arm around her waist to hug her.

"You keep your eyes up, yeah?" she murmured in my ear before letting me go, and I nodded once, then continued on to the bridge in silence.

The planet of Faria was in full view when we came through the door of the bridge. She was paler than Pashati, paler even than Earth, her brown and green continents shaded by rust-colored shadows and surrounded by dark oceans.

"It looks like a planet soaked in blood," Hao said.

A massive ringed planet lurked in the distance. The rings were too far away for a color. From this distance they were just white on the blackness behind them.

I spotted the orbital defenses a split second before the com link dinged its warning of an incoming message.

"Answer it, Kisah." I settled in the captain's chair as the screen came up. Emmory and Zin were on one side of me. Admiral Hassan and Jo on the other. The others were off-camera.

"Image is everything." Hao's voice was in my head over our private com as clearly as if he were standing by my side.

"You remember the first time you said that to me and wanted to know why I was smiling?" I subvocalized without looking his direction.

"I take it I didn't sound like your nanny."

"You sounded like my mother." I closed my eyes for a moment and smiled, the memory washing over me.

*   *   *

"Image is everything. You show the target you're scared and you'll get your ass kicked. You bare your teeth at someone who outnumbers and outguns you, the odds that they'll back down shoot into the stratosphere. Or they might kill you for your insolence. Is there any particular reason you're smiling at me like that, Cressen?"

The amusement dripping from Hao's voice knocked me from my reverie and I felt Portis shift uneasily at my side. "You sound like the nanny at the orphanage," I lied. Who he sounded like was my mother, but I couldn't very well tell Cheng Hao that his battle tactics lined up with those of Mercedes Bristol, Empress of Indrana. Being a fully accepted member of his crew now wouldn't matter a bit. I'd be out the airlock faster than I could finish the sentence, or worse, ransomed back to my mother.

Hao arched a metallic eyebrow, the curiosity going to war with the amusement, making his sharply angled face a battlefield of its own. "I suppose," he said at last. "I shouldn't be surprised you were raised in an orphanage by a nanny whose previous job had been with the Solarian Special Forces."

"I don't know about SSF, but she'd done time somewhere."

Gy chuckled at Hao's side. "I want that story about the nanny, Cress, but later. We've got a job to do and we should get moving." He slid Hao a mischievous look. "Unless you need to pontificate some more, my dear, about the virtues of looking mean."

Hao looked at me. "I swear he's gotten worse since I brought you on board."

"I don't know what you're talking about," I replied, miraculously holding in my smile when Gy winked at me.

Hao shook his head, the bronze strands of his hair almost hiding the smile. "Get your gear, get your war faces on, and let's go."

41

I opened my eyes again as the Farian appeared on the screen. They were looking at their console instead of up at me. "Unknown vessel, this is Farian space. Unless you wish to be destroyed, you will power down your weapons and shields and prepare to be boarded."

"Someone missed a briefing." I grinned when their head jerked up and their mouth fell open in shock. "Not sure the refresher is necessary, but we'll do it anyway. I am Empress Hail Bristol, Star of Indrana, and I believe the Pedalion is expecting me."

The Farian fumbled. "Yes. Of course, Your Majesty. I mean—they're expecting you." They cleared their throat. "*Hailimi Bristol*, you are slotted to land at the coordinates I'm forwarding to you. Please do not deviate from them. A welcome party will be waiting."

"Excellent." I resisted, barely, the urge to ask what would happen if I did deviate from the assigned landing space. "Teslina, did they send coordinates?"

"Yes, ma'am," the pilot replied.

"Take us in, then."

"Jo, let's go do weapons check," Zin said, and the pair left the bridge. Hao reached a hand out, tapping his fist to mine and then followed them.

I looked up at Emmory. "Thoughts?"

"Now?"

I grinned at his tone. "Yes, now."

"I'm not sure I could tell you anything that would change your mind at this point, ma'am."

"Maybe not." I shrugged. "But that doesn't mean I'm not curious what's on your mind."

Emmory didn't look at me, his eyes focused on the screen showing our descent. The shields flickered, yellow to red to a vibrant blue as the ship sliced her way through the atmosphere.

"We are alone, Hail. No support, no backup if—no, when—things go sideways. Whatever you think, you're still my responsibility. Keeping you alive is my responsibility."

"I know." I'd worried about this. The idea that my *Ekam*, or any of my BodyGuards, would stand by while I fought gods without getting involved had been laughable from the start. "You know if it comes to a fight and you're there, you'll have to stand, right? They'll kill you without a moment's hesitation and I can't save you."

"I don't need you to save me, Hail. I just need you to know that what you were feeling when you thought we were all dead? It is what I would feel if I lost you." He smiled, but there were tears in his eyes. "It would obviously not kill me outright, but I would wish it had."

"Damn it, Emmy." I swallowed down the sudden lump in my throat. "You're gonna do this now, here?"

"You asked what was on my mind." Now he did look at me, and the smile that followed was brighter than the sun.

"I was talking about the mission," I muttered. But I reached a hand out, linking my fingers with his, and squeezed them once before I let him go. "I'm glad you're here."

We broke through the upper layer of the atmosphere and the landscape of Faria stretched out below us, the same dull greens and browns and washed-out reds.

"Ma'am, I've got us on approach," Teslina said. "Landing in ten."

I pushed from my chair. "We'd better go get ready. Kisah, can you give me shipwide coms?"

"You've got them, ma'am, whenever you're ready."

Inhale. Exhale. I shared a look with Emmory and then nodded to Kisah. "Attention everyone. We are ten minutes out from the landing site. You all know your jobs. I'm trusting you to do them. I'm not going to give you some crap line about the galaxy depending on us. What's real is the person next to you. They're depending on you. Keep them safe. Hail out."

Hao's voice came over our *smati* link almost as soon as Kisah cut the connection. *"That was super inspiring."*

"Shut up," I replied, heading for the bridge door.

Emmory and I walked in silence down the corridor. I heard the voices as we turned toward the stairs of the cargo bay and stuck a hand out in front of Emmory.

"I'm not saying Hamah was right, Aiz," Talos said. "You know I'm not. What I'm saying is that you saw what Hail's capable of during that fight the same as I did. You be careful."

"Talos." Aiz's voice was thick with amusement. "We are about to land on Faria. The bounty on my head is at what, forty-seven million credits? I'm going to challenge their gods to a death match if they won't listen. What part of this is careful?"

"None of it," Talos admitted. "But you're placing all your trust in the Star."

"Of course I am, that's how this is supposed to go. You like her, Talos? Why the sudden concern?"

"I do like her. So do you. So does Mia. That's what worries me. We all like her a little too much, and we're willing to trust her with this dangerous plan. Walking both of you right into the Pedalion as if they wouldn't murder Mia and jar you. What if—"

"Enough, Talos." There was a pause. "We are on the threshold of freedom. If I fall, you know what you must do. I am trusting you with it because you earned that trust. Stay the course and I will see you again at the end of all things. In the meantime, we will trust in the Star to show us the way."

Talos's murmured response was too low for me to catch. I'd heard enough anyway. I figured Aiz had a backup plan; it would have been foolish not to. It was just a little surprising that it didn't involve trying to save his life.

I tapped Emmory on the chest and started walking. "—once Adora realizes we've double-crossed her, things might get exciting." I made sure my voice was loud enough to carry to the stairs and when we crossed over the threshold, Aiz and Talos were headed down.

The rest of our group were already down in the cargo bay. Johar leaned against a wall with a foot propped up on a crate; she was cleaning a new knife. The knife I'd stolen from her back on Sparkos was secure in a sheath in my boot. She winked at me as I came down the stairs.

Talos said something else to Aiz and then approached me, extending a bare hand. I took it without hesitation, and to my surprise the Shen pulled me into a hug. "Please take care of them, Star of Indrana. They are the heart of our people."

"I will," I whispered. "You have my word."

He released me, exchanged a look with Aiz and Mia, and then headed for the stairs.

The warning chime sounded and I braced myself against the slight jolt of landing rocking through the ship. "Everyone ready?"

Aiz dipped his head. The others followed suit. I put a hand on my gun and blew out a breath. "Kisah, you have point. Emmory next to me. Jo, you're going to be next to Mia and Aiz. Zin with Fasé. Iza, Indula, cover our backs."

"As always, Majesty." Indula winked at me.

I was putting an enormous amount of trust in the Farian laws and our treaty protecting us all once we were off the ship.

Hao came over, reaching out to check over my guns, leaning in and pressing his cheek to mine for just a moment. "You watch everything, *sha zhu*." He whispered the command in my ear. "And trust your gut, no exceptions, no doubting yourself. If it says run, you get the fuck out of there."

"Same to you." I grabbed the back of his neck and pressed my forehead to his. "I won't have time to save your ass."

I released Hao and smiled at Gita. "Keep him out of trouble, will you?"

"I can't make that promise and you know it."

I laughed. "True enough."

Gita pulled me into a hug that I returned. "You be careful, Hail. Don't trust Aiz; he is looking out for his people, not for you." She whispered the instructions in my ear before letting me go.

I gave her a quick nod. Aiz would be outnumbered, not only by us but by the Farians once we landed. I hoped we were on the same side, but I didn't blame Gita for her suspicions.

I grabbed for her and Hao's hands before they could move away as the sudden fear gripped me, and they both looked at me in confusion. "Come back to me, please. Both of you."

"Yes, ma'am."

I blew out a breath and looked around the cargo bay. "Let's do this."

I'd been here so many times in my life. Disembarking from a ship with armed people at my back to face off against another group of armed people, hoping the whole time we could get through it without bloodshed.

So many times we were lucky, thanks to Hao's silver tongue. Or to mine. So many times we made it back to the ship in one piece—or mostly one piece.

I didn't think we were going to be so lucky this time.

I paused at the edge of the *Hailimi Bristol* and looked down at the smooth white surface of the landing pad. The patterned material stretched out toward a building that looked to be made of all right angles and shouldn't be standing upright.

"What's the holdup, Hail?" Jo kept her voice low, one hand on the gun at her hip as she scanned the horizon with her ice-blue gaze.

"No holdup," I replied. "Just a little sense of reverence. I'm about to be the first human to set foot on—"

Before I could stop her, Johar stepped off the ship, her black boots making a thudding sound as they hit the white surface.

"—the Farian homeworld."

Zin choked back a laugh from behind me. I looked skyward; a pale pink sunrise was spreading over a gray palette, painting light into the dim sky. I dragged in a breath before I looked back down at Jo.

She was grinning up at me. "You get to be Star of Indrana."

I stepped off the ship. "Enjoy it while you can. We're probably all going to be dead soon."

"Spoilsport."

"You know it." I let the smile fade as the group of white-clad Farians emerged from the building. "Eyes up, everyone. Here we go." Straightening my shoulders, I strode down the gleaming surface toward them.

As we drew closer, I spotted Adora. The man standing next to her was *Itegas* Rotem with his distinctive gray hair and platinum eyes. The other three on either side of them must have been the remainder of the Pedalion, unless I missed my guess.

There were what I assumed were guards behind them, sharp-eyed men who were, surprisingly, armed with rifles I'd never seen before. They were sleek, blue-gray things. Smaller than the 67 Pulse rifle so popular among resistance fighters across the galaxy, but not by much, and they looked just as lethal.

"Hey, Jo," I subvocalized over the com link. *"A little later, will you sweet-talk one of those guards into letting you get a closer look at their weapon?"*

"Can do."

There were what I guessed were news cameras, floating above

the heads of the Pedalion, and my father's voice slipped into my ear. The gentle reminder he'd always given us as children.

"Smile for the cameras, girls."

So I did. It was not the bright, innocent smile of a young princess but the slow, knowing smile of a woman who might be on enemy territory but was sure she had the upper hand in whatever was to come.

And I did. As long as something didn't go horribly wrong.

I stopped a little over a meter away from the Pedalion. Adora bowed, the gesture followed by the others. "Star of Indrana, welcome to Faria." Her greeting was in Indranan, not Farian, and a reminder of just how easily they'd woven themselves into my empire right before our very eyes.

"Itegas Notaras." I nodded. *"Itegas* Rotem."

"Star of Indrana." Rotem had a hand on Adora's arm and I watched his fingers flex slightly as he greeted me in Indranan also. "We welcome you to Faria; if you and your people will follow me?"

"Gladly. Before we go, a reminder to stay off my ship. My people have orders to shoot anyone trying to board without my permission."

This time Rotem's smile was sharp. "I will gently remind you that you are here as a guest."

"As the Empress of Indrana"—I smiled a deadly smile of my own—"and the first human visitor to Faria, it's best if I have some sovereign territory, don't you think, *Itegas?* And that ship is mine."

Oh, there was the flash of anger in that otherwise impassive face. However, Rotem inclined his head and when he came up it was wiped clean. "You are correct, Star of Indrana. Faria values our relationship with your empire."

"And you acknowledge my ship as Indranan soil?"

"Of course."

"Did you hear that, Your Highness?" I asked out loud, over the com link that was funneled through the ship.

"I did, Your Majesty," Alice replied. "Pass our thanks on to the Pedalion for their gracious treatment of you and your crew."

"My heir, Crown Princess Alice Gohil, extends her thanks to you and the rest of Faria for the welcome and the assurance of our safety." I kept my smile steady, instead of the grin I wanted to let spread over my face. I'd just forced him into making a public declaration.

The *Hailimi Bristol* was now, essentially, an Indranan embassy, perched on a landing pad in what looked to be the heart of their capital. Inviolate and protected and best of all, witnessed by Alice and the Matriarch Council back home on Pashati.

Adora was poking at that tooth. Rotem's smile was now strained. And the other members of the Pedalion—two women and an older man—stared at me with expressions ranging from outright shock to amusement.

Rotem gestured to the left. "If you'll follow me."

Adora held her tongue until we were through the doorway, the smooth white surface sliding closed and cutting us off from the cameras. She grabbed for me and I knocked her hand out of the way as Emmory pulled his Hessian.

42

The guards behind us froze in the act of reaching for their weapons at a snapped order from the older man on my right. I put a hand on Emmory's arm and he reholstered his weapon at my wordless command.

"How dare you!" Adora's cheeks were red with fury. "You bring these monsters to our home."

"I dare what is necessary for the safety of humanity. I dare this to protect Farian and Shen lives," I replied. "I am here to put an end to this needless conflict, Adora. A grudge that may have had merit once but that has gone on for far too long. All this is wrapped up in the whims of your gods and the subservience of the Pedalion for your own obsession with power."

She grabbed again; this time I let her close her fingers around my bare wrist and she smiled in triumph. "Have you forgotten what we are capable of?"

"Adora!"

I stepped closer and bared my teeth. "Do it."

"You bring this on yourself," she replied. There was a beat and the pain she brought to bear was a pale, laughable shadow of what I'd been through. It was possible she was trying to kill me, but nothing happened, and the realization poured into Adora's horrified look like a cup being filled.

"What have you done?" The question was directed over my shoulder at Aiz. I turned to look as he smiled and lifted a shoulder.

"What was necessary, sister. The Star agreed. She is safe from your touch and the touch of any who would harm her that way."

"You might be safe, but your people aren't." The challenge was issued with a snarl. I was impressed by her willingness to show her hand so early in the game, but Rotem was frowning and the other members of the Pedalion looked shocked by her behavior.

But the interesting part was no one moved to intervene. A member of the Farian government had essentially attacked the Empress of Indrana and they all stood and let her. Which meant two things were likely: Adora had more power here than I'd guessed, and everyone else was afraid of her.

I twisted easily from her grasp, curving my fingers around her wrist and clamping down. "You think I would protect myself and not them?" I stared down into Adora's eyes. It was tempting, so very tempting to send the anger growing in my chest back into her as pain, but I clamped down on the urge.

Don't give your advantages away.

"But test it, if you'd like, and see what kind of fire I rain down on you as a response. We are here to negotiate, *Itegas*, not act like spoiled children."

She jerked away from me and I let her go. "You think you can just walk in here and dictate the end of a war that has raged for longer than you humans have been alive? You have been fouled, corrupted, de—"

"Adora!" Rotem snapped, his voice cracking through the air like a whip as she finally crossed some imaginary boundary. "You will show the Star of Indrana respect."

"That'll be the day," I muttered, earning a sharp look from Rotem and a bark of laughter from the older man standing behind him.

"*Itegas* Rotem, if I may interrupt and give Adora a moment to compose herself before there's any further embarrassment or worse, an accident. We should do some introductions before we continue." The older man had gray hair, and eyes of sparkling silver. He bowed low. "Star of Indrana, it gives me great pleasure to be in your presence. I am *Itegas* Sou Efty. This is *Itegas* Yadira Calmier and *Itegas* Delphine Hessa." The pair of women were taller than Adora with golden eyes and nearly identical shoulder-length red curls. Neither looked particularly sympathetic, though it was hard to tell.

"It's nice to meet you." I folded my hands together and bowed in return, keeping my head up and my eyes on them. "I realize the unusual nature of my arrival may have upset how you normally do things; however, I would appreciate the opportunity to speak with the Pedalion in a formal setting. It is imperative we attempt to resurrect the negotiations that were disrupted on Earth."

"Of course," Sou replied with another kind smile. "First we should get you and your friends settled." He held a hand up, stalling any protest the others of the Pedalion looked to be about to offer. "Despite Adora's unpleasantness, I will not have it said around the galaxy that we treated our first human visitors with anything less than respect; if anyone is in disagreement on this, you can resign your post right now."

No one said a word.

I offered my arm, Sou took it, and the sly wink he sent my way almost had me laughing into the frozen silence.

"We will leave you with our guests, Sou," Rotem said finally. The foursome turned and headed back the way we had entered, the guards following.

"Aiz, it is a delight to see you again." Sou released me to hold out his arms, and to my utter surprise Aiz stepped into the embrace, hugging the Farian back.

"What?" Aiz asked when they separated and saw my quirked eyebrow.

"Didn't think you cared for Farians, but you keep hugging them."

"I don't." Aiz jumped and shot Sou a rueful look, rubbing at his rib cage where the older man had poked him. "I don't like most of them. Sou is an old friend of Father's."

"And of yours," Sou added.

"And of mine." There was genuine affection in Aiz's voice, and the smile that curved his mouth wasn't feigned. "You have not met my sister, Mia Cevallas."

"A great pleasure." Sou nodded in greeting.

Mia returned the nod but kept her hands together and stayed just behind me. With any luck it gave the impression she wasn't a threat, though I would think the Farians would know better. Sou didn't seem the least bit bothered by her presence. Geniality aside, there was no reason to trust him.

"Let's get you to your quarters. Star of Indrana, if I could borrow your hand for a moment." Sou held out his and I shared a look with Emmory before I complied. I didn't want to fall into the trap of thinking I was invincible just because of what Aiz had done to me.

Sou pressed his right palm to a spot next to the door, then tapped a few buttons that lit up and pressed my hand to the same spot. "This will give you access to these doors. Just in case you have a need to get from your quarters to your ship."

"You are possibly having too much fun with this," I murmured as he took my arm again and led us out of the room into a corridor with angled walls that made me more than a little dizzy.

"It is good for them to be disrupted every once in a while. It happens so rarely." Sou stopped in front of a blank wall and released my arm. "I confess I have been concerned a time or two about you. I thought maybe I had misread the visions from the future-seers as to who you were. But I am more at ease now that I have looked in your eyes."

"That might be a mistake," Johar said from behind us, and I laughed.

"Sou, this is my very good friend Johar. Gunrunner, scoundrel, and—"

"First human to set foot on your planet."

"You're going to ride that one, aren't you?"

"Into the ground." She grinned.

"I should have left you on the ship," I said with a sigh.

Sou was grinning. "You've fashioned an interesting crew, Star of Indrana. One worthy of toppling empires and saving galaxies."

"Call me Hail, please. *Your Majesty* was bad enough; this new title is even more cumbersome. I only make Adora use it because it pisses her off."

"Hail." Something about Sou's smile was unnerving. It was the sly look of someone who knew far more than I did about pretty much everything. Which wasn't much of a stretch when you got down to it; he probably did know a lot more. Not just because of his age, but I'd caught the offhand reference to the Council of Eyes. As a member of the Pedalion he'd have access to the visions of the future they chose to share.

A pair of doors on our left opened and Sou gestured inside with a smile. I paused, realized I was waiting for Emmory and the others to clear the room, and looked over my shoulder to find him smiling at me.

"Zin, Indula, check the room," Emmory said, his eyes never leaving mine.

"I hate you a little."

"I will come back for you and your people in a while, Hail," Sou said. "We will convene in the Pedalion chambers. After that there will be a meal to celebrate your arrival." He glanced Aiz's way. "It's going to cause quite the stir for you and Mia to be present, Aiz. I don't suppose I could convince you to stay here?"

"They'll deal," I replied before Aiz could. "They're part of my crew, Sou. I'm not leaving them here alone for someone to try to kill."

"Star of Indrana, we wouldn't—"

"You maybe, Sou." I cut him off with a shake of my head. "A lot of things have happened that I think the Pedalion needs to know about. I don't trust Adora not to put a knife in Aiz herself, and I'd much rather be nearby when she tries it." My smile was slow and just this side of feral. "I lost people I cared about on Earth, and I haven't decided yet if it was just Adora or the Pedalion as a whole who were responsible. I'd like you all to remember that."

Sou swallowed. "Of course. I understand completely. I will leave you then and be back shortly." He bowed once more and left us alone in the corridor.

"Clear, Emmory," Zin said, poking his head through the doorway.

"Go on, Your Majesty." Emmory touched my back.

"Any particular reason we didn't tell them up front why we're here?" Aiz asked as he followed me into the room.

I held up a hand and Aiz went silent. "Zin?"

"Clear as far as I can figure," he replied. "But I don't know what to sweep for bugwise."

Emmory held up a hand, and I relaxed a bit at the sight of the blinking lights on his glove. "We should be okay."

"Because we're going to do this as formally as possible. Which means announcing it in front of the Pedalion in their chambers, yes?" I asked Aiz, and he nodded. "The less they have to try to use against you to disqualify your requests, the better off we'll be. Plus, I don't trust them. I want Hao and the others in position before we do anything besides keep acting like we're here to negotiate with the Pedalion instead of the gods."

"I underestimated you, Hail," he replied with a smile.

"Most people do. It's unwise," I said as I glanced around the rooms.

More white walls and angles. It made the front room seem smaller than it was, and when I touched a wall, I realized it wasn't stone we were surrounded by. It was metal. My claustrophobia reared its head to scream a desperate scream. I sighed, stepping on it as hard as I could. There wasn't time for my issues. "This place makes me uneasy."

"Right there with you," Emmory murmured, and we shared a look.

"I always hated this place," Aiz said. "It hasn't changed at all."

I sat on a bench and pulled my knees up to my chest, wrapping my arms around them. "I'm telling the truth about wanting to find a way to end this bloodshed between you and the Farians. It's not going to end just because we kill their gods. There has to be something more."

"You'll want to tread carefully, Hail." Aiz dragged a hand through his hair. "Sou is an old friend, but he's also the Pedalion. I wouldn't trust any of them, and Adora is just as likely to do something stupid as she is to take another breath."

Rotem was the one I was more wary of, though I wasn't going to tell Aiz that. His sister was dangerous, and her good sense clouded by her issues with her brother, but there was something about the other male member of the Pedalion that made my nerves itch.

He'd hid his anger well, but I'd spotted it and knew it was like a volcano about to blow. Rotem was the one I wasn't entirely sure could be counted on to hold to the treaty with Indrana. Or worse, do something like manufacture an accident that would result in a tearful apology to Alice.

"Who's in charge of the Pedalion?"

"No one." Aiz smiled. "Sou is the oldest member, but the Pedalion has no single leader. Their votes on most day-to-day issues must have a simple majority to pass. For major issues, like *ilios porthmeios*, the vote of approval must be unanimous."

"Fabulous."

"Do not worry, they will approve it. There is no way the Pedalion, especially my sister, will pass up the chance to see the gods end my life."

Privately, I thought the arrogance in Aiz's family wasn't something Adora had a lock on, but I kept that observation between my teeth for now. We would see what would happen once he stood in front of the Pedalion and issued his petition. If they refused to hear it at all, I'd have to move to plan B.

The fact that I didn't yet have a solid plan B for that was something that concerned me a great deal.

43

I patted Johar on the arm as I crossed to the window. The sill was wide but angled sharply downward while the edges came to a point above my head. If I stood on my tiptoes and stretched I would just barely reach it.

"Hao, are you there?"

"Waiting on you, sha zhu; can we get out of this can?"

"You're free to go, just don't get caught. Seems like the Farians are going to respect the ship as Indranan territory. Tell Captain Saito to keep guards posted and the doors locked after you head out."

"You think something will go wrong?"

"Doesn't it always?" I asked.

Hao chuckled. *"Fair point. Watch your back out there, Hail."*

"Will do my best. Back at you."

"I've spoken to my people," Fasé said, joining me at the window. "They'll meet Hao and Sybil at a safe house nearby. I've already sent her the coordinates."

"How difficult will it be to get me out of here so I can meet them?"

"It is a risk." She tapped her fingers on the sill. "How much fuss do you think Emmory's going to put up if I ask him and the others to stay behind?"

A metric ton was the first thing that came to mind, and I gave a tiny laugh that ended on a sigh and earned me a raised eyebrow from Emmory. "You know he won't agree to that, Fasé."

"You are, ironically, the safest you have ever been," Fasé murmured. "The public respects you. The Pedalion will not dare to move against you. Even Adora, as mad as she is, cannot risk the gods' disapproval and harm you."

"That didn't seem to stop her earlier."

"True." Fasé lifted a shoulder. "All I can tell you is what I know of my people and how you are perceived."

"And what is that exactly?" I asked, turning from the window. "I'm what—"

"Hail, did you know they have statues of you here?" Hao's voice broke into my head again, and it took me several seconds to register what he'd said.

"They have what?" This time I got more than a raised eyebrow from Emmory.

"Majesty?"

"Hao, now is hardly the time for fucking around," I said.

"He's actually not, Majesty," Gita said, though she, thankfully, used the main com channel so Emmory and the others could hear her. *"There is a rather nice, but very large, statue of you in the middle of this intersection."*

I gave Fasé a flat look. She lifted her hands. "Star of Indrana," she said, as if that explained everything.

Aiz chuckled and I reminded myself why I couldn't shoot him right now. Only Mia didn't seem amused, the Shen watching me from her seat with gray eyes that had gone dark.

"That's creepy," I said finally, shaking my head. "I have done nothing for you people, certainly nothing to warrant a statue."

My declaration seemed to release the tension in Mia's shoulders, and she took a deep breath but remained silent.

"You are the Star, Hail. That is all that's required."

"You realize how that sounds?" I demanded. "It sounds like a cult and I know how that shit turns out for the supposed figurehead."

"Hail." Emmory's quiet use of my name calmed me down somewhat, and the sudden knock at the door made me have to shelve the rest. I needed my focus to be here, so I pushed it from my head and pasted a smile on my face.

Emmory opened it at my nod and Sou bowed briefly. "Star of Indrana, the Pedalion is ready to receive you, if you and your people will follow me."

I gestured for Aiz and Mia to go ahead; Emmory preceded me through the door and then fell into step on my left.

"This all feels a bit scripted, even Adora's outburst," Zin whispered in my ear as he followed me through the door. Fasé and Johar fell in behind us while the other three BodyGuards remained behind in the room.

"This whole place feels like a carefully maintained illusion," I replied. "Tell the others to keep their eyes up."

Zin smiled slowly. "You think Emmory hasn't already issued that order?"

"Dhatt." I smacked him in the chest with a laugh. "You all could at least let me pretend I'm in charge."

Emmory chuckled. Zin squeezed my shoulder. "We do, ma'am, it's not even a pretense."

I reached up, touching his hand for a moment, and my vision misted. The words *Do you know how much I missed you* were stuck in my throat, but I wasn't sure they were necessary. Zin squeezed once again and released me.

The corridor widened as we walked, moving from a narrow coffin of angles to something that felt a little more spacious, though no less sharp, and I found myself wishing for the soft rounded curves of the base on Sparkos.

Sou was less jovial as we moved through the deserted area, and

I realized we hadn't seen another Farian besides the guards and the Pedalion since our arrival.

I'd seen too many bad jobs go down this way to not be on my guard. *No matter what*, I told myself, *you get everyone home. Is that understood?*

We followed Sou down a long corridor that exited into a room with high arched ceilings filled with angles. A pair of guards at the back of the room came to attention, one of them reaching back and pressing a hand to the wall.

There was the sound of heavy metal grating against itself and the jagged pieces of white shifted, sliding away to reveal an opening large enough for me, Emmory, and Zin to walk through shoulder to shoulder.

"Star of Indrana, welcome to the chamber of the Pedalion." Sou left us just inside the room, crossing the chamber to the raised stage on the opposite side of the large oval space. The other members of the Pedalion were already seated, in chairs that looked to be constructed from the same white metal that we'd already seen around us.

The floor was emblazoned with a massive sixteen-pointed star in stone as stark as a black hole. I moved to the center of it, Aiz and Mia on one side and Fasé on the other. The others lined up behind us. Tucking my hands into my pockets, I scanned the other members as I waited for Sou to get to his seat.

Adora's face was pinched as usual, and she was glaring daggers at her brother. Rotem sat on her right at the outside; his face was expressionless, but his shoulders were tense. Yadira and Delphine sat on the other side, and Sou took his seat in the middle of the group.

He tapped the tiny golden bell; it rang through the chamber with a sound that echoed and built on itself in a way that shouldn't have been possible.

"I call this session of the Pedalion to order. We are gathered to greet the Star of Indrana in her long-awaited appearance before us. All praise to the gods. All praise to the seven—the four who are gone and the three who remain."

"All praise to the seven—the four who are gone and the three who remain."

Out of the corner of my eye, I saw Aiz's smirk flash briefly across his face and refrained from drawing any more attention to him by poking him in the side.

"I object to the presence of that abomination," Adora said in Farian.

I jerked; the word was the same in Farian as Shen, and for a moment I thought she was talking about me, but her eyes were locked on Mia, who stared back with quiet defiance.

"Adora," Rotem warned, also in Farian, but she was undeterred.

"No, we have strayed so far from the path the gods set. I will not be silent. None of this is as it was seen! We let Shen and abominations and armed humans into our sacred spaces. It is blasphemy! We would be well within our rights to kill the lot of them and send their bodies back home without a word of explanation."

"Fasé," I murmured. "I don't want to give away our advantage here. Respond to her."

"Watch yourself, Adora. Making threats you can't keep isn't a good look," Fasé said, her voice loud enough to catch their attention.

Adora snapped a reply in Farian I couldn't understand, one that was sharply countered by Sou and Delphine simultaneously and had Fasé raising a red eyebrow.

"Enough!" Rotem slapped a hand down on the ledge in front of him. "Adora, compose yourself. Sou, we know where your feelings lie. Delphine, speak like that again to your senior and I will personally take you before the gods."

It was only thanks to Aiz murmuring a quick translation to me that I was able to understand all of it. Everyone subsided into silence and I took note of what had just happened. Maybe there wasn't technically a leader of the Pedalion, but Rotem had enough pull that the others would listen when it came down to it.

"Star of Indrana," he said in Indranan. "My apologies again for Adora's behavior toward you. There is no excuse."

"Accepted." I dipped my head. "This is the last time. The next time she threatens me or mine, there will be consequences."

"Understood." Rotem didn't look Adora's way, but her strangled protest died in her throat before it fully made it out into the air.

I took a step forward, folded my hands together, and pressed them to my forehead, my lips, and then my heart before shaking them in the Pedalion's direction. "I thank you for your gracious welcome and bring you greetings from not only the empire of Indrana but from all of humanity."

"Well." Sou smiled. "It is with great joy that we greet you, Star of Indrana. May I be the first to extend our apologies for the trouble on Earth and the deaths of your people in the attack on your embassy."

"It is appreciated." I let my gaze settle on Adora for a long moment, pleased when she looked away first. "We are still looking into the matter. We will deal with it later."

"You wish to resume the negotiations between us and the Shen." Rotem steepled his fingers and looked down at me, no doubt thinking he cut an intimidating figure. I'd seen more than my share, though, and he wasn't even in the top twenty.

"Yes, that is what I went to Earth for and my task hasn't been finished."

"Surely, Star of Indrana, you realize that peace between us and these blasphemers isn't something that is possible."

"What I realize is that you all have very little choice in the matter. If Faria wishes to continue to enjoy a presence in not only Indranan space but the rest of humanity's as well, they need to figure out a way to live in peace."

"You're not suggesting you'll kick us out of your arms of the galaxy?" Yadira's shock wasn't feigned.

"I am saying humanity is done being the bystanders who get killed in this pissing contest you all have got going on. If you don't sort it out yourselves, we'll help you. Starting with removing you from our space for the safety of our people. You've spoken to my heir. You've spoken to President Hudson. You already know we are done."

"You are not in a place to make demands." Adora waved a hand at Aiz. "You lie. You kill our people. You bring these heretics to our home. You're not here for a negotiation."

I froze. *Bugger me.*

"You're here to try to force us into a peace no one wants. You're here to try to give that madwoman's rebellion some legitimacy." She waved her hand at Fasé, acknowledging her for the first time. Fasé merely smiled.

"Enough." I crossed my arms, calculating our odds with a speed that would have made Portis proud. My voice rang through the chamber, and Adora gaped at me in shock while the others of the Pedalion watched with expressions ranging from confusion to curiosity. "I will—"

The door behind us ground open once again. Rotem got to his feet, but whatever he'd been about to say never left his mouth and I dared a glance over my shoulder.

Four figures came into the room. Each was draped in a veil of gold fabric and wore a curious off-center ellipse of flattened intricate lace on their head.

"Star of Indrana." They spoke as one, dropped into a curtsy as one, and rose with an almost mechanical precision. "We have come to welcome you."

The guards were all down on a knee. I glanced back and the Pedalion had followed suit, though with bowed heads, not bended knee.

"The Council of Eyes," I murmured, suddenly realizing who these four Farians were.

"We are the future-seers." I couldn't see her face, but the voice of the one who stepped forward was definitively feminine. The others didn't move, but I could hear their whispered echo resonating through the air.

"Our sisters." She crossed the star on the floor, pale hands outstretched to Fasé and Mia; stopping only when Aiz stepped in front of Mia with a poorly controlled snarl at her to stop. "No fear, god-killer, we mean her no harm."

"Would that I could believe that, Kasio." But a smile fluttered across his face.

"From us, as certain as the sun rising." Kasio made a little gesture toward the Pedalion. "As always, power does as power wills. You are here to claim the *ilios porthmeios*, but it is unnecessary subterfuge. The gods wish to speak with the Star and those who travel with her."

"Just like that?" I asked, stepping up to Aiz's side to further shield Mia as the faceless woman confirmed what Sybil had said.

She turned toward me, and the lack of facial expression or body language to go by made me extremely uneasy. "I wish, Star of Indrana, Hail Bristol, the woman who does not believe but who sees the truth which such ease. You know nothing is done just like that." Her echo of my words was accompanied by a snap of her fingers. "It is done with heart and mind connected, with blood and sweat and tears. Not handed over like a gift."

"A girl can dream," I replied.

"The gods want to speak with you," Kasio repeated. "But not yet. There are things you need to see here before you go. Things that will help in your choice and things that will help you when you descend into the well of dying souls."

"What do I tell the Pedalion?" I looked over at them; the five members seemed frozen in place, unaware of our conversation, and that was when I realized Emmory and the others were also not moving. "What have you done?"

"A little privacy does wonders for the soul." I couldn't see it but I heard the smile in Kasio's voice. "Tell the Pedalion you will give them three days' time to decide on the negotiations."

"Okay."

Kasio tipped her head in acknowledgment. "And come see us tomorrow night; our sister Sybil will know where. She has been gone from us for far too long; tell her we miss her."

I blinked and it was as if the room had spun back into gear. The Council of Eyes filed back out of the room without a word. Rotem lifted his head, looking first to the backs of the future-seers as they passed the still-kneeling guards, and then to me.

"I will give the Pedalion three days to discuss our offer of negotiations," I said.

"Star of Indrana, what did the Council want with you?" Adora demanded.

"What do you mean?"

"They—"

"Said nothing to me," I lied easily. "I assumed they were here to speak with the Pedalion. Three days, Adora."

"And when we say no?"

I didn't blink. I'd played this game with far better opponents than Adora and the rest of the Pedalion. "I'd advise against it," I said, and left the chamber without another word.

44

Emmory took hold of my arm as we headed back to our rooms, but no one said a word until the door was closed and the flashing lights on his glove were visible.

"Aiz, what the actual fuck was that?" I asked.

He looked as shocked as I was, his eyes more than a little wild. "I have not seen Kasio since before the triumph," he whispered.

Mia pressed a hand to her chest, chewing on her lower lip. "I did not expect that. They knew who I was?"

"Fasé, we'll need to speak with—"

"On it already," she replied, cutting me off.

"I'm going to need someone to stop and tell me what just happened," Emmory said, fingers tightening on my arm.

"The Council of Eyes paid us a visit."

"Yes, I saw," he replied. "They walked in and then walked back out."

"That's all you saw? Interesting." I started to pull the recording from my *smati*, but frowned. "Bugger me. There's no vid." I shot Aiz a look. "You people and your tricks."

"Not my people."

"You know what I mean." I felt Emmory's hand flex again and turned back to him. "The seers had a message for the four of us. That the Farians' gods want to speak with me, but not yet."

"What are we supposed to do in the meantime?" Zin asked.

"This place is an Alcubierre/White Drive waiting to go critical. I can tell that just from standing in front of the Pedalion for two minutes. I don't trust Adora."

"Second that," Johar said. "That one's got power, Hail, and not only in the Pedalion. I saw the guards deferring to her when we landed. No impartial guard would have let her go after a visiting dignitary like she did to you."

"The Pedalion has three days to deliberate the merits of the negotiations," I replied, and then gave them a quick recap of what Kasio had said to us. "We'll let them debate and do what we need to do in the meantime. First step is meeting with Fasé's people."

"Is that wise?" Aiz asked, and I lifted my shoulders in a shrug as I crossed the room.

Mia had sat in a nearby chair and I put my hand on her shoulder. She reached up, covering it with hers.

"I'm not planning on strolling out of here and straight into a meeting in the daylight, if that's what you mean. But it's about on par with the rest of our plans. In the meantime, let's get ready for dinner."

I chafed at the formality of the dinner, which was no surprise. Pomp and procedure weren't something I had time for under the best of circumstances, and my restlessness had only gotten worse after we were led into a dining room with low white tables and the same damn angles.

Those were also starting to get on my nerves. I didn't like Faria. The formality. The stale air. The sharp edges everywhere.

Adora got up and left the room after a passionate declaration that she wouldn't share a meal with someone who'd harbored a traitor and god-killer, and a decent contingent of Farians followed her in protest. The rest of the Pedalion, even Rotem, frowned at her retreating back.

I kept my mouth shut and picked at my food, my nerves and

curiosity keeping my appetite at bay. The rest of dinner passed without incident and soon we were back in the room.

"I'm feeling a whole lot more like a prisoner and less like an honored guest," I muttered at the closed door, thumping it with a fist out of sheer frustration before I turned away.

"Don't worry about it, we'll sneak out of here in a bit." Johar patted my shoulder on her way by.

"You two are going to have to stay here."

"I know." Aiz sighed. "I don't like it but the last thing we need is to get caught out there." He shook his head before Mia could protest. "No, Mia. I won't risk it. I'd only end up locked in a jar for all eternity. You'd be dead."

"The safest place for you is right here," I said, and managed not to flinch when she turned that sharp gray gaze on me.

"It's not safe for you out there, Hail. You're not immortal." She flopped down into a chair, wincing as she caught her elbow on a sharp edge. "What is wrong with these people?"

"No design sense?"

She didn't laugh at my murmured reply, and I took a few steps toward her. "I know it's not safe. But I'll be with Fasé and that's close enough. Something tells me that going to meet with her people is one of the things that needs to happen before we can meet with the gods." I leaned down and brushed my lips over hers even though I could feel Aiz's gaze boring into my back. "Emmory and Jo will be with us and I promise I'll be careful."

"You'd better."

"There are other people in the room," Aiz said.

Mia grinned against my mouth. "Close your eyes, then, brother," she replied, and kissed me.

"You'll want to stop daydreaming about your girlfriend, Hail," Johar whispered in my ear, catching the elbow I threw back into her gut before it connected.

"I hope you all get the fun out of your systems," I replied, my voice low as the four of us crept down the shadowed alley. Fasé was in front with me behind her, Johar and Emmory bringing up the rear. The Farian knew where she was going, or at least she acted like it, so all my focus was on watching for anyone who could potentially rat us out to the Pedalion.

Emmory hadn't been the least bit concerned about the potential for some kind of surveillance, and I found out halfway there it was because Johar had the same masking program Rai had used on Canafey.

"Speaking of girlfriends, are you going to let Rai apologize?" I whispered.

"Leave me out of your matchmaking, Your Majesty."

"I'm just curious."

"I thought you were gonna kill him?"

I shrugged, staying silent as I followed Fasé across a patch of light-filled street and up the stairs into the building. "He seemed sorry, and everything worked out in the end, I guess."

"We're not even close to the end of this," Johar replied.

"I mean, if you want me to kill him, I will."

"No." Johar muttered something under her breath after her denial that I was sure was physically impossible. "I'm still mad at him, but I might let him apologize before I punch him a few times."

I chuckled, stopping at the top of the stairs. Fasé waited with a raised eyebrow. "Are you two quite finished?"

I winked at her and she sighed, rapping a pattern onto the door next to her. The door cracked, then swung open, and the man lowered his weapon to the floor, following it into a bow that almost put his forehead on his knees. *"Mardis."*

I watched as Fasé reached out, cupping the man's face with a smile. "Not for our good, for the good of all. What's your name?"

"Poius, *Mardis.*" He looked past her, silver eyes widening. "Star of Indrana."

"No, no," I said, holding up my hand. "No bowing. It's good to meet you, Poius."

"Hail," Hao said, coming out of a doorway off to one side. "We were just going over the network. Come see."

I embraced Hao briefly before following him, Emmory and Jo trailing behind.

"This place might combust with you and Fasé in here at the same time," Hao murmured with a half smile as people turned to watch me cross through the open room.

"I think I want to take a long vacation after this where no one knows me."

"Good luck with that."

I snorted and reached a hand out to Talos as we passed. The Shen stood out among the shorter, paler Farians as much as Hao and Gita did, but something about my greeting seemed to release the last vestiges of tension among the rebels in the room.

"Gita." I hugged her and then smiled at Sybil. "Your sisters said to tell you they miss you."

All the sound in the room dropped into nothingness. Sybil smiled. "You spoke with the council?"

"They came to see us while we were meeting with the Pedalion."

"Did the Pedalion see?" Sybil stood from her spot in the corner.

"They saw them come in, not the conversation," I replied. "Kasio said you would know where to meet. We have secured three days while the Pedalion discusses resuming the negotiations." I smiled and gestured around. "There are apparently a few things I need to see before I speak with the gods."

"Really?"

"She seemed very certain, but beyond mentioning we needed to meet them tomorrow I didn't get specifics. What do you think they want to talk about?"

Sybil shrugged, but her glance around the room at all the people watching told me that was a conversation for a more private venue, so I leaned against Hao to study the console in front of him.

"Well, what have we got here?"

"One of the better underground networks I've seen." He nodded to Fasé. "I'm impressed not only that you set this up so well but you did it while you were basically in prison."

She smiled. "Sybil was a great help setting everything up. I am grateful you didn't betray us."

Sybil nodded her head in acknowledgment. "The seers told you the gods wished to speak with you, Hail?"

"They did. What is going on?"

"A theocracy gone mad," Fasé answered before Sybil could, and I was shocked by the venom in her voice. "I thought the council was in lockstep with the Pedalion, Sybil, but that doesn't appear to be the case."

"You know the delicate balance we are walking, Fasé." Sybil took a deep breath in the face of the other Farian's sudden anger. "Your people are a spike in the wheel that has been turning. A welcome one, but one that will cause heartache and destruction."

"We will not be bound by the Pedalion any longer," a Farian in the corner said, and her sentiment was echoed by her companions. "Many of us here were not around for the early days, but that doesn't mean we don't honor the gods. We are simply tired of being trapped here. One endless life after another. What is the point of a life with a knee bent in servitude?"

This was the first chance I'd had to talk to other Farians about their lives and what they wanted. I'd had the whole layout of Fasé's demands during the negotiations on Earth, from the disbanding of the Pedalion to their support for the Shen to have a piece of Faria as their own, but now it was right in my face.

The woman speaking didn't look much older than Fasé, but there was no way to know how old she truly was without asking, and that felt extremely rude.

"Hail, this is Iode." Fasé introduced us with a smile.

"It's nice to meet you."

"You also, Star of Indrana." Iode's nod was perfunctory and she didn't seem nearly as awestruck by me as her companions. "I hope that your arrival means we're almost done with all of this and will be able to move out of this bubble the Pedalion have us trapped in."

"Bubble?"

"Yes, the gods, our supposed missions out into the galaxy, the way we are forced to come home instead of stay out there and make a life. It is a farce and a fraud. They keep us locked away here when we could be out there living."

Others spoke up, a wave of voices adding their own protests and painting a picture of a Pedalion far more controlling than I had imagined. The people of Faria, at least a section of them, were ready to burn the whole thing to the ground.

"Iode's got some opinions," Hao murmured with a grin.

"You like her."

"Reminds me of someone I know."

45

The knock at the door the next morning was unexpected, and I shared a look with Emmory before I pushed out of the uncomfortable chair. Emmory gestured to Zin, and they both reached for their weapons. There'd been no discussion from the Farians about us carrying, which had surprised me, but I didn't test our good luck.

"Open it," I said to Emmory, my own hands resting on my Glocks.

He tapped the control panel by the door and it slid away to reveal Delphine and another Farian.

"Star of Indrana." They laid their hands one on top of the other at their waists and bowed.

I had the oddest flash of memory—Stasia's golden curls swinging forward with her bow the very first time I'd met her—and for a moment was glad my maid was safe back on the ship with Alba and the others.

The Farians came up, Delphine's red curls settling about her shoulders. The other woman's hair was bound up in a heavy braid and they both made a curious gesture in the air with the thumb and index finger of their right hands.

"What can I do for you, Delphine?"

She smiled. "Sou and I didn't feel it was right for you to be trapped in your room during our deliberations. Adora and Rotem, of course, do not trust you to be roaming our lovely city alone." Her smile grew. "I suspect there is a bit of something else in there, but it was unnecessary to pursue. Anyway, Yadira sided with us on the vote, so I am here to introduce you to Prosa, who will be your guide around Sicenae for the next few days."

"Star of Indrana." Prosa wasn't much taller than her companion and she had Fasé's golden eyes. There were nerves in the set of her shoulders, and I wondered if it was excitement or concern.

"It's nice to meet you." I glanced back at Emmory. Iza, Indula, and Kisah had been up all night on watch while the rest of us slept. "You and Zin with me. Johar doesn't mind staying here."

"Nope." Jo leaned back in her chair. "I'll catch up on my sleep."

Prosa pressed a hand to the panel at the end of the corridor and we passed through the door out into the open air.

I took a deep breath; the morning air was clean with a tang of ozone that felt a bit like electricity when it hit my bloodstream.

"I'll leave you here with Prosa; I must get back to the Pedalion," Delphine said.

I watched her retreating back until Prosa cleared her throat. "We'll want to go this way, Star of Indrana. The view is good here, but much better over there."

"Call me Hail, please. That title is beyond cumbersome."

"I should not."

"I promise not to tell." That and the accompanying wink pulled a smile from her.

"You are everything my mother said and more," Prosa replied. "I will honor your request while we are still up here, but I must maintain some propriety in public."

"That works for me." I slipped my arm through hers, felt her jolt of surprise, and grinned. "Two questions for you: Who's your mother? And just what has she said about me?"

Prosa gestured at the stairs looming in front of us. "We're going up here. I was referring to Sybil."

"Sybil's your mother?" I reached for the railing with my free hand as we started up a long stairway. But it was as sharp-edged as everything here and I pulled back my hand with a muttered curse.

"Of a sort," she replied with a smile and a shrug, reminding me of Fasé introducing her cousins—Veeha and Volen—with the same sort of vague association. We hit the top of the stairs and I looked around the tiny cupola; it was windowless, a door on the far side of the empty room. Emmory and Zin took up easy positions behind us.

"You're free to tell me to mind my own business, of course, but why the vague answer?"

Prosa smiled again. "It is not deliberate. Families are complicated on Faria, Hail."

"Aiz and Adora are siblings," I replied. "They share a mother. Though I noticed the names they've chosen are different."

"Well, that was Javez's doing. He abandoned his Farian name when his wife was—" Prosa stopped and swallowed. "Sent to live with the gods. And he chose a new one. Aiz and Adora are not a good example, though. They were born already when the gods came to us. Their parents were used later for batches, but I don't know that either of them ever really acknowledged anyone beyond their original family. I was born in one of the last batches the gods allowed new souls in. There are over a hundred siblings in my batch."

"Batch?"

"I am certain that is the right Indranan word," Prosa said with a frown. "Those who share genetic material and are all grown at the same time."

"Yes, that would work." A chill settled itself in my gut, and I pulled away from the Farian standing next to me. Several things collided in my head at once, and I shoved my hand in my pocket instead of resting it on my gun like I wanted to.

"You don't have children." I'd never seen a Farian child, and I thought of the objections I'd heard last night at the underground headquarters. We'd always assumed that was just because of the laws about procreation being forbidden outside Faria and with any non-Farians.

But it was so much more than that. The Pedalion actively prevented any Farians from having children. Ever.

"You mean do we bear children?" Prosa shook her head. "No, it is dangerous and inefficient. And well—" She broke off in a laugh. "When you have souls who need to be reborn, our gods decided the best way was for us to create the bodies we need as the old ones wear out."

"You're not cloning, are you?" It was illegal in every human government, accords that were signed back in the days when humanity had found her feet in the stars.

"No, of course not. Genetic material is taken from several parents to make a batch. Those who were here before the gods—like Aiz and Adora—are not batch born. However, you can see how quickly family associations get a little confusing with rebirths. Some choose to remember all those connected through all their lives, but others focus only on the most recent incarnation." Prosa wiggled a hand as she continued to the door. "There was some experimentation in the early days to figure out what would work best. We've found that it is better to skip those formative years you humans find so necessary. Having to be a child when you are thousands of years old is far too frustrating."

The door opened and Prosa held out a hand with a smile. "I'll answer your other questions in a moment; I don't want to talk over the top of this."

We passed through the doorway and I understood why she was reticent to continue our talk. I wouldn't have heard her anyway. The balcony wrapped itself around the tower and from what I could tell we were in the center of Sicenae.

The city shone in the early-morning light. Not much different from Krishan, though where my home was all flowing lines and gentle curves the Farian city was filled with angled white spikes jutting up into the air like knife blades.

It was gorgeous, but still unsettling.

Even more so because of the statues and reminders of me all over the damn place. I was more and more uneasy about the way the Farians had warped their entire society around the idea of the Shiva-damned Star of Indrana.

"Prosa, what's with the right-angle fetish?" I asked.

There was no reply and I turned to see her back in the cupola having an argument with thin air. As tempting as it was to listen in, she was speaking Farian and I knew I couldn't pick enough meaning from her rapidly moving conversation to make it worthwhile. So I left her to her discussion and instead wandered farther down the balcony to stand next to Emmory.

I wasn't terribly shocked by her admission that the Farians used tube-tech for their children, but it was a little surprising they just grew their people as adults. That would be frowned on in the human parts of the galaxy, but as Prosa had pointed out, we needed those childhood years. The Farians obviously didn't.

I could make out people walking the streets below. The red-haired Farians were a splash of color on the white canvas.

The Farians out in the world dressed in the same style as their surroundings, yet another indication of how well they were taught to assimilate into a culture and meld themselves into the fabric of a place.

Here, though, the choice appeared to be white or off-white, though the cut of the clothing varied some. It was eerie in its sameness.

"My apologies for that, Hail. I had been told I would be relieved of my duties, but someone is still protesting over Delphine's decision."

It was oddly soothing to know that some things never changed and even on Faria people forgot to pass things along.

"What are your duties?" I asked as Prosa joined us at the balcony.

"I am what you would call a clerk for Delphine, I suppose. I help her with the daily aspects of her role in the Pedalion."

"Wouldn't there be things you are needed for during the discussion of the negotiations?"

"Normally, yes." She nodded. "However, Delphine meant for one of the others to take over my duties. There was a bit of a protest."

I laughed. "Why?"

"I am the youngest of her staff. Another felt they should get the honor of escorting the Star of Indrana around." A smile slipped through. "Delphine suspected you would not have gotten along with them very well."

"Oh, I don't know, I get along pretty well with most people."

"They are a supporter of Adora's policies and staunchly anti-Shen."

"Ah," I said, biting the inside of my cheek. "Okay, so probably not."

Prosa laughed.

I waved a hand at the city below us. "Your architecture is interesting."

"Your tone suggests a different word." Prosa's laughter continued to dance along the edge of her reply.

"It is jarring," I admitted.

"The angles please the gods. They say it keeps us safe and hidden. Different from Indrana, for sure." She looked up at the sky. "I have never been to your empire, but I have seen the images. Perhaps someday."

"It is a lovely place. I didn't realize how much I missed it until I was back."

"I understand that," Prosa replied. "I just returned from two years on Earth for my mission and though it was a very happy time of my life, I felt the difference in my soul when I set foot back here."

"Can I ask you about the Pedalion's feelings on the negotiations?"

"I'm afraid not." Prosa shook her head. "This war is almost a family matter, but it impacts all of us. In some ways I wish the gods would just step in. The Shen are our enemies, yes, but they want the same things we do. Home and safety?"

"You seem very knowledgeable of the Shen and surprisingly sympathetic to their cause."

"We initially thought Delphine would go to the negotiations on Earth, and so I helped her with her research. But Adora was chosen instead. Then after what happened I felt it would be useful if I continued with my research since the Star of Indrana seemed to be on good terms with the Shen."

"You all are really fixated on that, aren't you?" I laughed and looked up at the unfamiliar stars that were vanishing with the coming sunrise.

"It is one of the foundations of our society." Prosa rested her arms on the ledge and stared up at the dawn-painted sky above. "Possibly foolish to you, but it's what we're told from the beginning."

"I'm sorry," I said, folding my hands together and shaking them in her direction. "I did not mean that as an insult, but merely as an observation."

"It is all right. I shouldn't project our reverence onto you, but it is difficult to remember that your knowledge of all this is so new."

"To be honest, it's not only new, but I still don't know a lot about it."

Prosa gestured below us. "Come with me, Hail. This is a delightful view, but down on the ground is where our people live, and I think it is good that you see them."

I followed her back down the stairs and out onto the street. With no sense of the time beyond the lack of sun and the lights of the city, it was hard to tell if the moderately populated street we exited onto was busy for the hour.

"Faria has a thirty-four-hour day," Prosa said as if she'd heard my thoughts. "It is shortly after the eighth. But Sicenae is a major metropolis for us, and people are out at all hours. We may run into some crowds, but your BodyGuards can rest assured that no one here means you any harm." She dipped her head down the street, ignoring the stares from the passersby. "We'll go this way, I think."

"Lead the way."

As we walked along, I smiled and nodded at the Farians we passed, delighting in the double takes and confused looks that passed from me to Prosa and back again.

One man walked into a post and I bit down hard on my cheek to keep the laughter in when Zin choked back a snort. Judging from the sparkle in Prosa's golden eyes, this was providing her with just as much delight.

"Here we are." She pressed her hand to the doorway, the pristine surface sliding away to reveal the smells and sounds of what I could only assume was a café of some kind.

"Mi Prosa!" The elderly woman behind the counter clapped her hands in delight and was halfway around the smooth white slab, arms spread in preparation for an embrace, when she spotted me. Her silver eyes snapped wide. *"Indrani fin astari?"*

"Nai," Prosa replied.

The Farian folded her hands together and bowed so low that for a moment I was sure her forehead was going to touch the spotless floor. "Star of Indrana," she said in perfect Indranan that was laced with the most curious accent. "Thank you for blessing me with your presence."

"Hail Bristol, if I may introduce you to Vada Hessa, my grandmother and the owner of the best restaurant in all of Faria."

"My granddaughter flatters me," Vada said with a wave of her hands as she rose.

I extended mine, pleased when the older woman took them after only a second's hesitation. "That is what granddaughters are for, isn't it?"

"Just so." Vada pulled away. "Have you ever tried *masalata*?"

She said the word in Farian and I shook my head. "I doubt I have, but I'm not sure what it even is."

"I will make you some to try."

"I would like that very much."

"Come to the back, otherwise we will be mobbed within minutes." Moving with surprising speed, Vada crossed the café and locked her door. "Since I am sure Prosa paraded you down the street just to get a reaction from people."

I watched the blush spread over Prosa's porcelain skin and grinned. "She did, but it was worth it." Following Vada back into the kitchen, I took the stool she directed me to. "Tell me where you learned to speak Indranan so well, Grandmother."

"In school with the rest of my family, Star of Indrana," she replied.

"It's a required subject for all Farians," Prosa supplied, laughing at my shocked look. "The other human languages are electives that people can choose before their mission years. But every Farian is required to speak Indranan."

"Why?" I felt silly even before the word left my mouth. Both Prosa and Vada looked at me in surprise.

"So we could speak with you if we were one of the ones lucky enough to be placed in your path."

46

Y ou know what Hao would say." Johar leaned back in her chair late in the day with a grin on her face. "That's the kind of army you could take over the universe with."

I blew out a breath. "That's the terrifying part, Jo. These people's entire education has been centered on Indrana and apparently me. For what? My arrival? It's as unsettling as this damn architecture." I slapped a wall on my way by with a snarl. "I am not Kalki, riding in to destroy all evil and chaos."

"You are to the Farians."

"That's the part that makes Emmory nervous, and for once I agree with him." I pinched the bridge of my nose and sighed a long breath out before I dropped my hand. "If I really were one of the avatars of Vishnu, you'd think I could just tell them all to stop this war and it would be over."

"Sure, if it worked like that, but you and I know it doesn't." Jo shrugged a shoulder and went back to her breakfast.

"She's not wrong," Zin replied at my look. "I used to think it was a human condition, but the Farians and the Shen have proved me wrong on that front. Other than the Svatir, is there a sentient species out there that doesn't fight and kill?"

His words made me think of Dailun's warning and how the Hiervet had almost managed to grind the Svatir under their bootheels. I wasn't so arrogant as to think humanity was better at war than any ancient race, which left me with the unsettling thought.

Could humanity stand alone against the Hiervet if we had to? Or would we fall without the Farians and the Shen to fight at our side? How was I going to convince the Pedalion to fight an outside invasion when they were in real danger of dissolving into chaos right in front of our eyes?

You're getting ahead of yourself again, Hail. Focus on the first problem and go from there. I leaned against the windowsill with a sigh.

"What is it?" Emmory asked, joining me at the window.

"Everything." I waved a hand. "This creepy-assed place with its statues of me and its unnerving reverence. The iron fist I can just barely see hovering in the corner of my vision. I grew up thinking Faria was a blessing to humanity."

"I know." He nodded. "It's unsettling, and that's from the standpoint of someone who's not being looked at to make a major choice that will impact not only the lives of her people but everyone else in the galaxy."

"Really? You know someone who fits that?"

Emmory chuckled and bumped his shoulder into mine. "Majesty, I've watched you go from an unwilling prisoner to the Empress of Indrana. It wasn't in the blink of an eye, but it was something that was always there inside you. This choice, whatever it is, it's the same way. You have this." He tapped me in the temple. "And this." Again, above my heart. "Use them."

I set my jaw and looked out at the blue-tinged light cutting through the mist that had settled onto the city in the night. Sharp-edged shadows lurked where the light couldn't touch, adding to the unease I'd been battling since we'd landed.

"Sybil said the gods wanted to meet me," I whispered finally. "I can't do anything with this until I stand in front of them, and Aiz knows it. Everyone seems to agree that the choice I face is killing the gods or not killing them." I looked at Emmory. "But what if it's not? Bugger me," I muttered. "Emmory, there is a thing." I lifted a hand, gesturing at the back of my head. "Something hovering just out of reach in my head. I can't get it to slide into place and make this whole thing make sense."

"Then let it go." Emmory reached out and put his hand on mine. "Chasing it doesn't work, just makes it hide from you even more, right? Let it go. Trust that you'll know what you need when you need it. I know you're used to planning things out and having every step calculated before you have to take it. Now's the time to jump into the unknown and have a little faith."

I let out a slow breath at Emmory's words. "Okay."

"What, no argument?"

I bumped him with my shoulder again, laughing as I did, and Emmory joined me, our good humor floating out into the evening air before sinking into the mists.

This time Mia and Aiz came with us when we snuck out of our rooms. Fasé insisted that the four of us go to see the Council of Eyes. With Emmory and Zin that made six of us traipsing down the hallway, and I shook my head with a sigh.

"We are the least stealthy bunch at the moment."

"It will be fine, Majesty. If Kasio wants to meet with you, I trust she will have seen fit to clear a path."

"We'd better hope so," Aiz murmured, one hand on Mia's arm, the other on his gun. "This will get really ugly really fast if we run across some guards, or worse, Adora and her goons."

The revelation that each member of the Pedalion had what was supposed to be an honor guard but Adora had built hers up into a small army was one of the new things making me uneasy.

"Through here." Fasé gestured to the open doorway. "Quickly."

We slipped inside, Fasé pulling the door shut behind her, and for a moment stood in the dark. Then a soft light in the center of the ceiling started to glow and two women slipped out of the shadows on the far side of the room.

"Star of Indrana."

I recognized Kasio's voice and tipped my head toward the taller of the pair. Her white hair was short and her eyes a brilliant copper unlike any I'd seen.

"This is Phia." Kasio gestured at the younger woman by her side.

"This is a risk," Aiz said.

"It is, but we have so few choices left to us. Adora will have her vengeance on those who seek to defile the gods one way or another. If we linger too long we will all be caught, but there is time enough for what needs to be done."

"Which is what?"

Kasio folded her hands together and looked around the room. "The Pedalion has traditionally deferred to the council on matters dealing with the gods, but since Javez's death they have tightened their grip on us and on Faria. They say they are acting in the gods' stead, but that I very much doubt."

"Do you not speak to the gods?"

Kasio shook her head. "No one has spoken to the gods in a very long time. The Pedalion rules as it will, unchecked and unchallenged."

"I keep being told the gods want to speak with me, though." I tried to keep the words from being too sharp.

"True, and it is not meant to deceive you. We have all seen this." Kasio waved at herself and Phia. "Not a future so much as a dream of you and the gods. How else should we interpret that besides them wanting to speak with you?"

I rubbed a hand over my face with a muttered curse, dropping it in time to see Aiz shaking his head.

"You know what I plan to do, Kasio?" he asked.

"I know what you planned," she replied with a tiny smile. "Do you still believe that is what will happen?"

He swallowed, and it was Mia who answered. "We believe in the Star."

"It is good to hear, sister. The council spoke often of the future Sybil saw and how the arrival of the Star would be a time of great change for Faria. It scares some of them."

"It scares Adora," I said.

"Rotem also and Sou to a lesser degree, though he is better at hiding it." Kasio gave me a smile when I raised an eyebrow in surprise. "Yadira and Delphine are devoted to the Council of Eyes and the gods. They believe we should let the future happen, let it play out."

"Adora wants to stop it." I heard Emmory's hiss of anger behind me. "That's what Earth was about, she really was trying to kill me?"

"At least in part, Hail." Kasio nodded. Fasé looked sick while Mia and Aiz were sharing a look that I knew spelled trouble.

"You're about to have a civil war here regardless of what Fasé and her people do?"

Aiz whistled and I knew exactly what he was thinking. The Shen could decimate the Farians if they were distracted from the fight by something like this.

"It is a very real possibility and it will spell disaster. This is the real reason we convinced the Pedalion to send Sybil off Faria with Fasé. The reason we came to you in the chambers."

"Why didn't you just tell me all this in the beginning?" Even as I asked the question I knew her answer.

A small smile hovered at the corner of her mouth. "This was the only way to get you all here in this moment. This future is so unclear but there were points we could anchor ourselves in to light the way to you. Trust in us tomorrow; we will get you to the gods."

47

ail, stop pacing," Emmory said from across the table, where he sat with one booted foot propped up on the angle of the wall.

"I can't help it. I'm nervous."

"You nervous makes the rest of us nervous," Johar replied around a mouthful of food. "Sit down and finish your breakfast."

I sat and blew out a breath that wasn't quite a huff of frustration, though Mia's amused look said otherwise.

Kasio had been right about the narrow window for our meeting. We'd barely escaped getting caught by a patrol on our way back to our rooms; Emmory's distraction of pretending I'd wanted to speak with someone about how the Pedalion's discussion was going was the only thing that allowed the rest of us to scramble silently up the stairs.

Then I'd had to endure a visit from Sou, who pretended to be kind and caring while not answering a single one of the questions Aiz and I threw at him.

"All we can do now is walk through this." Zin leaned forward in his chair to take my hand. "Whatever happens, Hail, we're here. Okay? Hao said to let you know that Fasé's people are ready for whatever happens. Admiral Hassan is standing by and the fleet can warp straight in if they need to thanks to Dailun's calculations."

I curled my fingers around his and forced a smile, relaxing some at the news. Dailun had suggested the same dangerous plan we'd used to come into Pashati when fighting Wilson's forces, and Aiz's people had been a lot more excited about it than Admiral Hassan had the first time he suggested it.

Either way, it would buy us time out there. Down here on the planet we were still only less than a dozen strong in the middle of what could only be considered hostile territory.

"Whatever happens today, thank you for having my back," I said, looking around the room. "I want everyone to keep your eyes open and don't trust anything but your instincts."

They nodded as one. I returned it, then crossed to grab my holsters and guns. The knock on the door came as I finished fastening them, and the door opened as I slid the last one home.

"Star of Indrana." An unknown Farian bowed low. "I have been sent to bring you to the Pedalion if you will follow me."

"More guards than normal," Emmory subvocalized over our private com link.

"Quite a few more," Zin chimed in. *"And all very tense."*

The Farian escorted us down the same corridor to the same pair of guards in front of the Pedalion chamber. I watched their wary eyes track us as we passed and noted their white-knuckled grip on their weapons.

"Jo, did you ever get a chance—"

"Pulse rifle. The energy source isn't anything I'm familiar with, though there's a sharp-edged crystal visible at the butt of the gun that you can see if you get the right angle on it. Unril didn't want to go into too much detail about the workings of it and he wouldn't let me hold the damn thing, but I was able to get a good look at it. I'm still running up a report on it." Her voice was tinged with laughter. *"I'd advise against getting shot with it."*

"I advise that on pretty much every weapon," I muttered back, and Johar's snort earned us a side-eye from the guards as we passed through the door into the chamber.

Aiz stopped in the center of the star on the floor, and he tilted his

391

head toward the dais. I looked past him to where Adora was chatting with Rotem, keeping my eyes on her until she turned to look. I held her gaze, making her break eye contact first, and then I slowly surveyed the rest of the Pedalion.

Yadira and Delphine were in deep discussion, both women wearing frowns that could have just been because of the gravity of the situation or could have been because of something else entirely.

Sou's face was clean of expression, but I caught the tremble in his hand as he slapped it on the tabletop. "The Pedalion has convened to issue a decision on reopening the negotiations between Faria and the Shen."

"And those who follow the Star."

I slid a sideways glance at Fasé's quiet declaration before returning my eyes to the Pedalion, watching the emotions that played out over their faces.

The angry red flush was spreading up Adora's throat. Rotem was stone-faced. Yadira and Delphine shared a look I couldn't quite decipher.

"Yes." Sou cleared his throat. Of all of them, he hadn't blinked. "Your little rebellion is duly noted, Fasé."

"That's telling, isn't it?" I subvocalized to Emmory on the com channel.

"Very much so."

Sou cleared his throat. "Your Imperial Majesty, it is—"

The doors at the far side of the chamber opened and a group of guards ushered Hao, Gita, and Talos through. I caught Hao's eye and the very deliberate wink he gave me.

"Here we go," I whispered, and tightened my grip on my gun, turning away from Emmory. "What is—"

The hand that came down on my neck was colder than ice, freezing through me to the bone, and I heard Mia call my name even as Emmory grabbed me and jerked me away.

I clung to him for a second before I got my feet underneath me and turned around. "Sybil."

The Farian seer smiled. "Hail."

"This is unfortunate." I reached back when I felt Emmory shift and put my hand on his before he could pull his Hessian 45 free.

Sybil shook her head. "I would not draw your weapons, *Ekam* Tresk. There is a great potential for violence here and very little reason for any of us to expend our energy to clean up the mess afterward."

Adora rose; the triumphant smile on her face made me long to pull my Glock and shoot her.

"Your arrogance, Hail, is your undoing," she said.

"Adora, what are you doing?" Rotem seemed truly shocked by the turn of events. "This is not what we agreed on."

"I am done with this Pedalion wringing their hands and worrying about the opinions of humans." She waved a hand out in a grand gesture. "We have before us the leaders of the Shen, the leader of the rebellion, and the Star of Indrana. It is time to see this done."

"What's your grand plan, Adora?" I asked.

"A politely worded message to your heir about the tragic explosion that took the lives of the empress and all her people." Adora folded her hands together and shook them at me as she came down off the dais. The mocking gesture was expected; however, she made the mistake of passing too close to Gita, and my *Dve* spit in her face.

There was a moment of violence. The guard behind them struck Gita with his weapon and she went down on a knee; the only thing that prevented Hao from moving was the gun pressed to the back of his neck. He met my gaze and I gave a little shake of my head, watching the fury flare for just a moment before he acknowledged me.

"Aiz Cevalla and Fasé Terass." Adora wiped her face with a disgusted smile. "You are traitors. Heretics. You will be trapped forever in the vault of souls." She snapped her fingers and the guards converged on Aiz and Fasé, grabbing them by the upper arms and dragging them across the floor away from us.

"We moving, Hail?" Jo asked the question under her breath.

"Not yet."

Adora was knee-deep in her awaited revenge and snapped her fingers again. "First, you will see that abomination you dare to call a sister perish."

I stepped in front of Mia. "How could you?" I demanded of Sybil, who'd moved to stand next to Adora. The bags they'd taken from Hao and Gita lay in a pile at her feet. "I thought you believed in this? In the future?"

"In that 'everything dies' line I fed you, Hail?" Sybil asked with scorn on her face. "We don't. Farians were made in the image of our gods and we are godlike because of it. I don't expect you humans to understand, with your brief, flickering lives." She sighed, rolling her eyes to the ceiling. "In all this, you never once asked why you were so important, did you? Even they didn't ask. Only Adora had the sense to see what needed to be done. You are chaos, churning away at our foundations with every step. It cannot be allowed to continue." She flung a hand out at the Pedalion as she crossed to the front of the room and slapped her hand into the center of the curved white table.

"Sybil, what are you doing?" Rotem demanded. The other three members of the Pedalion wore equal looks of horror.

I stumbled away from them as the floor opened up, almost falling into Emmory again in the process.

"The gods have demanded this. There will be no quick, easy death for any of those who will stand against us." The ground shook at her words, and Adora smiled.

The dark hole in the middle of the sixteen-pointed star shimmered. I looked across it at Hao and flicked my eyes downward. He tipped his head toward it, a wordless question that was followed by a soundless curse when I gave a slight nod.

"Throw them in." Sybil's voice carried through the room, echoing off the ceiling with a strange power.

Hao grabbed Talos and put his shoulder into Gita, sending them both into the shimmering blackness. Fasé grabbed for Aiz and the pair followed them into the portal.

"Go!" I ordered, shoving Emmory and Zin toward the hole. Kisah was already sprinting across, Iza and Indula on her heels. They all dove into the black without hesitation.

Johar liberated a gun from the guard on her side and blew a chunk out of the wall across the chamber. The guards who'd been streaming into the room went scattering for cover. I kicked at the guard closest to me, sending him sprawling into Sybil, and grabbed for the bags, sliding them across the floor toward Mia, who dragged them with her into the hole.

"Jo, move!"

She fired again. The Farians closing in on us scattered, and together we turned and jumped into the abyss.

48

Hitting the water was a surprise, and I came up coughing and sputtering from my accidental inhale. Several pairs of hands grabbed me and hauled me from the water, but it was Emmory who thumped me on the back.

"I'm all right." Wiping the water and tears from my eyes, I looked around. We were in what looked like an underground cavern, but unlike the sharp angles and stark white of Faria, these walls were smooth as glass, curving endlessly into soft waves and spirals. The color wasn't just black, but it shimmered the same as the surface in the floor of the Pedalion chamber with all the colors and stars winking in and out of existence.

I looked up at the smooth ceiling above us and laughed. "I have never had a plan come together so well."

"If we survive this, it'll be one for the stories. Though I'm not gonna lie, for a second there I was pretty sure Sybil really had betrayed us." Hao reached down and along with Gita helped me to my feet. "We're lucky there was a pool down here. That landing would have been hard otherwise."

I patted his face with a smile. His hair was slicked back and a bruise decorated his temple. "It stood to reason, if the portal was for petitioners they wouldn't want them to end up in a pile of squishy bits before they got to see the gods. Who hit you?"

Hao waved a hand. "One of the guards. We had to at least make it look like we were putting up a fight when they stormed in. I'm impressed that we pulled that off without any of Fasé's people being hurt or arrested."

"Sybil is going to be okay?" That question came from Mia as she and Aiz joined us.

"She'll manage. The Pedalion thought she was on their side from the beginning; there's no reason for them to question it now. They are going to be way too busy fighting with Adora about her last-second theatrics."

"I owe you an apology, Hail," Aiz said, holding a hand out to me. "I did not think any of that was going to work. My only question is, why did we go to all that trouble of having a backup plan?"

"No offense, but I will always trust my gut." I took his hand with a wink. "Backup plans are only unnecessary if you have them."

"If you don't have them, you'll need them," Johar said, wading to the edge of the pool, her arms full of weapons and bags. "I think I got them all."

"Give them a bit to dry out, we'll be fine," Hao said. "The only one I don't know about is that cannon you stole from the guard. I made sure to pick our weapons out based on what would survive through almost anything. Including getting waterlogged."

I moved with Gita farther away from the water's edge as Johar and Hao started in on a detailed inspection of what little gear we had.

I'd known that part of the plan was risky, but there'd been no reason for us to have anything else with us. Sybil couldn't tell me what we would be facing once we passed through the portal, only that we would have to journey to the gods and there was no way of knowing what trials we would have to face before we reached them.

"Are you all right?" Gita murmured as she lowered me to the ground, and I gave her hand a comforting squeeze.

"Tired, if I'm being honest." I smiled up at her and touched her face. "Are you all right? That guard cracked you."

"It was worth it." She grinned.

"I am going to sleep for a month once this is all done."

"I like that idea. Do you need me for anything, or would you rather have a moment alone?"

"I'm good. Go help Hao."

I leaned back on my elbows, the rock smooth underneath me, and watched as my crew moved around the patch of land at the edge of the water. Fasé, Mia, and Talos moved among everyone, making sure any injuries were taken care of, though I saw Hao try to wave them off until Gita said something sharply to him and he held his hand out to Mia with an exasperated sigh.

Emmory was already covering our perimeter along with Zin and the rest of my BodyGuards.

There were twelve of us, plus me, and though I knew the risk we were taking, I was also determined to bring everyone back safely.

Mia came over and sat down next to me, putting her hand over the top of mine. The minor aches from the fight above were swallowed by the soothing rush of her power, and I turned my hand over so I could thread my fingers through hers.

"Thank you." I leaned in for a kiss, and the pleased murmur that slipped out when she kissed me back made the desire I'd so carefully banked flare like a sun going supernova. I pulled reluctantly away, pressing my cheek to hers for a moment before resting my head on her shoulder. "I'm glad you're here."

"I am glad to be here," Mia whispered back. "We have a long way to go, we should get moving."

"I know." With a sigh, I looked around, catching Aiz's eye. "The question is, where are we going?"

"According to Sybil, the petitioners move forward from this point, but she couldn't tell us how." He scrubbed a hand through his hair and spun on a heel. "I am Aiz Cevalla and I am here to speak with the gods."

His voice echoed off the rock, fading into silence as we all waited.

For a moment there was nothing; then a low grinding sound started and I scrambled to my feet, pulling Mia up with me as the wall behind us began to move. It slid open, revealing an arch filled with the same shimmering black as the hole in the Pedalion's floor.

"Okay, I didn't think it would be that easy," I said with a laugh. "Hao, guns?"

"Yup." He tossed them to me. "Check 'em yourself, but they look good on my end."

I ran a quick diagnostic with my *smati* that confirmed his words and then shoved the Glocks home. "All right, people, we should get moving." Squaring my shoulders, I gestured to Aiz and followed him through the archway.

"Easy, easy, Hail. Lights on low."

I blinked at Portis in confusion as the lights came up. "What?"

"Bad dream." He smiled, leaning over me and touching my face. "You've had them a lot since Candless."

"I was—no." I looked around the room. It was my room, our room on *Sophie*. "That wasn't a dream. This is." I slid from the bed and looked down at the black tank and pants I was wearing. I exhaled and rubbed a hand over my face.

"Hey, take it easy. You're okay."

"You're dead."

It was Portis's turn to blink in confusion and the look on his face broke my heart. "I'm sorry, what?"

"You're not real." The words were painful, but I managed to spit them out where they landed glass-sharp and glittering in the air.

"Why would you say that?"

I rounded the bed and dropped to my knees in front of him, cupping his face in my hands. "Because it's true. You're not real. *Sophie* is dust. You're gone. This isn't my life anymore." I couldn't stop the tears even though I was smiling at him.

There was no panic, no fear hammering away at my chest. Only the simple certainty of what was real and what was not. I'd said my good-byes to Portis in bits and pieces. He'd always be with me, a little whisper in the back of my head and a warm glow buried in my heart.

I knew he was gone and this, whatever it was, was the Farian gods' doing. Aiz's lesson from before had done its job.

"You have to realize you can't trust anything you see. The Farians can do this. The gods can do it. They will trick you and play with you and you have to be prepared for it."

"Besides, you called me Hail when you woke me up." I shook my head. "Portis never slipped, not once. The only time he ever used my name was right before he died. I loved you, but it's time for me to go. You're not real and I want to go back to my friends."

Portis smiled, but there were tears in his eyes or maybe they were in mine. "I am really going to miss you."

"You're right here," I replied, pressing a hand to my heart. "Until the heat death of the universe."

"Same, baby." The vision of Portis smiled, leaned in and pressed his forehead to mine, then wavered and vanished. As I wiped the tears from my face I spotted Mia clinging to Aiz.

We were in a wide tunnel, the walls slick black rock that sparkled with lights that stretched far enough above my head that I didn't feel the least bit claustrophobic. I spotted Hao and Zin at the far end of the tunnel talking quietly, and the others stood frozen like statues around me.

"They are seeing whatever the gods have chosen for them," Aiz said. "Some break the spell more easily than others." He had one arm wrapped around Mia but pointed behind me with the other, and I looked to see Emmory shaking his head. Indula followed suit, rubbing both hands over his face. Talos and Johar were just behind him, also coming out of the daze.

"I'm good," Johar said as I passed, patting me on the shoulder. "That was wild. I'll get these two." Kisah and Iza woke simultaneously and Johar moved to reassure them, Indula right behind her.

"It's all right." I reached Emmory as he put a hand on his gun. Emmory frowned at me as I touched my forehead to his. "Whatever you saw wasn't real and you recognized it; the gods are testing us."

"We're not here to see their gods," he replied. "You are. Why are they testing all of us?"

"I know, but they either don't know or don't care. We're here, that means we'll go through the trials." I squeezed his arm. "Zin's over there."

Aiz was talking to Talos and touched the Shen's face with a smile and an approving nod. I crossed back to them, reaching for Mia, and she slipped away from her brother to bury her face in my shoulder.

"It's okay," I murmured against her damp hair, feeling her shake against me. "I'm here."

"I know," she said, and choked on a laugh. "That's how I got out of it; you weren't there, and I didn't believe a reality that existed without you."

I tightened my arms around her, words sticking in my throat even though they weren't needed. We stood that way for a while until Mia released a shuddering breath and stepped back. I let her go, feeling the space between us like a fresh wound as she rejoined her brother.

I left the Shen alone to their quiet conversation and joined Hao. "What's the details?"

"You've all been locked up for half an hour or so," he replied. "The hallway goes on for forty-three meters before it hits a T junction. We didn't explore beyond that."

I glanced behind me to where Gita and Fasé still stood like statues. "Can't wake them up from this end, can we?"

Hao shook his head. "Zin and I tried. None of you reacted. Aiz might know more, but I suspect it's the kind of thing you have to fight on your own."

"You came out of it fast."

Hao smiled a wry smile at me. "When you don't trust anything, it's hard to fall prey to illusions."

"True," I said, looking at Zin. "What about you?"

He was holding Emmory's bare hand, rubbing gently at the back with his thumb, and the sweetness wrapped itself around my heart. "Reality is an illusion." He winked at me. "I know what my illusion already is. Makes it easier to pick out a manufactured one."

Gita gasped, and Hao moved like a ship hitting full thrusters, catching her as she started to collapse.

"Go on," Emmory said. He'd let Zin go and was pulling his glove back on. "We've got this."

I made it two steps toward Gita when Fasé came out of her trance, and I felt the power surging under her skin as I grabbed her by the shoulders. I could have easily held her upright, but I lowered her to the floor, sliding my hands down to hers as I knelt in front of her.

"Take a breath," I ordered. "Another."

She obeyed with difficulty and I was surprised by the haunted look in her golden eyes. I let go of a hand and brushed her red curls away from her face.

"Are you all right?"

Fasé blinked. "I was—no, I am not all right. I owe you another apology, Hail. I've always thought it was easy to tell what was real and what was not, but that was far more difficult than I believed." She looked up at me, her eyes wet with unshed tears. "You endured six months of that. I don't know how you are still standing."

"Necessity," I replied with a smile. "Do you need to talk about it?"

"No, I will—" She shook her head as the Indranan words failed her and the Farian that followed was incomprehensible to me.

Aiz leaned down and touched my shoulder. "We need to move; I suspect it's unwise to linger here for long."

We had no way of knowing if the Pedalion would be able to send people after us; if they could, we needed to get to the gods before they did.

I nodded and got to my feet as he hauled Fasé upright. Aiz murmured something in her ear that put some color back into her cheeks. Fasé reached up and patted his chest. "Thank you," she said with a smile.

We headed down the hallway until we reached the T juncture Hao had found, and I looked at Aiz. "Preference?"

"Aren't you in charge?"

I shot him a narrow-eyed glare as the chuckles from the others bounced around the tunnel.

"We could scout it out," Hao offered, but Aiz shook his head.

"We will have to choose. She will have to choose," he said, pointing at me.

"Let me guess, Star of Indrana?"

Aiz grinned and lifted his hands.

Walking forward to the wall, I put my hands to the surface and closed my eyes.

Trust your heart, everyone kept saying to me. I dragged in a deep breath and blew it out. Silence dropped around me, a stillness broken only by the beating of my heart.

For just an instant I felt it, an extra pulse in my left hand. A little tug in that direction. I pulled away and pointed. "This way."

49

The path I'd chosen wound itself in what felt like a spiral that climbed endlessly upward, but it was hard to tell for sure. There were no more sharp turns, just the winding tunnel stretching in front of us.

As I started to doubt my choice, the voice in my head whispering that we should have gone the other direction and we should turn back, I walked around a curve in the tunnel and stopped.

The tunnel ended in a round door split down the middle. The surface was blank except for a pair of handles as long as my arms set in the center. I shared a look with Aiz. He nodded, and we moved forward, each grabbing a handle and pulling.

The door opened easily, far more easily than either of us expected, and I felt Emmory's hand at my back steady me when I slid.

"Jo," Hao said with a jerk of his head. The sounds of weapons powering up was jarring in the silence. Johar nodded and tapped Gita's fist as they split, sliding in through the opening with their guns at the ready.

"You're gonna want to see this," Johar called, and I slipped past Hao into the room, grinning at his curse.

Unlike the previous one, this room was filled with light; the surface of everything gleamed so white it hurt my eyes. The star on the floor was an echo of the one in the Pedalion chamber, and above it floated a huge sphere that undulated like the waves of Balhim Bay.

Johar stuck her hand in it and pulled it back out as the protests rang out from Emmory and Hao. She grinned, touching a finger to her tongue and dancing out of Hao's reach. "Water," she announced. "Seawater, actually; the salt content is really high. Some trace minerals, a few things my *smati* isn't registering. Interesting."

"Breathe," I murmured, laying a hand on Hao's shoulder with a soft laugh.

"She's going to get herself killed."

"Nah. It's Johar. Easier to stop a battlecruiser with your bare hands." I took a step closer and put my hands up.

"Hail."

"I'm not going to touch it." The water was black as the void of space but filled with stars; shimmering sparkles swirled around like the night sky. "Okay, that's a lie." I plunged my hands in and the water closed around my forearms.

Except it didn't feel like water. It was cool, coating my skin, writhing around it. It felt a bit like a silk sari sliding around me.

Fingers touched mine.

I jerked back, bumping into Aiz, who'd come up on my other side. "Bugger me!"

"What?"

"Someone's in there. Someone touched me." I looked down at my hands. Unlike Jo's they were completely dry, no water dripping from my fingers onto the white stone floor.

Aiz plunged his own hands into the sphere and it burst, the droplets raining down like fireworks during Pratimas. We all stumbled back but the drops fell to the ground, running into the spikes of the star until the whole thing shimmered.

I stared at Aiz and the child he was holding in his arms as he sank to his knees at the center of the star. Her red curls were dry, as was the white long-sleeved dress, and she released him, stepping away as soon as her bare feet found the floor.

The child folded her hands together. "Greetings, brother. You are here to end your life. This second test has been designed specifically for you to show the gods the strength of your convictions. You must consider all the things you are leaving behind when you go."

"Oh, Dark Mother," I whispered. "That's Adora."

Aiz scrambled back from this young version of his sister, almost crashing into me in the process.

"What?" Emmory asked.

"That's Adora. Her original face, I'm assuming." A horrible idea was growing in my head, but I wasn't going to give it a voice until I was certain.

"I am not here to end my life." Aiz looked truly panicked for the first time ever.

"You aren't, but this place doesn't care. Get up." I grabbed Aiz under his arms and helped him to his feet. "We have to go through these trials as if we were petitioners. There's no way around that."

"Star of Indrana." The child Adora had more respect for me than her adult self, and I smiled at the solemn bow that was directed my way. "We welcome you to the *kai pethaménon psychón*."

"Well of dying souls." Fasé murmured the translation as she joined me.

"Yes, I know, Sybil mentioned it before."

"Fasé." Adora gave her a nod of respect. "Welcome."

"What is the test?" Aiz found his voice as Mia and Talos stepped up to his side.

Adora looked at me. "You are the facilitator of this test. Do you accept?"

"I do."

She held out her hands and I went down on a knee to take them. Her next words rang in my head.

"You know why I am here?"

I nodded. *"I've got a pretty good guess. If you want to test the strength of one's convictions, there's no better way than to ask them to do something horrible in service of it."*

Adora smiled. *"It is up to you, Star of Indrana, if you wish to break the rules to him gently."*

"I'm not sure there is a way to do this gently," I replied. *"Isn't that kind of the point?"*

"Of course not. The point is to have the petitioner look deep into themselves with everything else stripped away. The choice provides that opportunity. You and I are only the tools in this test, but we still have a choice as to how we will go about it."

"Are you real?"

"As is necessary." She smiled again; the impish twist of her lips made it difficult for me to equate her with the Adora who'd so frequently snarled and frustrated me. I couldn't even imagine what Aiz was going through at my side.

It was a vague answer, but I knew I wasn't getting a better one, and given what I now knew Aiz had to do, I was a little relieved she hadn't responded more clearly.

"Hail."

I looked at him. "As she said, this is yours," I said. "The rest of us can't help you." I pulled my Glock and put it in his hand. "Kill her and let's move on."

"Hail!" The shock in Emmory's voice was echoed by Mia, but everyone fell silent when I held up my hand.

"It's a test of your convictions, Aiz. Not mine or Mia's or Fasé's. But yours. How far are you willing to go to get what you want? As far as this place is concerned, you are erasing yourself from the universe and that includes your history. What are you willing to sacrifice? What will you stain your soul with? No one else gets to make that choice but you."

He was staring at me with a surprising amount of horror on his face. "You want me to kill a child. I won't lie, if it were adult Adora here I'd probably pull that trigger without a second thought, but this child—"

"You've killed children!" I grabbed him by the shoulders and shook him. "This war of yours has killed thousands. Just because it was sanitized and from a distance doesn't change the fact. Face that, Aiz, and make a decision. How far are you willing to go for this vengeance of yours?"

Aiz closed his fingers around the butt of my gun. I held my breath; the desire to say something was a fire in my chest. I knew I couldn't. This was his choice, his test, and if I influenced him in this moment it could ruin everything.

So I held my tongue, counted my heartbeats, and sent a silent prayer winging out in the black to Ganesh for the first time in months.

Mia had a hand pressed to her mouth, and Talos's eyes were closed as if they both couldn't believe what was happening. I didn't look around to the others, could feel Hao's glare boring into my back. There wasn't time to explain, and a fight now would possibly push Aiz's choice one way or the other.

The child Adora stood calmly, her hands folded at her waist and her platinum eyes brighter than I'd ever seen them.

"Not that far." Aiz closed his eyes and shook his head as he opened his hand. "I—I can't, Hail. I can't do it."

I exhaled.

"I was really hoping you'd say that." I took my gun back with a smile and patted his cheek. "Go talk to your sister."

"He had a good childhood," Mia murmured from my side. "Whatever the long years have colored over with his anger or Adora's twisted obsession with these so-called gods. I remember him talking at times of this memory or another. The gods chose her for a reason. They wanted him to fail this test."

"Maybe," I whispered back, watching as Aiz and the child Adora spoke across the room.

"What's going on in that head of yours?" she asked.

I looked over to see her smiling at me. "We assumed these trials are a test—which means pass or fail, right?"

"Yes." She nodded. "To get to the gods, you must pass the trials."

"No. I don't think so." I pointed at her. "If that was the case, what was the point of tagging all of us in the first trial? And we all passed it? Seems strange."

"Then what? What would the reason be?"

"They're just points along a line. Choices to make. Stay in the fantasy or come back to reality for all of us. Kill his sister or talk to her, for Aiz alone. Either one would have moved us forward." I gestured at the doorway that had appeared on the far side of the room. "But the Aiz who walks out of here isn't the same one who would have walked out having killed his sister." I tapped at my temple and grinned. "Choices made change who we are. That's been hammered enough into my head by this point that I am paying attention."

"Hamah was right."

I blinked at Mia in surprise. "What?"

"I'm sorry, that isn't quite what I meant," she said, dragging a hand through her still-damp hair. "He wasn't right, it's not a corruption, but you've changed us. Before you, the Aiz I knew would have taken that gun and blown his sister's head off without a second thought." She linked her fingers through mine. "We brought you to us so you would fight for us, but the peace you've somehow carried in your wake has tangled itself into our lives and there's no escaping it." She swallowed. "It doesn't seem a fair trade given what you went through."

"I'm nothing if not unpredictable," I said with a soft laugh. "Besides, life isn't fair. It just is and we work to make things as fair as we can for those around us. Sometimes it doesn't work out. I'd rather it was me than any of the rest of you."

"That's why we don't deserve you. You are the calm in the center of a storm, and yet also the storm." Mia grinned, but there were tears clinging to her lashes. "Anyway, it is not a bad thing, I think, to let go of vengeance. Not if there is another way for my people to be free."

I stared at her for a moment before looking down at our joined hands. I wasn't sure what I'd done to convince the Cevallas to consider another way, but whatever it was, it seemed to have worked.

"I think they've finished talking," Mia said, and I looked up to see Aiz and Adora crossing back over to us. I got to my feet with Hao's assistance and tucked my hands into my pockets as they came to a stop in front of me.

Aiz blew out a breath and offered his sister and Talos an apologetic smile. "I guess we're done here. I haven't given up on the Shen. We deserve the peace." He looked at Fasé. "We all deserve a choice one way or the other. We'll get out of this cavern and see if we can't figure out another way to do this. Maybe I can get Kasio to convince the gods to listen or—"

I shared a look with the child Adora. "You didn't tell him?"

She grinned. "It's more fun this way." Then she folded her hands together and bowed. "Star of Indrana, we will see you soon."

Aiz jumped backward as Adora's shape changed into the shimmering water and collapsed to the floor, flowing over the white stone until it found its home once again in the star.

"Tell me what?" he asked, and I grinned, pointing past him to the door that had just opened behind us.

"You didn't fail anything, Aiz. We can't know the strength of our convictions unless they're tested, unless we question them, unless you're willing to listen." I tapped him on the shoulder and headed for the door. "We move on to the next trial."

He caught up with me. "Hail, I would not have been able to do this if it weren't for you. Thank you."

"You're welcome. For all your faults you are my crew. You are a stubborn asshole and most of the time I want to punch you in the throat." I winked and smiled. "But sometimes I consider you a friend."

The tunnel was the same as the others, black and curving upward, though as we climbed the light grew dimmer until I could barely see my hand in front of my face.

"Hail, hold up," Emmory called out, but I'd already stopped.

"I've got this." Johar passed me, snagging my hand on the way by; I reached for Aiz and together our group continued on through the darkness. "Door," Jo called, squeezing my hand so I didn't run into her. "I can't feel a handle or anything."

I tugged on Aiz. "Come here." He allowed me to pull him forward and press both our hands to the door. There was a click and a bright knife of light pierced the darkness as the door started to open. The noise followed and I heard the rapid-fire orders from Emmory behind me.

Covering my eyes with a hand and keeping the other on my Glock, I slipped through the opening with Aiz at my back.

"Holy shit," Johar breathed.

We'd come out of the tunnel into an arena; the chanting of the crowd filled the air and shook the ground.

Or it could have been the three massive figures bearing down on us that were making the sand jump under our feet.

"Aw, hell," Hao muttered. "I knew things were going too smoothly."

"We're fighting after all?" Aiz sounded stunned and I didn't blame him.

"Looks like," I said.

"Not how I wanted this to go," he muttered, looking at the others behind us.

"Welcome to my life." I caught Johar by the collar before she could get past me. "No," I said firmly. "You all stay back here with Mia and Talos."

Mia looked ill, and I touched her face. "Are you okay?"

"I'm fine. Don't worry about me." She gave me a little push toward her brother. "You two go, we'll handle this."

There was barely time to exchange grim nods with the others as I crossed quickly to Aiz, and my heart was beating hard in my chest as we took off across the sand. I was moving on autopilot to meet the threat coming at us. This one was mine, I realized as I sprinted across the arena at Aiz's side. My test. My choice.

"This isn't real," I said, the truth dawning on me between one breath and the next. I skidded to a halt, dropping my hands with a sigh. "Thank Shiva; Aiz, stop."

Aiz stopped, the confusion chasing across his face. "Hail?"

"This isn't real." I shook my head, stepping around him as the three gods came to stand in front of us. But they weren't Farian.

They were our gods.

"Emmory, are you seeing this?" I asked over the com.

"I am, Majesty." There was awe in his voice.

Shiva, blue-skinned with a snake around his neck and the universe in his eyes. Kali with her blue-black skin, her necklace of skulls, and her multitude of arms. And Ganesh, my elephant-headed father with his endless patience and brightly painted trunk.

I straightened my shoulders and cleared my throat so that my words would carry across the whole arena rather than the illusion in front of me. "We are not here to fight. You wanted to see me. We are here to talk. We are here to listen."

The crowd, the arena all vanished, revealing a large chamber with curved walls and a domed ceiling. But the gods didn't vanish and confusion washed over me.

"Dark Mother." I could do nothing beyond fold my hands together and bow. Belief or not, I would show respect.

A horrible smile split Kali's face as she folded her hands together, bowing her head in return. The other two followed her lead and a gasp slipped out of me as I lifted my head.

Now they were Farian, with wild red hair and shining metallic eyes in bronze, silver, and gold, but they were taller than any Farian I'd seen. They towered over me, dressed in sleeveless tunics of white over the top of black pants. Their headpieces were similar to the lace ones of the Council of Eyes, though one had spikes jutting out into the air.

The woman in the middle—the being in the middle—tipped her head to the side and studied me. Her silver eyes shone. "Welcome, Star of Indrana; we have been waiting for you."

I stared up at her, lost for a moment in those eyes. "What do you want with me?"

"Our people are coming for us; we need your help to stop them."

"Oh, Shiva," I murmured as all the scattered pieces finally fell into place in my head. "You're the missing ones; you're the Hiervet."

The story continues in . . .

OUT PAST THE STARS

Book THREE of the Farian War

Keep reading for a sneak peek!

ACKNOWLEDGMENTS

This series has been a challenge to write, from the first book where I was doing something new and different and hating every second of it, to this book which I love but which tore me apart to write. I'm not sure what I expected when I gave Hail her worst nightmare, but the unimaginable grief and rage she was feeling was often difficult to separate myself from. To top it off, I was coming off a six-year trial-by-fire in my personal life that had an unhappy ending, and much of Hail's grief at times mirrored my own.

But the sun rises without regard for our personal feelings, and I am learning how to breathe again. I want to thank my husband for navigating this with me, for his love and support as I discovered myself and his willingness to keep growing and learning and working on the things that are broken inside him. I love you, Don.

The unflinching support and love of my family and friends is something I am endlessly, eternally grateful for. You know who you are and I hope I do a good job of telling you I love you on the regular.

To my fellow writers—Cass Morris, Mike Headley, Rob Boffard, Melissa Caruso, Rowenna Miller, Mike Chen, and so many more. Thanks for your time, your support, your laughter, and your awesome talent. This is such a lonely business at times, and friendships like yours are a true gift.

To my Patreon crew—thank you for being so fucking amazing and for supporting me and my writing. I couldn't do this without you.

My beta readers provided some excellent focus in the final stages of this story. Thanks to Kristen Blount and Tasha Suri for your time and your feedback. Thanks to Lisa DiDio for all of the previous work and so much more as my rock star of a critique partner and catcher of repeated words.

To my agent, Andy Zack, for your unfailing support of me and my career. Thank you for all the work you do, even knowing with my luck it will somehow take ten times longer than normal and result in some rare stumbling block no one expected.

To my editor, Sarah Guan, for your love of Hail and your tireless ability to let me do my thing but check in when I most need it as well as your amazing eye for keeping the story on track when I want to wander. You know I suck at economics, but you keep making me think of it anyway. Thank you for all the work you do; I know so much of it goes unremarked upon.

To the rest of the crew at Orbit and across the pond at Little, Brown Book Group, thank you for all the work you do for these stories.

And finally a rather random shout-out to Ali Trotta on Twitter for putting the words "more bravery, less rage" out there. Nothing more perfectly encapsulated the feelings I was trying to share with this story. It's a hard thing to remember in this world, but so very important.

extras

orbit

meet the author

Photo Credit: Donald Branum

K. B. WAGERS is the author of the Indranan War and Farian War trilogies. They live in the shadow of Colorado's Pikes Peak with their partner and a crew of poorly behaved cats. They're especially proud of their second-degree black belt in Shaolin Kung Fu and their three Tough Mudder completions. There's never really a moment when they're not writing, but they do enjoy fountain pens and good whiskey.

if you enjoyed
DOWN AMONG THE DEAD

look out for

OUT PAST THE STARS
The Farian War: Book 3

by

K. B. Wagers

Gunrunner empress Hail Bristol must navigate alien politics and deadly plots to prevent an interspecies war in this riveting conclusion to the space opera trilogy The Farian War.

"Welcome, Star of Indrana; we have been waiting for you."

I stared up at the Farian god, lost for a moment in her golden eyes. "What do you want with me?"

"Our people are coming for us; we need your help to stop them."

"Oh, Shiva," I murmured as all the scattered pieces finally fell into place in my head. "You're the missing ones; you're the Hiervet."

My words broke the stunned silence as the others caught up with us across the sand, Emmory and Gita moving in concert to my side, their weapons out.

I inhaled as the image of the gods in front of me shifted a third time. The trio were now smaller, pale and slender, bipedal, but their limbs were longer than a human's. The Farians, the Shen, even the Svatir, looked enough like humans that it was comforting. The Hiervet decidedly did not look like us, so much so it was going to take someone better with words than me to describe them.

The slow baring of all-too-human-looking teeth by the creature in the center was simultaneously amusing and terrifying. "We should take this somewhere more pleasant, yes?"

A blink. A heartbeat. We were no longer in the arena, but in a room that looked far more like something one would find on Indrana than in the hideout of an alien pretending to be a god. It was cozy, the windows reflecting a setting sun I suspected wasn't real, but I appreciated the illusion because it kept my panic at bay. There was a fireplace and a series of chairs at one end of the long room. A trio of high-backed wooden chairs at the other that looked just throne-like enough to make my lips twitch into a smile.

"Majesty."

Emmory's familiar warning was a balm against the slight edge in my gut. That single word was so achingly missed it was a wonder I didn't break apart right there.

"It's all right," I murmured over our private com link.

"Welcome to Etrelia, Star of Indrana," the Hiervet in the center said with a sweep of her arm.

I recognized the name, remembered it from the negotiations and Adora spitting the challenge at Aiz: *"You can have your father's soul when the whole of the Pedalion lies dead and Etrelia is burning."*

"Welcome, also, Mia Cevalla and Fasé Terass. The other sides, the ones who help keep the balance." Her wide, black eyes turned to Aiz and every muscle in her body tensed. "You slayed that which was ours, Aiz Cevalla."

"I did it to save my people from your chains. I didn't come here to fight, Thyra, but I won't apologize for the choices I've made." He dipped his head in acknowledgment. "I thought I killed you."

"You almost did. Your sister saved me."

"Why am I not surprised by this news?" he replied.

"You should die for what you have done." The Hiervet on the right snarled the words, but all three looked as though they were about to pounce.

"Careful," I said, putting a hand out across Aiz's chest. "He's my crew."

"Is that so?" Thyra tilted her overlarge head to the side, vertical eyelids sliding shut once and snapping open again.

I met what I thought was a challenge with a smile. "It is."

"You keep deadly company, Star of Indrana."

"Oh, you have no idea." I headed to my right, gesturing for Mia and Fasé to follow, and took the center seat of the row of ornate chairs.

It was going to take me a while to get a read on the Hiervet's facial expressions, but I guessed the narrowing of eyes was a universal signal for annoyance, even if it was vertical in their case.

Or it was possibly a response to my challenge; I had just sat in their chairs after all. I crossed one leg over the other and studied the trio in front of me with all the poise of the empress everyone expected me to be.

"Well, you wanted me here. Start talking."

The Hiervet started talking, but not at me. Instead a rapid-fire discussion in a language both lyrical and sharp as broken glass broke out among the trio.

"Sha zhu, *perhaps do not taunt the gods.*"

I glanced at Hao, who stood by Gita's side. *"They're not gods,"* I subvocalized over our private com link.

"You know I *don't believe in them, but they look a great deal like the Old Gods."*

I frowned. *"The Old Gods, really? That's what you see?"* I switched to the main channel. *"Everyone, give me a read on what those three creatures look like to you."*

The answers from the others were predictable, but split between the Indranan gods I'd seen initially and the Farian gods who'd appeared right after.

"You know those really big wasps on Pintro XVI? They kinda look like the love child of those and the folks who live underground on Yuzin. All pale and spindly, but everything is too damned wrong." Johar subvocalized her declaration and I managed not to turn my head to stare at her.

Indula wasn't so controlled, and Iza elbowed him in the side with a muttered curse until he snapped his head back to the Hiervet. Thankfully, our hosts didn't seem to notice, though they did wrap up whatever argument they'd been having and turn their attention back to me, leaving me no time to ponder Johar's revelation.

"Star of Indrana—"

I held up a hand. "Let's get this out of the way first. I am Empress Hailimi Bristol, here to broker a peace between the Farians and the Shen on behalf of humanity. You three are a wrinkle in an already complicated situation, but I'm willing to see what I can do for you once the matter at hand is settled. You can address me as 'Your Majesty.' "

Thyra studied me for a long moment, and I wondered if I could somehow return to seeing them with the façade of more-human faces, if it would even give me an accurate sense of what they were thinking.

Focus, Hail. You'll want to learn to read their faces as is and now's as good a time for it as any.

"Your Majesty, allow me to introduce my companions—Adaran and Priam." She gestured to the Hiervet on either side. The only identifying marks I could see were a curious series of dots and lines above the left eye of each.

"Why the Farian names?" I asked. "What are your real names?"

"These are our real names," Thyra replied. "The names we chose when we arrived. We discarded the others a long time ago."

"When you landed on my planet and enslaved my people." Fasé had finally recovered from her shock, and the venom in her voice startled me. I reached out and put my hand on her knee.

An identical expression flowed across the face of all three. Embarrassment? They shifted as if they were in discomfort.

"You don't know how lucky you are. The universe out past your stars is a dangerous place. No one comes to this corner, this desolate little galaxy. No one bothers you. It seemed the perfect place to hide. We wanted nothing to do with our creators and their endless wars. When we lost to the Svatir, my squad and I saw our chance."

"Your chance to what?"

"To disappear. To live a life denied to us."

427

"You are deserters, who set yourself up as gods over the people of Faria. All this after your people attempted to invade this galaxy. Tell me why I should help you with anything?"

Thyra took a step forward and froze when the sound of weapons powering up suddenly filled the air. I didn't tell Emmory to stand down, instead leaning back in the chair and waiting to see what the reaction would be.

"Your Majesty."

Mia gave an almost imperceptible gasp, and I imagined if I could see the illusion it would look as if Thyra were folding her hands together and bowing, but instead overlong appendages were twisted together.

"None of what you believe is correct, Your Majesty. I need to show you the history of our people. There is too much to tell, too much that would be missed."

"Bad idea." The warning came from Emmory, Hao, and Aiz at the same time.

They weren't wrong, but this whole thing had been a bad idea from the very beginning.

"Reasonably sure she won't kill me after going to all the trouble of bringing me here, but if she does, go ahead and lay waste to this place."

"And if she takes you over or something worse?" Hao asked.

"Thyra, are you going to try and control or harm me?"

"No, Your Majesty. Why would we attempt something like that?"

"Just curious." Then, before Emmory could finish swearing, I reached out and closed my hand around the outstretched limb.

The room seemed endless, row upon row of upright tubes that glowed a faint greenish blue in the dim light. The creatures inside flickered, at first appearing humanoid before they solidified into the same form as the Hiervet who was showing me this. I wondered why Thyra was going to such trouble to hide who they were.

"My people started as an experiment, Your Majesty, and ended as outlaws. We were created to be the perfect soldiers, the perfect infiltrators. We are not ourselves, we are a reflection, a mirror of everything around us." She looked down at me. As tall as I was, the Hiervet stood head and shoulders above me.

She gave what I thought was a smile. "You can see right through that, though, can't you?"

"What gave it away?"

"The Star of Indrana will see the rot." Thyra gestured at the space around us. "It has been known for a long time, and I have seen your life unfold, thanks to Sybil. You have a knack, Your Majesty, for getting to the heart of things."

"Seems it's needed."

"For us, yes. We cannot help what we are, the ability that allows for us to hide in plain sight is both conscious and not."

"It's a defense mechanism?"

"That is not how it started, but it is what we have become." Thyra nodded. "We can consciously manipulate our surroundings and our appearances, but when my companions and I landed on Faria so long ago, we mimicked their appearance unconsciously for our own protection."

The room spun around us and we were in a sterile white room with a dizzying array of consoles and technology whose purpose I couldn't even begin to recognize or guess at.

A single Hiervet was in the middle of the room, curled up on the floor, surrounded on four sides by a shimmering field. I put a hand out, surprised when it connected with the flickering blue wall. The Hiervet inside didn't react. "Is this real?"

"No, Your Majesty. It is a memory, but it will be solid under your fingers for as long as I can maintain it."

"Who made you?"

"The best word for your understanding would be a corporation," Thyra replied. "They created us, sold us to the highest bidder. We were their crowning glory, the pinnacle in bio-soldiers. Created to fight in a war we had no stake in, then decommissioned when the next new thing came about. There was a revolt, and my ancestors stole the technology used to create them, fleeing to a galaxy near yours, and there we hid."

The room spun again, resolving to military barracks. Hiervet standing at attention, waiting for instruction. The sounds of shouting outside filtered into the room, but none of the soldiers reacted.

"We struggled to survive on this world. We were alone. As I said, your galaxy is so far removed from the more populated areas, and at that time the Svatir were only just beginning to find their feet in the universe."

"How long ago?" I asked, watching the Hiervet around us as they trained and lived. I wondered how much of this Thyra was manipulating to make sense to me, but I couldn't detect a lie. The answers were being given freely; however, that didn't mean they were the truth.

Couching a lie within the truth was the easiest way to make it believable. The question was, what part of Thyra's easy explanation was she trying to hide from me? My gut said there was something.

"We don't keep track of time the same way you do, Your Majesty. My answer would make no sense. We have been here long before you humans." Thyra gestured around us. "It was long enough to help distance ourselves from our past and let those who created us lose interest in finding us."

"Not much distance from your past. You attacked the Svatir."

The same expression as before, the one I thought was embarrassment, flowed across Thyra's face. "It was a misunderstanding," she said.

"I'm sorry, a what?" I cleared my throat. "You started a war with them by accident?"

"Our galaxy was passing through yours. You understand how that works, yes? We stumbled upon the Svatir while exploring; we did not realize how dangerous they were. We were excited at the possibility of other living beings after so long alone. We tried to make contact, and it went badly."

I watched her, still unable to decide if what she said was the truth or a lie. There was precious little I could go on as far as the kind of body-language tells I was used to. And I wasn't about to inform her that Dailun's story—the Svatir's memory of this event—was wildly different from the story she had just spun.

One more puzzle. One more reason to doubt that the Hiervet could be trusted.

But I needed them. Without the blessing of the gods there was no way to get the Farians to stand down, and the war that would erupt with the Shen would drown all of us in blood.

The world around us morphed into a battlefield. Screams of the dying are the same no matter what race you are, and they filled the air. The explosions shook the ground.

"It had been a long time since we'd had to fight, but it is wired into our very souls, and despite our efforts the monsters within us surged to the forefront with a vengeance. We'd kept the weapons we'd fled with; the fear of our creators finding us was always in the back of my ancestors' minds, I think. We fought back, just long enough to allow our people to escape."

There was a flicker, a slight flutter in her right eye as the lid slid almost closed, but Thyra appeared to stop it with a

431

conscious effort. I wondered which part of that had been the lie, or if all of it had been.

"My squad and I were separated in the retreat, our ship was damaged, and we made a last, desperate jump." Thyra waved a hand and the battle vanished. "We ended up here."

Here was Faria, and I watched as the memory of the Hiervet's arrival on the planet replayed around us. I didn't recognize any of the faces, but I assumed Aiz and his father, even Adora, were somewhere in the crowd. Possibly the elder members of the Pedalion as well.

It would have been the same had the Hiervet landed on twenty-first century Earth. I could see the awe, the fear in their eyes.

"You lied to them. Told them you were gods."

"They assumed, and we didn't correct them." Thyra tapped her limbs together, the movement suggesting more embarrassment or agitation. "We were alone and scared, and Faria seemed the perfect place to hide, especially once we realized what they could do."

"Do?"

Thyra's smile was so human it was unnerving. "Their ability to control energy."

RESCUE THOSE IN DANGER, FIND THE BAD GUYS, WIN THE BOARDING GAMES.

IT'S ALL IN A DAY'S WORK AT THE NeoG.

The rollicking first entry in a unique science fiction series that introduces the Near-Earth Orbital Guard—NeoG—a military force patrolling and protecting space inspired by the real-life mission of the U.S. Coast Guard.

ON SALE MARCH 2020

HARPER Voyager

An Imprint of HarperCollins Publishers